Readers are raving about the beginning of the Grady-Garrett partnership

CUT & RUN

By Madeleine Urban & Abigail Roux

Urban and Roux are the masterminds of a terrific novel, over 300 hundred pages of solid goodness.

—*Rainbow Reviews*

Ty and Zane were so heartbreakingly beautiful and so realistic that these two will go down as two of the most fascinating characters written in this genre.

—*Literary Nymphs*

The plot was a stroke of genius….

—*Erotic Horizon*

An action-packed, angst-filled story where the sparks fly around Ty and Zane both in and out of bed.

—*Joyfully Reviewed*

A touching erotic romance as well as an intriguing murder mystery.

—*Romance Junkies*

OTHER BOOKS BY
MADELEINE URBAN AND ABIGAIL ROUX

Caught Running
Cut & Run
Love Ahead
Warrior's Cross

BY ABIGAIL ROUX

The Archer
My Brother's Keeper
Unrequited

BY MADELEINE URBAN

Far From Home
Man of Mystery
The One That Got Away (with Rhianne Aile)
Snowed In (with Rhianne Aile)
Sutcliffe Cove (with Ariel Tachna)

STICKS & STONES

MADELEINE URBAN
ABIGAIL ROUX

Published by
Dreamspinner Press
4760 Preston Road
Suite 244-149
Frisco, TX 75034
http://www.dreamspinnerpress.com/

Sticks & Stones

Cover Design by Mara McKennen

ISBN: 978-1-61581-382-7

Printed in the United States of America
First Edition
January, 2010

eBook edition available
eBook ISBN: 978-1-61581-383-4

Sticks and stones may build your homes,
but words will lift your spirits.

~CHAPTER 1~

"THIS has got to be a fire hazard," Ty Grady complained in a strained voice as they inched the heavy pool table across the scarred wooden floor, his broad shoulder pressed to the side of the table as they struggled.

Zane Garrett grunted as he pushed the table with his ass braced against the end. "Would you stop with the fire hazards?" he asked in annoyance. "This wasn't really what I had in mind when I said we should take some time off, do something for ourselves," he grumbled.

"You turned down my black market orchids," Ty reminded. He looked up to see that they'd pushed the table far enough and stopped with an irritated huff. He turned and grabbed a nearby stool, sat it on the pool table, and climbed up on top of it, cursing as the stool wobbled beneath him. He pushed the access panel in the ceiling experimentally. It didn't budge. He banged it with the heel of his hand. It rattled but didn't pop free.

"The one thing in this place that's built solid," he muttered as he looked around for something to use. There was nothing. There wasn't anything but the pool table and a pub table with two stools in the deserted pool hall. It didn't even have pool cues!

He grumbled under his breath and punched the access panel, causing it to crack down the middle. With his movement the stool wobbled dangerously beneath his feet, and he threw his hands out to the sides to catch his balance. The stool stopped rocking almost as suddenly as it started, and as Ty glanced down, he saw Zane had grabbed it with both hands to hold it steady.

"Careful there, Twinkletoes," Zane said with a half smile.

"Thank you," Ty said to him as he shook his hand. "About time you did something useful. Watch your head," he warned as he shoved at the pieces of the panel, which fell to the pool table below him with a muted clatter. He looked back down at Zane. "Come up here so I can stand on your head," he said with a slight smile.

Zane snorted as he hefted himself up onto the table next to the stool. "You just want me for my body," he said as he stood up, his shoulders even with Ty's waist.

Ty petted him on the head with one gloved hand, then reached through the nearly foot-thick ceiling, placed his gun on the roof of the building, and gripped the edges to lever himself up. He growled in annoyance as he hung there, almost stuck in the opening due to the bulky body armor hindering his progress. He managed to pull himself through, grunting as he scratched and clawed his way through the opening and crawled out to flatten out on the roof. He yanked the protective helmet from his head and tossed it away, breathing in the crisp air in relief.

He stuck his head back over the edge and hung his arm down, offering Zane a hand up with a hint of dread. He never knew lately whether Zane would accept help or bite his head off for offering it. The abrupt mood swings and other problems Zane had been having since the Tri-State serial killer case were the reason they were doing jobs like this instead of working back at the Bureau.

But Zane was apparently still in the good mood he'd exhibited so far, because he took Ty's arm without comment as he climbed up on the stool to follow him. Just as he pushed off with his long legs, there was a loud bang on the door.

Ty saw the flimsy door rattle, and he yanked at Zane with everything he could muster while still lying flat on his stomach. "Battering ram," he warned in a strained voice.

Zane huffed and pulled himself up with Ty's help, growling as soon as his feet were through the access hatch. "Clear," he said under his breath. A second later a loud bang echoed in the pool hall underneath them as the door was forced open.

"Move, move, move," Ty hissed to Zane as he grabbed his gun and mask and ran for the edge of the building, easily leaping to the next. They needed to be several buildings over before the team that had found them could relay their position.

Zane was right behind him. "Three buildings over. Fire escape." He'd memorized the downtown layout the night before while Ty worked on today's plans with Benson and the rest of the crew. Of course, those plans were now blown to hell. At least Ty still had the walking map with him.

They kept low, hurrying along the rooftops until they came to the fire escape Zane had mentioned. Ty glanced over the edge. The only problem, of course, was that the top of the metal stairs didn't reach the roof. It was an eight-foot drop to the top level from where they were.

"I hate this fucking town," Ty grumbled as he secured his gun and glanced over his shoulder. He could hear shouting, the various patrols communicating to each other; they obviously didn't possess the same sort of gear he and Zane were using to stay in touch with their comrades.

He looked back down at the fire escape. It was their only way down unless they fancied trying to fly.

They were almost out of options, and not just because they were stuck on a roof. They'd planned for this contingency, though. There were three two-man teams in town today, each equipped with enough charges to blow one of three targets and radio receivers linked to each set. Bravo team had achieved its objective—blowing up a television station that doubled as the town's communications center. But in doing so they'd moved too early and announced their presence before Ty and Zane could even reach their own target.

While Bravo team had done its job, the two men hadn't survived long enough to celebrate. Alpha team had managed to set its charges at the supply stores at the end of the street, but the men had been assaulted on their way out and hadn't managed to blow them. They were now involved in a running gunfight through the streets, taking their radio receivers farther and farther out of range as they went. They were screwed, much like Ty and Zane were about to be.

Ty climbed over the edge of the brick and lowered himself slowly until his feet dangled just a couple feet above the metal platform below, Zane following suit. To jump would have made too much noise, and they couldn't afford to be captured or killed before they laid their charges. One target out of three was unacceptable. Two targets was still a failure, but it was better than nothing. Ty wanted all three targets, even if he had to do the last two himself.

They made their way down the fire escape quickly, causing only the occasional clang or bang as they hurried. When Ty's booted feet hit the pavement, though, a shout from the corner of the building met them.

"Stop! Federal agents!" the man behind the protective mask warned as he held his gun up.

Ty turned without a moment's hesitation and fired at him, two quick shots, and red bloomed across the letters on the man's chest. He fell back, and Ty and Zane ran toward him rather than away, firing at the other agents who rounded the corner. Before the other two men in the patrol could retreat or call for backup, both took shots in the chest and dropped with pained cries.

Zane lowered his gun and pulled off his headgear. His dark hair, longer than it used to be and brushing his collar, was ruffled up now, and a curled wire from the ear bud ran along his scruffy cheek. He turned his chin to look at Ty. "We can still make the objective. This is the right street." He nodded to the road at the nearby crossing.

"Lead on," Ty told him as he tossed his protective mask at the agents lying on the ground. He didn't plan to wear it anymore; if he took one in the face it wouldn't do him much good anyway, and he couldn't think with it on.

Zane's safety gear hit the ground as well as they loped past the fallen men, and at the end of the alley they flattened against the vinyl siding of that building so Zane could look around the corner.

The town's main street was a long, paved corridor lined with shops. Laundromat, barber shop, diner, movie theater, the deserted pool hall they'd fled just a few moments ago, and several other buildings. Some in use, some not. At the very end of the street was the large brick building that served as the area's supply storage, its front lined with garage doors for freight trucks to drop off provisions. The munitions dump was several stores over on their side of the street, concealed in a computer repair shop. That was their objective.

Ty knew that the big problem was not the distance they had to travel, but the teams of agents that patrolled the streets. He and Zane had nothing but the charges and receivers, the guns they held in their hands, and their communications gear. And a bottle of hairspray Ty had taken from the drug store down the street when they'd ducked inside to avoid a patrol.

Their biggest ally now was stealth.

They made their way to the corner of the block undetected, swiftly coming up on the ammunition cache.

Shouts came from their right, and then they heard a muffled gunfight. The commotion continued, followed by the pop-pop of the guns and the screams of their team members in their ear buds.

"That'll be Alpha team," Ty said flatly as they continued to move.

First Bravo team, and now Alpha team was down as well— *without* completing their mission of blowing up the supply stores at the end of the street. Ty and Zane still had to set their own charges at the munitions dump and blow them, and now they also had to get within range of the storage building to blow Alpha's charges if they wanted to complete the mission.

"Stupid. They should have blown the charges when they had the chance," Zane muttered, looking behind them quickly as they made their way to the door of the computer repair shop. He held up three fingers to indicate the number of people Benson's intel had said would be guarding the ammo dump. Zane stopped beside the door and looked at Ty seriously. "Ready?" he asked almost inaudibly.

Ty nodded as he popped a fresh cartridge into his gun. He looked up at Zane and grinned widely. He fished out the bottle of hairspray he'd pilfered from the drug store up the road as they had dashed through it earlier, shaking it vigorously.

It wouldn't blow up. Hell, it wouldn't do anything but roll when he threw it. But it would look enough like a flashbang as it flew through the air to make everyone inside duck. It might give them enough time.

Zane looked at him incredulously and then rolled his eyes. "Christ," he muttered. He crouched down next to the door, gun ready. "Go."

Ty stepped up to the door and kicked at it, just below the doorknob where it was weakest. He tossed the hairspray into the room and followed it immediately, firing to his right in a wide spray of bullets.

Still crouched, Zane shifted inside behind him and fired to the left, taking out an agent caught ducking from the fake flashbang. Zane got to his feet just in time to take a step into the room and be hit from the side by a heavy body.

Ty turned and watched as Zane hit the floor under the other man's momentum. Zane pulled up his knees and kept rolling while the agent scrambled, trying to reach for a gun sitting out on the sales counter nearby. Zane's boot in his gut stopped him, and the man dropped, gasping for breath.

Rolling his eyes, Ty simply shot the man in the back to stop the oncoming brawl. The agent fell forward without a sound, his eyes still registering shock as he lay on the ground.

Ty shook his head at him and then looked around the room at the mess they'd made. The walls were running with red. He clucked his tongue and shook his head as he looked around at the bodies littering the floor.

"Complacent," he chastised. He went over to the weapons locker, beginning to stuff extra cartridges into his pockets as he whistled. He realized belatedly that the tune was the chorus of "Battle Hymn of the Republic." He was having more fun than he probably should have been.

"What are they teaching these idiots?" Zane asked as he picked up the extra gun from the sales counter and slid it into his waistband. "No wonder the Bureau's going to shit," he muttered. He joined Ty at the cabinet to pull out cartridges for himself.

Ty nodded as he hummed. He finished loading up with extra ammo and went to the agent he'd shot in the back, kneeling down beside him. He patted him on the head. "Shoot first next time. Tackle later," he advised, and then he stood and went to the doorway.

"You have a really morbid sense of humor, you know that?" Zane said as he stepped over the body while sliding the new cartridge into his gun. "Let me have those charges," he demanded, holding out his hand.

Ty gave a careful glance around the door frame, peering down the street. "Set 'em quick," he ordered as he pulled them out and handed them to Zane. He looked out again, looking at the brick building down the road with its open bays and garages. "You think we're in range here?" he asked as he fished out the switch that would trigger Alpha Team's charges and looked at it. He pushed the button, uncaring of the teams of demolitions agents who were swarming the building, trying to defuse the charges. He peered out at the building. Nothing happened. He pushed the button a few more times just in case.

Zane shook his head while setting the charge inside the stack of boxes. He didn't even look outside. "Still eighty yards out of range. We have to get to the office building on the corner to be close enough." He glanced over at Ty. "Would you quit pushing the damn button?" he said in exasperation. "What if you break the connection? Then what're you gonna do? Waltz over there and set it off by hand?" He set the charge frequency and clicked on the receiver.

"Worth a shot," Ty said defensively. "Do these things have batteries?" he asked as he shook the receiver near his ear and listened for something to rattle inside it. Zane ignored him, and Ty looked back down the street critically. "Nowhere to hide," he commented. He glanced back at Zane. "We'll use this explosion as cover. Maybe buy us enough time to clear out."

Zane finished programming their detonator and joined him at the window. "I guess it was too much to ask that Benson had his shit together. I knew I should have taken Stanford's bet that he'd flop against the Feds. I could've bought a new Glock."

"Whatever, man," Ty grunted, not really paying attention to Zane's grumbling. "Let's go blow shit up," he said with relish as he moved out of the building.

They hugged the storefronts, moving along the street toward the target.

Ty was examining the entrance to the alley coming up when Zane abruptly grabbed his arm and yanked him down just as something hit the brick wall over their heads with a dull thump. The shot had barely missed his head.

Zane already had his gun up, shooting indiscriminately at the two-man team that had appeared out of the door of a nearby building. The two agents retreated back into the barbershop under the hail of bullets Zane sent their way.

"Move!" Zane hissed.

They scuttled along the side of the building, no longer concerned with stealth. The mission now was to blow the ammo dump they'd just left—their assignment as Charlie Team—and then they had to get close enough to fulfill Alpha Team's failed objective using the coordinated triggers.

Ty skidded to a halt as they reached another narrow alley and peered around the corner. Agents were running along the length of it, and more were coming up behind them. He and Zane put their backs to each other and fired in opposite directions, forcing the encroaching patrols to dive for cover.

"The cars!" Zane said harshly, and they darted across the street toward a row of parked cars, the action getting them closer to the building even as it offered cover. As they ran, Zane pulled the detonator he'd just programmed out of his pocket and flipped it. Behind them, the weapons cache blew, blowing the door open, making a mess of the windows and the street in front of the building.

It bought them just a little more time as the agents in pursuit ducked and covered or turned to look.

But after no more than half a block, they were forced to duck behind a Lincoln land yacht as more shots came at them from across the street. Zane flinched as a shot smacked the bricks ten feet away. They were pretty damn well pinned down; Zane took a glance over the hood and quickly hunched back down as more ammunition skimmed over their heads.

"Ten fucking yards," he said harshly, turning his chin, his dark eyes meeting Ty's.

Ty smiled at him, barely resisting the urge to grab him and kiss him. "We could pull a Butch and Sundance," he suggested.

"I don't know about you, but I did not come here to die today," Zane said smartly as he put a fresh clip in his gun. Despite his annoyed tone, he looked amused and his eyes sparkled wickedly. "Don't have a better idea, though." After a moment, he gave Ty a half-smile. "It was fun, yeah?"

Ty grinned back at him and nodded, switching out his empty cartridge and pulling out extra guns to set them aside. "Always knew I should have gone the Dark Side route," he mused.

Zane laughed quietly and was checking his two guns when they heard "Federal agents!" shouted by one of their pursuers.

Looking under the car, Ty could see the feet of the dozen or so agents surrounding them.

"Toss out your weapons and come out with your hands behind your head!" one of them called out.

Ty shook his head. "Did we ever sound that stupid when we said that?" he asked as he consolidated his supply of ammo. With two guns, he had enough for a last stand.

"I don't know. I was more the 'drop it or you're getting it in the head' kinda guy," Zane muttered. He winked at Ty and turned so he was facing the car where he crouched.

They had one advantage. The agents who were swiftly surrounding them would have to wait until no other option existed before they fired on their quarry. They would have to give warning, just like the good little Feds they were.

Ty and Zane were no longer constrained by such delicacies.

"On three?" Zane suggested.

Ty glanced over at him and then to his side, toward the building that was just out of range of their receiver. They were so close. Ty narrowed his eyes and looked at Zane again speculatively. Two out of three just didn't sit well with him. "Ready," he answered.

"One," Zane said under his breath. "Two. Th—"

Before Zane could stand, Ty reached out and grabbed him around the neck, yanking him up and to the side, putting Zane between himself and the agents as he dragged him sideways around the car they were using as cover.

"What the *fuck*?" Zane squawked, heels kicking out as he struggled to get hold of Ty's arm around his throat that was bowing his body back.

"I thought you liked it when I did this, darlin'," Ty breathed into Zane's ear with a smirk.

"Goddamnit," Zane huffed, sounding like he was trying not to laugh.

At least a dozen agents leveled their guns at them. Some knelt in the middle of the street behind large black ballistic shields in pairs. Others used the cars parked along the street as cover.

Several agents were yelling at them, telling them to stop, to drop their guns, to hit the ground. Ty ignored them, moving slowly toward the building, hiding behind Zane and pointing his gun at the agents who followed.

When a couple of the agents looked like they might be getting brave, Ty moved the gun to point the muzzle at Zane's head, grinning as he shouted, "Stop moving or I shoot him!"

The agents paused, looking at him warily and giving each other confused glances, but then they resumed their advance, following as Ty drew them backward.

Zane turned his head to the side, eyes shifting to look around them as he growled, "If they don't kill you, I will!" And then with no warning, he stopped struggling in Ty's arms. "Now," he hissed.

Ty pushed the button of the switch he held in his hand, tightening his grip on Zane so he couldn't get away. The building down the street—Alpha team's objective—gave off a muffled whump, dust flying off the roof and the bricks as the charges made a mess of the inside. The agents flinched and ducked before continuing to shout at them to drop their weapons.

"Happy trails, Lone Star," Ty breathed to Zane as he raised his gun under Zane's arm and fired several times, hitting the shields with dull thumps, just as Zane did the same with his two guns.

But when the agents returned fire, Ty ducked his head behind his human shield. Zane howled in pain, and his body jerked hard as he took the volley of shots right in the chest. When he started to collapse, Ty let him go and turned, running for cover.

A SERIES of piercing whistles sounded from one of the building tops.

Agents began filtering out from their locations, some of them covered with red paint where they'd been shot. The other two "terrorist" teams were brought out as well, all four of them covered in the blue paint of the FBI agents-in-training.

When everyone gathered in the middle of the street around the instructors who'd been observing from various points through the town, Special Agent Ty Grady emerged from the spot of safety he'd managed to reach, completely unscathed.

And Special Agent Zane Garrett sat up from where he lay sprawled on the asphalt, his chest soaked with blue paint.

He may have been covered in blue, but he was seeing red. Zane looked over his shoulder right at Ty and glared at him evilly. "You bastard. You cut and run?"

Ty shrugged unapologetically as he walked up to stand over him. "Every man for himself, partner," he said with a wide grin. "Last man standing," he announced triumphantly with his arms spread wide.

"I can change that," Zane promised darkly, torn between being angry and surprised or amused and resigned. Ty had not only used him as a distraction to make his escape but also left him behind. Zane wasn't even sure if it should bother him at all either way. It was just a training game, after all. And as he saw how relaxed and happy Ty looked, Zane could only sigh and set his arms on his propped-up knees, shaking his head.

"Trainees! Not only did all three points receive fatal damage, and not only did we not capture a live prisoner to interrogate, but you let one of the terrorist agents get away!" Special Agent Jason Stanford announced angrily, his voice booming out of his lanky frame. He was wearing a gray FBI sweatshirt and khakis like all the trainees. "But before I rip you all new assholes, let me introduce the men who just ran the table on you. This is Special Agent Ty Grady, who was raised by wolves, if that makes any of you feel better about getting your asses kicked," he said, pointing at Ty.

"I thought they hired actors for these things," one of the trainees called out. "We didn't know we were up against trained agents."

"You expect to face actors in the field?" Zane pointed out as he stood up and shook his hands while he glared at the newbie agents. Blue paint splattered on the asphalt as it dripped off him. How many paintballs had hit him? Those little fuckers hurt!

Stanford looked at Zane with a smirk. "And this is the very dead Special Agent Zane Garrett, who was apparently raised by Kevlar," he told his agents-in-training. "Nicely done, Special Agent Garrett." Zane glared at him, too, just for good measure.

"That was cold, man," one of the trainees muttered.

"No shit," Zane muttered, glancing Ty's way again. Ty studiously ignored him, though, blatantly pretending not to notice the look.

Stanford went on to introduce the other four agents participating as Zane swiped at the paint along his chest and arms. Ty stepped slightly away from Zane as the paint spattered, wiping delicately at a spot on his leg that may or may not have had blue paint on it. Zane narrowed his eyes as he watched him, considering what his chances were of tackling his partner to the street and kicking his ass. Or at least smearing him with paint. There was such a thing as enjoying oneself too much at your partner's expense.

At least he wasn't humming or whistling anymore. Or, God forbid, singing. Zane always knew there was trouble coming when Ty started making up his own words to "Battle Hymn of the Republic."

"The special agents participating today are on loan to us for this exercise," Stanford continued with a smug smile. "Give them all a hand, if you will, and be sure to try to learn something from them."

"That was kind of awesome," one guy said from the back of the crowd. The back of his sweatshirt had one small red splotch to indicate where he'd been shot. He was the man who'd tackled Zane. "Took three of us out without even saying anything to each other."

"After years of working closely with your partner, you too will develop that skill," Stanford said, blithely disregarding the fact that he knew Ty and Zane hadn't been officially partnered for more than five or six weeks. Zane suppressed the urge to smile. "It's something that can't be taught," Stanford added.

"Partners use each other as human shields often?" one of the group asked wryly.

"Never underestimate your enemy's will to live or his mental instability," Ty advised with a smirk. "You may be taught never to leave a man behind. Doesn't mean *they* are. Expect anything."

"Thank you, gentlemen. You were a big help today," Stanford said to Ty, Zane, and the other four special agents. He turned and started lecturing the trainees, many of whom peered around him to watch Zane turn on his partner, hands on his hips, looking none too pleased.

"Last man standing, huh?" Zane asked, voice dropping dangerously low. His chest was starting to ache under the protective vest he was wearing.

But Ty merely smiled at him and held up the switch he'd used to trigger the pyrotechnics in the targeted building. "We won," he said happily.

Zane made a disgusted sound in his throat even as his mouth threatened to turn up at the corners in the face of Ty's childish glee. "You're too damn pleased with yourself."

"But we won," Ty repeated, grinning widely in his pristine uniform.

"Keep talking," Zane dared him. "Please. Keep talking." Ty was only about four feet away, and Zane figured it was even money that he could take him down. Ty would probably kick his ass in the end, though, and it would also ruin Ty's good mood. Zane grimaced.

Ty looked down at the switch, still smiling. "Spoilsport," he said to Zane in a low voice, and then he tossed the switch to Stanford with a nod. The man was watching them in amusement, his smirk indicating that he was just as eager to see if Zane would retaliate as his class was.

"Next time try not to leave the place in pieces," Stanford said to them with a smile.

"No promises," Zane said, hands up as if to ward off the future. "They don't let Grady out of his cage often enough." Then he remembered something that actually made him smile. "C'mon, Grady. You drove today, remember?"

Ty pursed his lips, glancing at Stanford as he tried not to smile. He shook the man's hand, thanking him for the opportunity to come blow shit up and shoot people, and then he joined Zane as they headed out of the little mock-up FBI town called Hogan's Alley.

"You brought a change of clothes, right?" Ty asked Zane as he looked him over critically.

Zane stopped in place and just stared at him. He could feel the paint dribbling down his neck, into the collar of his jacket, and curling along his palms and fingers.

"What?" Ty asked innocently, his eyes wide.

Zane crossed his arms, heedless of how it spread the paint more across his jacket. "I didn't expect to turn into a wide-open target."

Ty's lips twitched, and it was clear that he was desperately trying to hold on to the innocent facade. "How many months have you been my partner?" he inquired.

"On the books or off?" Zane asked with equal nonchalance.

Ty finally let a smirk play across his lips, and he stepped closer. "Either way, you should know you're always a target," he advised, his voice low and teasing.

Zane rolled his eyes. "Funny guy." He uncrossed his arms and looked down at himself. "I'm a mess, and it's *your* fault. What are you gonna do about it?"

"Make you walk home," Ty answered seriously as he twirled his car keys around his finger and turned to head off for his Bronco again.

"C'mon, Grady," Zane complained as he followed. "I brought you down here, didn't I?"

"That's right," Ty acknowledged. "If it weren't for you, those could have been *real* bullets and bombs we were playing with," he said pointedly. "But no," he drawled out in disappointment.

Zane stopped at the side of the truck. "I passed the tests, okay? Should be any day now we get the word from Burns." He opened the back door and pulled out a duffel bag.

"Did you really bring a change of clothes?" Ty asked in surprise as he tossed his gear into the back seat.

Zane favored Ty with an aggravated look, but he was still pleased enough with the day not to get pissy about it. "I figured you'd find some way to fuck me over," he said. "You've been bouncing off the walls for over a week now, and I'm your favorite target lately."

"Are you still pissy about the rubber band cannon?" Ty asked him in exasperation.

"Ugh." Zane started unbuttoning the BDU blouse. "You're lucky that guy from accounting didn't know it was you when his toupee went flying. He might have rerouted your next paycheck to Greenpeace."

Ty began snickering softly, obviously trying to hold in the laughter. He closed the back door and leaned against the rear of the Bronco to look at Zane critically. "All the puns in my arsenal, and I can't think of a single blue joke," he said mournfully.

Zane carefully pulled the heavy green and black camouflage jacket off, turning it totally inside out as he did. "Off your game, Grady," he said distractedly as he set the folded-up blouse on the pavement next to his feet and started digging in his duffel for a towel.

"You're just pissed 'cause you got riddled with holes," Ty grunted as he turned to head for the driver's side door.

Zane had to smile as he shook his head. Ty had been going crazy in the office for the past five weeks, so when he'd heard about the chance to come over here to Quantico for the day, Zane had jumped at it and dragged his raving-mad partner along. With a sigh, Zane wiped pretty much all the paint off his hands and swiped under his chin a couple times before folding up the towel and shoving it and the now-blue uniform blouse in the duffel.

Ty had the truck running when Zane got into the passenger seat and shut the door.

Ty was looking at him with a crooked smile. Zane raised one eyebrow. "What?"

"That was fun," Ty told him in a pleased voice, one Zane hadn't heard much lately.

Whatever annoyance he'd been feeling faded in the face of Ty's unholy glee. "I'm glad you enjoyed it," he said, giving his partner a tolerant look. Maybe Ty would be a little easier to live with for a day or two. Which would in turn make Zane a little less cranky as well. It might just be a decent week after all.

Ty gave him a wicked laugh as he pulled the Bronco out of its spot, pointing them back toward DC.

~CHAPTER 2~

"SO, SPECIAL Agent Garrett, I understand you've finished your evaluations," the Assistant Director of the Criminal Investigative Division said from where he sat behind his large mahogany desk. The desk stood out against the drab colors of the paint and carpet and matched the wall of bookshelves that warmed the room.

FBI Special Agent Zane Garrett stood at the window, looking out at the wet, dirty streets of Washington, DC, and desperately wishing he could be anywhere else. He could see his boss in the window; the man behind the desk held several files in his hand as he looked at Zane with raised eyebrows.

Zane sneered at his own reflection in the window. The shadows under his eyes and wrinkles from his frown were pronounced above his slightly crooked nose, giving him a rough and tumble appearance even though he was clean-shaven. The scraped cheeks were in sharp contrast to his slightly overgrown dark brown hair. Looking at himself, he acknowledged that, despite the muscular build cloaked in black slacks and a royal blue dress shirt, he wasn't any prize right now.

He had been assigned to the DC office for five weeks, along with his partner, after they'd been reunited in this very office following five miserable months apart. Upon receiving the new assignment, they had both been relegated to deskwork for various reasons, not the least of which was the physical and mental aftereffects of the turbulent past year or so. For him, it had been an especially rough year. Ty seemed better able to shake off the past than he did. Zane took a steadying breath and slid his hands into his pockets, shifting uncomfortably in place.

He winced and turned to look at Richard Burns. He'd known the meeting today would be... rocky.

"You passed the academic and physical testing, but you know that already. You also know you managed to flunk the mental evaluation that would have cleared you for field duty," Burns said in concern.

Zane didn't answer as he folded his arms in front of himself, wondering what he could say to explain. There was so much shit bouncing around in his head that he wasn't sure himself why he'd had such a tough time with an evaluation he should have been able to bullshit through easily. He just hadn't been able to focus.

"If there's a legitimate reason you can't get your head out of your ass, I'd like to hear it," Burns invited as he looked back up at Zane. He paused, probably waiting to see if Zane would say anything. When he received no comment, Burns continued. "Is it your partner?" he asked carefully.

Zane's shoulders stiffened, and he shook his head quickly. His partner had a reputation throughout the Bureau for being hard to work with; Zane had found in the last five weeks that he got more apologetic looks from his co-workers now that he was working with Special Agent Ty Grady than he'd gotten when his wife had died. But Zane didn't have a problem working with Ty. Not for the same reason others did, anyway.

"It's been hard," he hedged. "Getting over what happened."

That was an understatement. The truth was that he'd been fighting insomnia, acute headaches, and suffering through nightmares when he actually *did* sleep alone. Tracking down a serial killer intent on not being caught was hazardous to your health, both mentally and physically, and nearly getting killed in a vicious car wreck during the hunt almost six months ago had contributed to his problems. He'd recovered surprisingly well—physically. He'd attended his rehab appointments and gym times religiously. But the rest....

He'd been able to ignore it as long as he'd had Ty in bed next to him. When Zane first got into his company-issue extended-stay hotel suite, Ty had been there almost every night, only going home to Baltimore once or twice a week to switch out his clothing. Over the next five weeks, though, as they'd languished in deskwork waiting to be cleared for the field, the overnight stays had tapered off until Ty showed up only once or twice a week, if at all. The less Ty showed up, the less Zane slept. And while it did wonders for his physical rehab and workout schedule, it was also one of the reasons Zane had been feeling somewhat disconnected, both from his job and from his partner.

Burns watched him knowingly. "That's certainly understandable," he finally agreed. "Which is why I've decided to give you a few more weeks of vacation before your *official* evals take place."

"What?" Zane asked in surprise. While he felt a wave of relief that he was getting a reprieve, he also felt his stomach plummet nervously. There was always a catch with Dick Burns.

"How's your partner, Zane?" Burns asked.

Zane blinked a few times at the unexpected query. "Grady?" he asked warily.

Burns' mouth turned up in a half smile. "Do you have another partner I should know about?"

"No," Zane said quickly. "He's fine." He and Grady got along. Most of the time. Mostly in bed. The last few weeks had been a disappointing stretch, though; apparently not having a psychopath trying to kill them was slightly detrimental to forming any sort of personal relationship.

"*Fine*," Burns repeated.

Zane waved a hand around. "Yeah. Fine. I guess. Trying to stay busy." He rolled his eyes, thinking about the whirlwind of attitude and energy from Ty he dealt with every day. "He can't sit still," he told Burns.

Burns looked highly amused as he tipped back in his leather chair. "No, he can't. He never could. But then, neither can you," he pointed out, looking significantly at the comfortable wingback chairs in front of his desk.

Zane shrugged uncomfortably but took the hint and moved to the chair Burns had indicated. "Grady spends most of his free time at the gym, as far as I know," he said, hoping to move the focus off himself. "At the office we try to keep him distracted so he doesn't burn down the building."

"How's he handling deskwork?" Burns asked knowingly.

Zane glared at him, clearly communicating that he knew it was a bullshit question. "He's about as helpful as you'd figure."

"Yes, I heard about your little day trip down to Quantico," Burns said as he frowned and pulled back his white shirtsleeve to check his watch.

"We did pretty damn well in that exercise," Zane pointed out.

"If you consider going down in a blaze of glory and paintballs 'doing well,'" Burns said with a hint of a smile. "The real test will come when you're back in the field. If you ever get there," he said seriously.

"You know how much Grady likes to win," Zane muttered.

Burns pursed his lips and nodded. He seemed torn between amusement and concern. "Well, take comfort in the fact they weren't real bullets, I guess," he offered finally.

Zane leaned forward to brace his elbows on his knees and laced his fingers together. Although Ty's actions at the time had been surprising, Zane figured he understood. It was just a game. Ty wouldn't leave him alone when it counted. Not if there was anything he could do about it. "Real bullets change everything," he answered.

"Remember that when you're back in the field," Burns requested wryly. "You have another evaluation set up in three weeks' time," Burns told Zane, his voice soft. "At which point I expect you to pass with flying colors. Your place is in the field," he asserted. "If I can't put you there after your vacation, I have no further use for you. Do I make myself clear?"

"Yes, sir." Zane swallowed hard on the bile in his throat. That meant either a forced transfer to a desk job in another division—which would be terrible—or early retirement. Zane didn't even want to think about that. He wouldn't have anything left without this job or his partner. Without Ty.

"Enjoy your time off, Zane, starting right now," Burns offered sincerely. "Grady is getting several death threats a day from the office staff, so he's been 'granted' two weeks of his own," he added in a long-suffering voice. "What you do with your time off is none of my concern. Just don't do it here."

Zane suppressed a groan. The last vacation he'd taken was a disastrous trip back to Texas to see his family. Most of it had been spent *avoiding* his family. "All right," he agreed, his tone resigned. At this point, sitting alone in his hotel suite would just make things worse, but he really didn't know what else to do. He hadn't felt this lost in a long time, and unlike the past, he didn't have drugs or alcohol to blame or to turn to. This time it was all on him.

Burns was watching him closely. "Have you thought about seeing a psychiatrist?" he asked carefully.

Zane flinched. He'd known this was coming, but it didn't make hearing it any less painful. He really didn't want to go that route if he could avoid it. He wouldn't wish all the shit in his head on *anybody*.

"When you get back, there's someone I'd like you to speak to if you're still having difficulty," Burns told him with a sigh. "He's not a Bureau doctor. He's just a friend of mine who is very good." Zane nodded slowly, and Burns took pity on him and smiled slightly. "Don't worry, Garrett. It'll be all right. Find a hobby or something. Take up knitting," he suggested with a twinkle of amusement in his eyes.

"Knitting," Zane repeated flatly.

Burns nodded as there was a knock on the door to his office, and his harried assistant opened it. Burns waved her off as a man pushed past her to enter. Zane turned to see his partner and looked back at Burns with a frown, wondering what was going on.

"Come in, Special Agent Grady," Burns greeted pleasantly, completely unfazed by Ty's entrance. "Good to see you."

"You're a lousy liar, Dick," Ty Grady muttered as he ushered Burns' secretary back out and shut the door in her face. He turned back around and glowered. "I just got off the phone with my dad," he announced accusingly. "Said he was looking forward to seeing me this week. Know anything about that?"

Burns merely cleared his throat and smiled.

Zane ran his eyes over Ty, skimming over the close-cropped hair and clean-shaven face before moving his attention down over the sand-colored suit and black shirt he was wearing. The tailored suits he'd been wearing while on duty in DC looked incredible on him, though Zane knew Ty hated to wear them. He managed to look loose and comfortable in them despite the almost constant fidgeting they caused him. The tie took the brunt of the fussing during the day. It was usually gone by lunch.

It was amusing to watch him, and Zane did so every day with not a little sympathy. Although, Zane admitted silently, it was worlds better to see his partner like this than as the still, silent ghost of himself Ty had been after the major concussion he'd suffered on their last case.

Right now, Ty looked annoyed, the slight wrinkling of his narrow nose matching his furrowed brow and sparking greenish eyes. He was angry; it was obvious in the sharp and annoyed movements of his lanky, muscled body and the tightness in his jaw.

Ty moved further into the office, glancing at Zane as if he were just noticing him there. He pointed at Zane accusingly. "What's he done now?" he demanded of Burns.

"Why would you suppose he's done anything?" Burns asked. Ty opened his mouth to speak, but Burns was faster. "From what I understand, you two are wreaking more havoc amongst the office drones than you ever did in the field. Got anything to say to that?"

"Yeah," Ty huffed in response. "Stop giving my dad progress reports!"

"He's an old friend, Ty," Burns said to him in a low voice. "And I will talk to him whenever I goddamned please. Sit down," he ordered.

Ty hesitated stubbornly for a moment and then reluctantly moved to obey, flopping into the seat beside Zane. He glared at his partner, as if his being there were somehow Zane's fault. Zane rolled his eyes and turned his chin so he was looking back out the window.

"Why are we here?" Ty asked impatiently.

"To embarrass me for jackassing my eval," Zane muttered.

"You're here to amuse me," Burns corrected in a sarcastically sweet tone. "But now that you mention the tests...."

Ty glanced over at Zane and frowned slightly. "What's going on?" he asked, the annoyance draining away, replaced by growing concern.

"Why would you think anything's going on?" Burns asked curiously. "Smell something in the wind, do you?"

"Uh huh," Ty responded warily as he looked between them, either oblivious to Burns' sarcasm or ignoring it.

"Garrett is going on a little vacation," Burns answered as he leaned back in his chair.

"What? How long?" Ty demanded.

"Three weeks."

"What?" Ty repeated, slightly more panicked. "But who will I get to do my paperwork?"

"Jesus Christ," Zane swore quietly. Burns was practically kicking his ass to the curb, and all Ty could think about was the paperwork. Classy.

"I'm still filling out forms from throwing his gun at that cab!" Ty told Burns.

Zane's lips quirked. Every bullet fired from a service weapon had to be accompanied with a written report for the Bureau. Ty had fired… quite a few bullets at the cab that had almost smeared them across the highway in New York City. Zane didn't know what paperwork you had to fill out for throwing your gun at something. He'd never tried that before. Hell, he'd never even *thought* of it before.

"Don't worry about the paperwork," Burns told Ty with a grin. "You can finish it when you get back."

Ty went silent, pursing his lips as he gave both Burns and Zane measuring looks. "Where am I going?" he asked carefully as he looked between them again.

Zane knew Burns sometimes sent Ty off to mysterious places that never produced paperwork. He had yet to find the right opportunity to ask about that though. Ty probably thought he was being sent on one of those trips now. "I'm going on 'vacation,' remember?" Zane reminded him, internally bracing for impact.

"What, I have to go *with* him?" Ty asked incredulously. "Why the hell am I being punished too? Jesus Christ, Dick, I'd rather take his damn tests for him than be sent off into exile!"

"Would you do any better?" Burns asked pointedly.

Ty leaned forward in his chair and smacked his hand against the desk. "I have never fucked up an eval," he protested in a hurt voice.

Burns slowly raised an eyebrow. He leaned forward and pushed the folders on his desk around slowly. Then he picked one up and tapped it on the desk, giving Ty a significant look.

"What?" Ty asked, his tone suspicious.

Burns silently slid the folder across the desk.

"What is this?" Ty asked as he took the folder and opened it.

"Your latest psych evaluation," Burns answered without commenting further.

Ty frowned as he looked at the file and began shaking his head before he snapped the folder shut again, tossing it onto the desk. "Is this medical leave then?" he asked tightly.

Zane sat quietly, taking in the news that Ty must have failed his most recent psychological exam as well. He was surprised. While he himself—usually—was pretty damn good at lying his way through just about any test, Ty was an expert at hiding things he didn't want other people to know, and mental problems would be at the top of that list. Zane frowned. Ty must not have recovered from the trauma suffered at the hands of the Tri-State killer as well as he claimed. Zane could understand that. He knew Ty had faced almost certain death when Tim Henninger had bricked him into a catacomb and left him in the dark to die. That had to affect a man, especially one whose sanity already teetered on the edge on a good day.

"As I told your partner, these results will never see the light of day," Burns was informing Ty. "Your real evals will be given in two weeks. Zane's in three. Until then, you are both officially on vacation."

Ty was silent, staring at Burns until Burns actually shifted in his chair as he met Ty's eyes.

"My dad knew you were sending me on vacation," Ty stated. "He know what's in that file too?" he asked him softly.

Burns gave a shake of his head in answer. "You know better," he chastised. "But your father asks after you, Ty," he said in a surprisingly gentle voice. "He worries. Maybe if you called home more often I wouldn't have to give him news when I talk to him."

Zane shook his head imperceptibly, feeling suddenly uncomfortable about being there. There'd always been something more between Grady and Dick Burns than merely a relationship between agent and director. Now he had some idea of what it was. Burns knew Ty's family, and fairly well, from the sound of it. While their relationship seemed nice on the surface, he could imagine it was a nightmare for Ty, who was so protective of his privacy. Zane didn't want to think about what he'd do if Burns had a direct line to his own father. He shifted to study his partner, whose face was stony and blank.

"Garrett, we're done," Burns announced without looking away from Ty. "Would you excuse us?"

Zane hesitated for a long moment and then murmured, "Yes, sir," before standing and exiting the room without looking at his partner again. Once he got out of the main office and shut the door, he leaned back against the wall and exhaled heavily.

Well, it could have been worse.

TY LOOKED down at the file on the desk again, waiting until he heard the door click, and then he looked back up and met Burns' eyes.

"I'm fine," he said in a low voice.

"For now," Burns answered. "Maybe."

"Don't do this, Dick," Ty pleaded. "You take this job away from either of us, and we're both done," he said with a tap to his own temple.

Burns raised an eyebrow. "Is that so? Both of you?"

Ty cocked his head, trying not to react too obviously to anything Burns said or did. But Burns didn't look away; he just watched and waited.

"What?" Ty finally asked, feeling uncomfortable under the older man's piercing gaze.

Finally sniffing, Burns relaxed back into his chair. "I have it on very good authority that without this particular job, you would have three more waiting for you," he said with a sigh. "From organizations that would be less concerned about your mental health than I might be."

Ty shifted, trying not to fidget.

"I know why you stay here, Ty, and I'm grateful to you," Burns went on in a gentler tone. "But I begin to wonder how long I can keep you here before you just go stark raving mad on me. They're still cleaning up paint in Hogan's Alley."

"That wasn't all me," Ty reminded defensively.

"You don't owe me your dad's loyalty," Burns told him, ignoring his interruption. "Don't think I don't know that."

Ty swallowed heavily and linked his fingers together, trying harder not to shift around in the creaky old wingback.

"It's not necessarily you I'm worried about here, kiddo," Burns continued. "If abnormal psych evals from you concerned me overly much, I'd never get any sleep." He paused. "Tell me about your partner, Ty," he requested. "How is he?"

Ty met Burns' eyes carefully, wondering just how much the man knew about him and Zane. But it was safer to play dumb than it was to try and find out. No matter how well Ty knew Burns, something like fucking around with his partner wouldn't go unpunished.

Ty shrugged, deciding to bypass the other comments for the one he was comfortable talking about. "He's struggling a little," he answered.

"Why haven't you done anything? Or said anything?" Burns asked, his voice flat.

"To who?" Ty asked calmly. "You? You telling me you didn't know? Thought he'd be okay right back in Miami after all we went through?" After healing up from his injuries in New York, Zane had been pitched right back into undercover work. It hadn't gone particularly well, and although he'd kept away from the drugs and the drink, he'd definitely been a mess in the head when he'd gotten back to DC to be re-partnered with Ty.

Burns' face took on a pinched look, and he shook his head. "I made a mistake, Ty. It happens to the best of us."

"Yes, it does," Ty agreed. He nodded at the file on the desk. "My marks are low, but they're acceptable. So I'm guessing you want me gone for a reason. Tell me what's going on."

"I'm juggling some paperwork here," Burns informed him, his shoulders sagging to show how exhausted he really was. "In order to bury these current tests, I have to have both of you make yourselves scarce for a while. Nothing more sinister than that," he assured Ty.

"Dick," Ty protested weakly. He hated the thought of sitting on his ass, twiddling his thumbs.

Burns raised his voice, speaking over Ty's objections. "After these evaluations go through, you'll both be reassigned to the Baltimore office. I bet you'll be happy to return home."

Ty eyed Burns warily. It would be good to get back to Baltimore. He had buddies there, and he considered the city home after nearly four years. He was still living there through the temporary DC assignment, making the commute every day and occasionally shacking up with Zane in his DC hotel room when he didn't want to go home.

The drive back and forth was murder.

A move back to Baltimore was good news. But he knew there was something he was missing here, some catch in the arrangement that Dick was about to throw in. He had a feeling he knew what it was too.

"Have a nice trip, Ty," Burns offered with a smile. "Say hello to the family for me," he told him with a hint of mischief in his eyes.

Ty stared at him. "The family," he echoed. "My family?"

Burns just smiled and pushed the folders in front of him into a neat stack once more. Ty warred with himself. He wanted to ask questions, but he didn't feel like getting into it with Burns about his family. Or about Zane. "Is that all?" he asked after a long moment of contemplation.

"Unless you want to talk about which part of your training gave you the idea to use your partner as paintball repellant?" Burns inquired with a raised eyebrow.

Ty pursed his lips to keep a smile from forming.

"That's what I thought," Burns replied with a shake of his head. Ty saw his lips twitch in amusement. "Then yes, Special Agent Grady. That is all," he confirmed without ever allowing the smile to surface.

"Next time can you do this on the phone?" Ty asked as he stood and turned away, heading for the door with a frown. "It's a long fucking drive from Baltimore."

"Say hello to Earl for me," Burns requested, a smile in his voice.

Ty didn't respond as he exited the office. He walked through the outer office, head down and face set in a worried frown as he contemplated the next two weeks. It was quite clear what he was supposed to do. A trip to West Virginia was in his immediate future. He ignored the hateful woman at the receptionist's desk as he left the office and headed for the elevators.

"Grady."

Ty stopped abruptly and turned in place to look back at Zane in surprise. He hadn't expected him to stick around. "Hey," he responded, unable to think of anything else to say.

Zane's face was blank, and his shoulders were pulled back stiff. He was obviously expecting some sort of bitching out over the evals. He was all geared up for a fight. It seemed like Zane was always geared up for a fight lately, and Ty was running out of ways to handle him. It was tiring, and he'd been seeking solitude more often than not just to give himself a break.

Ty gave him a jerk of his head. "Come buy me some coffee," he requested as he hit the button for the elevator.

Zane frowned and walked slowly toward Ty and the elevator. "You don't drink coffee," he said with a suspicious note in his voice.

"So?" Ty responded with a slight tilt of his head as he looked sideways at Zane, who held his gaze only for a moment before dropping his eyes. Ty frowned. They weren't connecting like they had been, and he wondered when it had happened and why neither of them had noticed. The only time they seemed to click on all cylinders was when they were working—or playing—and the thought made Ty slightly sad and maybe a little hurt. He brushed it off, though. There was no point in forcing the issue. Things like that came and went, whether you wanted them to or not.

Zane shrugged. "Fine. Coffee." He looked at Ty speculatively. "What did Burns tell you?"

"That you're fucked in the head," Ty responded as he turned and looked at Zane with narrowed eyes, taking in how on edge Zane seemed. Defensive. "What have you been doing about it?"

"I've been busy."

"Doing what?" Ty asked in amusement. "Aside from me?" he added.

Zane's lips compressed, but then his eyes closed for a moment, he half smiled, and some of the tension eased. He slid one hand into his pants pocket. "Planning my next chance?"

"Don't get your hopes up," Ty muttered as the elevator doors opened. He stepped in and punched the button for the ground floor. "Come on," he said to Zane with a sigh. "I have to go home and pack."

"You're actually going somewhere?" Zane asked in surprise.

"I have not-so-subtle orders to go see my family," Ty answered wryly. He cocked his head as he studied Zane again. "You're going to spend three weeks just sitting around your hotel room and moping, aren't you?" he asked knowingly.

Zane sighed and crossed his arms. "I don't really know where I'd go. I'm not going to Texas again."

Ty hesitated, looking him up and down. The thought of inviting Zane to accompany him to West Virginia was appealing, in a way. If things went south, Ty could throw Zane in front of his parents just like he had the paintballs. Use him as a sort of human sacrifice. And then there was the added benefit of having Zane close every night. He'd come to enjoy that when it still happened, despite how he wanted to throttle Zane sometimes.

"You want to come with me?" he asked tentatively.

Zane stared at him, obviously thinking it was a joke. "I don't need a babysitter."

"Maybe, maybe not. But I need you," Ty told him as he reached out and stopped the doors from closing. He knew Zane well enough to know how to manipulate him. If Zane thought his partner was showing vulnerability, he'd fall for it every time. It was an amazingly predictable habit for his unpredictable partner. And there was more than a grain of truth in the words. "Come on," he repeated.

Looking faintly surprised, Zane got on the elevator and stood next to him, waiting for an explanation. Ty remained silent, enjoying watching the other man struggle with the fact that he would have to ask for it. Zane actually lasted almost the entire elevator ride to the parking garage before he huffed softly. "Fine," he said grudgingly. "What do you need me for?"

Ty smirked as he looked over at Zane, but the smile faded as he cleared his throat. "If I'm going home, I need something bigger than me to hide behind," he said as he gestured to Zane's larger frame.

"That actually did work out pretty well for me in the end last time," Zane drawled, raising an eyebrow. He was obviously remembering the night after the trip to Quantico.

Ty let his eyes rake over the man suggestively. "You have other uses too," he agreed.

"Home," Zane said slowly, smiling a little at Ty's playful words. "To West by-God Virginia? And you want me to just… tag along?"

"Yes," Ty answered with a curt nod. That was exactly what he wanted. If Zane could survive a trip to West Virginia to meet the Gradys, he could live through anything. Like a cockroach.

An amused smile slowly pulled at Zane's lips as the elevator doors opened onto the parking deck. "Just what is it you're afraid of?"

Ty pursed his lips and waited a moment before moving out of the elevator without bothering to answer.

Zane huffed quietly and followed him. "Grady, you're going to answer my question."

"And you're going to sprout wings and fly," Ty shot back over his shoulder. "Do you have camping gear?"

"Camping… why the hell would I need camping gear in DC?" Zane asked, throwing up a hand. "Answer the question."

"There are places to camp in DC," Ty answered as he headed for his Bronco.

"Yeah, if you're homeless in a city park," Zane retorted. "Answer the question, Grady."

"I did," Ty said to him with a smirk he tried to hide. He seriously enjoyed riling Zane up. The results were often… heated. "I mean, if you want *specific* places to camp, I'm gonna need a map. And maybe some squeaky pens, you know, the ones that smell good?" he rambled, knowing it would annoy Zane and trying not to smile as he said it.

Zane stopped in place as Ty kept walking. After a long moment he shook his head and changed directions, heading for the far side of the parking garage. Zane had learned not long after they'd been reassigned that he didn't have to stick around to deal with Ty's verbal sparring. In some ways it was a nuisance, because now Ty had to work harder to annoy him, but it was refreshing, too, in that

Zane wasn't willing to be batted around like a mouse being taunted by a cat anymore.

"Hey!" Ty called after him with a melancholy smile. He did miss the verbal sparring sometimes.

"What?" Zane yelled back as he kept walking to his Valkyrie, parked in the corner about thirty yards away.

"You want to know why I don't like going home?" Ty asked as he jangled his keys, the sound echoing in the cement parking garage.

"I believe I asked what you were afraid of, Grady. Two different things," Zane responded as he picked up his helmet from the seat of the motorcycle. His voice bounded off the concrete of the parking deck and reached Ty almost as an echo.

"I'm afraid of the dark," Ty answered immediately with a tilt of his head, his voice soft and serious.

Zane paused and turned back to study him. Ty smiled slightly. They were both still dealing with hang-ups and problems. While Zane certainly had a harder time dealing than Ty did, every once in a while it did Zane good to be reminded that he wasn't alone in his struggles.

"You really want me to come?" Zane asked him uncertainly.

Ty nodded.

"What are we going to do while we're there?"

"Eat home cooking and take a little hike in the woods," Ty answered with a negligent shrug.

Zane's shoulders relaxed. "There's a difference between a little hike and needing camping gear."

"Is there?" Ty asked innocently. He shook his head. "We just go up on the mountain. Stay there a week, maybe ten days," he explained.

"Ten days," Zane repeated flatly.

"Sometimes less," Ty answered.

"I've never been to the mountains," Zane said doubtfully as he set his helmet down.

"All the more reason to go," Ty countered, though he was silently wondering how in the hell Zane had lived all his life without going into the mountains. Any mountains.

Zane nodded slowly. "Are we still getting coffee?" he asked after a moment.

"If you want it," Ty answered with a shrug. "We need to go shopping. You're gonna need some boots," he told his partner with relish.

~CHAPTER 3~

IT WAS warm enough that they could leave the windows of Ty's Bronco down as they drove along the winding roads that led to Bluefield, West Virginia. The fall leaves had turned, making the road a blinding corridor of oranges, yellows, and reds. And even though the sun had just barely risen, the sky was an amazingly clear blue as they headed higher into the Appalachian Mountains.

Ty didn't say much as he drove. He didn't even have the radio on. He was obviously distracted, resting his head in his hand as he propped his elbow on the open window. Even behind the dark aviator sunglasses and the mangled straw bullrider-style hat that sat low on his head, shielding his face, he was frowning unconsciously. He'd purposely taken the scenic route, avoiding the highways as much as possible, but he got more and more tense as they got closer to their destination.

Zane was distracted as well, but more by the scenery than by his thoughts or by his companion's mood. He'd never been up in the mountains, and while Texas had trees, it didn't have trees like this. Trees in every direction, up the mountains, down the mountains, as far as the eye could see.

He frowned and shifted his jaw from side to side, trying to pop his ears. "I need gum," he muttered, looking over to Ty. "You could have warned me. I didn't even think about altitude change."

"Hold your nose and try to blow air through it," Ty advised seriously.

Zane peered at him, trying to decide if he was joking. With Ty, it was usually a safe bet that he was jerking him around, no matter how serious he sounded. But since his partner still looked as distracted as before, Zane decided to try it. And damn if it didn't work.

"Does it all look like this?" he asked as he pulled at his ears. "All the trees and sky and nothing else?"

"The sky is usually there, yeah," Ty answered with a firm nod. "So are the trees, come to think of it," he added thoughtfully.

Zane thwacked him, earning a surprised, "Ow!"

Ty glanced at him and grumbled as he rubbed his chest. Grinning, Zane shifted in the seat to extend his legs across the floorboard as they drove into the town of Bluefield. It wasn't what Zane had expected. It was large and fairly modern, nestled in a valley and sprawling across a gently rolling landscape. There were sections that were older and slightly dilapidated, but for the most part it looked like Bluefield was doing pretty well.

They drove through the Main Street area, historic buildings that had been rejuvenated and hosted little boutique shops and cafés. An old man on the corner of the street waved at Ty as they drove past, apparently recognizing the Bronco, and Ty raised his hand out the window and grinned as he waved in return.

Zane was smiling slightly as Ty took the truck through several turns. Then they were heading further up the mountain. Zane's brow furrowed as he watched the rustic scenery pass, and he asked, "You don't play banjo, do you?"

Ty looked over at him quickly, shock written plainly on his face even behind the sunglasses. "Did Dick tell you that?" he demanded.

Zane stared at him for a moment and then broke down laughing. "Oh hell, no. I was just making a *Deliverance* joke!"

Ty glared at him for as long as he was able before he was forced to look back at the road. "I learned when I was little," he finally said defensively. "Banjo, fiddle, guitar. The whole family plays."

"That's great," Zane said once he calmed down a little, though he couldn't resist another snicker. That just seemed out of character for tough guy Marine Ty Grady. It was almost charming.

"Shut up," Ty muttered. "And FYI, *Deliverance* took place in Georgia. In West Virginia we kiss our cousins."

Zane laughed softly. Soon they were out of the city, climbing even further up into the mountains. He had to yawn a couple times to pop his ears again.

Another five minutes and they were turning off the paved two-lane and heading up a winding dirt road. Ty was getting more and more fidgety, shifting in his seat as he put the Bronco through its paces. Just when it looked like the road might be tapering off into rugged wilderness, Ty turned onto a narrow gravel drive that seemed to go straight up into the heart of a mountain. He glanced at Zane again and smiled. "You can get a car up here, but you better hope the weather sticks." Then he frowned and slowed the truck further. "Here we go," he murmured as they topped the steep incline and a house came into view.

Zane's lips compressed. Ty was still edgy, and it was getting to him. He leaned forward to look out the windshield at what awaited them.

The house was a classic old farmhouse, but well-kept, with a stone foundation, white siding, dormer windows on the second story, bright red shutters, and a matching tin roof. A porch wrapped around the entire front and side of the house, complete with an array of old rocking chairs and oversized stairs leading up to the front door. The outbuildings were in worse shape, the paint peeling slightly on the clapboard frames; some of them tilted precariously. Several of them were nothing but cedar beams and tin, while a few were cinderblock and much sturdier.

In the gravel driveway were four other vehicles: a crew cab Ford F-150, a Chevy Blazer, an old Ford Ranger, and a brand new black Lexus coupe. Ty parked beside the Lexus and cocked his head, peering at it curiously.

A man drew Zane's attention when he came out onto the porch, pushing through the screen door and shielding his eyes as he stepped into the morning sun. He was young, much too young to be Ty's father. He still bore a striking resemblance to Ty, though his hair was a little longer and lighter, and he was taller and thinner. He had to be Ty's brother. The man thumped down the stairs, walking with a pronounced limp, and Ty opened up his door and slid out of the Bronco as he came closer.

Taking his cue from Ty, Zane got out as well but stood just inside the door as he looked around at the towering trees that surrounded them. He tore his eyes away from them to watch Ty approach the house. He felt like he should hang back for now, at least until after the reunion.

Ty grinned as he and his brother embraced. He gave the man an affectionate pat on his cheek and then turned and gestured for Zane to come closer.

"'Bout time y'all got here," Ty's brother said to them.

"Shut up," Ty grunted at him. "Zane, this is my brother, Deacon," he said with a wave of his hand at his brother. "This is Zane Garrett."

"Special Agent Zane Garrett, I assume," Deacon said with emphasis as he stepped forward and took Zane's hand, pumping it hard. His voice wasn't as deep as Ty's, but it still had that gravelly, drawling quality to it that Zane liked. "You can call me Deuce."

"Okay, Deuce," Zane agreed. He liked him already; he seemed like a friendlier version of Ty. "Nice to meet you."

"Likewise," Deuce drawled, grinning. "Come on in," he invited as he turned and threw his arm around Ty's shoulders. "Mom's fluttering," he said to his brother, trying unsuccessfully not to laugh.

"As long as she's cooking while she's doing it," Ty muttered. "I'm starving. Did you get a new car again?"

"You like it?" Deuce asked.

"No," Ty answered candidly with a shake of his head and a glance back at the Lexus.

"It has Bluetooth," Deuce answered with a grin, unperturbed. Ty groaned and shook his head.

Zane walked up the steps behind them, rubbing his hands together to ward off the slight morning chill. He'd pulled the jacket off when they'd gotten in the truck at the last rest stop. He'd known it would be cooler up here, but it had to be a good twenty degrees cooler here than in DC. He spared another look around and shook his head. It was so totally different from any other place he'd been— Washington, LA, Baltimore, New York. Texas. Especially Miami.

Ty stopped at the door and looked back at him. "Welcome to West Virginia," he murmured as he held the screen door open. The smell of frying bacon and fresh bread wafted out to them.

Zane nodded and followed Ty inside, where it was quite a bit warmer, and the smell of the bread made his stomach growl. "Oh Lord. Fresh-baked bread."

Ty sniffed at the air as he tromped through the house toward the back, where the dining room opened up into a large kitchen. "Morning," he greeted as he stepped into the kitchen.

The woman at the stove turned and smiled widely. Ty went over to her and hugged her close, kissing her on the cheek as she patted his back without letting go of the spatula in her hand. She was a tall woman, the top of her head hitting past Ty's broad shoulders, and her round face was almost devoid of wrinkles until she smiled. Her graying hair had once been the same color as Ty's, and her eyes were a bright, striking green.

She stepped back from Ty and took his face in her hands, the spatula smacking against his temple. "'Bout time you got here," she said to him. She looked over Ty's shoulder at Zane and smiled again. "You must be Zane," she said as she unceremoniously pushed Ty aside. She went up to Zane and pulled him into a hug as well, just like he was another son she hadn't seen in some time.

Zane's eyes widened in surprise, and after a beat he halfway closed his arms around her, not sure what to do. "Uh. Hi," he said weakly, patting her shoulder gently.

"Zane Garrett, Mara Grady," Ty introduced with a smirk as he met Zane's eyes.

"Nice to meet you," Zane said as she patted his back, oblivious to his discomfort. Then she turned away and bopped Ty in the head with her spatula.

"Ow!" Ty protested with a surprised laugh.

"Shoulda been home months ago," she scolded. "Sit down, Zane dear, breakfast is almost ready," she said in a much sweeter voice.

Zane swallowed a laugh, although he didn't even try to hide his smile. "Yes, ma'am," he said, pulling out a chair on the far side of the table next to the wall so he'd be out of the way.

Ty sat down opposite him, grumbling. "You got bacon grease in my hair," he said to his mother as he rubbed at his head.

"Serves you right," Mara responded. She tossed the spatula into the sink and fished out another from a nearby drawer.

Deuce sat next to Zane and plopped an empty glass in front of each of them, snickering softly and avoiding meeting his brother's eyes.

"Where's Dad?" Ty asked as he made a rude gesture at Deuce. Zane could feel his smile grow wider.

"Went up to the mine early this morning; someone called about some kids messing with the gates," Deuce answered. At the mention of the mine, Ty tensed visibly, and he nodded and looked toward the back door uncomfortably.

"If he's gone much longer," his mother said to them, "I want you boys to go fetch him."

"Yes, ma'am," both brothers answered in automatic response. Zane had seen Ty snap to attention for Dick Burns before. He'd always assumed it was some latent response from his military training. But it clearly went back further than that.

He also noticed Ty's reaction to hearing about the mine, and he remembered what little Ty had told him about growing up here. Ty had always been scared of the mines, afraid of something happening to his father while he was there, and terrified of being trapped in them himself. After his experience in New York and being buried in a dark hole where he thought he'd never see light again, the thought of going into those mines now had to be outright terrifying. Zane had to admit Ty hid it well.

Mara set down a platter overflowing with biscuits, warm slices of fresh bread, bacon, and sausage links. Then she set down a bowl of grits, two jars of what looked like homemade jam, and two pitchers of orange juice. Last came a bowl full of scrambled eggs.

She tapped Ty in the back of the head as he reached for a piece of bacon. "Manners," she reminded as she wiped her hands on her apron before beginning to untie it. "You go ahead and load up, Zane, you're going to need a full stomach to deal with these two all day," Mara advised.

Zane nodded but stood up. "I need to take a quick break first. We didn't stop much during the drive," he explained.

"Out that door and first tree to the left," Deuce told him as he pointed at the back door.

"Put a sock in it, Deacon," Mara scolded. "It's the door under the stairs, dear," she told Zane as she sat at the head of the table.

As he walked out of the kitchen in the direction she'd pointed, Zane got a better glimpse of the rest of the house. It was a typical old farmhouse with scuffed hardwood floors covered by handmade rag rugs. The plaster walls were covered with neatly framed black-and-white photographs; some of them had to be a hundred years old, and some of them were new enough that Ty was wearing his FBI windbreaker in one.

Zane looked at a few of them, stopping for a little longer when he found a photo of Ty in uniform. He looked much younger, and while it was the same hard, unsmiling face he'd seen in every

Marine's photo, there was a hint of something in the hazel eyes that Zane didn't think he'd seen in Ty before. He couldn't quite place it. The man did look good in a uniform, that was for sure.

Zane stared at it for a long time before pulling himself away and going to find the staircase.

"Grandpa!" Zane heard Ty exclaim in a pleased voice from the kitchen.

Zane shut the door with a smile. About five minutes, later he stood in the doorway of the kitchen again. An old man had joined the table, and he sat next to Ty, holding his hand and patting it affectionately.

"Grandpa, this is my partner, Zane," Ty said as soon as Zane sat. "Zane, Chester Grady."

"FBI agent, huh?" the old man said to Zane with narrowed eyes.

"Most of the time," Zane admitted.

"Won't hold that against you," Chester said. "Yet," he promised.

Zane arched an eyebrow at the old man. "I'll keep it in mind."

"Behave, you old goat," Mara chastised. "We'll start without your daddy," she told the rest of them with a frown. "He better be stuck in a hole somewhere," she grumbled as she bowed her head.

Zane glanced around the table as he slowly crossed his hands, figuring a prayer was coming, and his eyes stuck on Ty, who looked even more tense than before.

"One of you say grace," Mara ordered after waiting for one of the brothers to take the lead. Ty looked up, meeting Zane's eyes. He opened his mouth to speak, but the screen door creaked and interrupted him.

"Those damn kids are gonna blow themselves up down there," the man who entered pronounced as he shrugged out of his jacket and hung it on a hook beside the door. "Morning, boys," he said, as if having his sons there for breakfast was nothing unusual.

"Morning, sir," both men responded in unison.

"Dad, this is Zane Garrett," Ty added with a nod to his partner. "Zane, Earl Grady," he introduced as Ty's father came over and patted Ty on the shoulder in greeting.

Earl was an imposing man, tall and broad-shouldered. The man made Ty look like the runt of the litter. His graying hair was cut short and neat, and he was clean-shaven and almost as devoid of wrinkles as his wife. Zane decided it must be the altitude.

Earl reached across the table to offer his callused hand to Zane. "Hello, sir," Zane greeted as he stood to shake Earl's hand.

"Good to meet you, son," Earl responded as he shook Zane's hand. His voice was deep and gravelly, with the same twanging, almost hoarse quality Ty's was apt to have at times. His accent was more pronounced. "Ty has told us absolutely nothing about you," he informed Zane as he sat at the other end of the table, opposite his wife.

Zane's brows rose. He was mildly surprised, first by being addressed as "son" and second by Earl's comment about his presence. "Ah." He looked to his partner sitting across the table from him. "You *did* tell them I was coming, right?"

"Yes," Ty answered defensively.

"Oh, don't you worry, dear," his mother said with a pat of Zane's hand. "Earl, say grace so Zane doesn't starve," she ordered. She bowed her head again as Earl said a few words over the food, and then as soon as he was done she lifted her head and started passing around the dishes. "Eat up," she invited.

Giving Ty a dubious glare, Zane picked up the serving fork and started filling his plate and then offered the platter to Deuce, who took it with a murmur of thanks and dished out his own breakfast before passing it to his father.

"So Zane, Richard tells me you two have had some interesting times," Earl Grady said as he took the platter.

"Richard? Richard... Burns?" Zane asked, his fork pausing over his plate. Earl looked up from his plate and raised one eyebrow.

"Interesting times," Zane quickly answered. "If you were reading about them, I guess," he added.

"Reading about them," Earl repeated as his eyes traveled to Ty. "That what you been doing, son? Sitting behind a desk and reading about them?" he asked his son.

Ty sighed and sat forward to lean his elbows on the table. "Dad, don't be silly," he said with practiced patience and sarcasm. "You know I don't read," he assured his father.

Earl smiled slowly before passing the platter on around to Chester. "You like desk work, Zane?" he asked, his voice still mildly curious.

Zane screwed up his face in distaste. "I've done more than my fair share."

"Earl, leave the boys alone," Mara ordered.

"Hell, Mara, I'm just being friendly," Earl protested.

"You're interrogating them," Mara corrected. "Eat your bacon," she ordered. She patted Ty on the head protectively as he took the platter from Chester and started scooping food onto to his plate. He didn't even react to the gesture.

Zane wondered if Ty was a mama's boy. He tipped his head to the side, watching them as he picked out a piece of warm bread, and thought maybe so. Not that he would ever voice that opinion to Ty until he was good and ready to die. He supposed, though, with a father as imposing as Earl Grady seemed to be, his sons would need a protective and loving mother. With a soft hum, he started picking up jelly jars and examining them.

"That there's plum jelly, and the other's cherry, honey, you help yourself," Mara told him. "You like hiking, Zane? I've never met one of the boys' friends who could keep up with them on the mountain," she went on cheerfully.

"Haven't done much hiking, I'm afraid, unless you count running around out on the flats," Zane said as he peered into the jars and finally chose the cherry. "And that was a long time ago."

Earl and Mara both stopped what they were doing and looked at him in surprise. Chester began to laugh delightedly as he continued eating. Zane glanced among them, waiting for an explanation.

"You've never been out on the trail?" Earl asked dubiously.

"Sure I have. Just not in the mountains," Zane said, glancing between Earl and Ty.

"He'll be fine, Dad," Deuce said through a mouthful of food. "If I can do it, so can he," he pointed out with a tap of his knuckles on the table.

"Gonna be cold out there," Chester interjected gleefully.

"Maybe you boys should think about not going," Mara said. She sounded worried.

"Zane'll be fine, Ma," Ty assured her, unconcerned as he looked at Zane. Zane shrugged with one shoulder, not sure what Ty wanted him to say. Ty cocked his head and gave him a quick wink, and Zane gave him a small smile in response.

"Well, Zane, you must have proved yourself somehow," Earl observed wryly. "The last person Ty took on the mountain was Recon. And we carried *his* ass back home."

"He got bit by a snake, dad," Ty said in protest.

"Well, hell, you told the dumbass not to poke it," Earl argued. Ty pressed his lips together tightly, trying not to laugh as he looked back at Zane.

"I'm betting it's cool enough not too many snakes will be out," Zane said dryly. "But I'll do my best not to poke them."

"You do that," Earl said with a nod.

"Probably don't want to poke at the wild boar either," Deuce added helpfully. "Or the bats. Or the bears."

"Sounds like lions and tigers and bears, oh my," Zane said as he helped himself to more scrambled eggs.

"Bears, sure. Lots of coyotes. And you just might see yourself a lion if you're really lucky," Earl said while he buttered a piece of toast.

"We have varying definitions of lucky," Deuce interjected.

"Seen a black panther out there once," Chester offered, unconcerned.

"Was that through the end of a moonshine jug?" Ty asked him with a smirk.

"Watch that tongue, sonny," Chester warned with a wag of his crooked finger in Ty's face.

"Better if you plan to restrict your poking," Deuce told Zane helpfully. "Lots of endangered animals up here aside from Ty. Snails. Peregrines and a lot of other birds, mostly. And a salamander."

"Don't forget the freshwater mussel," Ty drawled.

Deuce toasted him with his orange juice. "And the freshwater mussel."

"How do you even know where to walk?" Zane asked flatly. Ty rolled his eyes and waved Zane off.

"What's the plan today?" Deuce asked Ty as they ate.

Ty shrugged. "Haven't really got that far," he answered. "What about you, Garrett? Got anything you wanna do before we take you up there and leave you?"

"Sleep?" Zane suggested, ignoring the playful threat. "Or something equally relaxing. We're supposed to be on vacation, remember?"

"Vacation?" Deuce asked in surprise. "I thought you used up all your vacation already."

Ty looked at him, pursing his lips. The two brothers stared at each other expectantly for a tense moment. "I don't wanna talk about it," Ty said finally.

"Neither do I," Deuce assured him gratefully as he went back to eating.

"Talk about what?" Mara asked distractedly.

"Nothing," Ty insisted.

"Ty and his partner are on punishment," Earl told her, frowning. Zane's head popped up in surprise.

"Did Dick tell you that?" Ty demanded angrily.

"No, Ty, I figured that one out all by myself," Earl answered with a tap to the side of his head. Eyes darting from side to side, Zane leaned back a little out of the line of fire.

"If you two are gonna fight, you take it outside," Mara told them, unaffected by the suddenly tense atmosphere. "Zane, honey, how long have you been with the Bureau?" she asked.

"A little over twenty years, ma'am," Zane said hesitantly.

"You'd think twenty years would get you better than Ty," Deuce muttered as he reached for the orange juice.

"Well…" Zane drew out, smiling a little, "no. Afraid not."

Ty glared at them both. Earl watched Zane with his head slightly cocked. He had the same quality Ty did, the one that always made it look like he knew something more than he was letting on.

"I believe it was more Ty getting stuck with me than me getting stuck with him," Zane clarified as Ty gave him a gesture that probably meant for him to shut the hell up.

"Why do you say that?" Deuce asked curiously.

"I was transferred from another division, and Assistant Director Burns dumped me on him with no warning," Zane said, trying to talk around it enough that Ty might not kick his ass later.

"So you consider each other punishment?" Deuce asked as he set his elbow on the table and leaned forward in interest.

No way was Zane touching that one. He'd let Ty throw the first insult.

Ty wagged his fork in his brother's direction. "Stop psychoanalyzing us," he warned.

"But that's my job," Deuce protested.

"If I wanted to see a shrink, I'd go to the one Dick told me to," Ty told him. Zane did a double take between the brothers.

"Why do you need a shrink?" Earl asked Ty.

"We really don't like to be called shrinks," Deuce informed them in annoyance.

Zane's chin turned toward Deuce. "You're a shrink?" was out of his mouth before he could stop it.

"I'm a psychiatrist, yes," Deuce answered. "Ty didn't tell you?"

Zane snorted. "I know as little or less about you all than you know about me. I didn't even know Ty *had* a brother 'til this morning."

Ty's fork clattered into his plate, and he held up his hand. "Can we stop sharing, please?" he requested in frustration.

"Why do you need a shrink?" Earl asked him again.

"I have daddy issues," Ty answered with a smirk.

Earl pointed his fork at him and narrowed his eyes as he chewed, though there was a hint of amusement in his expression. It seemed all of them enjoyed brandishing that quick wit. If Zane weren't so off balance, it would have almost been fun to see Ty bested by someone else.

"If Richard said you needed a shrink, then you need a shrink," Mara told Ty with certainty.

"I don't need a shrink," Ty insisted with a gesture of his hand to calm his mother.

"We really don't like to be called shrinks," Deuce repeated again in annoyance.

"Honey, you're lucky that's all we call you," Mara told Deuce as she dished out more grits.

Ty snorted, and Deuce grumbled at them both.

"I think Burns just enjoys yanking us around," Zane said under his breath.

"He doesn't enjoy much about either of you lately, son," Earl told him, growing serious once more.

Zane glanced up at him, surprised. He wondered what the two men could legally even talk about. Ty—maybe. But certainly not himself, except in the most general of terms. With a quick look, he saw that Ty wasn't paying him any attention. His eyes were closed, and he was pinching the bridge of his nose.

"Ty?" Zane said significantly. He hated the thought of someone checking up on him without his knowledge. Especially if it was someone who might really care and be upset by hearing about Zane's ups and downs. He could imagine that Ty didn't like the idea, either.

Ty opened his eyes and looked at Zane through his fingers as he covered his face with his hand. He shrugged helplessly, as if to say he had absolutely no control over what was happening. Zane wrinkled his nose and resisted the urge to reach across the table and smack him one for being absolutely no help. Instead he turned his attention back to Earl. "Just how well do you know Assistant Director Burns, Mr. Grady?" he asked curiously.

"You're welcome to call me Earl, son. And I've known Richard for almost forty years," Earl answered. "We went into Vietnam together, and we came out together," he said with a hint of pride.

Very good friends, then. Zane sighed and sat back. Earl might not know much of anything about him. But he also might know more than Zane would want to admit to anyone, much less Ty's father, of all people. He leveled his eyes on his partner and waited.

"What?" Ty asked defensively. "It's not my fault," he protested as Earl chuckled.

Zane felt his lips curl up. It was actually amusing to see Ty's reactions to his family. "What isn't he enjoying about us?" he asked, going back to Earl's first comment.

Earl shrugged as he handed his plate to his wife, who was now rounding the table collecting dishes. "Apparently you're making him do more paperwork than he wants to be doing. He mentioned something about throwing handguns and blue paint," he said with a bemused frown. Ty snorted and covered the laugh with a cough. Earl looked at him with narrowed eyes and then back at Zane. Zane was hard-pressed not to chuckle. "He also told me he was worried about you both," Earl continued. "He's always worried about Ty, but him saying he's worried about Ty's partner is new," he informed Zane as he studied him closely. "Ty usually takes care of his partners."

Zane automatically handed his plate up when Mara held her hand out for it, but he kept his eyes on Earl, not sure if there was more to hear.

"Why's he worried?" Earl asked him pleasantly.

"Dad," Ty said in warning, but Earl continued to look at Zane expectantly.

After a long moment of silent standoff, Zane just shrugged one shoulder. He didn't know what the man wanted him to say. Anything he could think of was far too personal. Earl's eyes transferred from Zane to Ty without a word. Ty merely raised an eyebrow at him and bit into a piece of bacon with a loud crunch, obviously more immune to the gaze than Zane was.

Deuce gave Zane's arm a gentle pat, and he scooted his chair back noisily. "Come on, Zane, I'll show you the mountain," he offered under his breath.

Zane glanced to Ty before moving to follow Deuce out. His partner was on his own with this one, and Zane wanted out from under Earl's knowing eyes before he said something he shouldn't. It wasn't really Earl's reaction he was worried about. Zane didn't have to go home with *him*.

They went through the back door, which was the nearest exit, and Deuce had to grip the railing as he thumped down the old wooden steps that led into the back yard. The grassy part of the yard rolled slightly and then dropped off suddenly into a deep ravine just twenty yards from the back of the house. The thick woods started at the edge of the far side, seeming to enclose the area with a wall of trees. Deuce took a few steps toward the ravine and waved at the land beyond it. "And there's the mountain," he told Zane with a small smile.

Zane took a deep breath of the clean air and gave him a smile. "Thanks," he said with a nod.

Deuce waved him off. "Don't let Dad get to you," he advised. "If you can deal with Ty, Dad should be a cakewalk for you."

"I don't care about offending Ty," Zane answered. "Although I do have to work with him, so I try not to piss him off too badly."

"A fair plan. And Dad isn't easily offended," Deuce told him with a smile. "What are you worried he knows about?" he asked curiously.

"I don't exactly have the best track record in the Bureau," Zane said quietly as he looked around at the trees.

"You're still in it, though, and I know Ty doesn't rate second-hand partners," Deuce countered.

Zane would have answered in the affirmative, but he wasn't quite sure if he really fit the bill. "I guess I'm a little off balance," he said vaguely, gesturing to the surroundings.

"High altitudes will do that," Deuce replied, the sarcasm practically dripping from the words.

"You talk like him," Zane said wryly, hearing the smartass echo in Deuce's voice that so reminded him of Ty.

"How's that?" Deuce asked in interest.

"That tone of voice," Zane said, fixing his eyes intently on Deuce. "Ty sounds like that all the time. Droll. Like he's humoring me."

Deuce laughed. "I apologize," he offered with an open, honest grin.

Zane's smile was more genuine this time. "I'd say you don't know how annoying that can be, but...." Deuce laughed harder as the screen door creaked behind them.

"We're gonna have to start slipping Dad Valium or something," Ty muttered as he joined them. He handed Deuce a thick cigar that he'd had hidden in his pocket.

"Cuban?" Deuce asked in delight.

"Cuban," Ty answered with a nod as Deuce slid the cigar under his nose and sniffed it.

Zane frowned. "Where's mine?"

"You haven't earned illegal Cubans yet," Ty informed him seriously.

"Earned?" Zane asked, voice rising toward the end. He looked at Deuce and jerked his thumb toward Ty. "See? This is what I deal with almost every day." He sniffed. "Earned," he muttered, shoving his hands in his pockets.

"I thought acting as a human paintball shield qualified you for illegal Cubans?" Deuce asked Ty in an innocent voice. Ty began snickering before he'd even finished speaking.

Zane rolled his eyes. "I still have bruises," he said plaintively.

"Boo hoo," Ty offered. "You smoke too much for cigars," he reasoned.

Zane shrugged at Ty's logic. He was used to it by now. "Better hope no one with a grudge catches you with one of those."

"Everyone has a grudge," Ty told him with a smirk.

"My brother has no morals," Deuce sang lightly, and he cackled gleefully as he slid the cigar he'd been given into his pocket.

Ty grunted at him. "I'm running low, and Charlie's getting discharged in three months, so enjoy it while it lasts," he told Deuce in a disgruntled growl.

"You'll just have to find some other shady character at Gitmo," Deuce counseled seriously. "I'm gonna go unpack some things and sit with Grandpa before he gets the shovel out," he added with a smirk. He gave Ty a pat on the arm before walking away, leaving them alone in the cold, fresh air.

"Shovel?" Zane questioned.

Ty shook his head. "Later," he promised.

Zane shifted his weight and tried to let the tension from breakfast go as he pulled out a pack of cigarettes and lit one up. He took in the sun rising above the trees, and there was a full minute of quiet before he spoke. "Your family is… nice," he said with difficulty.

That caused Ty to start laughing. Hard.

~CHAPTER 4~

SOON enough, Ty was making his way around the house toward his Bronco to retrieve the bags of camping equipment they'd brought with them. Zane remained in the back yard for a moment, finishing his cigarette in the cool, crisp air and looking around at the peaceful surroundings. For some reason, he couldn't imagine Ty having grown up here.

His lips twitched. In the barn, maybe.

As he joined Ty at the truck, Zane caught sight of Chester sitting in a rocking chair on the porch, eyeing them silently. He also saw that the old man now held the aforementioned shovel across his thighs as he rocked.

Zane leaned over toward Ty. "Is that *the* shovel?"

Ty hefted a bag out of the back of the Bronco and glanced up at the porch. "Yep," he said with a smile. "He sleeps with it, too, so don't go sneaking around at night."

Zane took one of the bags. "He sleeps with it," he repeated.

Ty hummed affirmatively. "Not sure where he keeps it, but I can tell you with certainty that he wakes up swinging. He goes everywhere with it." He pointed to the old blue and white Ford Ranger that had a gun rack mounted in the back window. "When he drives, there's a cane and his shovel in that thing."

"It's not *that* weird. I sleep with a gun," Zane said with a shrug, though he was bemused. "You used to sleep with any number of weapons. Why not a shovel?" He paused and bit his lip. "What kind of damage can he do with that thing?"

"Broke my nose when I was fifteen," Ty answered with a fond smile. "He can hit a snake from ten yards away. Moving target's iffy since his eyesight started going," he added seriously.

Zane couldn't stop the laugh. "Broke your nose? What were you doing?"

"Sneaking in," Ty said unashamedly as he pulled out another heavy pack and thumped it on the ground. "Me and Deuce. I was on point that night. Turned the corner and *bang*!" he said as he waved his hand in front of his face.

Zane snickered. "After curfew," he said knowingly.

"You bet," Ty said with a nod. He looked over to the house and smiled at his grandfather, who was rocking contentedly, the shovel held loosely in his fingers. "Grandpa fought in the Pacific Theater in World War Two," he told Zane in a low voice. "Grandma always said he came home with a shovel and never put it away." He glanced at Zane and shrugged. "On the Pacific islands, sometimes a shovel was a Marine's only defense from enemy fire. Dug for your life," he explained. "We always figured something broke up there," he said with a tap to his temple. "The shovel made him feel... whole."

Zane nodded slowly as he picked up one of the bags and hung it on his right arm before picking up another. "It's great that you still have him."

"He's still here most of the time," Ty responded with a sigh. "Sometimes I think he's putting on just so he don't have to deal with us," he added with a smirk.

"Like I haven't seen that before," Zane said, nudging Ty in the ribs with this elbow.

"I don't play at crazy," Ty warned with a smirk he couldn't quite hide. He reached into the Bronco and dragged out one last bag, throwing it over his shoulder. Zane fixed a look of disbelief on his partner. "What?" Ty asked angelically as he picked up the first bag and began heading for the house.

"You don't play at being an asshole either," Zane informed him as he followed him.

"No, I don't," Ty agreed happily as he tromped across the yard with the bags.

"Oh, the things I could say," Zane muttered, reminding himself Ty's family was around.

"What was that?" Ty asked with a look over his shoulder. He was grinning widely, his hazel eyes sparkling in the sunlight.

"You heard me," Zane drawled, his heart skipping a beat or two. Ty was rarely in this mood lately. Not since New York, in fact. Ty winked at him and thumped up the steps.

"Hey, sonny," Chester said to him as he rocked. "How far's the trek this time?"

"Too far for you, old man," Ty grunted with a smirk.

"Damn straight," Chester said happily as he looked back out at the mountain and patted his shovel lovingly.

"Maybe I'll stay here and keep him company," Zane suggested. "He can protect me from the snakes."

"Ain't no snakes this time of year," Chester scoffed. "Damn fool federal agents," he muttered sorrowfully with a shake of his head.

Zane chuckled. "Sorry. There's snakes year-round in Texas."

"Garrett," Ty warned under his breath, shaking his head.

"Does this look like Texas to you, son?" Chester asked irritably. He easily picked up the weighty shovel with one gnarled hand and waved it in Zane's direction.

"No, sir," Zane answered smartly, stepping a bit behind Ty. "I'll be sure to pay better attention."

"Smartass," Chester muttered as he returned his attention back to the view and began rocking again.

Ty reached behind him and patted Zane's hip, urging him to get inside as they sidestepped past. Zane cleared his throat as he allowed Ty to shuffle him inside. Ty just shook his head again and dropped the heavy bags inside the living room. "Don't piss him off," he warned in a low voice as he headed for the kitchen.

"I think he puts on being pissed off to keep you in line."

"It works," Ty returned immediately.

Zane chuckled, trying to keep it quiet. "Wow," he observed.

"What?" Ty asked defensively.

"It just explains so much about you."

Ty turned to look at him, circling the kitchen table warily. "How?" he asked in confusion.

Zane braced both hands on the tabletop and leaned toward him. "It's not just you. Your whole family's cracked, but somehow, you all make it work. That's so unfair." A hand slapped him hard on the back of the head just as he finished speaking. "Ow!" His hand flew up to rub the sore spot.

Mara whisked past with a bushel of apples on her hip. "Be nice," she chastised distractedly.

"It was a compliment!" Zane protested as Ty laughed.

"I know bullshit when I hear it, kiddo. I raised that one," Mara told him with a jerk of her thumb at Ty as she plunked the apples down on the table. "Get out of my kitchen or help me," she ordered as she wiped her hands on her apron.

Ty went to the nearest cabinet and opened it, extracted a white tub labeled "Flour" from the highest shelf, and set it on the nearest counter. He gave his mom a kiss on the cheek and then promptly headed for the door. That was apparently all the help she'd get.

Zane trailed after Ty into the living room. Ty flopped onto the couch and looked at him critically. "Shut up," Zane said as he sat opposite him in an armchair.

"You really think I'm crazy?" Ty asked him curiously.

"Crazy, yes. Cuckoo off your rocker, no. There's a difference," Zane answered. "Ask your brother," he tacked on. Ty raised an eyebrow at him.

"Ask your brother what?" Deuce called as he thumped down the stairs into the living room. He had changed clothes into something more appropriate for the mountains rather than driving from Philadelphia in a Lexus.

"Whether I'm crazy," Ty answered as he leaned back and slumped into the soft cushions.

"Completely certifiable," Deuce provided without looking at either of them as he examined a bowl full of peanuts on the coffee table.

"There's a difference between crazy and cuckoo off your rocker," Zane repeated.

"That's true," Deuce agreed as he looked up at Ty and nodded. "Are these Dad's?" he whispered as he pointed at the peanuts. Ty merely nodded, not looking away from Deuce. Zane glanced between the two, interested in watching them interact. There didn't appear to be any rivalry. In fact, they seemed to be truly at ease with each other. Deuce deflated a little and abandoned the peanuts. He sat in the old wooden rocking chair near the fireplace and sighed heavily.

"Zane thinks we're all crazy," Ty told him with a smirk.

Deuce was nodding even before Ty finished speaking. "Right on, brother," he said to Zane as he held his hand up in a fist and then smacked it down on the arm of the rocking chair.

"See?" Zane shrugged. "I said it was a compliment. Deuce understands."

"I wouldn't call it a compliment," Deuce argued. "Doesn't mean it ain't true!" he added cheerfully.

Zane couldn't help but laugh and relax a little into the armchair. "Refreshing."

Deuce cocked his head and studied Zane. He looked remarkably like Ty when he did it. The whole family, even Chester, was capable of the same expression, like they knew something about you and didn't plan on telling. The longer Deuce peered at him, the more Zane wondered what was up. "Something on your mind, Deuce?"

"Not usually," Deuce responded with a grin. "I'm just sort of curious," he added thoughtfully as he looked over at Ty. "About you two," he clarified.

Zane's eyes slid to Ty to check his reaction. His partner had narrowed his eyes at his brother, but he was still smiling slightly, like they were about to play a game he enjoyed.

"Another interrogation?" Zane said, amused. This could either go well... or not. There was potential for all sorts of questions Ty might not want answered for him.

"I don't interrogate," Deuce answered with an easy grin. "That's my brother's job. I just listen when you give me answers."

"I'm sure you listen very well," Zane allowed after a long moment's pause. But before he said anything else, he glanced over at Ty for some sort of comment.

Ty rolled his eyes. "You don't have to dance around it. He knows."

Zane's brows jumped. "Knows... *what*... exactly?"

Ty tilted his head and gave Zane a look that asked him not to make him explain. Zane leaned back into the chair and considered. He suspected Ty was talking about them fucking around. But if he wasn't....

"Interesting," Deuce drew out with an obvious smile.

Zane took his time speculating how this conversation might go. Deuce merely smiled at him widely and rocked. Zane shook his head; he hated playing head games with shrinks. It took a lot of concentration that he just didn't want to muster. He was supposed to be on vacation, after all. "I just might learn to dislike you," he said conversationally.

"You won't be the first, Slick," Deuce responded easily.

Even if he wanted to, Zane honestly didn't know if he could manipulate Deuce. The man was too much like Ty. Zane shifted in the armchair and shrugged. "What are you curious about?"

Deuce narrowed his eyes and glanced at Ty again. "You got him on the hook, man, ask away," Ty advised, smiling slightly.

Deuce nodded and glanced back at Zane speculatively. "I think I got my answer. But we'll talk later," he decided as he pushed himself out of his chair. "Right now I gotta see a man about a shovel," he said easily as he walked past and toward the front door.

His lips curving into a rueful smile, Zane watched the man walk out, knowing he'd let himself be outplayed. Now, Deuce would know he could broach the subject at any time, and he knew Zane would have been thinking about it and dreading it all the while. "Goody. Something to look forward to," he muttered before looking up at his partner.

Ty was watching his brother, smiling slightly as Deuce let the screen door bang shut. The look in his eyes was almost one of pride. "Pain in the ass, ain't he?" he asked softly as he looked back at Zane.

"Like someone else I know," Zane said pointedly, though he smiled to offset it. It was obvious Ty loved his brother very much. It was odd to find brothers just two years apart in age and not see at least one point of contention between them.

Ty shrugged unapologetically. "He's a hell of a lot smarter than I am," he warned.

"That's what I'm afraid of," Zane said. Then the proverbial light bulb came on. He shifted his full attention to Ty. "That another reason you brought me here?" he asked mildly. "Your shrink brother?"

Ty met his eyes and sighed. "If it was, would you be pissed?" he asked.

The corners of Zane's lips turned up. "Probably," he admitted. "But I suppose I'd forgive you."

"Good," Ty grunted. "'Cause you caught me."

"I'm too comfortable to kick your ass right now. Remind me, and I'll do it later," Zane said, leaning his head against the back of the chair, scooting his feet on the floor so his legs stretched out. Ty nodded agreeably, looking like he thought he might have dodged a bullet. But Zane wasn't ready to let him off the hook. "What does your brother know?"

Ty cleared his throat and looked toward the kitchen, where his mother was making quite a bit of racket as she prepared her pies. He stood and nodded for the front door. "Let's take a walk," he murmured.

Zane sighed before pushing himself up and out of the chair, and he gestured for Ty to lead the way. Ty pushed through the screen door and put a hand on Chester's shoulder in passing before clomping down the steps into the front yard. When they got into the soft grass, Zane started patting his pockets, looking for his cigarettes.

Ty shook his head and held out a pack, shaking it at Zane tauntingly. Zane grimaced and swiped at it. Ty easily evaded him and slid the pack into a hidden pocket inside his jacket. "No ruining my mountain air with cigarette smoke," he said sternly. He didn't hint at when, where, or how he'd gotten Zane's cigarettes from him.

Zane growled softly. "And you can ruin it with cigar smoke? I'm not even smoking half a pack a day," he reasoned. "I could sure use one right now."

"Why? What's to stress about?" Ty asked easily. "You're on vacation, Garrett."

"Think about that question real hard, Grady. Put yourself in my place," Zane instructed. "I'm in a strange place with strange people, and I'm really afraid I'm going to say something wrong."

"I don't lie to my family, Zane," Ty murmured. "Although if you tell anyone but Deuce that we're fucking there might be problems," he amended. He gave Zane a wry smile and shrugged. "They'll find out eventually. But not this weekend," he said good-naturedly.

"It's not something I'd make normal dinner conversation out of," Zane said, wondering about the "eventually" comment. "But you can tell me why Deuce knows, when I didn't even know he existed until about... eight hours ago?"

"He's my brother," Ty answered seriously. "We have very few secrets."

"But *we* do," Zane finished for him.

Ty opened his mouth to respond but closed it again with a sigh. His lips quirked in a smile. "I wasn't keeping my brother a secret from you, Garrett," he said wryly.

Zane jerked his head to the side in silent comment but was smiling slightly when he again made eye contact. "That's not a denial."

Ty rolled his eyes. "Of course we have secrets. Everyone does," he claimed as he turned and started walking again. "I don't want to know that you keep your *Maxim*s under your mattress, and you don't want to know that I cry when I watch *Bambi*. That's what makes partnerships work," he rambled with a wave of his hand.

A soft laugh forced its way out of Zane, and he shook his head at his partner. He raised a hand to stifle a sudden yawn. He'd slept a few hours in the late afternoon yesterday, but not since then. Ty noticed it and sighed, stopping their walk and turning to veer back toward the house. He took Zane by the elbow first, though, and pulled him closer until their chests almost touched. "Try to relax, huh?" he said in a low voice. He just barely let his lips graze Zane's. "You're no fun when you're tense," he whispered mischievously.

"Ah, but I *am* fun otherwise," Zane said as he smirked.

"Only when you're naked," Ty assured him as he stepped away. "Come on. You can nap on the couch while Ma makes me and Deuce peel apples," he added, almost sounding as if he looked forward to the prospect.

TY HAD just left Zane on the couch and was heading for the door again to track down Deuce when Mara stuck her head out of the kitchen doorway.

"Ty?" she called after him. "I need your help for just a minute," she requested before moving back into the kitchen.

"I'm gonna get you a stepstool for Christmas this year," Ty told her with a smile as he came into the kitchen behind her, obviously anticipating needing to get something off a high shelf for her.

Instead, Mara set out a plate and sat down in front of it, knowing Ty would sit opposite her. The plate was filled with rolled strips of leftover pie crust, baked and covered with cinnamon and sugar. She always made the little rolls out of her leftovers, and Ty had loved them since he had had to stand on a stool to see over the countertops.

"Oh, yeah," Ty said with relish, and he reached out to grab one, popping it into his mouth as he pulled out a chair and sat down. "What's up, Ma?" he asked in amusement. The roll was stuck in the side of his cheek like he was storing it for later.

Mara smiled fondly at him, but the smile fell quickly, and she frowned. "You brought your partner here to hide behind him," she observed. "Why?"

Ty sighed and leaned forward, resting his elbows on the table. He was silent as he chewed, either contemplating how to answer or planning on remaining silent until they were interrupted.

Mara knew how her son's mind worked, mostly. She didn't understand his deep love for that Bronco or his absolute hatred of the Yankees or his desire to go out on his days off and shoot paintballs at his buddies. But she did know her boy well enough to know that she wouldn't get answers out of him if he didn't want to give them.

Even before he'd been trained by the Marines in case of capture, Ty had always been good at playing it close to the vest. If you found out something about him, he either wanted you to know it, someone else betrayed his confidence, or he was trying to get out of bigger trouble. The day he'd come to her when he was eight years old and admitted he'd broken a window with a baseball was also the same day she'd discovered he'd shot the oven with a BB gun.

Her lips twitched as she remembered. She still had that BB gun in the top of her closet. He'd never get that thing back.

Ty was looking at her speculatively, still trying to decide how or whether to answer. She took the opportunity to look him over with the critical eye of a mother. He looked worn and tense. His middle finger was slightly crooked, and she wondered how he'd broken it. His wrists also had light scars all the way around each of them. She knew the origins of those marks only because Richard Burns had called them while Ty was in the hospital recovering from being chained to a wall and bricked into a hole by a serial killer. She wondered how many other scars her son had accumulated that she couldn't see.

Ty leaned back and sighed heavily. Finally, he shook his head and said, "I've been sort of... lost." He shook his head in frustration as he searched for the right words to explain. "And Zane, he's not himself lately either," he continued. "I don't know what's wrong with him or with me or how to help either of us. I guess I'm hoping coming up here will give us some... answers."

Mara nodded in understanding. She didn't like to give advice, and she knew Ty would ask for it if he wanted it. Since he hadn't, she moved on to the one thing she knew always helped Ty when he was antsy. "Feel like some hard work?" she asked him hopefully.

"Yes, ma'am," Ty answered without hesitation.

"Got a whole pile of wood needs chopping," Mara told him.

Ty was already standing. He grabbed several more of the crust rolls and tossed them into his mouth as he pushed his chair in. "Make sure I got time to shower before dinner," he managed to say through the mouthful, and he was heading for the back door.

"Holler if you need help," she called after him with a smile.

He raised his hand and waved over his shoulder before disappearing out the door. Mara smiled and shook her head. He wouldn't call if he needed help. He never did.

ZANE inhaled sharply and opened his eyes as he woke with a jerk. He was looking up at an exposed beam wooden ceiling, and after a moment, his brain caught up. He sighed and let his eyes flutter shut for a long moment before he yawned and sat up. He actually felt pretty decent, even if the couch wasn't the most comfortable he'd ever napped on.

He stood up and stretched his arms toward the ceiling as he listened to what was going on around him. He could hear the faint sound of music somewhere, a regular series of thudding noises, and the clatter of dishes from the kitchen. He walked over to the entryway and looked in to see Mara Grady turning away from the sink with a large bowl full of apples and a paring knife.

She jumped slightly when she saw him standing there, and then she relaxed and laughed at herself. "Not used to having you boys home," she said with a grin. "Did you have a nice nap?" she asked.

Zane felt a smile pull at his lips, and he let it loose. *Home.* "Yeah, I did, actually," he said, hearing the faint surprise in his own voice.

"Well, good," Mara said happily. She sat at the table and reached for the first apple. "You want something to eat? I think Ty may have missed a few of these," she offered as she pushed a plate of rolled dough toward him.

"Thank you," Zane answered, a little bemused by her cheerful nature. Ty certainly hadn't inherited *that*. "Mind if I get a drink?"

"Help yourself, honey," Mara answered as she worked on the apples, peeling and slicing them and tossing them into a bowl.

Zane moved over to the fridge and checked out the selection, choosing a pitcher of what looked like iced tea. He'd seen her pull glasses out of a cabinet at breakfast, so he knew where to find those. He was pouring the tea when he happened to glance out the window over the sink and froze mid-pour, the tea splattering a bit on his shirt and the countertop.

In the small clearing behind the house, Ty was working on a pile of logs, splitting them easily with powerful, arcing swings of the axe he wielded. He'd taken off the shirt he'd been wearing and hung it on a nearby tree branch, leaving only his thin T-shirt to cover hard muscles Zane was intimately familiar with. The material was soaked through with sweat, clinging slightly, and the words were almost obscured by the darkened material. Zane could still read them, though, and they brought a smile to his face. He hadn't seen one of Ty's T-shirts in quite a while, and this one was right on par with all the others. There was a police car on it, and the words "The police never think it's as funny as you do."

As Zane watched, Ty stopped, set the axe down, and yanked the T-shirt over his head. He wiped his face with it and then tossed it aside.

Zane had to blink a few times as his gut cramped. Jesus. It wasn't like he'd never seen Ty shirtless before. Clearing his throat, he set down the pitcher and picked up the damp dishrag to wipe up the mess he'd made.

"Is that a bad batch?" Mara asked as she turned to peer at the tea. "Sometimes Earl makes it and it could peel the paint off an outhouse."

"Oh, no, it's fine. I just, uh, missed the glass a little," Zane said weakly, turning on the cold water to wash out the rag, keeping his body facing the sink. It probably wouldn't do for Mara to see how tight his jeans were all of a sudden. It was indecent how sometimes just one look at Ty was all it took.

"All the time you boys spend at the shooting range you'd think your aim would be better," Mara said with a smile evident in her voice.

Zane snorted as he got himself at least somewhat under control. He moved to put the pitcher back in the fridge. "It's vacation. I wasn't really *aiming* to do anything remotely resembling work." As he picked up his glass after shutting the fridge door, he couldn't help but glance back out the window.

He could hear the pop of the axe hitting every time Ty swung it. Each log split cleanly, no match for the power Ty could put behind the swings, lifting the axe up in a jerky motion and then bringing it down with frightening speed. Zane could see the thin layer of sweat on Ty's skin, glistening in the dying light as his muscles bunched and shifted. His frame wasn't bulky, but Zane knew he was solid. Solid and strong. Especially since the Bureau's gym was as close as Ty could get to action lately. Zane shook his head and made himself turn his back on the sight before he got caught staring. With a settling breath, he joined Mara at the table, sitting across from her and pulling the plate of baked dough pieces a little closer.

"He ain't cut any limbs off, has he?" Mara asked wryly.

"All accounted for," Zane said as he took a bite of a dough roll. "So far, anyway."

Mara smiled without looking up from her apple. "I never worried about Ty when it came to sharp things," she told Zane with a mixture of amusement and sadness. "Deacon, now he's another matter. He's not even allowed to peel apples."

"Deacon," Zane mumbled before swallowing the rest of the cookie. "Unusual name."

Mara was nodding. "Deacon was my mama's maiden name. It's a tradition 'round here, starting to die out, though," she informed Zane as she dumped a handful of apple slices into the bowl and reached for another.

Zane remembered now. Tyler wasn't really his partner's first name. Burns had introduced him as B. Tyler Grady. Ty had warned him off asking questions about it, and Zane had promptly set it aside. Zane smiled as he nabbed another cookie. "Ty's not fond of his first name, huh?" he chanced.

Mara was shaking her head, her eyes on the apple she was peeling. The rhythmic thwack of the axe splitting wood reached them as they sat there. "Always hated it, even when he was tiny. I think that's why he makes up his own names for everyone."

"You mean his nicknames?" Zane asked fondly.

Mara nodded again. "How many has he got for you?"

"I really couldn't tell you," Zane said in the same wry tone. "Although Lone Star seems pretty popular." He glanced to the window but couldn't see out at this angle. "When we first met it was a different one every hour."

"No telling how that boy's mind works," Mara muttered. "He has friends he's known for twenty years, and I still don't know their real names."

Zane laughed and leaned back in the chair, extending legs to the side of the table and crossing them at the ankles. "He's still got friends back that far, huh? Pre-military," he commented.

"Oh yeah," Mara answered in a surprised voice, as if that should have been obvious to Zane. "If he's in the area much longer they'll start showing up at the door too. His best friends, though, they came from the service." She sighed softly and shook her head.

"Nothing wrong with that," Zane said slowly. "Marines are pretty good guys."

Mara glanced up at him, eyes wide. She nodded. "They are. For the most part. I wonder about a person who'd choose to be one of his own accord," she admitted, her voice low. "Grady boys have been Marines for a long time. Drafted, every one of 'em. When Ty was born, and then Deacon, I swore they'd be the first who didn't have to fight for a living. And then Ty went and volunteered," she said with a sorrowful shake of her head. "I was proud of him, mind you. But I cried for a month."

Zane didn't know what to say to that. From what he did know of Ty, he could imagine his partner had been on fire to *move* when he graduated high school, and the Marines gave him his way out. He wondered if Ty knew what it had done to his mother.

Mara looked up at him, her cheeks flushing. "I'm sorry, Zane, I didn't mean to go into that."

It was easier than he thought to meet her eyes. "He's talked about you a few times. Good things," he said quietly.

Mara smiled, the wrinkles around her eyes and mouth appearing briefly. "He's a good boy. I just wish he didn't like to shoot things quite so much."

Zane couldn't stop the sharp laugh, marveling at how Mara seemed to be able to take everything in stride. "Well, I guess we'll have to disagree, since he's watching my back."

Mara nodded as she dumped another handful of apple slices into her bowl. Her face was set in a frown now, her brow furrowed and her eyes thoughtful. In the silence, Zane could hear Ty chopping wood, the occasional grunt of exertion accompanying the thwack of the axe hitting.

"He's probably about done with that pile," Mara observed. "If you want a shower before dinner you best go do it now before he gets in," she advised.

Zane scooted back and stood to take his glass to the sink. As he set it down, he looked back outside and watched for a long moment. "I'm going to see if he has any other plans. Otherwise I'm good for tonight." He turned around and offered Mara a smile before walking to the back door.

Mara's chair creaked as she turned to look over her shoulder at him. "You're a good boy, Zane," she told him as she went back to peeling her apples.

Zane paused on the doorstep to look back at her in mild surprise. He wasn't sure what that was about, but it seemed a motherly thing to say, so he decided not to think on it and just appreciate the sentiment. He stepped outside, let the screen door snap shut behind him, took a few paces along the stone path, and stopped a healthy distance away to watch and wait for Ty to stop.

It only took a few more minutes for Ty to finish the pile. Once he'd arranged the last few halves into a woodpile that wouldn't topple, he picked up his T-shirt and swiped it over his damp body. He looked up and stopped briefly, betraying his surprise at seeing Zane standing there.

Raising an eyebrow in mimicry, Zane tipped his head to the side. "Didn't know I was here?" he asked, amused.

"Thought you were asleep," Ty answered as he moved closer. He was slightly out of breath, his hair wet with sweat.

"Woke up about fifteen minutes ago. Sat with your mom and had a snack." Zane didn't even try to look away.

Ty narrowed his eyes and looked him over. "What?" he asked suspiciously.

Zane waggled his eyebrows and smirked, dragging his eyes up and down over Ty's sweaty and very appealing body.

Ty looked down at himself and then rolled his eyes. "I know," he muttered as his cheeks colored. "All I need is the long blond hair, right?" he asked wryly, poking fun at himself even though it was obvious he was embarrassed. He wiped himself down with the T-shirt again and walked over to pluck his other shirt from the branch he'd hung it on.

"Don't change anything on my account," Zane murmured, sliding his hands into his back pockets. "Different than a gym workout, you know?"

Ty moved toward him, his shirts hanging from his hand. "You a little turned on, Garrett?" he asked with a smirk, his tone surprised.

"More than a little, Grady," Zane said under his breath. He sighed as Ty approached, eyeing him warily.

Ty hummed wordlessly. "Too bad there's no wood to chop back home then," he joked.

Zane shrugged slightly. His smile was just as obvious as before. "I'm sure I could find you some wood to work on," he said evenly, eyes twinkling.

Ty's lips twitched as he tried not to smile. "That's after-dinner talk, there," he drawled before he started laughing. "We've really got to work on your word play," he said as he moved closer and, to Zane's surprise, put his arm around Zane's shoulders as he turned him toward the house. He smelled of a mixture of sweat, wood, shampoo, Old Spice, and… Ty.

Zane chuckled and they bumped against each other randomly as Ty maneuvered them up the walk to the door. "There's always *something* you want me to work on," he complained. "We're supposed to be on vacation, for Christ's sake."

Ty merely squeezed Zane's shoulders before releasing him, and Zane grinned at him as he opened the screen door and motioned him inside.

~CHAPTER 5~

IT HAD been an incredible dinner—a huge, tender pork roast with all the trimmings, hot yeast rolls, and apple cobbler for dessert. Zane had finally sat back from the table, stuffed to the gills. It had been a nice, relaxing day. He'd napped, been shown around the place, been told stories of the havoc Ty and Deuce had wreaked upon the community in their youth, and had taken a short trip into the town of Bluefield to load up on supplies for the hike.

Ty had promised him a better tour of his hometown at a later date, and Zane was actually looking forward to it. He hadn't seen much more of Ty's parents. Mara had spent the day cooking and making various and sundry edible things for them to take with them on the trail, and Earl had headed back to the mines.

Ty had carefully avoided anything even remotely concerning the mines or accompanying his father. Zane didn't blame him. They'd sat on the front porch and relaxed for the remainder of the day, not even really speaking much as each of them tried to unwind and accept their forced vacation for what it was.

Once dinner was over and they were sitting around the table enjoying the last cup of coffee for the night, Mara stood and tapped Ty on the top of the head. "Come help me make up the couch," she requested.

Ty sat back and frowned at her. "I have to sleep on the couch?" he asked her incredulously. "I've slept on rocks more comfortable than that thing!"

"Then you go out back and find yourself a rock so you'll feel better about it," Mara suggested.

"Couch?" Zane asked in a low voice as he leaned closer to Earl, an eyebrow rising.

Earl was smiling widely. He nodded when Zane looked to him. "My wife has made up Ty's old bedroom for you," he told him in a low voice as Ty and Mara argued over the merits of the couch cushions versus the rocks out back.

"Oh Christ." Zane laughed, falling back in his chair. "He won't let me forget this. Losing his bed to me."

"Well," Earl said with a sigh, "it's either that or fight his mama over it." He sat and watched Ty and Mara for a moment, sipping at his coffee contentedly. "Ain't none of us ever won *that* fight," he told Zane flatly.

"Me and Zane'll just bunk together," Ty was arguing.

Mara laughed at him. "You two boys won't fit in a double bed any more than I'll still fit in my wedding dress," she scoffed.

"But—"

"I know Zane would end up on the floor when you're done with him," Mara continued, "and I will not have a guest in this house sleeping on the rug, so come help me make up the couch."

Ty glanced at Zane, his lips twitching at the irony of what his mother said. They would fit in a double bed together just fine, but only because they had a lot of practice with occupying the same space while horizontal.

"I'll make a pallet on the floor, Ma," Ty assured Mara. She looked at him dubiously, but he just smiled at her innocently. "For myself," he added.

Mara rolled her eyes, smiling as she turned away. "Fine," she agreed. "As long as *he* don't end up on the floor," she warned.

"Not like tomorrow night, when we'll *all* be on the floor," Deuce mumbled.

"Outdoors in the cold," Earl added from behind his mug.

"With the rocks," Ty concluded as he glanced sideways at his mother and smirked.

"Buncha dumbasses," Chester muttered as he stood and shuffled out of the room.

"Get out of my kitchen, all of you," Mara ordered with an irritated wave of her hand.

Ty and Deuce practically scattered, leaving Zane to fend for himself. Earl remained where he sat, finishing his coffee and laughing softly. Shaking his head at their retreat, Zane said his goodnights and walked up the stairs. Earlier in the day, he and Ty had brought their bags upstairs to the spare room—Ty's former bedroom—and now he pushed the door shut with a soft click as he sat down to pull off his boots.

Looking around the room, he realized that it wasn't so much a spare room as it was *still* Ty's bedroom. The walls were still adorned with the trappings of high school life: pictures, awards, trophies, and knickknacks lined the shelves and hung from the walls.

It was enlightening to see a younger Ty, before the FBI, before the military. Zane stood up and started around the room, smiling at some of the photos. Ty's wide grin was clear, so much more so than now. He'd been happy and unbothered by life's problems.

As Zane surveyed the items displayed on the shelves, he gained little pieces of insight into what had been important to Ty then. There was an old football with faded writing on it, as well as several ribbons that signified first and third place finishes, but they didn't tell what they were for. There was a fiddle case on a shelf near the window and an old guitar beside it, and Zane smiled as he remembered how appalled Ty had been when he'd admitted he knew how to play.

Almost every photo on the wall had Ty's brother in it as well. They'd obviously always been close, even more so then than now. One of the most prominent pictures was of the two of them standing together in front of the old garage that still stood beside the house. They were both covered in grease, wearing nasty coveralls, holding wrenches as they wrapped their arms over each other's shoulders and grinned at the camera. Behind them was an old motorcycle, halfway through being restored.

As he stared at it, he wondered again why Ty hated the Valkyrie so much.

He wasn't sure how long he'd been standing there before he heard the click of the door and felt that he was no longer alone.

"Snoop," Ty accused softly as he moved into the room quietly.

Zane smiled. "Kind of hard to miss photos when the walls are papered with them."

Ty lowered his head and smiled as he slid his hands into the pockets of his jeans. "I left a week after I graduated high school," he said. "Ma never touched this room. I don't think she's even vacuumed it." Zane turned to face his partner. Ty was staring at him, his head slightly cocked. "She was afraid I'd never come back," he said with a hint of melancholy. "Wanted it to stay like I left it."

Zane nodded slowly. "Mine feels the same way," he said quietly. "They love you, though."

Ty raised an eyebrow and nodded. "You saying yours don't?" he asked as he moved closer.

Zane's shoulders tightened. "No. Doesn't mean I don't wonder about my mom sometimes." He watched Ty approach and slid his hands into his jeans pockets to mirror his stance.

Ty stopped just inches away from him, studying him with an unreadable expression. "I'll get Ma to bake you a pie, make you feel better," he offered finally, his tone of voice and his expression entirely serious. The only way to know that he was teasing was the slight glint in his hazel eyes.

Zane's lips twitched at the ultra-dry humor. "Can't say I've ever had a pie baked for me before. My mom's more the cookie type."

Ty snorted in disdain and turned away, heading for the double bed. He flopped down on the end of it and bent to begin unlacing his boots. "She always has one waiting for us when we get back from a hike. Apple, usually. Good stuff, man."

"Sounds good," Zane agreed. He was glad he had his hands in his pockets; his fingers were itching to touch Ty, but he had no idea what Ty would allow, especially here in his parents' home. He toed out of his running shoes and unbuckled his belt, his gaze not wavering.

Ty seemed to sense his eyes on him, and he looked up at him questioningly as he pulled off one boot. Zane shook his head very slightly and glanced to the door Ty had left half-open. Ty followed his eyes and then smiled as he looked back at Zane.

"Getting a little antsy?" he teased.

"Yes," Zane said immediately.

"Why?" Ty asked.

"We're in the bedroom you grew up in," Zane pointed out. "I'm not sure what to expect with you here."

Ty began to laugh softly, and he bit his lip to keep from laughing harder as he pulled his other boot off and set it carefully beside the first at the foot of the bed. "We're not doing anything wrong, Garrett," he pointed out. "We're just sleeping here," he said with a wry twist of his lips as he stood back up.

Zane rolled his eyes and decided some reciprocal teasing was in order. "Fine. Then you can close your eyes and 'sleep' while I undress," he proposed innocently, pulling his hands out of his pockets and pulling his shirt over his head, letting it fall on the foot of the bed. He knew Ty enjoyed this part of their time together; he did too. The chemistry between them seemed to click just a little better when they got up close and personal.

"Cocktease," Ty accused in a low voice, and he moved closer, took Zane's face in his hands, and kissed him.

Smiling against his lips, Zane hummed quietly and slid his arms around Ty, settling his hands at the small of his back. Ty continued the kiss for one more breath before pulling away. He turned and went to sit down on the end of the bed again to pull off his socks and continue getting ready for bed.

Sighing, Zane got out of his jeans and moved to sit near him on the side of the bed with the lamp. He pulled his feet up and leaned back against the headboard, propping his elbows on his knees and lacing his fingers together, his dark eyes riveted on Ty. He watched the muscles of his back move beneath the thin white shirt he wore, and he mentally cursed. They'd never been in a situation where they wanted to fuck and couldn't. The only restrictions they'd ever encountered had been each other. This was a new and disconcerting feeling. Zane didn't like having obstacles between himself and what he wanted.

"Stop it," Ty warned without looking back at him, obviously knowing what he was pondering.

Zane smiled slightly. That just meant Ty was thinking the same thing. He could still hear the other members of the household moving about, preparing for bed. Until the house settled, they would need to at least pretend they wouldn't jump each other at the first chance.

The lights on the landing were still on, and Ty stood to go turn them off and shut the bedroom door. He flicked off the light beside the door, throwing the room into temporary inky darkness. When Zane's eyes began to adjust, he could see Ty still standing by the closed door. Zane smiled again. He hoped Ty remembered to wake up to do whatever he had planned, because Ty definitely had something in mind. Sex would be great, of course—it always was—but Zane would be happy to settle for simply holding him. Something about hearing Ty breathe, so calm and close, was reassuring in ways Zane didn't examine too closely.

"Good night, Ty," Zane murmured as he scooted under the sheet.

"Shut up," Ty grumbled as he moved through the darkness toward the blankets on the floor.

IT WAS nearly pitch black outside when Ty finally got restless enough to sit up. He sat cross-legged on the cold floor, staring out the bedroom window for a long, dull moment before he pushed the blanket aside and stood. The cool air hit him and made him shiver all over as he looked down at Zane, asleep in the bed.

Ty stood looking over him in the faint light from the moon through the window. He looked older, worn thin and worried even in sleep. Tense. It was something Ty had tried for weeks to fix, trying to get Zane to just let go of the past and enjoy the present. But the more Zane had resisted, the less Ty had cared about trying to help him. He didn't like where that left them, but he didn't know how to change it. The only things they really seemed to be good at were getting into trouble or getting into each other.

Ty reached over and brushed his fingers against Zane's cheek. His fingers had barely grazed skin when Zane reacted. He shot up and shoved hard with both hands, sending Ty back to the floor. Just as quickly, his hand was digging under the pillow, scrabbling for his gun. Ty hit the floor with a thump and immediately rolled to his side, covering his head and hoping Zane's gun either wasn't loaded or wasn't there.

"Goddamnit," Zane hissed when he didn't find it, and he swiped at the bedside lamp, almost knocking it over and having to grab for it before fumbling to switch it on.

Ty was already shaking with silent laughter as he rolled onto his back. He looked up at the side of the bed in a mixture of relief and amusement.

Zane groaned and flopped back onto the bed, throwing his arm over his eyes. "I knew it was a good idea to leave my gun in my bag," he muttered half into the pillow.

"I appreciate that," Ty assured him in a whisper as he got to his knees and rested his elbows on the side of the bed. Rolling to his side, Zane squinted at him obstinately. "You didn't want me to wake you?" Ty asked him with a knowing smile.

Zane relaxed onto his back, his eyes focusing as he looked at Ty. Ty smiled up at him, silent as he listened to make sure no one was coming to check on the noise. When he was convinced that everyone was still asleep, he climbed up onto the bed and lowered himself carefully to rest on his belly beside Zane. Zane threw the covers over him.

"Thanks," Ty whispered as he settled into the warmth. "I used to wake up swinging when I came home on leave," he told Zane quietly after a moment. "Almost decked my mama once. Dad made me sleep in the garage the next night."

"No wonder you don't visit your family a lot."

"Oh, a summer spent without being relegated to the garage was a summer wasted," Ty told him fondly. "I don't visit as much as I should," he answered guiltily. "Since the Tri-State case I haven't at all."

"Is it weird for you? Me being here with you?" Zane asked softly.

"Yeah," Ty answered with a small laugh. "I rarely bring anyone home with me," he admitted. "If we had an extended leave and one of the boys couldn't go home, I'd bring him with me. Maggie was the last one I brought home, though, and that's been about five years," he told Zane with a shake of his head.

"Maggie?" Zane's voice was careful.

"Stray dog," Ty answered with a look at Zane and a small smile. He knew he probably shouldn't, but he still enjoyed those little hints that Zane might want him enough to be jealous. Zane merely nodded and smiled. "Try going downstairs to Grandpa's bedroom, you'll trip over her. Right before you meet the shovel," Ty advised as he tried not to laugh at the thought of that damn shovel. Chester Grady woke at the drop of a feather and would whack you in the face with that thing first and then wait until morning when it was light to see who you were and if you needed an ambulance. They did not want to meet that shovel tonight.

Ty licked his lips and looked at Zane seriously again. "But as far as anyone… someone who wasn't a stray, you're about it."

"I'm honored, then. I like your family. They're absolutely nuts, but I like them," Zane added.

"Well," Ty said with a shrug of one shoulder, "with them, pretty much anything goes. If you stay away from religion, politics, and the designated hitter, you're gonna get along fine."

Zane chuckled and shifted uncomfortably, pulling the pillow slightly under his chest and tucking his hands under it. "How's the floor treating you?" he asked.

Ty grinned and stretched toward the lamp to turn off the light. He waited a couple minutes in silence until he could see again in the darkness that followed and scooted closer to Zane. "I like it much better here," he whispered.

Zane grunted in agreement, grasped Ty's chin, and pulled him sideways into a soft kiss. Ty responded eagerly, shifting closer and sliding his hand over Zane's waist to tug at him. He rolled until he had Zane under him, but his actions were gentler than they usually were—he was trying to keep the noise down. He knew his old bed was liable to creak and groan even if you weren't being overly active.

Zane obviously sensed that he was trying to be quiet. He didn't do anything that might be heard, keeping his hands under the pillow and leaving his mouth upturned to receive more kisses. Ty let his hands slide up Zane's arms to his wrists; he pulled them free of the pillow and held him against the mattress, still kissing him slowly. Zane's hands splayed as he stretched out his fingers, but he didn't try to pull free. He chased Ty's tongue with his own, drawing the kiss out. It was a disconcertingly tender moment, a rare thing for them.

It was long moments before Ty pushed himself up and looked down at Zane hesitantly.

"What, you having second thoughts now that I'm awake?" Zane prodded, dragging his wrists free of Ty's fists so he could slide his hands down Ty's back.

"Is it worth getting banged over the head with a shovel if we make too much noise?" Ty asked as he dug his foot between Zane's legs and pushed them apart, settling between his thighs.

Zane moved his legs without resisting and bit back a snicker. "You've been banged both by that shovel and by me. Is it worth it?" he parroted as he squeezed Ty's ass and slid one hand down the back of his thigh.

Ty grinned crookedly and began shaking his head. "Not really," he answered dryly.

"I'll risk it," Zane said, grabbing the back of Ty's neck and pulling him down for a harder kiss.

The bed creaked in warning with the rapid movement. Ty growled in frustration and pushed himself up, looking around the dim room briefly before he threw the blankets off them and tossed the pillows down to the floor. He grabbed Zane tightly and rolled them right off the bed, causing another muffled thud when they hit the floor. Thankfully, it was a low bed.

"Better," Ty decided as he pulled the blankets off the bed to fall back on top of them.

Zane groaned and gasped as he tried not to laugh. "Ow… what about being quiet?" he asked in a harsh whisper as Ty settled on top of him again.

"Give it a second," Ty whispered in return, cocking his head to listen.

Zane closed his eyes, and Ty focused on the sounds around them as he kissed lightly at Zane's neck and chest. He could hear Zane's soft breathing above the noises of the house, the creaking as it settled in the cold, the click and whir of the appliances downstairs, the hum of the large freezer on the porch just off the kitchen, the soft scattering of leaves scratching against the window.

Zane's eyes were still closed when Ty's lips brushed his again. He slid a hand under Zane's briefs and tugged at the elastic.

"Mmm. What do you want?" Zane murmured, shifting on the cool wood floor to give Ty's hand more access.

Ty shook his head and grinned. "Just you," he answered.

Zane smirked and held his arms out to his sides. "Go on then," he invited in a rough purr. "Snag the duffel."

Zane's bag was only an arm's length away at the foot of the bed. Ty reached for it, pushing himself down into Zane as he did so, getting a soft groan that made him smile. He got the bag between his fingertips and pulled it closer, pausing to steal a kiss.

Somewhere in the house, a door snicked shut, and Ty paused long enough to listen and hear the water running before he continued. Once the bag was next to them, Zane twisted around and dug through it, pulling out his shaving kit before pushing the duffel away again. He unzipped the bag and pulled out a familiar tube and a plastic packet. Ty waited impatiently for perhaps ten seconds before he pushed himself off Zane and began peeling off the rest of his own clothing.

They hadn't hit the stage in their relationship when foreplay was something important. Ty, especially, knew he was unlikely to even think about such nuances. Zane didn't need to be seduced. Ty didn't suppose that Zane *wanted* to be seduced, either. There was never any question that Ty wanted him in bed, and that seemed to be enough to keep Zane happy.

Ty fussed with his boxers and fell back to lay down to take them off, but then he struggled to get his legs untangled from the blankets in order to continue. It was all very difficult in the dark when he was in a hurry.

Zane groaned, rolling toward Ty in an attempt to get closer. He reached to slide his hands under Ty's T-shirt, gripping warm flesh, and then he tugged Ty's shirt off, making sure to touch lots of skin as he went. Ty slowly laid his back to the cold hardwood floor again, pulling at Zane to follow.

After kicking his briefs off, Zane leaned over to slide his tongue up the crease of Ty's thigh. Ty tensed below him, just like he always did despite his continued efforts not to. Zane had either stopped caring or started pretending not to notice. Ty was grateful, either way. He lifted his shoulders off the hardwood to arch his back as he handed the lubricant and condom back to Zane wordlessly. Then he rolled in Zane's arms, turning over onto his stomach.

Zane leaned over him, grabbing hold of Ty's wrist and squeezing it. "You sure?" he whispered into Ty's ear.

Ty didn't bottom easily or passively even under the best of circumstances, and they both knew it. "I'll be quieter than you are," he answered anyway. Zane didn't usually restrain himself when Ty was fucking him. It was a very vocal, very arousing experience, one that Ty rarely turned down the opportunity to enjoy. But…. "I'm not running into that shovel with my pants down."

Zane popped open the tube and soon slid his slick fingers between Ty's legs as he leaned over to nuzzle against his ear. Ty's fingers gripped the blanket, clenching slowly. He shifted again, pushing up onto his hands and knees, spreading his legs wider as Zane slid a finger into him.

"Don't have all night, Garrett," Ty hissed at him impatiently.

Zane shushed him and twisted his fingers harder and deeper before leaning back to grab the condom. Ty heard the crinkling plastic flutter to the floor and Zane's hand grasped one of Ty's hips, pulling him back as he leaned over him, one hand braced next to Ty's on the hardwood floor.

Zane was good at this, and Ty always reacted the same way: heartbeat racing, breaths shallow and fast, excitement and nerves churning in his gut. It was all part of Zane's charm.

Ty squirmed under him, pushing his hips back and lowering his shoulders, resting his head on the floor as he did so. Letting out a slow breath, Zane pumped his hips slowly, working himself inside. Ty groaned and bit his hand to keep from making any more noise as Zane forced his cock past the tense muscles and pain seared through him. It ebbed quickly, though, and he moved under Zane's weight to help, his entire body flooding with heat as Zane rocked deeper into him. It always felt so damned good; Ty was never sure why he didn't do this more often. But that just led to more questions he didn't want to find answers to, and he'd rather focus on what Zane was doing to him right now.

Zane drew a deep, quiet breath as he gripped Ty's hips and pulled back, starting with slow thrusts. Ty closed his eyes and bit his hand harder, telling himself not to moan as Zane moved inside him. But it was difficult to keep quiet when Zane was sliding into him with slow, deep thrusts. It wouldn't stay slow and sensual like this for long; it never did with them, no matter who took the lead or how determined they both were to make it last.

Zane's hand slid up his back until he was gripping Ty's shoulder, his fingers digging into Ty's skin. The blanket beneath Ty's hands began to slide, and Ty went with it, the weight of Zane's body on top of him stretching him and the blanket out on the floor. When Ty was flat on the floor, Zane shifted to plant his knees outside of Ty's. He pushed down on the backs of Ty's shoulders as he worked up to a steady, heated rhythm that would please them both sooner rather than later.

Ty found himself pinned flat to the floor, with Zane using his knees and shoulders for leverage as he fucked him. He gasped wordlessly against the blanket under him, liking the overpowering weight of Zane's body on him. Zane snapped his hips down, hard, and Ty had to bite his lip to keep from crying out. He bent his knees and lifted his feet, pushing his heels against Zane's ass to urge him on. Zane grunted quietly before lowering himself to hold Ty closer and speed his thrusts.

The sound of their bodies slapping together was loud in the otherwise silent room, and Zane slowed his thrusts again, grunting in Ty's ear. "Not much longer," he warned breathlessly.

Ty responded to his warning by tensing around the hard cock inside him, and he reached back to drag his short fingernails across the naked skin of Zane's hip. Zane grunted and trembled with restraint as he continued. Ty panted heavily against the blankets under him as his body tightened. He wouldn't last much longer either. He never did with Zane's cock inside him.

Zane bit the back of his shoulder, hard, and Ty grit his teeth against the shout of pleasure it almost produced. Zane pushed off him again, his hands on Ty's shoulders as he pounded his cock past the tight ring of muscle, heedless of the sound their bodies made as they met or of the fact that Ty's groans were steadily gaining in volume. It felt like his cock drove deeper and deeper, his grunts of exertion and pleasure in Ty's ears, until Ty could do nothing but whimper helplessly as his body convulsed. His fingers dug into Zane's hip, and he writhed beneath his lover as he spilled himself against the blanket.

After a few more hard thrusts, Zane froze in place and his grip tightened, his whole body locked in the fight between climax and silence, shuddering. He rocked into Ty a few more times before he finally relaxed and rested his head against Ty's back, breathing hard and trembling.

"Good job," Ty finally offered in a hoarse voice. Zane groaned softly before pulling free with a plaintive gasp. He lowered himself carefully to the floor beside Ty. Ty rolled onto his back, letting his body stretch out, investigating the aches. No matter how ready he was for it, Zane's cock inside him *always* left aches. That was part of the fun. "I would have bet money we couldn't be quiet," he whispered as he stared at the ceiling.

Zane smiled at him and shook his head. "Always glad to prove you wrong," he said.

Ty turned his head to look at him and laughed suddenly. "You wound up on the floor after all," he observed with a snicker.

"Funny guy," Zane grunted before climbing to his feet and offering Ty a hand.

Ty stared at him from where he lay flat on his back. Sometimes he wondered if Zane just tolerated him because he was a good lay, or if he truly enjoyed being around him as much as Ty did Zane. He told himself that was another question for a later time. Finally, he reached up and took Zane's hand, pulling himself to his feet. "Thanks," he whispered.

Lacing their hands together, Zane leaned to kiss him, just for a moment. He squeezed Ty's hands and nodded before loosening his grip. Ty sniffed daintily at the tender gesture as he turned away and bent to gather the clothing he'd shed. Well, maybe Zane did enjoy it a little.

As Zane grabbed his shirt and used it for a quick clean before pulling his briefs on, Ty pulled his pants on haphazardly and headed for the bathroom to do a slightly better job of cleaning himself. When he returned, Zane was gathering up the extra covers and tossing them on the bed. Ty watched him with a smirk as he slid his T-shirt over his head. "Might want to flush that instead of tossing it in the trash," he said with a nod at Zane and the condom he had yet to discard. "Ma'll be wondering what we were doing when she empties the trashcans," he joked quietly.

"You think?" Zane muttered. He left the room quietly as Ty straightened out the sheets and blankets left askew from their fun.

"Fucker," Ty grumbled affectionately as he made up the bed. He knew he might never explain to himself the emotions Zane caused in him. He didn't mind the mystery. It was another part of what made it fun. What he did mind was the uneasy feeling that Zane merely tolerated him rather than enjoyed him. Again, he told himself to worry about that later—much later—and he climbed into bed.

When Zane returned, he slipped under the covers beside Ty and immediately wrapped around him, pulling Ty closer just as he would the pillows he liked to hold. With a sigh, Ty pondered over the question of whether his doubts were unfounded or if Zane was just a cuddler. They hadn't had a lot of time to feel each other out. As partners, it seemed like they could read each other's minds. But as lovers—or even friends—they barely knew each other at all.

He sighed and scooted closer, twisting his body so he could brush an awkward kiss against Zane's cheek. "Sleep well, Zane," he offered quietly as he settled into the embrace. He closed his eyes and sighed again. Zane slept much better with Ty alongside him than he did when he was alone, and they both knew it.

"I will," Zane murmured, his breath warm against the back of Ty's ear.

BY THE time Zane got down to the kitchen the next morning, breakfast was on the table, and Ty and Deuce were sitting together, drinking orange juice while their mother bustled around them and scolded them for stealing some of her apples.

"Morning," Ty greeted as he gestured to an empty chair.

"Good morning, Zane dear, how did you sleep?" Mara asked as she came up to him and pressed a glass of orange juice into his hands.

"Ah, okay," Zane hedged, taking the glass out of self-defense. "I don't do too well sleeping in strange places lately, but…."

"Well, Ty's bed is about as strange a place as you can get," Deuce offered under his breath. He followed it with a muffled grunt as Ty kicked him under the table.

"Don't mind them, we dropped 'em both on their heads when they was little," Mara assured Zane as she moved back to her stove, where two different skillets sizzled. She'd been cooking for some time already; the kitchen was warm from the heated oven, and it was the smell of crisp bacon and fresh biscuits that had beckoned Zane downstairs.

Zane turned a look on the two brothers, his eyes narrowing slightly. Under the brown Western-style flannel shirt Ty wore, Zane was pleased to see that he was also wearing another one of his signature T-shirts. It was oddly reassuring to see it. It was brown with white writing on the front, two crossed paddles advertising "Schitt Creek Paddle Co." Zane didn't bother to hide his amused snort, but the others paid him no mind.

"Where's your daddy?" Mara asked them as she sat at the head of the table.

"Wasn't my morning to babysit him," Ty answered as he poured himself more juice.

"Well, you and your smart mouth go find him so we can eat," Mara responded without blinking an eye. Ty stood immediately, snatching a sausage link as he went. "And track down your granddaddy too!" his mother called after him.

Zane watched over the edge of his juice glass as Ty headed out of the kitchen, taking particular notice of the worn jeans that were molded to Ty's ass as he moved around the corner.

"Zane, tell me," Mara said, drawing his attention, "how do you enjoy working for the FBI?"

Surprised by the question out of left field, Zane hesitated as he pushed the visual of Ty away for later. "It's like any job, I guess. I like it some days, others not so much. Ty makes it interesting sometimes."

"My son does do that to people," she agreed with a sigh as she sipped at her coffee. "Both of them do," she added wryly as she glanced at Deuce, who looked at Mara with an obviously feigned hurt expression.

Zane chuckled and took a drink of his juice. "He makes up for it, though. He's a good partner."

"Is he?" Mara asked with true concern. Her brow furrowed, and she leaned forward, meeting his eyes questioningly.

Zane sighed and glanced at the door, weighing his options. Honesty and... honesty. "All right, he's a great partner. But don't tell him I said that."

The relief that washed over the poor woman was tangible. "Ty's ego was never one of the things I fretted over being broken," she assured Zane. "But I was so afraid after Jimmy was killed he would never be able to deal with a partner again," she explained as she looked down at her coffee and stirred it slowly.

"I don't think it was easy for him," Zane said slowly. Despite how they ragged on each other, he didn't want to say anything that might be construed as badmouthing Ty in front of his family. Zane could imagine how angry he would be himself if the situation were reversed. He also knew that the Jimmy Mara referred to was Special Agent James Hathaway, who'd been partnered with Ty for more than two years before he was killed in the line of duty. It wasn't a joking matter. "I won't say we get along all the time, but we make it work," Zane added.

"You handle him the right way," Deuce interjected.

Mara nodded in agreement. "You have to give Ty as good as he gives you."

"Yeah, and it's not easy. He can be hard to handle sometimes," Zane said vaguely rather than trying to make light of it.

"Try raising two of 'em," Mara said wryly with another pointed look at Deuce.

"You know I can hear you, right?" Deuce said in annoyance.

Zane smiled just like Mara did. "Ty gets that look on his face, too, when he's ticked off. Which is fairly often, so I'm familiar with the expression," he added earnestly.

"Shut up," Deuce offered grumpily as he reached for a sausage link, only to get his hand slapped by Mara's spatula for the effort. He opened his mouth to protest, but a call from the front of the house interrupted him.

"Hey, Ma!" Ty yelled as the screen door slammed. Zane could hear his booted footsteps coming closer, and when Ty appeared in the doorway, he was frowning slightly. "Grandpa's eyesight's getting worse, huh?" he asked.

"What makes you say that?" Mara asked in concern.

"'Cause he's out in the yard, killing your garden hose with his shovel," Ty answered with a jerk of his thumb at the window.

Mara balled up her fists and made a strangled sound of frustration as she pushed her chair back noisily and stood. "That senile old goat!" she muttered as she hurried out the back door. Zane made it until she was out of the room, but then he had to laugh out loud, covering his mouth with his hand.

Neither Deuce nor Ty were laughing, though, both of them treating it as if it were an everyday thing. "How's his aim?" Deuce asked Ty dubiously.

"Still pretty good," Ty answered in a surprised voice as he went to the window to watch, leaning over the sink. "He still sharpens the shovel tip, doesn't he?"

"As far as I know," Deuce answered as he poured himself a cup of coffee, unconcerned.

Zane's brows were nearly up into his hairline. Sharpens the shovel tip? Jesus. No wonder Ty had a penchant for weapons, growing up in this environment.

"Hey," Ty said as he waved his hand around at them, still looking out the window. "Y'all gotta see this. She's beating him with the hose," he told them as he began to snicker. "God, I love coming home," he mused as he sipped at his own juice. He made room when Deuce moved to stand next to him and peer outside.

Still laughing softly, Zane watched Ty closely, fascinated by the relaxation in his frame and the easy smile that curved his lips. What little tension that had been invested in him last night was gone. He was at ease with both himself and his surroundings, something Zane rarely observed in his partner. He was always alert and sort of twitchy when they were working or even when they were in Zane's hotel room, as if he always had a sense of impending doom and wanted to be ready when it came.

Seeing this new side to him made Zane's heart beat faster. He was just glad the two brothers were too busy watching Mara try to wrestle the shovel away from their grandfather to notice his intent focus.

"You boys just gonna stand there?" Earl Grady asked them in a stern voice from the doorway behind Zane.

Both Ty and Deuce jumped slightly—Zane did as well, actually, splashing a little juice onto his plate. He'd been so focused on Ty that he hadn't even heard Earl approach.

"Go help her," Earl ordered.

The brothers scrambled to set down their glasses without spilling the contents and get out the back door to do as they'd been told as quickly as possible.

Their father waited until the door had fallen shut behind them before he sat down at the kitchen table with Zane and smiled.

"Morning, son," he greeted nonchalantly as he poured himself a mug of coffee.

Zane felt another flash of mild surprise. These people treated him like one of their own; it was the strangest thing. "Morning, sir," he answered, reaching for one of the coffee mugs and the sugar bowl after sopping up the juice on his plate with his napkin.

"Is it the garden hose?" Earl asked before taking a sip of his coffee.

"Uh, yeah," Zane chanced.

Earl chuckled and nodded. "That's the fifth one," he told Zane in mild amusement. "He got in a fight with the rake summer before last that damn near killed all of us before it was over. You try taking that shovel from him, you risk getting it shoved up your nose."

His point was emphasized by a shout from one of the combatants outside. Zane had to laugh again, just at the ridiculousness of it all. "You all are something else," he stated, still chuckling. Each of them seemed to deal with life's little absurdities in stride, something Zane had never really figured out how to do. At least not without some form of chemical help. Zane envied them.

He also wondered if this was the root of why everyone in the Bureau thought Ty was batshit crazy.

"Something else," Earl echoed. "The boys call it the galloping crazies," he informed Zane seriously.

"Yeah," Zane agreed. "That's about right." He shook his head and scooped a teaspoon of sugar into his coffee. "My family is seriously normal. So seeing this"—he waved his hand around—"it's an eye-opener."

"Normal," Earl repeated, looking at Zane as if expecting him to expand on the notion.

Zane shrugged with one shoulder. "No arguing, no rocking the boat, mind your own business, show up for Sunday lunch or else. Nothing really extraordinary, but not much bad, either. They're just… normal."

"Not close, huh?" Earl commented.

"*They* are," Zane answered with a rueful curl of his lips. He was the odd man out and had been for a long time. He didn't spend any time thinking on his family if he could avoid it. There was too much to be angry or upset about.

Earl didn't respond to that other than to nod in understanding, apparently content with silence just like his son often was. Zane went back to his coffee, letting it go. Earl sat nursing his coffee for another moment before glancing at the window when there was another short shout. "I reckon *I* could go help them," he mused.

He was saved from having to do so by Ty stomping back into the kitchen with a length of mangled green hose in his hand. "Hose is a goner," he told them grimly as he let the piece of hose fall into the trashcan. He lowered his head as he washed his hands and moved to sit down beside Zane, crossing his arms over his chest and covering his mouth with one hand as he tried desperately not to laugh. The others came inside as he pressed his hand over his mouth and slouched further in his chair, and Ty studiously avoided meeting his mother's eyes as she glared at him.

Chester grinned at them all and sat beside Deuce, propping his shovel against the leg of the table carefully. "That was a big'n," he told them. "Cold for a big'n like that," he advised, which caused Ty and Deuce to break into uncontrollable snickers as they tried to hide their laughter from their mother.

Zane just grinned. "I hear you've got quite the eye," he complimented deliberately.

Chester narrowed his eyes and pointed his finger in Zane's direction, wagging it at him threateningly. "Smartass, eh?" he asked knowingly. "I ain't sure I like you," Chester claimed as his eyes narrowed further.

"How about breakfast, Ma?" Ty asked as he leaned forward and tried to distract his grandfather with the movement.

She responded by thumping a plate in front of Chester and sitting down with a huff. "Amen," she said in annoyance before beginning to dish eggs onto her own plate.

Ty glanced over at Zane and smiled at him, giving him a quick wink. Zane returned the grin and reached for the biscuits, taking two before passing the plate to Ty. Ty's knee occasionally brushed against his under the table as they ate, but the conversation died down as the food was passed around. It was an odd, remarkable feeling, to be eating breakfast with Ty and his family and feel not only welcome, but like he might belong there.

It was a feeling Zane tried to soak in and store for later.

When the breakfast was mostly over, Ty stood and scooped up the empty dishes off the table. They clattered as he dumped them in the sink. "Are we going to sit here all day, or are we going up the mountain?" he asked as he ran hot water.

The corners of Zane's lips turned up, and he turned in his chair to look at his partner. "Waiting on you, bus boy."

Mara walked by and smacked Zane lightly in the back of the head for his trouble. "Be nice," she chastised as she walked out of the kitchen. Zane just smiled.

Ty laughed softly, turned back to the sink, and rinsed his hands. "If we don't go now, we might as well wait 'til tomorrow," he added as he grabbed a dishtowel to dry his hands.

"Got a garage roof needs patching," Earl suggested as he poured himself more coffee.

Deuce stood hastily and made his way out of the kitchen. "I'll start packing up the truck!" he called as he went.

"My duffel's packed," Zane told Ty with a shrug. He already had on jeans and boots along with his thin T-shirt covered by a long-sleeved Henley.

Earl grunted and pushed away from the table. "We'll just patch that roof next time," he said to Ty with a smile before he strolled out of the kitchen, mug in hand.

Ty cleared his throat, snorted in annoyance, and looked at Zane with narrowed eyes.

"What?" Zane asked softly.

"I should've left your ass in DC," Ty muttered to him as he pushed away from the sink counter and moved slowly toward the table where Zane sat. He cocked his head to listen briefly, and then he bent and stole a surprise kiss before leaving the room.

Zane licked his bottom lip as he stood. He was smiling when he followed.

~CHAPTER 6~

THEY said their good-byes to Mara at the trailhead, each giving her a hug and a kiss—even Zane, Deuce noticed—and they each shouldered their packs. Deuce examined his walking stick, a long, thick piece of wood that had been hand-rubbed and stained dark. It had a length of survival rope tied around the top as a handle, and fixed into the wood of the tip was a small compass.

"That's quite a walking stick," Zane said, coming to a stop to stand next to him as he zipped up his heavy coat. He had Deuce's old pack hanging off his broad shoulders.

"It is," Deuce agreed readily. "Ty made it for me. Saw one at a gun show somewhere and thought it might come in handy."

Zane snorted. "Thoughtful," he said more genuinely.

"He can be," Deuce answered as he tightened the strap on his own pack.

Zane smiled a little. "Sometimes," he agreed, looking over to his partner, who was circling around one of the other cars in the gravel lot, frowning at it thoughtfully. "So," Zane sighed as he watched Ty for a moment. "Where are we off to? Just… up the mountain in a random direction?" He glanced up into the trees, and now that Deuce really looked at him, he could tell Zane was tense. Edgy, even.

"There are several different trails we can take from this point," Deuce answered. He tugged at one of the straps of Zane's pack and shortened it for him, making certain it fit snugly to his back.

Borrowing a pack was generally frowned upon on the trail because it was so important that they fit well. But Zane and Deuce were roughly the same height, and the pack wasn't too heavily laden, so Deuce wasn't worried about it. "We don't usually have a set path planned out. Just a general idea of how long it will take so Ma can pick us up at the other end. Ty's got the trail map."

Zane shot Ty a glare as Deuce spoke, and his brother just smirked evilly as he walked past them. It was easy for Deuce to see the dynamic between them. Ty and Zane seemed to get along best when they were annoying each other. They enjoyed the adversity, and Deuce was enjoying seeing all the puzzle pieces of their partnership and how they were starting to fit together.

"Great. He'll pick the worst one," Zane grumbled as Ty moved past them.

"Nah," Deuce answered with certainty. "He stays away from the really bad ones when I'm with him," he said with a tap of his walking stick on the ground to indicate his bad leg. Zane offered him an apologetic smile, but Deuce waved it off.

"You ready?" Ty asked them from where he stood at the head of the trail.

"What's with the car?" Zane asked as he and Deuce moved to join him.

Ty shrugged and looked at it again. "Expired inspection," he explained. "Been up here a while."

Deuce glanced over at the vehicle, wondering why Ty had even noticed and why Zane had felt the need to ask him about it. It had to be an FBI thing.

"You want to do something about it?" Zane asked Ty as they all looked at the dusty car. There were several stickers on the back for the Appalachian Trail, the Shenandoah Valley, the Great Smoky Mountains, The Black Cat in Boone, North Carolina, and several others in the same vein. The owner was obviously a hiker.

"Ten to one the driver has a hemp wallet," Deuce said to Ty wryly.

Ty snorted and shook his head, smiling. He gave the car one last look and shrugged. Deuce figured the car probably belonged to a long-term hiker who hadn't thought ahead to have the inspection done. Ty was apparently thinking along the same lines.

"We'll let it be," Ty answered carelessly. "Y'all ready?" he asked them. Earl had already disappeared into the trees.

Zane nodded, although he did give the car one more look before he started walking. Deuce started off down the trail just ahead of him, knowing Ty would take up the rear like he always did. It often didn't matter what trail they intended to take. Earl went where he pleased. That was why they had stopped even trying to plot their course years ago.

It was quiet on the mountain, cool and peaceful and wonderful. Deuce and Ty had grown up in these mountains, and no matter how many big cities he lived in or how much money he made, Deuce would always consider this home. He glanced back at Zane and then Ty as he followed a curve in the trail. Zane was looking all around him, and it was even clearer now that he was stiff in the shoulders. Wary. On guard somehow.

Very interesting. It could be as he said, that he just wasn't accustomed to the mountains, or it could be that this was how Zane Garrett always was. Deuce didn't want to describe it as a hair trigger, but it was close.

It usually made Ty cranky when Deuce started analyzing his friends, but he just couldn't help himself. "Is it the trees that make you nervous or just not knowing where you're going?" Deuce asked over his shoulder.

Zane glanced up at him. "Both," he said curtly, though he sighed and shrugged a little after that answer. "But I imagine I'll get used to it really quickly."

Deuce turned and glanced back at him more fully. Behind Zane, Ty was fixing a lime green buff over his head as he walked, not really paying attention to them. He had about half a dozen of them, each a different color and pattern, and he wore them underneath his straw hat to keep his ears warm and wick the sweat away from his short hair. Deuce knew he'd worn them through a variety of different Recon missions, and he was never without one on the mountain.

Deuce looked back at Zane and smiled. "Shout if you need to stop," he advised.

"Come on, ladies!" Earl called from far ahead of them. "Next twenty miles ain't gonna hike theirselves!"

Behind him, Deuce heard Ty begin to whistle the tune to "For He's a Jolly Good Fellow." Deuce knew, though, that in his mind Ty was singing "The Bear Went over the Mountain." Deuce grinned. It was going to be an interesting hike.

IT WAS well past midday of the second day of hiking when Earl stopped them for a decent break. Ty set his pack against a towering tree and took out the trail map. He held it up and tilted it into the broken sunshine that cut through the canopy of leaves. They were going over terrain he didn't recognize, and though Earl seemed confident in where he was going, Ty's father *always* seemed confident in where he was going, regardless of whether he knew where he actually was.

Ty was fairly certain they were already lost.

Deuce came over as Earl and Zane sat on a fallen log near the trail, eating the last of the sandwiches Mara had wrapped tightly in wax paper and packed up for them. "I think we're lost," Deuce muttered to him.

Ty snorted in amusement and nodded. "This trail here," he said, indicating the path they'd been following, "it's so overgrown I don't think it's been widely used in a few years."

"Think we should ask Dad if he knows where we are?" Deuce asked dubiously.

Ty looked at him askance. "And have to listen to him harp at us for not having our bearings?" he posed. "Not me."

"Good point," Deuce agreed with a sigh.

"You don't think this is another of his little tests, do you?" Ty mumbled with a frown as he turned the trail map sideways. "Is that crayon?"

"He wouldn't do that when you have a stranger up here," Deuce answered with a shake of his head, ignoring the second query. "Would he?" he asked doubtfully.

Ty shrugged and looked up at his father and Zane as they ate in silence. To his eye, Zane looked okay; he hadn't made a single peep about them slowing down or stopping yet. He was stubborn, and he'd tromped along with them gamely, even talking with Deuce about some of the places he'd worked. But Ty also knew his partner still wasn't sleeping at night, and this hiking was wearing on him. Zane tried to hide it, but Ty knew what to look for after the last few weeks. Sometimes even a nice rough roll between the sheets wouldn't help Zane sleep well.

Zane was wrong in the head somehow, and he wasn't getting better. Ty knew that was a big reason they'd not been put back in the field yet. It frustrated him to no end, and that frustration was beginning to wear on their partnership in more ways than one. That was one of the reasons he'd been keeping his distance; he didn't want to add any more stress to whatever Zane was dealing with, and Ty knew himself well enough to know that he caused stress even to the people who liked him.

Ty set those thoughts aside for later, hoping he wouldn't have to deal with the issue at all. "Hey, Dad, Deuce and me are gonna scout ahead a little," he called out, thinking to give Zane a little more of a break before they headed off again. And hopefully find a clearing and a landmark or two.

Earl gave them a wave of acknowledgment as he chewed. Ty turned and gestured for Deuce to come with him.

"So," Deuce said as soon as they were far enough away from the others to speak freely. "Is it really such a good idea to get involved with him?" he asked.

"What do you mean?" Ty asked with a distracted frown as he studied the surrounding area and looked down at the laminated paper in his hand. He was almost certain now a portion of the thing was drawn in crayon. They were not where they were supposed to be.

"Ty? Give me one minute, okay?" Deuce asked, and he held up one finger to emphasize the request. Ty looked up at him in surprise, pulling his attention away from the trail map. "One minute to have a serious conversation. Then we can go back to pretending we're not lost," Deuce bargained.

"Okay," Ty muttered warily, and he folded the map up and slid it into his pocket. "Shoot."

"Don't get me wrong, all right?" Deuce requested as he started walking again, using the stick Ty had carved to help him. "He seems like an okay guy. He's kinda… twitchy, but then so are you. And if you're going to be involved with a *guy*, I'd rather it be someone who can kick your ass," he informed Ty seriously. "But I've seen what you do to the people you're fucking, man. They fall for you; you dump them; they have a nervous breakdown. What happens when it ends? Can you request a new partner because of personal issues?"

"It won't go that far," Ty scoffed as he caught up to his brother and walked beside him with his head down, watching the trail. "And I do not give people nervous breakdowns," he added in an insulted voice. He glanced up to catch Deuce's disbelieving eye, and he shrugged defensively.

"You saying your relationship with him is purely professional?" Deuce asked.

"Yes," Ty answered stubbornly.

Deuce stopped walking and shook his head. Ty moved until he was standing in front of him. "You're full of shit," Deuce accused with a smile.

"Well, that's not new," Ty argued.

"So, you're saying if you weren't fucking him any longer, you'd still be okay working with him," Deuce posed, unwilling to be driven off track.

"Yes," Ty answered in annoyance. "You a couples therapist all of a sudden?" Deuce snorted and began laughing. "Really," Ty grunted as he turned away.

"You know how lovers' spats get, Ty," Deuce called after him.

"There's no love involved," Ty insisted as he turned back around and glared at Deuce.

"Maybe not for you," Deuce pointed out. "What about him?"

"Garrett?" Ty asked, his voice rising in tone. "He's not in love with me; are you kidding? He can barely stand me."

"Love and like are two entirely different things, Tyler," Deuce said knowingly as he started moving again.

"Yeah, well, save it for your clients," Ty muttered as he followed. His brother responded with a delighted whistle, and Ty shook his head, trying not to let on how disturbed he was by the discussion. Deuce was even more perceptive than Ty, a skill that served his brother well in his chosen profession. But there was no reason to think Deuce was right in regards to Zane. Ty knew his partner better than Deuce did. Zane had already known the love of his life, and he wasn't looking for another one. What that spelled out for them was absolutely nothing but enjoying the here and now.

Zane would no more fall in love with Ty than he would sprout wings and fly.

ZANE watched the brothers tromp off down a trail. He could hear them talking for a few moments, but then they were too far away.

"They seem close," Zane observed, shifting on the log to lean his elbows on his knees as he studied the greenery under his boots.

"They were tied together like a knot when they were little," Earl confirmed. "Caused all kinds of hell. But then, Grady brothers always have. Been that way since my daddy and his brothers was little."

Zane smiled. Trouble ran in the family, obviously. "Always wondered what it'd be like to have a brother," he confided in Earl.

"Well, you practically got one now," Earl pointed out as he gestured with his half-eaten sandwich.

Glancing at the older man, Zane tipped his head as he turned the half of his sandwich on its side to take another bite. "Yeah, I guess." He wouldn't exactly call his relationship with Ty a brotherly one. But then, they were in West Virginia…. His lips quirked before he took a bite, aware of Earl's scrutiny and trying not to laugh.

"Dick tells me you took care of my boy," Earl said a full minute later.

Zane slowly lifted his gaze to meet his eyes but didn't comment. He didn't want to talk about New York with anyone—and definitely not with Ty's father. Earl nodded, that look about him like he felt he might have an idea of what they'd dealt with. "Bad enough you don't want to talk about it, huh?" Zane swallowed hard and reached for his canteen, looking blankly out into the forest. "You military, Garrett?"

The abrupt change in the line of questioning threw Zane for a second. He figured at that moment that he ought to have expected it. All the Gradys did that jump-the-tracks train of thought thing; he suspected it was a way to throw their quarry off guard. It worked, he thought with a sniff. "No, sir."

"That's too bad," Earl commented sincerely.

Zane frowned and turned his chin back. "Why?"

"Military gives you a state of mind to deal with those kind of things," Earl told him sympathetically. "Man ain't made to deal without help."

Zane had to admit the man had a point. Truth was, he wasn't handling parts of his job-related past well, even with outside help. But the comment rankled, regardless. "Just because I'm not military doesn't mean I can't handle the job."

"Didn't say you couldn't, son," Earl told him evenly.

Zane nodded slowly, finishing the last couple bites of his sandwich and watching as Earl stood and walked a few steps away. Zane tipped his head to one side. He hadn't quite figured out how to take Earl Grady yet.

"Damn fool boy needs someone on his six," Earl murmured as he looked out into the woods where Ty and Deuce had disappeared.

"Ty's very good at his job," Zane defended quietly.

Earl nodded and turned back to him. "Yes, he is. You know anything about tracking?" he asked.

Zane raised an amused eyebrow, acknowledging another jump in the tracks. "Not on a mountain," he answered.

"Where then?"

"In a city. The Texas flats where I grew up. Or on a computer."

Earl wrinkled his nose. "Computers," he repeated with a shake of his head. "Can't wrap my mind around them."

"They're the new frontier," Zane told him wryly. "Not many places like this left," he said, pointing his finger up and circling.

"Mountains, they got their dangers, just like anywhere else. I been a lot of places. So has Ty. But these mountains are in my blood, and they're in Ty's blood too." Earl went quiet, looking around them speculatively. "They've served Tyler well," he finally decided. "If you can survive here, you can survive just about anywhere," he claimed.

"I guess I'll find out then," Zane finally answered. "But you won't be carrying my ass out," he said with a slight smile, echoing a comment Earl had made about one of Ty's Recon friends.

Earl snorted. "We'll see shortly," he said with a smirk.

A little bothered, Zane slid his empty sandwich wrapper in his bag and stood up, pacing away to the edge of the clearing. He didn't like the constant air of doubt Earl exuded, as if he wasn't quite sure Zane—or any of them, for that matter—was capable of doing what needed to be done. It was similar to the attitude Ty'd had toward him when they'd first met.

He stood in place for a while, arms crossed, looking down the hillside at the thick undergrowth that rambled over rocks and broken trees about ten feet below them, doing his best to zone out and listen to the woods around him. After several minutes, he took a slow, deep breath, sighed, and went to move, but he paused as a small mouse darted out of the brush and dodged around his feet before disappearing again. Zane nearly chuckled until more movement caught his eyes, and he looked down.

"Earl?"

"Yeah?"

"Come here, please."

Earl walked up behind him, and Zane pointed down.

There was a snake sliding out of the brush, its nearly camouflaged brown body stretching out as it slithered near one of Zane's boots, intent on the mouse it had been stalking. It kept moving, and Zane's eyes widened as the snake got longer and thicker.

"Never seen a snake before?" Earl asked as he frowned and squinted at it. "Cold for her to be out."

Zane turned a disbelieving glare on him. "Is this particular one dangerous or can I kick it away?"

"That's a rattler, boy," Earl said with a careless wave of his hand. "You just wait 'til she decides to move and hope she don't startle," he advised, as if it were the easiest thing in the world to just stand there while a poisonous snake slid around your ankle. "She knows you're there already; she can see heat."

Just at that moment, the snake coiled itself and raised its head, its tail moving and emitting the rattling sound Zane was all too familiar with from growing up on a horse ranch in Texas.

"Now she's pissed," Earl observed calmly, taking a cautious step backward. "Them boots of yours leather?"

"Leather and canvas," Zane answered, swallowing. But that wasn't going to help if she bit above them. She was within easy striking distance of his knees.

"That there's a timber rattler. Pretty rare. Not usually mean, but you must have interrupted her dinner," Earl said, keeping his voice down. "Real poisonous. But don't worry," he was sure to add. "Usually when a snake strikes defensively it's a dry bite." Zane glanced at him quickly. "Means they don't load up no venom before they bite," Earl explained, as if he was teaching a class rather than talking to a man about to be bitten by a snake.

Zane grimaced. "I don't really want to take that chance, thanks. So what now?" he asked as he eyed the snake that was coiled in front of him and still rattling. "I can't shoot the damn thing." He very slowly uncrossed his arms, his right hand settling at his left wrist. He was pretty sure his knife wouldn't help either, but it made him feel better regardless.

"No, they're endangered. Can't kill her. Don't move," Earl warned. He moved closer and circled behind the snake as the rattling became louder, but Zane wasn't about to turn his head to see what the man was doing.

"Fucking vacation," Zane said under his breath.

"Move," Earl barked suddenly.

As Zane shifted his weight and jumped sideways, away from the snake, it went after him, striking fast. Earl grabbed at it as it lunged through the air, its momentum making it impossible for the five-foot long snake to do anything but hiss and curl its body around Earl's hand as he held onto it, just below its widened jaws.

Zane stared at him, both appalled and impressed.

"Got to catch 'em below the teeth," Earl advised calmly as he carefully unwrapped the snake from his wrist and then tossed it with both hands into the underbrush, sending it sliding down the rocky hillside unharmed, away from them. "You all right?" Earl asked him as he turned to look at him.

Zane nodded numbly. Ty joked about West Virginia snake charmers sometimes. Zane had never taken him seriously, though. Maybe he should start. "Thanks."

Earl grunted and took a few steps to peer down the hill. Zane stayed back—no way was he tempting fate again. In Texas the general wisdom was that snakes traveled in pairs.

"Just a last big dinner before winter. Thought we wanted it," Earl drawled carelessly. "Warning us off is all."

"Well, it succeeded," Zane said vehemently.

Earl just chuckled. Before Zane could say anything more, Earl frowned and squatted down, moving aside some fronds of a ground fern.

"What are you doing?" Zane asked in confusion.

"Look at this," Earl said.

Zane went to stand behind Earl and look over his shoulder. But he kept one hand on his knife, just in case.

"SO IF you're not emotionally invested in this guy, why'd you bring him up here?" Deuce asked as he caught up to Ty again.

"Why are you so interested?" Ty asked desperately, wishing his brother would just back off for once.

"Because you're my brother," Deuce answered as he grabbed at Ty's elbow to stop him. "And I enjoy watching you squirm," he added as Ty glared at him.

"You want the truth?" Ty asked in frustration.

"No, Beaumont, I want you to lie to me," Deuce replied drolly.

Ty gave him a hard punch to the bicep in retaliation, and Deuce yipped and stumbled a bit, laughing as he grabbed for his arm. "You're a jackass, Deacon," Ty said with a grunt. "Don't you tell him my given name," he threatened seriously.

"I won't," Deuce agreed, still laughing. "Answer the question, Ty. You're never this stubborn unless you're trying to hide something. You're in love with him, aren't you?" he stated with a hint of surprise.

Ty sighed and looked away, staring out at the rise and fall of the mountain ridge through the breaks in the tree line. To this point, he'd been able to tell himself that Zane was nothing more than a friend and partner. Ty had never been in love. He didn't know what it was, and so he couldn't say for sure. He pressed his lips together and lowered his head. He rarely lied to Deuce, and he saw no reason to start now.

"I don't know," Ty said. "I don't know if I love him or not. I think… I think I *could* if he let me," he said, admitting more to Deuce than he'd even been willing to admit to himself. "But that has nothing to do with why he's here," he insisted as Deuce opened his mouth to speak. "Dick is on the verge of forcing Garrett into an early retirement," he told Deuce softly, looking around the trail at their surroundings as if someone might overhear them.

Finally thrown off the scent, Deuce straightened in surprise and took a step closer to Ty, lowering his voice when he spoke. "What's the reason?" he asked curiously.

After a moment of hesitation, Ty answered regretfully. "Our last case did a number on him. He's bombing his evals." It felt wrong, telling anyone about Zane's situation. Hell, it had felt wrong *hearing* about Zane's situation. But he trusted his brother, and he was hoping Deuce might be able to help. He was a trained psychiatrist, after all, and that was exactly what Zane needed, in Ty's opinion.

"Which evals?" Deuce asked, and Ty could practically see him switching over into professional mode.

It had always annoyed Ty before, but now it was almost a relief. "Psych ones mostly," he answered with a small huff.

"He seems pretty grounded," Deuce observed.

"It's an… ongoing thing," Ty answered. "Things from the past piling up. Then that car wreck in New York?"

Deuce nodded, not commenting on the fact that Ty hadn't called home to inform them about that whole ordeal until *after* he'd been released from the hospital.

"He got pretty torn up. And he doesn't know I know, but he ended up having to kill the man we were hunting. Then he got tossed back into an undercover gig that he wasn't ready for and didn't want, and there's drugs and alcohol and all kinds of shit involved from his past. He cleaned up but... it... he's not dealing well. He tries to hide it, but he's not," Ty went on in frustration.

"You brought him here for me to talk with him?" Deuce asked in surprise.

"Not... really," Ty answered with a wince.

Deuce was silent, staring at him, and soon Ty lowered his head, unable to look his brother in the eye. "Did Dick order you to bring him here?" Deuce asked uncertainly.

"No, that was all me," Ty corrected.

"But Dick ordered *you* here," Deuce reminded.

"It was a suggestion," Ty argued.

"A suggestion," Deuce repeated dubiously.

"A mild suggestion," Ty said with a nod of his head.

Deuce snorted. "The last mild suggestion Dick gave you sent you to Cuba," he reminded.

"Yeah, well, I kind of enjoyed Cuba," Ty muttered as he looked away and squinted back in the direction they'd come.

"I assume he doesn't know this?" Deuce asked.

"I'm pretty sure Dick knows I enjoyed Cuba," Ty said with a smirk he couldn't hold back.

"I'm talking about Zane, numbnuts," Deuce said. "And don't try to confuse me, I'm immune," he added. Ty sighed and looked back at his feet. "Does Zane know why he's here?" Deuce prodded.

Ty shook his head and looked up at his brother pleadingly. "I told him I wanted him to come along to run interference with the family. That *was* the original idea, actually, but the more I thought about it on the way up, the more I thought maybe you could help. I don't know what else to do. I'm not sure he'll *let* me help him."

Deuce was silent, studying Ty for a few minutes. Finally he nodded, taking pity. "I'll talk to him," he promised.

"Thank you," Ty said in relief.

"Ty! Deuce!" Earl called out suddenly, his deep voice echoing in the thick woods. The tone of his voice caused Ty to turn and run instantly, leaving Deuce to keep up with him as best he could on his bad leg.

Ty skidded into the clearing where they'd been resting, and he glanced around until he saw his father crouched in the woods at the edge of the clearing, looking down at the ground. Zane was standing behind him, and they wore matching frowns.

"What?" Ty demanded irritably as his heart began to calm. Deuce clambered out of the woods behind him and ran into him, almost toppling them both to the ground.

"Quit messin' around and come look at this," Earl requested calmly. Ty shoved Deuce gently before stomping over to join his father.

"Don't *do* that," he requested as he knelt beside Earl.

"Do what?" Earl asked in confusion.

Ty just shook his head. "What is it?"

Earl pointed at a track in the dried mud in front of him. He was pulling the leaves of an overgrown plant away in order to see it, and Ty wondered briefly how he'd even found the tracks to start with. They were standing only a couple feet from a drop-off to a creek in a ravine.

"Is that from an ATV?" Deuce asked as he leaned over them, his hands on his knees.

"It's definitely a tire mark of some sort," Ty murmured as he looked up and over his shoulder, peering into the woods in the direction the track headed. Motorized vehicles of any sort were illegal up here. Even bicycles weren't allowed. So it was a concern to find a track like this. His eyes scanned the trees and underbrush, looking for signs of recent passage. An ATV trail wasn't hard to follow, but Ty could see no broken twigs or brushed leaves in the area, much less any more tracks.

"This is a pretty old track," he finally decided as his brother and father waited for him to speak. They knew his abilities, and they were willing to defer to him even though both men had been raised in these mountains as well. His father had been used as a tracker in Vietnam because of his skills, and he had taught his boys everything he knew. Ty had merely had more opportunity to hone the talent.

"When was the last heavy rain up here?" he asked his dad.

"Been about two weeks, to my knowledge," Earl answered thoughtfully. He gently replaced the fronds of the little fern he'd been holding back, and he and Ty both cocked their heads in the same manner as they looked down at the track beneath. "It was made before the rain," Earl realized as Ty nodded in agreement. "Plant protected it from being washed away," he told Zane as he stood and stretched his back.

"We'll report it when we hit the ranger station, all the same," Ty told them as he stood as well. "Person on an ATV up here is either up to no good or they're gonna get hurt," he said with a sigh.

"I don't see how a four-wheeler would get up here at all," Zane said. "So much of the woods, the paths are too narrow."

"If you don't care about trampling the underbrush or getting clotheslined by the occasional low-hanging branch, you can do it," Deuce told him wryly as he stood with one hand on his hip. He looked over at Ty. "Are you worried?" he asked.

Ty frowned thoughtfully but finally shook his head. "Marijuana, probably. Could be moonshine, but I don't know. We'll stop in at the ranger station, give them a location."

"They'll just kick it off to you Feds," Earl pointed out.

"Dad, if I call Dick with a case, even something like this, when I'm supposed to be on vacation, he will skin me alive," Ty pointed out. "Besides, what do you want me to do? Track them through the back country and take them on with Deuce's walking stick?"

"Don't be a smartass," Earl warned as he turned away and headed toward his pack. "Watch out for the snake," he added as he went.

"Snake?" Ty asked in confusion, glancing at Deuce and then Zane, who was shaking his head as he walked away.

~Chapter 7~

"WE'RE a few hours behind schedule," Deuce informed the group as Ty and Zane hunched over the fire and warmed their stiff fingers. Ty looked up at his brother and snarled quietly.

Zane knew it had gotten much colder than they had anticipated, and it was sapping their energy at a dangerous rate. It was only the second night, but they were all dragging a little. The last ridge they'd topped before stopping for the night had revealed snow on the highest peaks, and Ty had gone so far as to tell Zane he was beginning to fear it would get worse before they could find the appropriate shelter. That wasn't reassuring.

At least it was cold enough that surely *no* snakes would be out at all.

"I'd like to scout ahead a little," Earl told them. He was screwing the top onto a Thermos of hot coffee he'd boiled over the fire and looking off into the woods that awaited them. "Get clear of the roof and smell what the weather looks like," he went on as he looked up at the thick canopy of trees.

Zane looked up as well, only catching glimpses of the gray evening sky between the layers of colored foliage barely illuminated by the fire. He'd almost gotten used to the feeling of being underneath a huge tent that happened to move and sway with the wind.

"If we can't get to the next shelter in a day's trek, we might think about turning back," Earl was saying. "Keep to the lower elevation and familiar ground. Ty, load up."

"Yes, sir," Ty murmured as he stood again and began to extract things from his pack quickly.

"Catch up," Earl instructed as he headed off into the woods with his flashlight and canteen.

Ty glanced up and sighed in exasperation. "Damn fool, can't even wait for me to lighten my damn pack," he muttered under his breath as he knelt and moved faster. "Familiar ground, my ass," he grumbled.

Zane watched him, wondering about the relationship Earl Grady had with his sons. He seemed pretty good-natured and easygoing, and so did Deuce, for the most part. Although he wouldn't describe Ty that way on the whole, they all seemed to get along just fine and have a great deal of respect for each other. But when Earl gave an order, both Ty and Deuce jumped to obey it as quickly as possible. Easygoing or not, somewhere along the way Earl Grady had taught his sons to do as they were told without questioning it. Zane wasn't sure what he thought of that, and it was definitely odd to see Ty like this. Ty mumbled something to them Zane didn't quite catch before heading off into the dark woods after his father.

Zane leaned back against a rock that lined the clearing where they'd made camp for the night and stretched out his legs with a wince. He was in really good physical shape—lots of hours in the gym to offset all the sitting at a desk—but the hard hiking wasn't like running on a treadmill or lifting weights. He had kinks in his back from carrying the backpack that were bugging him.

The fire was putting out good heat now, so he pulled off his heavy jacket and set it to the side, not wanting to get overheated. Grumbling to himself a little, he twisted carefully from side to side to pop his back and then his neck.

He was tired. Bone tired, even. Maybe he'd be able to sleep more than a few hours tonight. He yawned, but movement to his side drew his attention. Zane flicked his eyes to his left to see Deuce rambling across the campsite. He was carrying an armload of small sticks and brush to fuel the fire, and he happily dumped them onto Ty's bedroll as Zane watched him.

He straightened and turned to meet Zane's eyes, and he cocked his head curiously when he saw him sitting there. He glanced off in the direction Ty and Earl had gone and began moving toward him. Deuce knelt beside Zane with a smile and then allowed himself to fall into a seated position in front of the fire.

"Tired, huh?" he asked knowingly.

Zane let himself smile a little as he slumped. "What gave me away?"

Deuce shrugged. "You have that 'please carry me' look to you."

Zane snorted. "Seen that a lot?"

"I have a mirror," Deuce answered with a laugh. He unscrewed the cap to his canteen and gave Zane a measuring look. "Why'd you come up here with Ty?" he asked.

Holding Deuce's eyes, Zane silently acknowledged the talk that had been pending. "He asked me to."

"I'm betting he asks you to do a lot of things," Deuce wagered.

Zane shook his head briefly. "You'd lose."

"Really?" Deuce responded in genuine surprise. "Interesting," he murmured as he again looked out to where Ty and Earl had disappeared down the trail. After a moment, he shook his head and looked back at Zane. "You like your job?" he asked suddenly.

Zane was still amused by the now-trademarked "interesting." "Sometimes. Not as much as I used to."

"Pain can color a lot of things," Deuce pointed out with a nod.

Zane nodded. "Yeah," he agreed.

"If you hadn't been hurt on the job, would you enjoy it more?" Deuce asked thoughtfully.

Zane considered whom he was talking to. This was Ty's brother, after all, not just some random bureau psychiatrist. "No," he admitted quietly.

Deuce pursed his lips and nodded. Then he leaned toward Zane slightly. "Is Ty a good partner?" he asked.

"You were there when I told your mom about Ty being a good partner."

"That's what you told my mom," Deuce pointed out. "I'm asking for the real answer."

Zane frowned slightly, not sure what Deuce wanted to hear. "Why would I lie about that?"

"So he's a good partner," Deuce concluded with a nod. He looked at Zane unflinchingly, studying him. "Are you?" he finally asked.

Zane was a little surprised by the question. "I hope so. "

"Of course," Deuce agreed with a shrug of one shoulder and a smile. "But are you?"

"I don't know," Zane answered defensively.

"Sure you do. You know what it takes. Are you someone *you'd* be comfortable putting your back to in a fight?"

Zane caught himself pausing. He'd been wrestling with his fears a lot in the form of nightmares, especially the fear of losing someone close to him. In the past, it had been Becky. Right now, it meant Ty. "I don't know."

"So you're not a good partner," Deuce translated for himself. "Very interesting."

Zane pressed his lips together, embarrassed and at a loss for words. "Has anyone ever threatened you over saying that word?"

"Not that I recall," Deuce answered sincerely. He was still smiling at Zane thoughtfully. "As a shrink, we're trained to listen and ask the relevant questions, not so much give advice," he confided in Zane.

"I thought you didn't like to be called a shrink," Zane said with a weak smile.

"It comes and goes," Deuce admitted carelessly. "And I'm going to offer advice to you now despite being a shrink, okay? It's good to be honest with yourself. And harsh, to a point. After that point it gets unhealthy," he said with a wince and a shrug. "But sometimes the cold hard truth is very effective in helping yourself. I tell Ty all the time, just admit that you're an asshole and make life easier." He went on, seeming to enjoy the line of conversation and rambling happily.

Harsh truth. Zane figured the worst of his nightmares was that sometime, somewhere, he wouldn't be able to protect the people he cared about—and that they'd be taken away from him as a result. As to how to fix it? God only knew, because Zane sure didn't.

"Once you admit to yourself that you are or aren't something, then you can begin searching for the reason why," Deuce went on. "And once you've found that, you can begin to take steps toward making it better. So, tell yourself you're an asshole, stop being an asshole, your problem's solved," Deuce said in a pleased voice. "He usually glazes over on me at that point," he added with a frown. "Kinda like you are."

"That's because he's an asshole," Zane said with a small smile before he huffed quietly. "He just seems to blow things off so easily. It makes me fucking crazy."

Deuce was frowning harder and shaking his head. "Ty takes things to heart," he told Zane, his voice losing the light, carefree tone and becoming more serious. "Most things he takes hard for about a minute, then he's moving on. Other things, they take him longer. Especially issues of fault. Failures hit him hard, but he processes them well. They don't stick to him. See, some people, they're sticky like Velcro. You're sticky. Your problems stick to you like fuzzballs from the laundry; you take them everywhere with you and people can see them plain as day. Ty, he's like spandex. Nothing sticks to him, and he's shiny on the outside."

Zane knew he was staring at Deuce oddly, but he couldn't stop himself. "You know, I don't know what's worse, that you just said that or that it actually made sense."

Deuce winked at him and grinned. "You just have to pick off the fuzzballs," he advised.

"I never was really good with laundry," Zane said with a self-deprecating laugh. "Not really good with dealing with 'things', either."

Deuce hummed in response. "Maybe if you tried doing the laundry more often, you'd be a better partner."

"Are we continuing the laundry analogy for the laugh factor?" Zane asked as he wrinkled his nose. "If we are, I'll say I'd rather dump it all at the dry cleaners and forget about it."

"You don't want a tiny little Oriental guy dealing with your fuzzballs," Deuce argued, barely restraining a laugh. "It's one of my better analogies," he went on, his grin widening as Zane did laugh. "I should write it down." He paused for a long moment. "Am I making any headway here?" he asked seriously.

"I hear what you're saying. But it's nothing I didn't already know," Zane said. He *knew* what was wrong. He just didn't know *how* to fix it, so he'd taken to ignoring it.

Deuce nodded in understanding. "So what you're saying is you don't *mind* being a bad partner to a man you claim is a great one."

Zane's face went very still as a flash of pain streaked through his chest. "I've been a good partner when it counted."

"It always counts, Zane," Deuce murmured gently.

Zane sighed, dropped his eyes, and then closed them for good measure. "Yeah," he whispered.

Deuce reached out and patted him on the foot. "We went over the whats. You ever want to get into the whys, you know where to find me," he offered.

After managing to get a breath into his lungs, Zane looked up at Deuce. He thought he should say something, but there just wasn't anything to be said. He settled on nodding and smiling weakly.

Deuce smiled lopsidedly at him. "Good, now help me up," he requested as he held out a hand. "Leg'll let me get down, but it's no damn help getting back up. I just roll around like a turtle on its shell 'til somebody shoves me with a stick."

Zane couldn't help but snort and smile. "I'm not sure I'm in much better shape," he admitted. "Your dad sets a fast pace."

"He always has," Deuce acknowledged.

Zane snorted, got to his feet fairly easily, and then offered Deuce an arm. Deuce clasped his wrist in a hard grip, and he pulled himself to his feet with Zane's help. He clapped Zane on the back and turned to head for the tree line again to gather more firewood.

Zane watched him limp away. "If you don't mind me asking, what happened?" he asked impulsively.

Deuce turned and looked back at him with a raised eyebrow. "What happened to my leg, you mean?" he asked to clarify. He patted his thigh as he turned back to face Zane. "I went over the handlebars of a motorcycle," he answered with a slight smile. "Got pinned between the bike and a tree. Broke all kinds of bones and tore some tendons below the knee. Couldn't be fixed to where I don't limp."

Zane nodded slowly. Sounded like normal dumbass kid stuff; he'd done his share. It just didn't end very well for Deuce. Then something clicked. "That's why Ty hates motorcycles, isn't it?"

Deuce nodded. "He gave me the bike when he went off to join the Marines. I was sixteen. He blames himself. You know the drill."

Zane nodded. It fit what he knew about Ty. "Yeah, he must. He doesn't like me riding my Valkyrie. And he's made it very clear he never will."

Deuce clucked his tongue. "Ty's got to place blame. He's a very black-and-white type of person. He needed something to blame for it, and instead of accepting that I was going ninety miles an hour on a dirt road and it was *my* fault, he blamed the bike. And himself," he explained. "But it all worked out for the best," he claimed, remarkably cheerful as he spoke about what had to have been a devastating, life-altering event. "I wouldn't have been a very good Marine," he mused. "And that's the route I would have taken, right down the path he did."

"You love him a lot," Zane murmured.

"He's my brother," Deuce answered, as if that should be obvious.

Zane nodded. "Of course."

"Do you?" Deuce asked without looking away.

Zane held Deuce's gaze as his lips quirked into a wry smile, and he had to go with his honest, gut answer. "No," he said softly, a slight tinge of regret in his voice.

"Huh," Deuce responded in genuine interest. "I would have guessed otherwise," he admitted to Zane.

Zane shrugged uncomfortably, unsure of how to respond to that. It was something he consciously avoided thinking about. "I do like having the asshole around," he offered.

"That's more than can be said for most," Deuce commented in amusement.

"So I've been told," Zane agreed. He rolled his shoulders slightly, trying to shrug off some of the tension. Deuce just watched him closely, narrowing his eyes and smiling. "You look very happy with yourself," Zane observed.

Deuce glanced off into the woods again and then took a step closer to lower his voice. "Try to be a better partner," he advised softly.

Zane held his gaze for a long moment. Finally he sighed. "I want him around."

Deuce merely nodded again. He glanced to his side, listening briefly. "We'll talk again later," he promised as he looked back at Zane and smiled.

"Yeah," Zane said as he acknowledged Deuce's help. Deuce had zeroed in on what bothered Zane so much in under five minutes—either the man was that good, or Zane felt that comfortable with him. Probably both.

He was distracted from his thoughts when he heard Ty and Earl conversing and tramping through the underbrush, coming closer. Deuce turned and limped back toward the tree line to continue his gathering.

"I don't smell dinner cooking," Ty observed after he broke through the tree line in a different spot than where he'd gone through. He tromped closer to the fire and glanced at Zane, giving him a quick second look over. "What's wrong with you?" he asked.

Zane blinked and shook himself. "Trying to recharge."

Ty looked him up and down dubiously, but then he nodded and unshouldered his pack. "All righty," he said agreeably.

"What'd you find?" Deuce asked them as he brought over another armload of wood and dumped it into Ty's bedroll.

"Hey!" Ty shouted with an accusing point at the firewood.

"What?" Deuce asked innocently.

Ty pointed his finger after Deuce threateningly. "I will beat you like a rented mule next time Daddy ain't watching!"

"Bring it on, G-man," Deuce invited with relish.

"Don't start," Earl warned as he sat down on a rock near the fire. "Deacon," he added, gesturing to the bedroll tiredly.

Ty and Deuce gave each other measuring looks as Deuce bent and pulled the bedroll out from under the woodpile. He held it up and waved it. "See? Good as new," he claimed.

"You're gonna wake up with a snake in your jeans," Ty growled softly.

"Too cold for snakes," Deuce reminded.

"Don't start with the snakes again," Zane said plaintively, getting a chuckle out of Earl.

"Chipmunk then," Ty decided.

"You're afraid of chipmunks," Deuce told him with a laugh.

"Yeah, 'cause they're... twitchy!" Ty explained with a little gesture of his hands.

Deuce laughed harder and waved him off. They were both smiling, though, and Zane could tell the little scene was a familiar one for them.

"We can make the trail cabins if we haul it tomorrow," Earl informed them in a loud voice, getting everyone's attention. "Cold front's a day or so off yet; we should be clear of it before it comes through."

"It might even hook west," Ty added seriously as he sat down beside Zane with a soft huff. "But we might not miss the rain," he added under his breath. Zane frowned and shifted uncomfortably.

Great. Cold *and* wet. What an awesome idea for a vacation. Next time—if there *was* a next time, because their vacations were fucking cursed—Zane was choosing, and right now a beach in Cozumel was sounding pretty damn good.

"So we go on?" Deuce asked.

"We go on," Earl confirmed with a nod.

THEY reached the trail cabin just as darkness was falling the next evening. It hadn't been a nice leisurely stroll through the mountains like the first two days. When the rain started as Ty had predicted, they'd had to double-time it in order to reach the shelter before the coming storm hit them hard, and when they finally made it through the door, they were all wet, cold, tired, and cranky.

Ty pushed back the hood of his slicker and glanced around the interior. These places were never cheerful, but this one had definitely seen better days. Desiccated leaves littered the floor because someone had left the door open last fall, and the exposed logs of the walls were all damp. The roof dripped, the floor was sagging, and there appeared to be moss growing on the outer rock of the fireplace. A fire already flickered there, though, barely warming the tiny cabin. There was a small supply of dry wood stacked in the corner that might last the night if they were careful.

A man sat on one of the four bunk beds in the room, watching them sedately as they darted in from the deluge. Once Zane had slammed the door shut against the rain, the man nodded at Ty.

"Hello," he greeted drolly. He was unshaven, his graying beard long and scraggly. Ty knew he was a through-hiker just from the smell. Soap wasn't an essential item when hiking from Maine to Georgia in one go.

"Evening," Ty responded as he dropped his pack and struggled out of the wet slicker. He threw it aside, headed for the fireplace without another word, and hugged the rock chimney happily.

Zane leaned back against the wall next to the door with a tired half-smile, shaking his head at Ty's antics. Earl had already dropped his bag by the other set of bunk beds, and as soon as Deuce shed his wet clothing, he claimed the lower one, sitting down hard and stretching out his leg.

Ty turned to them and shook his head. "No, no, I got the floor last time," he protested as he pointed at the bunks.

"And you'll get the floor this time because we'll offer the same arguments we did then," Deuce countered with a smile. "He's old; I'm crippled; what are you gonna do?" he posed carelessly as he pulled off his damp socks. Earl laughed softly and began stripping off his outer layers until he came to dry fabric.

"Damnit," Ty muttered. He turned and looked at Zane critically. They would have to fight over the last bunk. And it didn't matter how accustomed to a hard surface you were, sleeping on the floor when you knew there were mattresses was unpleasant. He glanced at the bunks. Okay, well, not mattresses. But up off the floor, certainly.

Zane had set down his pack and was pulling the slicker carefully over his head. He still had to shake his head when he sprinkled water drops all over himself as he took it off. He let it fall to the floor and pulled his shoulders back, trying to stretch out.

When he looked up at Ty, he raised an eyebrow in question. "I'm just going to be glad to be down for a while," Zane admitted. "I don't care if it's the floor."

Ty narrowed his eyes, looking Zane over carefully before sighing. It came out a heavy, dejected sound. "Take the bed, then," he told his partner.

"Quit being a bastard," Zane said mildly as he started stripping down.

Ty huffed at him and began shedding his wet clothing as well. He delved into his pack and pulled out a tight pack of clothesline, which he attached to the walls by slipping each end onto hooks that had been mounted for the purpose. It strung along the center of the cabin, dividing the bunks from the fireplace. Then he began hanging the wet clothes on it so the fire would dry them faster. They couldn't afford to go anywhere with wet, cold clothing on.

He could hear the storm worsening outside, pounding rain on the roof and a steady trickle of water through the shingles in the corner. Ty glanced over at the man who sat watching them all quietly as Earl and Deuce followed suit with their own clothing.

Now that he'd gotten the necessities out of the way, Ty could afford to be friendly. He took a step toward the bunk and offered his hand. The man took it and smiled at him. He was dry, obviously having made it to shelter before the storm broke.

"Ty," Ty offered as he shook his hand. "Zane, Earl, Deuce," he rattled off as he pointed at each of the other men in turn.

"John," the man announced in return.

"Made it in before the rain?" Zane said conversationally.

"Only just," John told him.

"Are you hiking by yourself?" Zane asked curiously.

John nodded as he crunched down on a piece of jerky.

"Started late in the season, huh?" Ty wagered.

John smiled at him. "Started early, just been going slow," he told them. "Figure it's my last one, so I'm enjoying the sights," he said serenely as he gnawed on his jerky.

Ty glanced to Zane. "Trail goes from Maine to Georgia," he told him.

"The Appalachian Trail?" Zane said, his voice rising a little toward the end. "That's got to be a couple thousand miles."

"Two thousand, one hundred and seventy-five," Ty said with a nod. He looked to John. "North or south?" he asked.

"Heading south," John answered. "You?"

Ty shook his head. "Just a local thing," he answered with a smile.

John tilted his head and smiled suddenly. "So then you'll know about the Romney treasure?" he asked excitedly.

Zane was staring at John. "You're hiking more than two thousand miles... for fun?" he asked incredulously.

"Done it every summer for twenty years," John told him.

Zane's jaw actually dropped. "That's... incredible." John merely shrugged.

"Lots of folks do it," Earl told Zane quietly as he pulled out some fresh clothes from his pack. "Through-hikers. I'm sorry, did you say you're looking for treasure?" he asked John after a moment.

John shook his head and leaned forward in his bunk. "Not looking for it, no. Just interested. Ever heard tales?" he asked.

Earl just shook his head in amusement. Zane was still peering at John with a peculiar look on his face, like he thought the man must be off his rocker.

"Romney," Ty repeated curiously. "You mean like the city?" he asked dubiously. The mountains were full of stories about buried treasure, lost gold mines, hidden caches that were never reclaimed. It wasn't unusual to hear about them from hikers who soaked up the lore and retold it as gospel. Ty himself knew quite a bit about a few of the treasure stories in the area, but he'd never heard one associated with Romney.

Muttering something about vacations under his breath, Zane stripped off his windbreaker and Henley, revealing the thinner long-sleeved shirt underneath, and dragged his bag across the small room to settle on the floor near the fireplace, leaning back against the hearth.

John scooted to the edge of his bunk and placed his elbows on his knees, looking around at all of them. "You've never heard of the Romney treasure?" he asked in disbelief.

Ty glanced over at Zane distractedly and back at John with a shake of his head. A crack of lightning outside was followed by thunder that shook the small cabin around them. It was close. Ty thought he might have gotten a whiff of ozone. Deuce gave a low whistle as he glanced up at the ceiling.

"I'm not from here," Zane said as he studied the roof above them, looking doubtful.

John nodded as if that explained it. "I teach about Appalachia back in Maine," he informed them. "Romney isn't exactly on the syllabus, but it's a good story," he said hopefully. He obviously wanted to relate it. Ty figured he probably hadn't had much in the way of conversation for months.

Ty glanced over at his dad, who was watching John with a hint of a smile. It was the same look most of the locals gave a tourist when they used the word "quaint," a look that said smile and humor them until they go away.

Ty cleared his throat against a laugh. "Well, why don't you tell it to us while my brother makes dinner," he said with a look at Deuce.

Deuce glared at him from where he sat huddled on the lower bunk, still shivering. "Fine," he muttered as he unfolded himself and began getting out the makings of dinner.

John sat forward on his bunk and smiled widely. "Well, as you probably know, West Virginia was just Virginia about a hundred and fifty years ago," he started.

Ty exhaled slowly. If this story started a hundred and fifty years ago, it was going to be a long night. He sat beside Zane, his back to the warm rocks of the chimney, and listened half-heartedly.

"Back during the Civil War, the communities of western Virginia were sympathetic to the North, despite the state of Virginia's allegiance to the South," John was saying. "Most of the fighting took place in Virginia, and the western portion was a particularly tricky spot. The South didn't want to lose it, and the North saw it as a strong position to attack Richmond from, populated with sympathizers who could offer help. The town of Romney in particular traded hands fifty-six times during the course of the war."

"This is why I slept through all my college courses," Ty muttered to Zane under his breath.

"Be nice," Zane said softly. "He's harmless."

"I don't like being nice," Ty reminded. Deuce cleared his throat pointedly as he handed out food.

"During the spring of 1863, two years into the War, there was a skirmish in nearby Burlington," John told them as his eyes danced with firelight. "A Confederate cavalry commander had captured twelve men of the Ringgold Cavalry. These men just happened to be the Cavalry's foraging party. Legend says this foraging party had stumbled over something, something spectacular. You know what it was?" Ty and the others shook their heads in answer. "Neither does anyone else, but the best guess is that it was the long lost fortune of Lord Fairfax, stolen from him in the 1700s."

"Who the hell is Lord Fairfax?" Ty whispered to Zane, who shrugged and closed his eyes.

"Stolen from him?" Deuce asked, whether to be polite or out of true interest Ty couldn't guess.

"By one of his land agents. Collected fees and rents that he never turned over to Fairfax. Rumor says it was hidden away until after any investigations could be done and the location was lost."

"Lost and spent sound a whole lot alike," Ty muttered under his breath. Zane jabbed him in the ribs, and Ty gave a soft grunt as he leaned closer to Zane and tried not to laugh.

"Some people believe that Union foraging party found it all those years later," John was saying.

"And that's the treasure that's supposedly buried up here?" Earl asked doubtfully. "Why didn't the Union army take it?"

"They did. That foraging party, they spirited it away, dumping out their supplies and using the sacks for the gold and silver they found. They even left their ammunition behind, blinded to the danger by the treasure."

"That explains how they were captured in a skirmish and not killed fighting," Ty muttered as he drew a circle in the dust next to him. Zane elbowed him again gently, and Ty bit his lip against a smile.

"When the Confederates went through their supplies, you can imagine what they thought. There was arguing over whether they should keep the money for themselves or send it to Richmond to finance the upcoming Gettysburg Campaign. They moved on to Purgitsville, where they themselves were attacked. The money changed hands again—"

"Before any official reports could be made about the money, of course," Ty interjected cynically. There were never any written records to accompany these stories.

"Of course," John agreed happily. "The Federals were then occupying Romney, and when the money reached the town, it was decided that the position wasn't secure enough to keep it there. As often as the town changed hands, you can see why."

Ty scrubbed his hand over his face. This was what being nice to people got him. Zane nudged him in the side yet again, and Ty was hard-pressed not to poke him back.

"The residents of Romney had been gradually taking their own valuables up into the mountains and hiding them, trying to keep them safe from the looting of the soldiers passing through. The man in charge of the Federal brigade, though, he had a sweetheart in Romney. The woman told him of the secret stash the town had hidden away, and one night just forty-eight hours before the town was attacked again, the Federals snuck all that gold and silver up into the mountains and hid it away."

"Are you saying that even though a whole town of people knew where this super secret hiding spot was, that it still got lost?" Ty asked incredulously.

John smiled widely and nodded, as if that was his favorite part of the story. "Over the summer of 1863, Romney was constantly occupied and switching hands or being watched by scouts from both armies. As winter came around, the fighting died down, but as you well know, you don't venture up into these mountains in winter no matter what kind of treasure is up here!"

Ty glanced at Zane and shook his head. Zane was trying hard not to laugh at him. Ty reached between them impulsively and squeezed his hand gently. It was nice to sit there with him and enjoy something physical that wasn't even remotely sexual. He couldn't really think of a time they'd even sat together like this, besides sprawling on the couch and watching post-season baseball to boo the Yankees together.

"So," Deuce said slowly as he looked at John in confusion. "What happened? Why didn't they ever go back for it?"

"The winter of 1863 was a harsh one," John answered. "There were collapses of caves, mudslides, flooding when the snow began to melt. It changed the topography, and so did four years of heavy fighting. The soldiers who'd taken Fairfax's gold and silver up there never returned to Romney. Those who'd been strong enough to drag the town's treasures up there in 1861 had all been sent off to war. They told their families how to get there, using landmarks as directions. By the time the war ended, those landmarks weren't there."

Ty scowled heavily. He was hesitant to admit that that made a certain sort of sense. Still, he didn't put much stock in treasure stories, much less the ones that had no proof of their existence.

"So it's up there somewhere," Earl concluded with a wave of his hand in the general direction of the peaks. He was smiling, obviously humoring the man.

"That's the story," John answered with a pleased nod. He shrugged. "It'd be quite a chunk of change, anyway!" he said as he pushed himself back onto his bunk and settled back.

Ty raised an eyebrow, hoping that was it for the history lesson. Beside him, Zane shivered slightly and reached into his pack to pull out a dry sweatshirt. He had a small hand towel draped over his knee; he'd obviously used it on his head because his hair was sticking up a little in a couple places. He was smiling too. He seemed pretty entertained. Ty turned to fiddle with the fire, stoking it and adding several more logs in the hopes they'd last long enough for him to get some good sleep. Then he sank back down beside his partner, his shoulder brushing Zane's. He watched idly as the others moved to get their beds in order.

"Tired?" he asked Zane softly.

Zane blinked heavily and looked up from where he'd been staring at the floor, meeting his eyes and smiling slightly. "Fresh as a daisy," he murmured.

"Yeah, you look it," Ty drawled. "Little out of shape, huh, Garrett?" he teased gently.

"Maybe a little." Zane played along, shifting back. "This isn't exactly like working out in the gym." He looked Ty over. "How about you?"

Ty patted Zane's leg sympathetically. "Got a little out of breath earlier," he answered with a quirk to his lips.

Zane chuckled. "I guess I don't feel quite so bad then." He started unlacing a boot.

"Get some sleep, gentlemen," Earl told them as he climbed onto the top bunk. John was already snoring loudly in his bunk.

"I'm too tired to sleep," Deuce muttered.

Zane started in on the other boot, and he turned his head to look over at Ty. "So this is your idea of a vacation, huh?" His voice was pitched very low.

Ty just smiled happily as he watched the shadows flicker around the cabin. He was in his element up here. He was happy up here, no matter how tired or cold or wet or hungry.

Apparently it was clear on his face, because Zane actually smiled genuinely. "So why not come up here more often?" he whispered as he pulled off the boots.

"Quit my job and become a ranger?" Ty posed with a small smirk.

Zane shrugged. "I can see you in one of those brown hats," he said, lips twisting against a laugh.

Ty snorted and nodded as he tilted his head to look up at the ceiling. The fire hissed and popped, and the light danced on the logs overhead.

There were plenty of reasons Ty didn't do this more often. One was the fact that the cell reception was shitty, and Burns usually had him at the ready. It was one of the first times that Ty had thought that with a hint of bitterness.

Zane studied him with a small frown that emphasized the furrows between his brows. After a long moment, he asked, "So why not visit more?"

Ty didn't move, blinking up at the ceiling as he tried to think of a way to answer. The truth was, most of his official vacation time was taken up by side jobs that weren't supposed to go in any records. But he couldn't tell Zane that even if he wanted to. Yet.

"Time, I guess," he finally answered, hoping it would satisfy. He could still feel Zane's eyes on him, but the other man didn't say anything else. Ty glanced over at him self-consciously. Zane was scrutinizing him, and he looked like he was considering what to say. Ty shook his head slightly and sighed, looking back up at the ceiling. It wasn't home that was the problem. He supposed he could let Zane believe that it was, though. It would buy him some time until he figured out what to do about Burns' black ops and whether Zane needed to know about them.

"Tell me something," Zane asked softly, gaining Ty's attention. "Something about growing up in the mountains."

"What, like... more story time?" Ty asked uncomfortably.

Zane shrugged one shoulder. "Some good thing you remember."

Ty watched him in the flickering firelight, frowning heavily and trying to think. "Good thing about growing up in the mountains," he murmured. He shrugged, at a loss. "It wasn't really all that different from growing up anywhere else, I guess. Every summer we'd come up here and Dad would teach us everything he knew. From the day school was out until football started up, we were running around outdoors."

"All those trophies," Zane said quietly. "You played lots of sports, looked like."

"I was decent," Ty acknowledged. "I liked them all, but football was my game."

"You're not exactly lineman size," Zane commented. "Wide receiver? Defensive back?" He smiled and bumped against him gently. "Quarterback?"

Ty glanced sideways at him and smiled. "You'll make jokes if I tell you now," he predicted.

Both Zane's brows raised. "Not near what *you* would if I told you what I did for extracurriculars in high school."

"True," Ty agreed shamelessly. "I was a tight end," he told Zane with another look sideways at him and a smirk. "Sometimes wide receiver if we were killing the other team."

"Big guy, fast runner," Zane said with a nod.

Ty nodded, waiting for Zane's love of bad puns to seize on the tight end thing and run with it. "What about you?" he asked to curtail the urge in his partner.

Zane snorted and rubbed a hand over his face. When he dropped it, his cheeks were surprisingly flushed. "Uh. Well, it was Texas, you know."

"Right," Ty said slowly. "So… you grew up roping longhorns and riding horses?" he joked.

"Yes," Zane said immediately, relaxing visibly. "On Granddaddy's ranch."

Ty narrowed his eyes at his partner. Zane had seized on that answer far too quickly and with too much relief, and he was obviously embarrassed about the subject. "You know, if you don't want to talk about it, I'm not that big on talking anyway," Ty offered softly. "I won't mind."

Zane sighed. "Nah. It's just silly." He winced. "I was on the square-dancing team."

Ty pressed his lips tightly together and closed his eyes, but he just couldn't help himself. He covered his mouth and tried to cover the laugh, shaking his head.

He heard Zane's soft laugh. "I told you," Zane said with a gentle elbow to Ty's ribs. "But I'll have you know we were in the state championship my junior year."

Ty snorted and laughed out loud, unable to contain it. "Oh God," he said as he covered his eyes. When he moved his hand, he saw Zane looking back at him, the corners of his mouth turned up slightly, but his dark brown eyes were shining in the firelight. "Next time just lie to me," Ty requested as he giggled.

Zane grinned and shook his head as he hefted himself up. "You love the ammunition. Though Lord knows why I keep feeding it to you. Glutton for punishment, I guess," he mumbled as he headed for the last bunk.

"I guess," Ty echoed with a soft smile.

~CHAPTER 8~

"YOU boys make it through that storm okay?" the ranger asked as he tipped his hat.

"We're here," Earl confirmed.

"So you are," the ranger answered. Zane noticed that Ty wasn't paying too much attention as he dug through his bag; he seemed content to let Earl handle the conversation. It struck Zane as odd that Ty didn't want to be in control of the situation like he almost always did, but maybe he was deferring to Earl as older and wiser.

Whatever the reason, Zane didn't think he'd ever seen Ty this relaxed. It was an attractive attitude on him, and Zane found himself hoping Ty would stay this way once they returned home. His T-shirt this morning was a black one that claimed "Only YOU can prevent forest fires!" and below that, in smaller letters, it added "Which is good because I've got shit to do."

Zane sat smiling at his partner as he mused over just how well that fit Ty.

"We found some ATV tracks up aways," Earl was saying, and the ranger frowned.

"Recent?" the man asked.

Earl shook his head. "No. Back before the last storms couple weeks back, we think."

The ranger nodded slowly. "We've had other reports the last few months."

"And the car," Zane added.

"Expired inspection," Ty provided as he stopped at Earl's side. "At the trailhead. Been there a while."

Earl supplied him with the specific location, actually giving the ranger the GPS coordinates. Zane was surprised. He'd not seen Earl with any sort of locator or battery-operated compass.

"We'll check it out," the ranger said as he took out a small notepad and started scribbling in it.

Zane leaned forward, his hands braced on the bench. "How far are we from the trailhead?"

"'Bout fifteen miles, as the crow flies," the ranger said.

"Means we've probably walked fifty," Deuce muttered. His legs were extended out in front of him in a mirror of Zane's.

"We're heading over to the nearest pass," Earl told the ranger.

"We've had some reports of missing hikers. Searchers ain't found no sign; it's too wet, and the cold doesn't help," the ranger told him, trying to impress upon them the danger. Earl nodded again.

"Missing hikers?" Zane asked Deuce.

"Yeah, happens sometimes. Usually kids running off and being stupid," Deuce said wryly. "But sometimes a through-hiker has an accident."

"Someone like John," Zane said.

Deuce nodded. "More often rookies, though. Or day hikers. People like John got enough experience to know the dangers and how to avoid them."

"Like snakes," Zane muttered, looking back over at where the ranger, Earl, and Ty were still talking.

"Don't worry, Zane," Deuce said, clapping him on the shoulder. "Like Grandpa said, it's too cold for snakes right now."

Zane resisted the urge to growl and instead stood up and stretched.

"We're going to refill our water and head out," Ty said as he walked over.

"Any more storms coming?" Zane asked.

"Ranger says no. It's supposed to be clear for the next few days."

Zane must have growled that time, because Ty gave him an amused look. "Man up, Garrett."

"Yeah. Sure," Zane muttered.

"Y'all be careful," the ranger said again, obviously not happy that they were planning to continue on. "The storm knocked out some lines and comm towers we got up there. Got no reception at all in some places. Other places it's pretty sketchy."

Ty pulled up short and turned to look at his father, raising his eyebrows in question. Earl pursed his lips, looking from Ty to the ranger again. "How's the shape of the trail?" he asked.

"It's intact, to our knowledge. Don't know what that storm did last night. There's some flooding around, swollen rivers and mudslides."

"Maybe we'll find buried treasure in one of them," Ty muttered under his breath. Earl looked around at them, his gaze settling on Zane doubtfully. His eyes flickered to Ty again. Ty shrugged. "I think we're good to go," he offered carelessly. "We're not climbing or anything," he pointed out.

Earl nodded. "Thanks for the updates," he said to the ranger, shaking the man's hand.

As they turned to go, the ranger called out to them. "Keep an eye out for snakes," he advised. "We don't know why, but they're still out and they're not happy. We think something's driving 'em down the mountain lately. Been lots of rattlers around."

Earl turned and smiled slightly, nodding his thanks before he walked out.

Ty made a disbelieving sound, shaking his head. "Snakes," he said to Zane derisively as he passed by, snickering as he stepped through the door.

Zane just stared at him for a moment before wiping his hand over his face and following him across the dirt clearing.

He stood at the water spigot where Ty was refilling the canteens for a few minutes, watching Earl and Deuce check their packs, seeing if there were any critical supplies they might be able to get from the ranger. So Zane had at least a few quiet minutes with Ty to broach a question that had been bothering him.

"Earl doesn't think I should be here, does he?" Okay, it wasn't much of a question, but it got his point across.

Ty looked up at him in surprise, jerking just enough to get his hand wet and splash water over his boots. "Damnit," he muttered as he looked back down to reposition the canteen. "Why do you say that?" he asked Zane, looking up at him again.

"Could be that somewhat doubtful look on his face every time he looks at me," Zane murmured.

Ty snorted and gave Zane a raspberry. "He looks at everybody like that."

"He stated quite clearly that the military would have toughened me up," Zane added.

Ty turned off the water and straightened to his full height, frowning at Zane as he screwed the cap onto the canteen. "Yeah, that sounds like him," he said finally. "He's not trying to be malicious," he told Zane softly. "It's just the way he is."

Zane wasn't exactly sure about that. "It's a hell of a contrast to his friendly greeting when we met."

"How's that?" Ty asked in confusion.

"I don't know," Zane murmured. "I just didn't like the implication that I'm not good enough to watch out for you." He took the full canteen and handed Ty an empty one.

Ty took it automatically and went about filling it as well. "I don't know what to tell you, Zane," he said as he watched the water. "He gives me the same looks he's giving you," he said without looking up.

Zane frowned. "What? Why?"

Ty shook his head. "I told you, that's just the way he is," he repeated, sounding a little irritated. "He doesn't mean any harm by it, but until you prove yourself to him, he's going to look at you like you don't know what the hell you're doing."

"That's a good way to describe it," Zane muttered. Then he straightened. "Are you saying he still expects *you* to prove to him that you know what you're doing?" he asked in a hushed but clipped voice.

Ty shrugged his shoulders uncomfortably and stopped the water again, standing up to fasten the cap on the canteen he held.

"Ty?" Zane said softly, now feeling some real concern. And it wasn't for himself.

Ty met his eyes for a moment, either trying to think of an answer or a way to avoid any more of the conversation. "Don't let it get to you," he finally advised as he handed the full canteen to Zane and took another empty one from him. Zane reached out and closed his hand loosely around Ty's wrist; Ty looked at Zane with a raised eyebrow. "What?" he asked as he gave his hand a tug.

"Do you follow your own advice?"

Ty pulled at his hand again and glanced over to where Earl and Deuce were. He pulled Zane closer and grunted, "Quit being weird."

Zane gave him a small frown but let go of his arm. "Galloping crazies?"

"You're the one from horse country," Ty reminded with a twitch of his lips.

"Yeah, takes one to know one," Zane muttered. "C'mon, partner. Many miles to go."

Ty grumbled as he filled the last canteen. "We're locking ourselves in a dark room for three days when we get back," he muttered, just loud enough for Zane to hear.

"Sounds good to me," Zane answered just as Earl and Deuce approached.

"You boys ready?" Earl asked them as he took one of the canteens and fixed it to his pack.

"Yes, sir," Ty answered with a sideways glance at Zane.

"Let's get moving, then," Earl said as he turned and headed off.

THEY spent the next day and a half making their way slowly up the trail, winding ever higher, going farther and farther into the backcountry where not even trail cabins interrupted the wilderness. Earl had slowed their pace to a near crawl, being careful of the treacherous trail made slick and unreliable by the most recent storms.

Every now and then Ty would check his cell phone, noting that he hadn't gotten even a hint of a signal since the storms had swept through. It made him a little nervous. He knew that you were pretty much on your own up here no matter what the conditions. You had to rely on yourself and your companions. But there was always that knowledge that help was just a day's trek away—and in the last ten years or so, a phone call away.

Now they were completely cut off, out in territory none of them had ever seen before. Why Earl had picked this particular hike to go trailblazing, Ty didn't know. He and Deuce had long ago stopped trying to figure out their father's mind.

During a lag in conversation as they all concentrated on the rough terrain they traversed, Ty began to notice a distinct lack of noise. He frowned and glanced around for wildlife, finding only birds in the trees. No squirrels, no rodents, no deer in the distance. Nothing. He glanced up at the birds in confusion. If there were danger, the birds would have been long gone too. Deuce looked over his shoulder to meet Ty's eyes, obviously taking note of the unusual silence as well. They both shrugged.

Deuce turned and kept going, but Ty picked up his pace, closing in on the men ahead of him. Something was setting off his warning bells, but he wasn't quite sure what it was. Something just felt off. He tried to tell himself it was the sudden change in weather or the exertion after so long stuck behind a desk. Earl hadn't stopped moving, so maybe he wasn't noticing the unusual quiet. Ty cursed under his breath, thinking they should have just turned back when the weather broke. Just as he caught up with Deuce, Earl stopped suddenly.

"It's quiet," Earl said as he turned to look at them. "Must be other hikers ahead of us," he reasoned. Ty nodded in agreement and looked back down at the trail they'd just traveled. "Damned litterbugs, is what they are," he heard Earl mutter under his breath.

He looked up to see Earl bending to pick up a faded Coke can someone had tossed to the side of the trail, just under the brush. Ty gasped for a breath as the scene triggered a full-fledged flashback: Earl blurred into a Marine ahead of him bathed in the green tint of night vision, kneeling to pick up a piece of trash on the side of a desert road.

"Dad!" Ty shouted in warning. He rushed past Deuce and Zane, who both instinctively ducked and covered, and Ty tackled Earl to the ground just as he picked up the can. But it was too late. A string attached to something inside the can pulled and snapped as they fell, and in the brush just off the path, something clicked loudly.

"Run!" Ty cried as he pushed Earl to get up off the ground. The four of them scattered, heading for cover anywhere they could find it. Just after throwing themselves over and behind a couple of fallen logs, a small explosion rocked the mountain around them, the booming sound echoing through the trees, sending debris raining down on them.

"I ain't seen nothing like that since 'Nam," Earl panted after a long minute.

Deuce groaned where he lay in the dirt next to Earl. "You saying Charlie's in the Appalachians trying to kill you?" he asked with a hint of psychiatric concern for his father's sanity.

"Don't be a smartass, Deacon," Earl snapped. "I'm saying that was a trap set to kill. Only thing up here worth booby-trapping is marijuana. But I ain't never seen marijuana growers use that kinda thing."

Deuce rolled and flattened on his back, extracting his cell phone to check if it had reception. He cursed. "So what the hell? What are we dealing with here?" he asked breathlessly.

"If it isn't marijuana, it sure as hell ain't moonshine," Ty offered as he lay on Earl's other side, his face still pressed to the ground where he'd landed. His heart was racing, and adrenaline sang through him just like it always had when explosives had been involved back in his Recon days. His head felt swimmy, and he would have sworn that if he raised it to look around, he'd be looking through the lenses of night-vision goggles.

"Doesn't help to jump to conclusions," Zane murmured from his sprawl next to Ty. "With the information available on the Internet, a grade-schooler would know how to create something like that."

"That's not just something you come up with for shits and giggles," Earl argued. "The Vietcong used to see how American soldiers liked to kick cans on the road as they marched through. They started setting up bombs set off by the kicks. That's what this reminds me of. Must have been held taut by the weight of the can, and the release when it snapped triggered it. Takes a little bit a forethought, anyway, and sure as hell means they meant to kill."

Ty swallowed hard. The Vietcong weren't the only ones who'd used those traps. He could still smell the stench of burnt flesh and dry heat surrounding them after that Marine had picked up that can. He breathed in the scent of the wet earth beneath him to calm himself and try to force his mind into remembering he wasn't in the desert.

"Whoever or whatever we're dealing with," he said slowly as he raised his head just enough to speak without eating dirt, "we need to concentrate on getting off this mountain safely and making sure the rangers close these trails off until we can get people in here and clear this shit out. God knows how many civilians come through here every year. That trap was intentionally set to kill a do-gooder."

"At least it's the offseason," Deuce whispered.

"How many people come up this far, anyway?" Zane asked in disbelief.

"Not many," Deuce muttered.

"Picking up litter on the mountain gets you killed," Ty whispered in disgust. He reached up and carefully pulled a few dried leaves out of his mouth and made a face as he spit out some of the twigs and dirt he'd practically inhaled when he'd landed. He was careful not to raise his head above the log, though. And he was relieved to see the damp woods around him rather than dry sand.

"Wait a damn minute. Are you saying we run?" Earl asked as he kept his face in the wet leaves on the ground too. Ty knew they both were dealing with memories of past battles, and Deuce and Zane followed their example.

"Yes, Dad, we run," Ty hissed in annoyance as he glanced sideways at Earl.

"The hell you say," Earl growled back at Ty. "The four of us is more than capable of taking on some pissant little backwoods pot growers, even if they do know how to lay trap. We know the signs, what to look for. Hell, we'd probably be back up here helping the search as soon as we report it!"

"Yeah, with guns and bomb-sniffing dogs and a lot of people who are carrying first aid kits and food," Ty argued.

"Someone could get hurt up here while we run off with our tails between our legs," Earl argued in outrage. "You remember those missing hikers the ranger told us about? God knows how many people already been hurt."

"Dad," Ty said in frustration. "We have two weapons with minimum ammunition, we're on unfamiliar ground, and we have very little supplies. If one of us gets hurt bad, we'll never make it off the mountain in time. And you're not twenty-five anymore!" he grated out, trying to keep his voice down.

"I may be an old man, Beaumont, but at least I ain't a coward," Earl growled.

The harsh words landed with force, knocking the breath from Ty's chest and wiping away any argument he'd been about to put forth. He blinked at Earl in shock before forcing himself to look away, resting his forehead against the ground again to make certain Earl wouldn't see the crushing impact the implication of the words had on him.

"That's enough, Earl," Zane hissed.

"No," Ty muttered as he raised his head again. He reached up and plucked off a leaf that had stuck to his forehead, looking at it dejectedly. "He's right," he told Zane as he dropped the leaf to the ground.

"You're damn straight I am," Earl told him angrily. "You and I both got enough deaths on the conscience. We can't afford anymore."

"There's four lives here to take care of," Zane snapped as he motioned among them with one hand. "That ought to register loud and clear on your conscience."

Ty pressed his lips into a thin line and nodded, not speaking in response to either statement. He began to move, pulling himself toward Deuce while still staying below the level of the log. He reached for Deuce's pack and gave him a shake of the head when Deuce opened his mouth to speak. Deuce snapped his mouth closed and glanced at the others. Then he closed his eyes and rested his cheek on the ground. Ty knew what Deuce was thinking. He was just as stunned as Ty was. They both loved and respected their father a great deal. He'd always been strict and expected the very best from his sons, but Earl had never been mean, and he'd never resorted to saying things that cut painfully deep in order to get his way.

Ty tried to let it slide. *Sticks and stones may break my bones, but words will never hurt me.* He shook his head as he snagged Deuce's pack, taking care to stay behind the fallen log as he pulled it close. Whoever came up with that stupid-ass rhyme deserved a few sticks and stones to the head.

He unzipped the outer pocket and extracted the small case that carried Deuce's extra set of contacts. He flipped it open and carefully lifted it, using the tiny mirror inside to peer at their back trail.

"Anything?" Earl asked.

Ty shook his head. "It appears to be an unmanned deterrent system," he reported in a low voice. He was surprised to find speaking difficult, and he cleared his throat quietly. "Early warning system, maybe. That's why it was so damn big. If there's anybody up here, they know we're here now," he decided grimly as he snapped the contact case shut and slid it back into Deuce's pack.

"Whether we're going or not," Zane growled, "we need to figure out what the hell to do next. Sitting here is not safe. We need a defensible position."

"If they're coming, they'll be coming soon," Earl agreed. He raised up slightly and peered over the log. "Be nice to see who we're up against from a safe distance."

Ty made his decision. "I may have an idea."

~CHAPTER 9~

TY LAY in the underbrush, unmoving, watching the trail. He and Earl had made a makeshift ghillie suit out of a few branches and the wet, dead leaves that littered the forest floor. He'd had nothing to cover his face with but dirt and debris, but it worked if he didn't move. Even blinking risked the cover as he lay near the edge of the clearing in hopes of hearing or seeing whoever came to check on the explosion.

It had been a long time since Ty had done this properly. And God, was he getting twitchy. It had only been fifteen or so minutes of lying there, and he already wanted to move. His biggest hurdle had always been the incessant rocking he did when he was tense or nervous or bored. Even lying alone in bed at night sometimes, he had to rock just to keep himself from going crazy. It wasn't nearly as bad when he was with Zane, if for no other reason than Ty forced himself to remain still so as not to disturb him. Zane slept precious little as it was, and he tended to jab Ty in the ribs when he rocked.

Luckily, he didn't have to wait much longer. A twig broke in the underbrush just yards away from where he lay. Ty resisted the urge to turn his head and check the positions of the others. He'd already made certain none of them could be seen; they were further away. Ty was only this close so he could hear.

Suddenly, two men moved through the overgrown foliage to his right. Ty could just barely see them out of the corner of his eye. They were both dressed in heavy, camouflage Carhartt jackets. The bigger of the two wore a hunting cap with earflaps, which were pinned up so they made him look a little like a moose in the woods. They both carried shotguns slung over their forearms and held in the crooks of their arms. Earflaps gave a low whistle as he peered out into the clearing at the crater the explosion had produced.

"We got somebody, huh?" he whispered to his buddy, who nodded and looked around wordlessly.

"No body," the smaller man observed as he chewed on what looked like a plastic swizzle stick.

Both men looked skyward, as if expecting to see a body in the trees. Ty caught himself almost rolling his eyes. They expected someone to have been blown up into the air?

"Must have been a lucky one," Earflaps decided quietly. "Got away," he murmured even as he turned his head and peered around the quiet forest.

Ty closed his eyes quickly and mentally cursed himself. He should have been more thorough with his camouflage. He should have known whoever was up here wouldn't be green city folks. He'd underestimated their opponent already, and he damn well knew better.

"Looks like he just got scared and ran," the thin, cruel-looking man with the swizzle stick said with a sneer. Ty risked opening his eyes into slits, watching through his eyelashes as Earflaps nodded wordlessly and continued to look around suspiciously. "Should we follow him?" he asked after a moment.

Swizzlestick shook his head and jerked his thumb over his shoulder. "No way he made it out without being hurt, and he's four days' hike from help. Mountain'll kill him before we have to. Let's get back."

The bigger man nodded, and they both turned to slink back into the woods. They moved quietly, and Ty was impressed. They were speaking louder now, though, no longer worried about being overheard.

"Radio back, let him know," Earflaps ordered. "He's all tetchy about people gettin' to his damn treasure before we do, he'll probably go nuts if he don't hear from us soon."

Swizzlestick nodded and stopped moving again. He reached for a small radio at his hip. He pushed the button and called, but got nothing but static in response. He sighed in annoyance and waved the radio. "Still don't work. Must be a tower washed out somewheres."

"Let's get goin', then," Earflaps said with a grunt. They pushed through the thick underbrush and disappeared into the forest once more.

Ty waited until he could no longer hear their progress. Then he waited some more.

ZANE lay still, breathing steady and low, eyes flickering about as he waited. More often than not, they moved to look about twenty feet to his right, where he knew Earl Grady was hidden. Zane gritted his teeth and forced himself to relax.

If he thought about what the man had said to his own son, Zane wouldn't be able to stay still, because he'd be over there kicking some sense into him. What kind of man called his own son a coward? Perhaps more specifically, what kind of man would call Ty Grady a coward? Zane knew without a doubt that had those words come from anyone but Earl, Ty would have taken off his head.

Zane closed his eyes. Ty hadn't been angry, though. The hurt he'd seen streak across Ty's face had been heartbreaking. Zane knew he should have said more, done something, but once Ty had quietly agreed with Earl, Zane simply couldn't contradict him.

And so Zane lay there, stewing, waiting for Ty to come back from a pointless recon to see who might have set that stupid trap. And while Zane thought Earl's plan to protect innocent hikers was a lovely, shiny idea, it was also naïve and dangerous.

Zane's fingers dug into the dirt, and he jerked in surprise when the underbrush stood up roughly five feet in front of him.

"Garrett," Ty muttered as he wiped the leaves and dirt off his face and shook off the rest of his camouflage.

Zane squeezed his eyes closed for a second before looking at Ty. "How'd it go?"

"This is trouble," Ty told him as he glanced around in the general directions of his brother and father. "They're carrying shotguns. Talked about following and killing. And there's another one somewhere."

"All we've got is your Smith & Wesson and my Glock, unless there are more guns I don't know about," Zane said.

Ty shook his head and wiped at his cheek again. "They were talking about treasure," he said with a wrinkle of his dirty nose.

Zane peered at him, incredulous. "Treasure?" He pushed himself up to kneel back on his heels. "Like from John's story?"

Ty shrugged and met his eyes. "I don't know," he muttered. "That's what they said. But I'm getting really fucking tired of hearing about treasure."

Earl and Deuce slowly separating from the foliage drew Zane's attention. "I don't like this, Ty," Zane said quietly, meeting his partner's eyes. Ty just shook his head helplessly, and Zane curled his hands into fists, unable to hide his aggravation.

"What did you see?" Earl asked once he reached their sides. Ty related to them everything he'd seen and heard, down to what each man had been wearing and the brand of boots each wore. "Treasure," Earl repeated in a flat voice after he was finished. Again, Ty just shrugged.

"Does it really matter?" Zane asked pointedly. "There are traps and men willing to kill us. Who cares what they want?"

"It matters 'cause money is a hell of reason to kill," Earl answered thoughtfully.

"You really think there's some sort of lost treasure up here?" Deuce asked doubtfully.

"Don't matter what I think," Earl pointed out. "Only matters what *they* think. And if they think they're gonna get rich up here, then it's trouble."

"All the more reason to get out of here," Zane said firmly, "before *we* get in trouble. We can't do much to stop them if we're dead."

"So we don't get dead," Earl said to him firmly.

"Swizzlestick did say we were four days' hike from help," Ty muttered, still fussing with the dirt on his face. "Either we walked through a time warp, they have no idea where the fuck they are, or they were banking on scaring anyone lost and eavesdropping."

"I vote time warp," Deuce said thoughtfully.

"Would make the retelling more interesting at the water cooler," Ty agreed in all seriousness.

Earl was rubbing at the bridge of his nose as he listened. "What's your point, son?" he asked finally.

"I'm just saying, they might've known I was there," Ty answered.

"Don't you think they'd have just shot you instead of playing mind games?" Earl countered.

Ty remained conspicuously quiet, his head down and staring at the ground devotedly. Zane felt his chest tighten as he looked at his partner. He'd never seen Ty back down from an argument when he thought he had a case to make. Anger bloomed again in Zane's chest and he turned on Earl to speak, but the older man beat him to it.

"We need to track them down," Earl decided. "Shut down whatever they got going and deliver them to the rangers to take care of."

"Is that all?" Ty asked drolly.

"Dad," Deuce started uncertainly.

"I will not have people gettin' killed in these mountains!" Earl snapped stubbornly. Deuce and Ty both looked at him oddly, obviously surprised by the vehemence. "Those men think they're safe up here, not being careful," Earl went on. "All the noise they was making, they're not trying to hide sign."

Ty looked at him doubtfully but remained silent, refraining from reiterating his opinion from a few moments ago.

"If they're setting more traps like this around, we may be the ones getting killed," Zane argued.

"Son, if you want to head on back and bring in the cavalry, you do it," Earl said with a look at Zane. His voice was calm and cold, and it raised Zane's hackles. "That goes for you too," Earl said as he gestured at Ty and Deuce. "But the next goddamn word I hear that ain't helpful is gonna be met with violence, that clear?"

Deuce didn't even look up; Ty was watching Earl calmly. Zane stared at Ty, gritting his teeth, waiting on his decision. This was a truly shitty situation, but he would not leave Ty behind. Ty glanced at him and met Zane's eyes for a moment. Zane had always detected a spark of enjoyment in Ty's eyes before, even in the most dangerous of situations. That spark was gone now, replaced by something more sedate and sad. Resigned. Ty sighed and looked back at Earl. "If we're going to follow them, we need to get going," he suggested softly. "Trail's getting cold."

Earl continued to fix a glare on Zane for a moment longer before he turned and nodded at Ty. He handed him a clean handkerchief as he passed by him. Ty took it and looked down at it with a mumbled, "Thank you, sir." He used it to wipe at his face as he turned and followed his father back toward the small clearing.

Zane clasped both hands behind his neck and just watched him go. He'd never seen Ty behave this way, as if someone had just taken all the spirit and fight in him and crushed it to dust. It was acutely painful to see, especially after seeing him so relaxed and carefree just a few hours ago.

Deuce stopped next to him, and they watched the other two move off. "He's not usually like this," he told Zane in a whisper.

"No. He's not," Zane agreed, fully aware that Deuce was talking about Earl and that *he* wasn't.

Deuce glanced sideways at him. "Can you blame him?" he asked finally.

Zane sighed, dropping his arms and watching the rigid line of Ty's shoulders as his partner walked away. How could Earl not see the pain coming off Ty in waves? "No," he said quietly. "I can't."

Deuce shook his head and started through the thick foliage, muttering to himself as he went. After another silent curse, Zane followed.

WITH Ty on point, following the trail through the dense woods, they were making excellent time. Earl watched Ty's back as he moved, the set of his shoulders, the somewhat jerky movements. Every time Ty glanced over his shoulder to make certain they were still on his six, Earl felt a pang of guilt. He knew what he'd said had been inexcusable and unnecessary and patently false. Ty was anything but a coward. Now, though, was not the time to apologize. It would keep until the danger had passed, he told himself.

Zane Garrett was getting on his bad side, though. The boy just didn't know when to keep his mouth shut. Earl glanced over his own shoulder to look back at the FBI man doubtfully. He wasn't certain why Ty didn't just demand Richard find him a new partner. He couldn't imagine how Zane was an asset to him.

Ty stopped and held up his fist to halt their progress. Earl slowed and watched as Ty stood with his head lowered, listening. Finally, Ty turned and looked back with a deep frown. Earl followed Ty's eyes; Ty wasn't looking at him. Ty was watching his partner. Zane patted Deuce's shoulder and walked forward, passing Earl without comment and joining Ty at point.

"What's up?" he heard Zane say quietly.

"This feels wrong," Ty responded with a shake of his head. He lowered his head closer to Zane's as they spoke. "A toddler could follow this trail. Why aren't they being more careful?" he asked.

"It's not like they're expecting trained Recon Marines to be tromping around," Zane said, just a touch of humor in his voice.

"But they know someone's close," Ty argued. "Someone who recognized that can for what it was."

Earl watched them silently, not intruding in the conversation simply because he was so fascinated to see them actually working together.

"And you said they dismissed it," Zane reminded Ty.

Ty looked at Zane for a long, silent moment before he lowered his head and rubbed at his eyes. "It just feels off," he murmured as he looked around almost nervously.

Earl frowned as Deuce came to stand beside him. Ty's behavior reminded him too much of the times he himself had seen ghosts in the shadows. An explosion like that could easily have triggered a few flashes. Earl knew something about those. He thought Ty would mention having that problem, though. His boy knew how dangerous they could become.

Zane nodded slowly as he tipped his head to one side, watching his partner. "We'll be careful. You know what to do," he said quietly.

Ty looked back at Zane, the frown still set on his face. But as Earl watched them, he could see a hint of calm come over his son. Earl had never seen anyone have that effect on Ty, and it truly surprised him.

Ty sighed heavily and nodded. "Just... be on your toes," he requested of Zane before he glanced at Earl and Deuce and nodded at them.

"Everything okay?" Deuce asked carefully.

Ty shook his head in answer. "We're gonna slow down some," he told them before giving Zane one last look and then turning around.

Earl watched Ty for a moment and then turned his chin to observe Zane as the man watched Ty walk off. Then Zane shifted his weight and took four long strides to catch up, and he stopped Ty by saying something quietly enough Earl couldn't quite make it out. Ty turned and responded just as quietly, reaching out in what appeared to be an unconscious gesture to fix the strap of Zane's pack before turning around again.

Deuce moved to follow, his head down as Earl stared after them all. He couldn't quite figure Ty and Zane out. He wouldn't call them friends, exactly. They were always mouthing off and antagonizing each other, much like Ty and Deuce did. But when the situation became tense, their relationship changed. The closest thing he could compare it to was him and Mara.

He wasn't sure which hole to peg them in.

Earl glanced at Zane as the others pulled ahead, narrowing his eyes at the man. Surprisingly, Zane's eyes flickered up to meet his own and actually hold them; apparently Zane was waiting for him to say something rather than running his mouth again. Earl merely nodded at him, unable to think of anything that needed to be said right then and there. Partners, friends, adversaries… none of the pegs fit anywhere.

DEUCE paused on the trail, watching Ty and Earl moving ahead of him. It was only a few seconds before Zane caught up with him.

"You okay?" Zane asked. He was looking tired himself. Deuce nodded, though he was leaning heavily on his walking stick. He wiped at the back of his neck with his bandanna as Zane spoke again. "I think next vacation I'm going to the beach."

Deuce barked a laugh and nodded. "I'll go in half with you," he offered as they started moving again, the walking stick taking a lot of the weight off his bad leg as they moved.

Ahead of them about twenty yards, Ty glanced over his shoulder to check on them. When he saw they'd fallen behind, he stopped and turned around to wait on them. Earl did the same, looking back at them as they approached.

Just as Deuce got to his dad, a small explosion right behind Ty caused him to pitch forward to the ground. It sent sticks and leaves and dirt skyward, the blast echoing through the woods, and they all ducked and covered their heads.

When Deuce looked up, Zane was already scrambling toward Ty, who was on his knees, coughing and picking leaves and sticks off his shoulders and out of his hair. Earl was standing, bent over with his hands on his knees and squinting at Ty.

"Jesus Christ, boy," Earl said before he was forced to cough again.

"Wasn't me," Ty insisted as he shook his head to clear it.

"What was it?" Zane asked as he crouched next to Ty.

Ty blinked a few times and looked up at Zane. Then he pointed upward. "Sounded like a grenade," he said breathlessly.

When Deuce looked up and off to the right, he could indeed see several grenades sitting precariously on the tree limbs above them, attached to what looked like weighted nets. The weights were perched on the thin branches, with the pins of the grenades attached to the trees, situated so that when you brushed one of the trees hard enough to make the upper limbs shake, the weight would drop, taking the grenade with it while the pin would stay in the tree.

It was a hasty job, even Deuce could see that. Something that had probably just been done minutes before they passed.

"That's the stupidest thing I've ever seen," Deuce muttered as he peered up at them.

"Great," Zane said under his breath. "Concussion?" he asked Ty. Ty shook his head and looked to Earl, but they both seemed to be okay. Luckily, the explosion hadn't been near enough to them to do them much damage other than to knock Ty off his feet. For once, Deuce was glad he was a slower hiker than they were.

"Must have been a squirrel or something," Ty grunted as he let Zane help him to his feet. "We gotta take cover," he said, brushing off his jacket.

They hid themselves quickly as far from the trail as they dared. Deuce flattened himself out behind a rise in the forest floor, Ty lying on his back beside him with his eyes closed. Earl wasn't far away, hidden amidst a thick patch of small trees. Zane lay on Ty's other side.

They were silent as they waited. A good ten minutes went by. And then another grenade dropped. Ty flinched beside Deuce, his eyes still shut and his hands folded calmly over his chest. After a third soon after, Zane spoke up quietly. "They must know we're here. No way do they keep those up there all the time."

Deuce nodded in agreement. Ty remained still, his eyes closed and his breathing slow and even. Zane growled as another one exploded. "Fuck. We can't stay here. We're pinned down."

"The thing is," Ty said conversationally, "they know it's not safe because of the fucking squirrels or evil chipmunks or whatever the fuck they are. So they're not likely to come engage us," he wagered without opening his eyes.

"Not likely?" Deuce repeated.

"But they know where to find us whenever they're ready," Zane said.

"And we'll know where to find them," Ty countered as he finally opened his eyes. He didn't turn his head to look at Zane, though. He didn't move. "If we move now, we put ourselves at even more of a disadvantage."

Zane didn't answer, Deuce noticed; he simply nodded once and shifted slightly where he lay on his belly, face settled against his forearms and hidden. Deuce looked between them, wondering what was next. Since neither man was forthcoming, he had to ask. "So what are we going to do?" he asked.

"I am going to lay here," Ty answered as he closed his eyes again. "And hope one of those things doesn't fall on me."

Zane made a noise that Deuce suspected was a smothered laugh.

Deuce rolled his eyes. "You're both insane," he decided, speaking under his breath.

Ty began to laugh softly. Zane didn't even look up from where his face was buried in his arms, but his back and shoulders were shifting in jerky little movements. Deuce glanced sideways at them. Ty was biting his lip, trying not to make noise as he snickered. Deuce looked away, pressing his lips together tightly, not wanting to laugh with them.

When the next grenade dropped, Ty snorted, unable to stop the laugh that followed. Zane's hand flashed out and smacked Ty in the ribs. Ty gave a muffled grunt and quieted, but Deuce could feel him shaking beside him.

"You kind of wonder what the squirrels think when they're being blown through the air to the next tree," Ty posed, trying not to snicker as he spoke. Zane smothered another laugh with his hand. "It's all fun and games 'til somebody throws a grenade," Ty recited sorrowfully. Zane snorted and used both hands to cover the sound.

"We're all gonna die," Deuce decided with a quiet groan.

After a few more moments of quiet snickering, Zane rolled up on his side and laid one hand on Ty's chest. "What if we threw stones or something and set them off?" Somehow he was serious again. Deuce narrowed his eyes at him.

"Yeah, Zane, let's make them all fall at once," Ty responded, his voice full of sarcasm. "That shouldn't leave a crater," he muttered.

"You mean to tell me you can't hit one so it falls without hitting the others?" Zane prodded.

"Never bring stones to a grenade fight," Ty advised sagely.

"I'm serious," Zane whispered.

Ty turned his head to look at Zane warily. "I'd have to get closer," he finally decided with a sigh. "It's not the aiming; it's the line of sight in the woods. Trees are too dense."

"How big a rock do you want?" Zane asked seriously as Deuce's eyes swung between them.

"You're going to throw stones at grenades," Deuce said. "And hit them."

Zane shrugged. "I've got better than average aim. Maybe if we set several off, they'd go ahead and come looking earlier, not expecting us to be ready for them."

Ty nodded. "Or," he said emphatically, "we could just lay here, take a nice little rest as shit explodes a safe distance away and then shoot them as they come over the rise," he offered with a flick of his finger that mimicked pulling a trigger.

"You are definitely having flashbacks," Deuce told him wryly. Ty nodded, unapologetic as he admitted it.

"That's a good idea too," Zane agreed without commenting further. "They'd be easy targets, even between the trees."

"Are you two seriously discussing shooting people?" Deuce asked, appalled by the nonchalance.

Ty turned his head to look at his brother with a frown. "Is that bad?" he asked with complete sincerity.

Deuce looked at Zane, who had the same expression on his face. "Yeah," Deuce concluded. "It is, Ty." Zane shrugged helplessly, though he didn't look particularly remorseful either.

Ty sighed heavily and raised his head just enough to look past his feet. "Dad," he hissed. After a moment, he tried again. "Hey, Dad!" he said in a harsh whisper.

There was no answer. Either Earl was too far away to hear them or he was ignoring them because he *could* hear them.

Ty sighed again and rolled, shifting his body into Zane's without comment as he slid around to his belly. "I'll be right back," he told them in annoyance before carefully slithering into the thick underbrush.

Zane swore colorfully under his breath. "We shouldn't be here," he tacked on to the end of it.

Deuce agreed with a firm nod as he looked over at where his dad and brother probably were. In Deuce's professional opinion, Ty needed to get off the mountain, and fast. Ty knew it too. No matter how grounded or well-adjusted or well-trained a man was, when things started exploding, anyone who'd been through battle was going to start losing their grip on their sanity.

"DAD," Ty tried once he was only a few feet away from where he thought Earl had hidden himself.

"What?" Earl responded in the same low hiss.

"Do we ambush, or do we go on the offensive?" Ty asked quietly as he pulled himself toward where Earl hid and hunched beside him, their backs to the same tree and their shoulders together.

Earl was silent for a moment. "I don't know," he finally answered. "Too many unknowns now."

"We've got to think of them," Ty said without pity, edging a shoulder in Deuce and Zane's direction.

Again, Earl was silent. Ty waited unhappily, holding his breath. He glanced over his shoulder to see Zane staring in their general direction impassively.

Finally, Earl answered. "Yeah," he said in a low voice. "We go for help."

Ty deflated, his eyes closing as he breathed a sigh of relief. Another grenade went off, much closer to Zane and Deuce than the others had been, almost like it had been lobbed at them. Ty jerked his head and saw Zane pulling at Deuce and scrambling for new cover, putting more space between them. Ty frowned and looked back at Earl.

Earl met his eyes briefly before nodding. "We go," he said more definitively.

Ty started to shift, to get them moving again, but Earl placed a hand on his shoulder and stopped him. "You were right, Ty," he said softly. "I'm sorry."

Ty blinked at him in shock for a moment before nodding curtly. "Yes, sir," he responded almost soundlessly. It took him a moment to compose himself, and when he finally did, he realized Deuce and Zane were even farther away.

He was about to give a low whistle to get their attention when three men with shotguns broke through the undergrowth just feet from where Zane and Deuce hunched. Ty jerked to rise to his feet, but Earl's hand on his shoulder stopped him. They watched together helplessly as the other two men were surrounded.

~CHAPTER 10~

THE leader of the three men was middle-aged and average in appearance, a man Zane wouldn't have looked at twice in passing. He wore glasses, a heavy red jacket, and a plain black ball cap to hide his receding hairline. He stood at the foot of a trail that led down the mountainside away from the camp they'd been led to. Zane took note that the path was well-traveled and marked with two ruts made by a vehicle of some sort. Probably the four-wheeler they'd seen sign of.

Swizzlestick jabbed Zane in the back with the barrel of the shotgun, forcing him forward. Zane took a stutter-step to keep from falling and kept his hands up in front of him as they were marched into the center of a clearing near the messy little campsite. He glanced at Deuce, who was also edging forward.

In front of them was a small clearing in the midst of the thick, overgrown forest and what looked like a satellite work site. There was the ATV, sitting off to the side. There were shovels and picks, a few sticks of dynamite, tarps, metal detectors, a single tent, and other equipment Zane didn't recognize. It did sort of look like they were hunting for buried treasure, though.

"Who the hell are they?" Redjacket demanded of his two lackeys, and he anxiously rubbed at his beard.

"They had to be the ones that set off the can," Swizzlestick offered.

Redjacket shook his head, walked over, and rifled through Zane's pockets none too gently. Zane gritted his teeth and suppressed the urge to first, knock him on his ass, and second, lean away—because the asshole smelled terrible. He knew what the man would find in the inside pocket of his jacket. Hopefully he wouldn't check the back of his waistband underneath the jacket.

Redjacket pulled out the badge when he found it and flipped it over. "Fucking FBI?" he asked in renewed outrage. Zane felt the muzzle of the shotgun dig harder into his back as Swizzlestick tensed with the news.

"What do you wanna do?" Earflaps asked as he gestured toward Deuce in distaste.

"They're Feds. We kill 'em and we got all kinds of trouble," Redjacket muttered, shaking his head indecisively.

"We can't just let 'em waltz off the mountain, neither," Swizzlestick argued, his narrow, pointy nose twitching, making him look like a fuzzy shrew.

Redjacket scowled mightily, and then he advanced on Deuce, grabbing him by the coat and yanking him forward. Deuce had no choice but to grab hold of the man to keep his balance. "What's a gimp like you doing up on this mountain? You're no FBI man," he snarled.

"You're right," Deuce said evenly.

Zane admired how calm Deuce was in the face of such obvious danger, but when Redjacket went to shake him again, Zane barked, "Leave him alone!"

The man pushed Deuce away roughly, causing him to stumble and fall onto the hard-packed dirt. Redjacket turned on Zane and threw a punch that snapped Zane's jaw to the side and caused him to stagger back into the shotgun. Zane regained his balance and turned on the man with a snarl, only to have Swizzlestick jab the shotgun in his back warningly. Zane glared at them both mutinously, but he kept his hands laced behind his head as the man with the swizzle stick hanging out of the corner of his mouth sidestepped around him and moved to stand next to Redjacket.

"Keep your damn mouth shut," Redjacket ordered as he poked Zane in the chest. "You're in *our* mountains now."

"We're not here looking for you," Zane grated out. "We're on a fucking vacation."

"I wanted to go to Cabo," Deuce muttered from his place on the ground.

Redjacket laughed loudly. "Shoulda listened to your boyfriend," he told Zane as he kicked at Deuce.

Zane's body jerked as he resisted the instinct to help. Swizzlestick stepped forward and poked Zane in the chest with the barrel of the shotgun. Zane swore right then and there that he would take that shotgun away from him and beat him with it. After the past week, his temper was seriously frayed.

"I don't give a good goddamn who the hell you are or why you're here," Redjacket snarled at them. "You stumbled onto the wrong damn mountain."

Zane could see Deuce's eyes scanning the equipment around them. There was one folding card table set up nearby that held an array of dull coins, one broken candelabra, and several other unidentifiable pieces. Deuce looked at them with a confused shake of his head. "You're actually looking for buried treasure?" he asked with ill-concealed disdain. "And blowing shit up all over the place to do it?" he added in growing anger.

"Can't have anybody finding out, now can we? Got to protect our investments," Earflaps sneered.

"How many people have you killed?" Zane asked furiously.

"Shut up," Redjacket growled at him.

"—over a few pieces of broken—"

"I said shut up!" Redjacket shouted as he raised his hand, prepared to hit Zane again.

A noisy tumble of pebbles and dirt from the treeline to their right halted him, and Earflaps turned to aim his shotgun at the noise as Redjacket pulled a gun from the waistband of his jeans. "Who's out there?" he shouted as he pointed his gun at Zane's face and squinted into the darkening woods. There was no response as every man in the clearing held his breath. Zane tried to turn his head just enough to peer into the forest, trying to see who or what it had been. He almost hoped it was some wild animal stalking them rather than Ty or Earl being careless. Swizzlestick pumped the action of his shotgun and pointed it at Deuce when the silence stretched further.

"Show yourself or both these men die right now," Redjacket called out.

Another movement answered the threat, and Earl slid down the small hill of the treeline and into the clearing gracelessly, his hands held up and out over his head as he stumbled out.

Zane grimaced and exhaled heavily. Fuck. This was both good and bad. Bad because now Deuce and Earl were both here and in the line of fire. But good because *Ty* was still out *there*. And these idiots would have no way of knowing.

Redjacket began cursing as Earl showed himself, and he turned just slightly, his attention wavering from Zane as he ordered Earflaps to go search Earl.

In the space of a few seconds, Zane calculated his chances: all three men were turning away, Deuce was mostly out of the way, Earflaps had his shotgun in his arm rather than ready as he approached Earl, and Redjacket and Swizzlestick were both in easy grabbing distance. Without even consciously deciding, Zane moved, shoving Redjacket hard in the back to tip him over and then lurching to grapple with Swizzlestick for the shotgun. In the midst of the struggle, Zane was aware of three quick shots coming from the trees to their left; Ty offering covering fire from his hiding spot and giving away his presence. Zane laid Swizzlestick out with a hard hook, but as he turned to face Redjacket, pain exploded in his cheek as his world went bright white and flared out.

EARL was on his knees, his hands laced behind his neck and his head lowered. He cursed himself for his clumsiness. Twenty years ago, he'd never have made such a misstep. When he'd seen the gun pointed at Deuce's head, he hadn't even considered not showing himself. It would be up to Ty now if they were going to get out of this.

The skinny guy with the swizzle stick was complaining loudly about his jaw as Earflaps rolled Zane over roughly. Earl watched as Earflaps rifled through Zane's pockets, looking for any sign that Zane might be conscious. The man was out, though, limp and unresponsive. He saw Earflaps pull out Zane's gun, and after a little more searching, he yanked sharp-looking knives from sheaths that were strapped to Zane's forearms. He watched Earflaps examine the knives before tossing them into a nearby sack. All this time, Earl hadn't even known Zane was wearing the weapons.

His eyes flicked to the side, to the woods where Ty's shots had originated. He knew Ty would be long gone, having simply disappeared into the forest after the treasure hunters regained control of the situation. He hadn't made a sound as he'd gone, Earl had noted with a hint of pride. He hoped the boy was halfway to the nearest ranger station by now, like they should have been to start with. But he knew that Ty wouldn't leave for help now. He'd stick around and probably get himself killed trying to save them. It was what Earl would have done. If these boys thought they had the upper hand, though, they were sadly mistaken. Ty was in his element up here.

"Fuck!" Redjacket shouted, the sound echoing through the clearing and off into the woods. "Where the fuck did they come from?" he shouted. "How many more's out there?"

"I told you they was trouble," Earflaps answered, unperturbed by the yelling.

"Well, no shit," Redjacket snapped. He looked around, his eyes landing on Earl. "What's your business up here, old timer?" he asked. Earl stared back at him wordlessly. He didn't even blink in response. "You FBI too?" he demanded. Earl just looked at him, betraying no expression.

"What about the other'n?" Swizzlestick asked as he gnawed nervously on the tiny, thin piece of plastic he had managed to salvage after Zane attacked him. "You want us to get after him?"

Redjacket turned away and looked out into the woods without answering.

"If he ain't smart enough to hightail it outta here, the mountain'll kill him before we could," Earflaps offered as held his shotgun at his hip. "Ain't none of 'em too bright, following us like they did."

Redjacket shook his head slowly, his eyes darting back and forth amidst the trees. He turned back to Earl and knelt in front of him. "You get sent up here or was this just your unlucky day, huh?" he asked Earl quietly. He stared at Earl, waiting for any sort of response, but all he got in return was another blank stare. Earl would be damned if he answered any questions while they held guns at their heads.

"That boy out there know the mountain?" Redjacket tried, getting nothing but silence in answer.

Zane groaned softly and tossed his head as he lay flat in the dirt. Earl's eyes flickered to check on him, seeing Earflaps shift as he stood over him, the shotgun pointed at the ground beside Zane's thigh. Zane would be awake very shortly, and God knew what that man would start saying once he was. Boy had a mouth on him to rival Ty's, just not the brains to put behind it. Earl moved his chin slightly so he could check on Deuce, who was kneeling, wincing in pain as he was forced to put too much pressure on his bad leg.

Redjacket watched him closely, following his gaze to rest on Deuce. "You'uns got a bit of family likeness to you," he murmured, and Earl's eyes darted back to glare at him. "That your boy?" the man asked knowingly with a nod at Deuce. Earl's jaw tightened, and his lips compressed against the words he wanted to say. Redjacket nodded. He stood and lifted his gun, pointing it in Deuce's direction.

"Stop," Earl said quickly as his heart stuttered and his stomach plummeted. He closed his eyes and breathed out heavily. Redjacket lowered the gun and looked at him expectantly. "We weren't sent here," Earl answered through clenched teeth. "We took a wrong turn on the trail, that's all." Swizzlestick snorted heavily. Earl didn't look away from Redjacket. "We don't want nobody hurt," he told him firmly.

"I bet you don't." Earflaps laughed as he nudged at Zane's hip with his shotgun. Zane shifted in the dirt and groaned again.

"So," Earl continued as if he hadn't heard the big man speak, "y'all just surrender now, and we'll see that you get back down the mountain in one piece," he offered charitably.

Redjacket looked at him oddly, then huffed a laugh and turned away. "Tie 'em up, we'll deal with this shit later," he ordered no one in particular as he walked away. They went about binding Earl and Deuce quickly, leaving Zane mostly unconscious in the dirt without bothering to restrain him. Earl prayed that would be a mistake as his arms were jerked behind his head and bound tightly.

Once they were bound, Redjacket stepped up to Earflaps and murmured to him at length. Earl watched them carefully, trying and failing to see a way out of this that didn't end with someone dead.

Once they'd formulated their plan, Redjacket kicked Zane's hip hard.

TY WINCED as he watched Zane contort in pain. Crouching further into his hiding place, Ty tried to slow his racing heart and think clearly. It had taken more discipline than he'd expected to restrain himself when he'd seen the man in the red jacket pistolwhip his partner and send him crashing to the ground.

But he had to be careful. He had to focus, despite his heart beating in his throat and his fingers shaking with adrenaline and absolute terror. Three of the people he cared for most in the world were in danger, and there was very little he could do about it that wouldn't involve bloodshed. The probability that at least one of them was going to get badly hurt was too high for Ty's liking. There had to be some way to do this without the guns, without violence.

He just wasn't seeing it.

He wasn't even seeing a way *with* violence that didn't end up with at least one of the three prisoners dead or dying by the end of the shootout. He wasn't even sure that he could get off three accurate shots—and they would have to be kill shots—fast enough to keep one of the treasure hunters from firing off one of those shotguns. It was too much of a risk to take, even if Ty didn't have serious issues with killing random assholes in the mountains. He'd offered covering fire when he thought Zane might have a chance to fight his way out. Now he regretted not taking the one kill shot he'd had.

Ty looked around the quiet woods with a hint of desperation. He was alone now, outgunned and out of options. There had to be another way.

AFTER the second kick, Zane jerked, and his eyes snapped open. Before he could move, though, a shotgun barrel appeared in his line of vision—lined up right between his eyes. He blinked up at it and remained still and silent, his hands limp at his sides. This was unfortunately a more common occurrence in his past experiences than he would have liked. Then the pain came crashing in. His face burned like it was on fire, emanating from the right side but causing his entire head to ache. It was nearly overwhelming, and he had to close his eyes and swallow hard as the nausea welled up and the agony washed through him.

He distantly heard men talking, and he knew on some level what must have happened. He shifted a little where he lay in the dirt, hissing slightly as his head protested angrily. He tried to carefully shift his jaw, but damn, it hurt. At least it didn't slide, which meant it wasn't broken. Thank God for small miracles.

Redjacket was standing over him, pacing, looking at Earl in annoyance. Zane rolled slightly to his side both to quell the nausea and to check on Earl and Deuce. He relaxed a tiny bit when he saw them both kneeling, looking relatively whole and unharmed even though they were heavily bound with rope and bungee cords.

"What's his name?" Redjacket demanded of Earl. Earl narrowed his eyes and looked at Zane. "The feller out in the woods," Redjacket snarled. "What's his name?"

Momentary relief washed through Zane when he heard the words. That meant Ty was still free. They still had a chance.

Earl swallowed hard but remained silent. He looked sideways at Deuce, who was watching him with wide eyes. Earl shook his head and looked back at Redjacket. Earflaps mumbled in annoyance and nudged at Zane's shoulder with the end of his shotgun. Zane jerked and groaned, rocking more to one side and curling up. If they thought he was hurt enough, they wouldn't consider him any more of a threat, and they might not tie him up.

He peered up at Redjacket, whose face was surprisingly composed as he and Earl stared at each other. Zane wondered what was going through his mind. He suspected whatever it was wouldn't be good for them.

"One more time, old timer," Redjacket threatened Earl.

"I don't know," Earl answered defiantly. "He ain't one of ours," he claimed steadily.

Earflaps kicked Zane in the hip again. "Maybe this 'un'll talk now that he's hurtin'." A choked groan escaped Zane as he rolled away from the man's foot.

Redjacket raised an eyebrow at Earl, waiting for him to say more. Earl's jaw tightened as he nodded at Zane, who was fully sprawled on his side now. "He's my oldest son," he told Redjacket calmly. "The other man, we came across him on the mountain this morning. Crazy son of a bitch. We don't know him," he claimed firmly. Redjacket turned to look down at Zane with narrowed eyes.

Zane very slowly raised a hand to his face and covered his cheekbone carefully. He glanced up at Earflaps. He was burly and solid, but Zane figured he could take him down if he had to. He was still aware of Redjacket's eyes on him. If Redjacket figured out that

Ty was invested in any of them, he could use them to force him out of the woods. Ty wouldn't just sit out there and let any of them be shot. Despite Ty's little game in Hogan's Alley, he wouldn't use any of them for cover, not willingly.

Redjacket looked from Zane to Earl and shook his head, obviously seeing something in one or both of them that didn't sit right. "Don't like to be lied to, old man," he said finally. He nodded at Earflaps and stepped away, holding his gun up and ready.

Earflaps grinned slowly and stepped closer to Zane, pumping the action of his shotgun and then pressing the barrel to Zane's forehead. Zane felt himself go cold all over. Cold with fear, sure, because this guy looked like he might just enjoy pulling the trigger. But also cold with anger.

"Don't do this." Zane's voice was low and level and not at all shaky. "You won't like the result."

"Neither will you, hot shot," Earflaps muttered to him with a smirk.

"Show yourself, friend!" Redjacket shouted into the woods where Ty had disappeared. "And we won't blow this man's brains all over the woods!"

"You pull that trigger, and you won't live to regret it," Zane told them quietly. "That's a promise."

He was aware of Earl's attention focusing on him, and Deuce's, too, but Zane didn't care what they thought. If Earflaps shot him, Zane had no doubt Ty would kill him. Ty would kill him, and the others, too, in front of his father and brother. It would be messy. And Ty would regret it later, if only because Earl and Deuce had to watch.

"You got to the count a three!" Redjacket called out to Ty. "You ain't a good enough shot to hit all of us before he dies!"

Zane kept his eyes on Earflaps, willing Ty to make something happen. He wouldn't take that bet against Ty, not when his family was involved.

"One!" Redjacket started as Earflaps began laughing softly.

"That's one stupid asshole out there," Swizzlestick observed in a detached voice. "Gonna get his friend killed."

"Two!"

Zane was vaguely aware of Earl trying to reason with them, telling them that if they shot Zane there'd be no reason for the man in the woods to hold his fire, but Zane and the men with the weapons all ignored him. Zane was keeping his attention on Earflaps. Although it wasn't his personal choice in the way to die, he would stare it down. Ty would be pleased with the method, anyway; it would be quick. He hadn't liked Zane's preference to die slow.

Redjacket took in a deep breath to shout again, but then Ty stepped into the clearing suddenly, almost ninety degrees from where Redjacket was looking, drawing everyone's eyes with the movement. Swizzlestick jerked his shotgun around and cocked it at Ty, who stood with his hands above his head obediently. In one hand he held his gun, hanging by the trigger guard off one finger. He dropped the gun as soon as they turned on him and then moved his hand to join the other, which was behind his head already. What he'd been planning to do was anyone's guess. He obviously hadn't had enough time or ammo to do anything but surrender.

Zane shifted back onto his elbows from his side to better see Ty. "Quit yer movin'," Earflaps snarled to him.

Ty stood stock still, watching them all impassively. Zane couldn't decide if he was glad to see him or disappointed that their last chance at escape might have just evaporated. But he knew better. There was no one better to get them out of this than Ty, even if he was unarmed now. And possibly in the midst of a mental breakdown. He didn't look like himself, nor had he been behaving like the man Zane knew for some time. Even now, he stood staring at them all sedately, no hint of anger or a challenge in his expression.

"What're we gonna do now?" Swizzlestick asked as he looked over their four prisoners critically.

Redjacket looked to Earflaps and nodded at Ty, as if giving him an order to go take care of him.

Ty's eyes slid from Earflaps back to Redjacket. He didn't appear too worried about the prospect as the big, burly man walked over and hauled off to punch Ty in the gut.

Reflexively, Zane sat up in a shot. Seeing Ty being attacked made something inside him clench, something that made him feel possessive and scared and angry as hell all at once. But the shotgun at his chest stopped him from moving further to help.

Ty didn't even try to defend himself. He kept his arms over his head. His entire body tensed, and Zane heard him breathe out hard as Earflaps grabbed him by the shoulder and rammed his fist into his stomach. Ty merely turned slightly, letting the punch hit him in his oblique muscles, along the side of his torso. He did everything Zane knew he could to lessen the impact of the direct blow to his torso.

The dull thud of fist hitting hard muscle seemed loud in the small clearing, but Ty barely reacted other than to wince with the impact. The punch should have leveled him. Earflaps looked at Ty in shock as he shook his hand and backed away a step, and Ty smirked at him.

"My turn," Ty told him with a grin before whipping his left hand around to smash his fist into the man's face. He held a rock in that hand, the one no one had thought to check. The crack of bone made Zane wince as his own face throbbed in sympathy. Ty could pack a punch, Zane knew from experience. He didn't want to think about the damage he could do actually wielding something solid. The moose hat went flying and blood gushed down the man's face as he fell back and landed in the dirt with a dull thump. Swizzlestick turned, raising his shotgun clumsily as he tried to aim it at Ty, and Zane surged to his feet.

Ty turned and threw the fist-sized rock at Swizzlestick, hitting him in the head and knocking him and his shotgun on his ass. Then Ty whirled around, intending to go for the gun he'd dropped.

He came to an abrupt halt when Redjacket calmly stepped up to him with his handgun and aimed it at his head. Something in the man's eyes must have told Ty he would fire, because Ty slowly put his hands up obediently.

Zane had almost reached the shotgun when Redjacket shouted forcefully. "Stop!" He deliberately pushed the barrel of his .45 under Ty's chin, forcing Ty's head back slightly.

Zane froze in place, fists clenched, a scowl on his face that he knew just highlighted the split lip and the quickly darkening bruises along his cheekbone that weren't hidden by his week's worth of beard.

"Son of a bitch," Swizzlestick wheezed from where he sat in the dirt, holding the gash on his head. "Shoot the bastard." Earflaps whimpered in agreement as he rolled on the ground and bled profusely.

Zane jerked his chin as Redjacket narrowed his eyes at Ty, obviously seriously contemplating doing it. Swizzlestick got to his feet, grabbed his shotgun noisily, and grunted at him in warning. Zane stepped back with his hands up, staring at Redjacket and Ty tensely.

Ty hadn't moved. He still stood with his hands in the air and his chin slightly raised, looking Redjacket in the eye as the man held the gun under his chin. He seemed to be holding his breath, waiting. For once, it looked like Ty didn't have any more tricks up his sleeve. Or rocks. He was just waiting to be shot, and the realization scared Zane more than he'd ever thought it would.

Finally, Redjacket moved, reaching out to push Ty's jacket off his shoulders warily. He yanked at Ty's shirt, ripping the buttons out of it, then pushed the sleeves off his shoulders so the shirt slid back as Ty stood still, watching him blankly. Zane held his breath, waiting for Ty to do something. Anything. But Ty didn't move as Redjacket patted him down to make sure he had no other hidden weapons or sticks or God knew what else Ty might have picked up out there.

He tossed away a few more rocks Ty had gathered, pulled a lighter out of his pocket and tossed it away, and removed Ty's hunting knife. He stopped when he pushed up one of the short sleeves of Ty's T-shirt. He stared at Ty's arm for a moment and then looked up at Ty warily. Zane belatedly realized that the man must have caught sight of Ty's tattoo.

"Marine, are you?" Redjacket muttered to Ty as he finally backed away from him, far enough that Ty couldn't reach the weapon as he held it on him. He gestured for Swizzlestick to help Earflaps up. "Think you're a smart guy, huh, Marine?" he said to Ty. "Think one broke face is gonna save you?"

"Made me feel better," Ty told him with a small smile.

Redjacket gave him a jerky nod. "On your knees," he ordered angrily. He turned his head to look at Zane. "You too," he snarled.

Next to Earl and Deuce now, Zane slowly went down in a crouch before dropping to his knees and settling his hands behind his head. Earflaps grabbed up his shotgun and practically shoved it in his face.

"Just one twitch, fella," he growled. "Gimme one little twitch, and I'll blow you to kingdom come."

Zane wisely chose not to move at all, hiding his emotions from long practice, and from the corner of his eye, he could see Ty in the exact same position. Zane wondered what Earl and Deuce must think of them, seemingly unaffected by such things.

Redjacket stood in the middle of them all, looking around at them and obviously realizing that it would be hard to keep them all under control. He glanced between Zane and Ty, common sense telling him that they would be the most dangerous.

"You watch him," he told Swizzlestick as he pointed at Zane. He handed the thin man Ty's gun, which Swizzlestick shoved into his belt. "And those two." He jerked his chin toward Deuce and Earl. Then he pointed at Earflaps. "You bring the Marine," he said as he pointed at Ty.

Earflaps nodded and took Ty by the elbow, yanking him off the ground and pushing him far enough away to hold the gun on him safely. It was disturbing that they seemed to know to keep out of reach with the guns. They had enough common sense and knowledge to make them scary. They stalked off with Ty in tow as Zane went cold.

As soon as the shotgun was pointed at Ty's back, Zane lurched. His body coiled as he saw them pushing Ty away from the clearing, but Swizzlestick was right over him and smashed the shotgun's hilt down onto his right shoulder. Zane crumpled with an odd, choked sound of pain, curling into himself, hugging his arm close as the pain in his head was eclipsed.

Swizzlestick laughed, obviously happy with seeing Zane curled up on the ground. "Aww, now see, I got the easy job," Swizzlestick said as he moved to stand next to Deuce, holding the gun on them as he positioned himself to where he could see his prisoners and still watch where his buddies were taking Ty.

Zane felt sick and incredibly helpless as he huddled there under watchful eyes, unable to move as his face and shoulder both screamed at him. When he heard the first blow land somewhere behind him, he turned his face into the soft dirt and closed his eyes. They could beat Ty into a pulp back there, and there was nothing he could do. And he knew Ty wouldn't fight back because of the danger to his partner, brother, and father.

It seemed like a lifetime before the hits and grunts stopped behind him, and Zane took a breath to try to settle his stomach. As far as he could tell, Ty hadn't made a sound. Far too long went by before they dragged Ty back into the clearing and left him on the ground, across the clearing from Zane and the others. Zane tried in vain to see his partner from where he lay, but the gentle curve of the ground blocked his view. To his immense relief, he heard Ty cough and the scuffle of his hands in the dirt as he tried to push himself up.

"Behave yourself," Redjacket warned as he walked back in front of them all, rubbing his fist like it was sore.

"I've met Iraqi women who hit harder than you," Ty told him, his voice rough and hoarse. But he had to cough and gasp as he said it. Zane closed his eyes and smiled slightly.

"Want some more, then, smartass?" Earflaps threatened.

"Give it a rest. I need to think on what we're doing next," Redjacket said crossly.

"I say we just kill 'em," Swizzlestick offered.

"We don't want every cop in the state crawling over this mountain looking for them," Redjacket responded.

"So what're you thinkin'? We don't kill 'em; they tell the Feds we're here. We kill 'em; the Feds come here when they don't check in. What's the difference? At least if they're dead, they ain't talkin'," Earflaps said as he stood over Deuce with his shotgun.

Zane cast his eyes around. No matter how much he pushed his eyes to one side, he still couldn't see Ty without raising his head. He could hear him, though, still breathing heavily from the punches to the gut they'd dealt him, no matter how hard he tried to play them off as if he wasn't hurt. Deuce was kneeling next to Earl in the dirt; tied up and considered less of a threat; the men were paying them little attention. Zane figured they were underestimating both of them. Earl was no fragile old man, and Deuce would put up a damn good fight if he had to—he was a Grady, after all. And if they were anything like Ty, those ropes wouldn't stop them when it got right down to it. They all seemed to be built of the same stone as these mountains.

Zane gave vent to some of his frustration and spat blood from where he'd bitten the inside of his cheek onto the dirt at the hunter's feet, using the opportunity to push himself up some. He saw Earflaps sniff and re-grip the shotgun in his hands. He still had Ty's gun in his belt, and Zane eyed it as he lay there.

"Well," Redjacket said thoughtfully after a long time of thinking it over. "I'm thinkin' they should just… disappear-like. Then they can't tell nobody nothing," he decided with a jerk of his head to the east.

Zane swallowed hard. Though it was four on three, these treasure-hunting bastards were armed with both their own shotguns and now Ty's and Zane's weapons as well. He and Ty were both hurt, although not incapable of putting up a fight. Zane and the others might have possessed the more experienced and capable fighting force, but they were seriously outgunned. You didn't bring fists to a gunfight.

"We could dump 'em down that old well we found yonder," Swizzlestick suggested as he held his shotgun on his hip.

"So now, Mister," Redjacket said, moving to stand in front of Ty as he spoke. Zane shifted slightly on his side, just enough to finally be able to see Ty where he lay in the dirt. "Let's talk," Redjacket said to Ty as he knelt near him. "How about you just behave yourself while you and hero over there take a little walk with us. No more tricks, and we'll leave those two alone." He waved his hand at Earl and Deuce.

Ty glared at the man, holding his ribs as he pushed himself up from the dirt and rocked a little. "You plan to let them go?" he asked finally in a rough voice. "They'll wander around lost for a few days, won't be able to lead anybody back to you."

Zane saw Earl frown and could tell he was barely resisting the urge to protest. Instead, he watched Redjacket, the de facto leader of this little trio of assholes.

Redjacket looked thoughtful as he considered Ty's request. "Could be, but they'd still know y'all were up here," he pointed out finally, nodding his head toward Zane. "They'd still send out search parties for you two," he said as he waved the badge he'd taken from Ty's pocket earlier.

Ty grunted in obvious annoyance. "Then how are you going to leave them alone?" he countered, possibly unable to help himself, considering the stress in his voice. "Lots of people know we're out here already."

Redjacket narrowed his eyes, looking at Ty as if he thought there might be some sort of mind-trick going on.

"If you want your prisoners to behave until you kill them, you don't *tell* them you're going to kill them!" Ty informed Redjacket irritably. He was very nearly shouting.

Zane narrowed his eyes, attempting to evaluate his partner as calmly as possible as his entire body trembled with adrenaline and fear. Ty was still slumped on his knees in the dirt and dried leaves of the little clearing, wincing and holding his side. Zane wondered if he had a broken rib or two or if he was just playing it up to look weaker. Hurt or not, he was definitely losing his grip on his sanity. Or doing a really good job of pretending he was. Ty continued to glare up at the man kneeling near him, his eyes flashing and his jaw clenching angrily.

"We won't be killin' you if we dump you in the well, now will we?" Redjacket argued.

"Holes don't kill people. People kill people," Ty pointed out mockingly.

Zane actually chuckled under his breath as he pushed himself halfway up. It was such a ridiculous conversation. Most captives didn't give their captors advice on how to go about doing things or argue with them over how to dispose of bodies, and this Redjacket character was growing more and more wary, beginning to look at Ty as if he might just be insane. Crazy captives were hard to deal with. And Zane quite honestly wondered if the man wasn't right.

"I'm thinkin' real hard on killin' this one anyway," Earflaps muttered as he kneed Zane in the back, nearly knocking him over again. Zane had to catch himself, palms down in the dirt, and he gave Earflaps an ugly look over his shoulder.

"Ain't nobody killing anybody yet," Redjacket declared as he held up his hands to calm them. He pulled off his glasses and rubbed at his eyes. "We don't wanna have to drag a body anywhere. Best thing to do is march 'em up there, and do it there."

Ty slammed both hands onto the ground suddenly, rustling the dried leaves and making an unsatisfactory thud. "I am sick and fucking tired of being threatened by amateurs!" he shouted in utter frustration. He pushed himself up to stand suddenly, turning on Swizzlestick and the shotgun, and he pointed a finger at the cruel-looking man. "If you're gonna shoot me, shoot me, but I'll be goddamned if you're gonna throw me in a hole and leave me!"

Zane's gaze wrenched up from the ground just as Earl and Deuce began begging Ty to calm down.

No one seemed to know what to do now that Ty was literally telling them to shoot him. Swizzlestick stood in front of Ty, gripping his shotgun uncertainly and glancing at Redjacket for guidance. As Ty threw his hissy fit, Redjacket moved closer to sort it out, his glasses in one hand and his gun in the other. Swizzlestick tossed his plastic stick away with a curse and gripped his shotgun tighter to point it at Ty threateningly, shouting for him to shut up and sit back down.

They circled around Ty, leaving Earflaps a good fifteen to twenty yards on the other side of the clearing. Alone with Zane.

Whether Ty did it on purpose was hard to tell, but it was Zane's opinion that he was just losing his temper and didn't care if they shot him, rather than purposely trying to divert their attention away from the rest of them. Ty did have a short fuse upon occasion, and Zane figured he had reason today. It was even possible that he was halfway lost in a flashback to his Recon days. If anything was going to cause one, this would. Ty turned to Redjacket as they circled him, both of them pointing their guns at him and shouting for him to get back on his knees. He ignored the orders and continued bitching about their tactics. "You don't *tell* your prisoners you're gonna kill them!" he shouted at Redjacket in annoyance as he took a step toward him.

It reminded Zane suddenly of the lessons Ty had been telling the rookie FBI candidates back at Hogan's Alley. Never overestimate the mental stability of your opponent.

Swizzlestick stepped forward and jabbed his shotgun into Ty's belly.

Zane's shoulders twitched, cold fear flooding him. He hoped to hell Ty knew what he was doing. There was no way he or Earl or Deuce could get to him to help when Ty already had a shotgun point blank in his middle.

Ty took another step, causing the barrel of the gun to dig against his abs and pushing Swizzletsick back a step. The man's trembling finger tightened slightly on the trigger.

"You give them hope!" Ty yelled at the man. "It keeps them docile and cooperative so they don't resort to desperate measures when you're not paying attention!" he said as he grabbed the barrel of the gun, shoved it away from his body, and struck out at the man with a left hook. The gun went off just as Ty let it go, the shot just barely missing Redjacket.

"Hey!" Redjacket yelled, raising his gun. Ty kicked back at him, hitting him square in the chest with his heavy hiking boot and sending him stumbling backwards before rounding on Swizzlestick again.

Earl and Deuce began to truly struggle with their restraints as all hell broke loose around them. Suddenly everyone was moving.

Zane was already twisting to slam his arm across the back of Earflaps' knees before giving him a heavy push, toppling the man over. He landed on his ass with a loud grunt, but he held onto his shotgun. Zane lunged at him, hand out to grab at Ty's gun, but Earflaps swung the shotgun, catching Zane in the face again, and the pain shattered through him. He was dazed for a moment, long enough for Earflaps to jab him in the kidney with the gun barrel before he shook the haze off and kicked at him. He could hear the cursing and yelling and scuffling going on behind him as Ty dealt with two men at once, but Zane couldn't get to them yet—he had to deal with this asshole first. Lurching to his feet, Zane grappled with Earflaps and slapped at his belt to dislodge the gun, getting a knee in the gut for his efforts.

"That there's part of the payback," Earflaps hissed as Zane collapsed to one side with a harsh gasp, trying to get air in.

Zane blinked hard, the others coming into focus for the seconds it took him to roll out of Earflaps's reach and get to his feet. Swizzlestick was on his knees, coughing blood and dazed. Ty had Redjacket down, holding him by the neck in a sleeper hold until he lost consciousness. Deuce and Earl were still tied, though Earl seemed to have almost managed to loosen his ropes.

Zane had to duck as Earflaps took another jab at him with the shotgun, too close to get off an actual shot with it, and he managed to get the man in the gut with a good punch. As Earflaps doubled over with a howl, the gun fell from his belt to the dirt, only to kick away toward the others. Zane stayed on him and kicked out viciously, his boot coming into crunching contact with one of Earflaps's knees and then his gut; Earflaps gave a series of pitiful howls and collapsed, falling over on top of his shotgun. Zane spun around, trying to find the sidearm.

Neither Earl nor Deuce were free yet. Ty still held Redjacket by his neck, and as Zane watched he rolled the unconscious man to the side and pushed himself up, reaching for the gun on the ground next to him. But before Ty could get to it, Swizzlestick raised his shotgun and aimed it right at Ty's back.

In that split-second, Zane reacted instinctively: he snatched Ty's gun up from the dirt and pulled the trigger without a single thought.

Three gunshots cracked loudly in immediate succession, echoing in the forest, and everything came to a sudden stop as Swizzlestick collapsed, thudding hollowly on the ground with three bullets in the chest.

~CHAPTER 11~

TY ROLLED to his side as soon as the shooting started, ducking and covering and then rolling into a crouch with Redjacket's gun, prepared to return fire. He found himself with his gun aimed at Zane, his finger on the trigger and ready to squeeze. Zane was on his knees, having turned his gun on Earflaps, who seemed frozen in place, shotgun loosely in hand, as he stared at Swizzlestick's bleeding corpse.

"Put it down or you're joining him," Zane said harshly to the stunned man, outstretched arm not wavering as he held his gun on him.

Ty gasped, his heart racing as he aimed the gun away from Zane. He turned his head to look at the man who lay dead. He was sprawled on his back, bleeding from three different expertly placed bullet holes.

Zane had killed the guy without even a blink of the eye. Ty had agonized over how to do this without bloodshed, and then Zane had just gone off and shot the guy. While he'd known that Zane was capable of killing, Ty hadn't seen it. Not like this. Not at all, now that he thought about it.

The gunshots had caused everything to cease long enough for Earl to finally free himself. He was cutting Deuce loose with a knife he'd grabbed from somewhere. Ty knew he should move to help, but all he could do was stay there on his knees and stare at his partner in stunned silence. He'd known Zane had killed Tim Henninger from reading the reports of what had happened in New

York. He'd never asked Zane about it, though, and on some level he hadn't truly believed Zane really had it in him to take a life so easily.

Ty shook himself and looked down at the dead man's body—the man had to have been right behind him, gun up and ready to fire. But Zane had beaten him to it.

Earflaps was so shocked that he hadn't moved. Zane got to his feet, walked over, and yanked the shotgun out of his hands. "Everyone okay?" Zane asked in a low growl. He hadn't even turned an eye toward the man he'd just shot down, and he ignored it as everyone stared at him, dumbstruck. Ty didn't move any more than it took to lower his gun. Deuce sank back to the ground and shook his head without speaking.

Earl looked from Zane to the body and back again. "Nice shot," he said finally, still breathing hard.

Zane's dark eyes flickered to the body and back before he tucked the shotgun in the crook of his arm and walked over to crouch next to Deuce, murmuring, setting one hand gently on Deuce's outstretched leg.

Ty found himself continuing to stare at Zane. Then he realized he was gaping and snapped his mouth closed. He shook his head to dispel the numb feeling, and he forced himself to stand. He spared a glance for Redjacket, who was still unconscious. He'd be out for a few minutes yet.

Ty looked at Earflaps, and he gestured toward the ground with the barrel of his gun. "Face in the dirt," he ordered in a hoarse voice. The man complied without argument. Ty turned to his father and was surprised to find him looking at him. Ty swallowed hard. "Okay?" he asked.

"Got a rib or two," his father answered gruffly. "Be fine," he added as he took the gun in his hand and turned it around to hand it to Ty, grip first.

"That's Garrett's," Ty told him quietly with a nod at his partner. He wondered what his father was thinking. The way Earl was looking at him was the same way Ty imagined he must be looking at Zane. Like he'd never seen him before.

Earl continued to look at him as he turned slightly and offered the gun to Zane. Glancing up from where he was kneeling next to Deuce, Zane took the weapon without comment and shoved it in the back of his waistband. Ty's gun was still in his left hand, though he'd laid the shotgun down next to Deuce. Ty finally shook off the stupor and moved toward them. "He okay?" he asked as he laid a hand on Zane's shoulder.

Zane nodded as he finished gripping different spots up and down Deuce's leg. "Not broken."

"Doesn't mean it doesn't hurt," Deuce muttered, still rubbing at his thigh.

"Man up, Grady," Zane said with a half-smile, but his tone was gentle.

"Shut up," all three Grady men mumbled at him.

Zane gave a sharp laugh and shook his head. "Let's get you on your feet and see how you do," he said to Deuce. Glancing up, Zane flipped the Smith & Wesson smoothly and offered it to Ty.

Ty met his eyes as he took the gun. He made sure to brush his fingers over Zane's. "Thank you," he said without looking away.

Maybe it was his imagination, but he thought Zane's eyes softened as he nodded. He shifted to slide one arm around Deuce's back to help him stand. Deuce hissed under his breath. But he was on his feet, standing unaided.

"We'll go find you a new walking stick," Earl told him as he looked him up and down.

"I'm gonna need one," Deuce acknowledged.

Ty was nodding as he looked down at his brother's bum leg. Not only did he need the stick, the compass embedded in it might have come in handy too. As would the survival rope around its handle. But it was long gone, lost somewhere in the woods.

They would need supplies in order to get home, and they would have to figure out what to do with their two prisoners. He frowned heavily and looked back at the men who'd tried to kill them. "They have ATVs," he remembered suddenly as he glanced back at his father with a raised eyebrow.

Earl pursed his lips and nodded, looking down at Earflaps. "Where's your main camp?" he demanded. The man shook his head stubbornly without raising his face from the dirt.

Ty walked to stand behind him and put his boot on the back of his neck, shoving his face into the dirt. He pressed the heel of his boot into the back of the man's neck, grinding it in retaliation for the beating he'd taken. "We'll find it ourselves," he declared as he looked around for what remained of their gear. "We're gonna need something to tie them up."

"I cut up all the rope and cords they used on us," Earl told him, a hint of wry humor actually entering his voice now that the danger had mostly passed.

Zane stood and walked past Redjacket to a satchel left in the dirt. He picked it up and started digging. "Ammunition, salt peter, slicker, bottled water... here we go," he said, pulling out a roll of nylon rope, still in store packaging. "Aren't we lucky," he said drolly.

"It'll do," Ty said as he gestured for it. Zane tossed the rope to him, and Ty began unwrapping it as he pondered the various and sundry ways to tie up the two men.

Between the four of them, he was pretty certain they could come up with something.

IT DIDN'T take Ty and Earl long to track the treasure hunters' trail back to their main camp. They obviously hadn't been worried about leaving sign; even Zane could follow it. It might as well have been paved with yellow bricks.

Despite the relatively simple task of herding the two men along the trail, Ty was in an incredibly sour mood. He was snapping answers to questions when they were asked and remaining silent otherwise as he walked behind the two prisoners with a shotgun at their backs. Zane glanced at him every now and then, but he had no plans to mention the behavior. Ty had every right to be in a shitty mood—they all did.

Zane briefly wondered if he ought to feel worse than he did about putting down Swizzlestick, but the farther he walked along to the soft purr of the ATV Deuce was riding behind them, the more certain he was that it wasn't worth the effort to work up remorse over something there was no way in hell he'd ever regret.

"Don't get clever with me, Ace," he heard Ty growl to one of the prisoners. The distinctive sound of the action on the shotgun pumping followed the threat.

Zane resisted the urge to look over his shoulder again. The biggest problem they'd had as they made their way over the roughly two miles of trail was keeping their two prisoners in line, and that hadn't really been much of a problem at all. Ty seemed to be taking some perverse joy in it. But Deuce had a bird's-eye view and hadn't objected to anything Ty had done yet, so Zane figured he'd let well enough alone.

Earl stopped ahead of him and turned slightly, gesturing at Zane. Frowning in surprise, Zane jogged ahead several steps to join him.

"Yeah?" Zane asked.

Earl had his head down, watching the others out of the corner of his eye. "You think we need someone else watching those boys?" he asked Zane seriously.

Zane raised a brow, figuring such a delightful question deserved a simple answer. "You going to tell Ty he needs to give you the shotgun and take point instead?"

Earl met his eyes briefly. "We don't want anymore bloodshed," he reminded neutrally. "Ty ain't exactly in the best frame of mind right now."

Pursing his lips, Zane exhaled slowly and glanced back at his partner, who was watching them as he stood with the shotgun trained on the two tied men. Would Ty really just off and shoot one of their prisoners? Even as rattled as he was? "He won't shoot someone who doesn't attack him head on," Zane settled on.

"Yeah, tell that to Mara's oven when we get home," Earl muttered under his breath as he looked out ahead of them.

Zane snorted at the silliness of it.

Earl nodded and glanced at Zane, turning to look over his shoulder at Ty and the prisoners.

"What's the problem?" Ty demanded in a sharp voice.

Earl looked back at Zane with a raised eyebrow. "No problem," he assured Ty as he gave Zane one last glance and moved on.

Zane winced slightly but kept moving with Earl. "It can't be much farther. We could all use a break," he muttered. Hopefully Ty would remember that his father and his partner were beyond the assholes he was herding. Not that he expected Ty to actually shoot....

The two prisoners obviously weren't as convinced, and thanks to the shotgun at their backs, Zane's repeated threatening glares over his shoulder, and some effective knots, the two men moved along relatively quietly. When they finally reached the main camp, the shelter and supplies were a welcome sight, as sparse as they were. Deuce parked the ATV out of the way and clambered down from it, groaning and complaining as he stretched out his bad leg. Ty kept the gun on Redjacket and Earflaps as Earl secured them to a tree with bungee cords and what little rope they had salvaged. Zane dropped his backpack and the satchel he'd carried from the other camp, and Deuce followed suit as he stepped up to Zane and spoke into his ear quietly while they were occupied. "I think he's having flashbacks," he confided in Zane with a tilt of his head in Ty's direction.

Zane felt a wave of something stronger than concern lap through him. He glanced at Ty furtively. Flashbacks meant military, and that was something Zane just wasn't equipped to handle. "We'll get some things settled, and I'll see if I can't talk with him a little, keep him with us," he murmured.

Deuce winced slightly and met Zane's eyes hesitantly. "He was a different person then," he told Zane in a whisper. "He's dangerous like this."

As Zane stared at Deuce, he realized just how much of himself Ty truly kept from his family, even Deuce, who seemed so close to him. Ty was dangerous anytime. Anytime at all. Right now he just had a shorter fuse. Zane nodded slowly, not seeing any reason to argue or try to enlighten Ty's brother just then.

"Well, we've got plenty to do, see what's here, get cleaned up." He lightly touched his own cheek, trying to evaluate it through the pain the pressure caused.

Deuce's perceptive eyes studied him, seeming to notice his lack of reaction and storing that information away. He swallowed hard and then gave a jerk of his chin. "Want me to doctor it?" he offered.

Zane raised a brow. "What kind of doctoring you think you can do?" he asked, a touch of humor in his voice. He figured the whole side of his face was one big bruise. There was nothing to be done if anything was fractured. The black eye couldn't be helped other than to keep the swelling down so it wouldn't swell shut. His jaw wasn't broken, and the only thing that really needed attention was his broken nose.

Deuce just raised one eyebrow. "I did my rounds in the ER just like everyone else," he reminded as he glanced over at Ty and Earl, who had just finished securing the two prisoners.

"Sure," Zane said with a shrug after peering at Deuce for a quiet moment. "You'd probably get the nose straighter than I would." He turned to look over at Ty and Earl. "What about them?"

Deuce watched his father and brother for a moment. "What's wrong with them, I can't fix," he finally claimed quietly. He dropped his pack from his shoulders and turned to limp toward a folding card table nearby.

Zane let out a long breath. After a good look around from where he stood, he went digging in one of the tents and came up with a first aid kit. At least the assholes were well-provisioned. He carried it out to the table where Deuce sat, letting the other man open it and survey the contents as Zane watched Ty and Earl going through the other tents.

"Earl's favoring his ribs," Zane observed.

"I'll wrap them," Deuce assured him. "If he lets me," he tacked on with a long-suffering sigh. He glanced up as Ty neared them, carrying a radio.

"Dad's got a broke rib," Ty informed them.

Deuce looked at Zane and smirked, but he nodded in response and looked up at his brother carefully. It was the first time Zane had ever seen a hint of true wariness in Deuce's eyes when looking at his brother. But Zane was too tired to pussyfoot around his partner, especially when it came to trying to take care of him. "What about *your* ribs?" he asked bluntly. "You took quite a beating."

"I'm fine," Ty replied immediately. He looked over Zane's face critically. "You're not," he observed. "Is it broken?" he asked with a frown as he reached out to brush his fingertips across Zane's bruised cheek.

Zane shied away from him and hissed at him. "The nose is. Deuce is gonna set it," he confirmed. "Not sure about the cheek. Hurts like hell, but it doesn't feel like anything's moving around that shouldn't be."

"Don't poke it," Deuce told Ty sternly as he rummaged through the first aid kit.

"I wasn't going to," Ty told him defensively. He placed the radio on the table and looked at Zane again.

"Need some help?" Zane asked, trying to keep his voice calm.

"I know how to work a radio, Garrett. You worry about your broke face," Ty advised in annoyance.

Zane bit back a retort, knowing that Ty would react badly. He almost didn't care. A good fight would help relieve some of the tension bottled up inside him. Inside both of them. But Zane also knew it would just make the situation worse, so he swallowed hard on the urge to argue.

Ty moved to sit down heavily next to Deuce and yanked the handheld radio from its cradle. Zane watched him silently as he started messing with the dials, and then he turned to submit himself to Deuce's tender mercies. As he sat and allowed Deuce to doctor, poke, and prod at his broken nose, he could hear Ty calling out over the radio in a tight voice, repeating the same words and requests for help as he switched frequencies methodically. There was nothing but static in response each time, but he continued on doggedly, waiting a few seconds after each attempt before moving on.

It was soon obvious that the radio would be as helpful as their cell phones. One of the storms that had passed by must have really done a job on the local towers, just like the ranger had warned them. Zane's eyes shifted across the camp to where Earl sat going through sacks of supplies, setting out some things, throwing others to the side. Earl stood with his hands on his hips as he surveyed his finds, then began to make his way over to them. He appeared to be favoring the arm on the side of his broken rib, but otherwise he looked okay.

Ty still sat with his head bowed, his eyes closed as he held his head in one hand and the radio in the other, calling out over the dead air for a response. "No joy with the radio?" Earl asked as he approached.

"No, sir," Ty answered quietly. He turned a dial and tried yet again.

Earl nodded solemnly, as if that was what he'd expected. He placed a hand on Ty's shoulder. "Best give it up then," he said carefully.

Ty immediately shoved the radio back into its cradle and sat back in his chair, rubbing at his eyes with the heels of his hands.

"This is gonna hurt," Deuce told Zane suddenly, and before Zane could fully drag his attention away from Ty, Deuce snapped his nose back into place with one quick motion of his hands and laid a small piece of first-aid tape across the bridge to hold it in place.

Zane inhaled through his mouth sharply and managed to keep his reaction to a twitch. After a still, silent moment, he released a long exhale as he blinked his eyes against the tears that streamed down his cheeks. He winced again as Deuce packed little fluffs of cotton up his nose.

"Damn," he said faintly when Deuce was done.

"Sorry," Deuce offered as he gave Zane's shoulder a pat. "All better," he added cheerfully. "Dad, your turn."

"Hell no," Earl replied without hesitation.

When the tears finally cleared from Zane's eyes, he found himself meeting Ty's as his partner watched him. It wasn't uncomfortable this time, Earl and Deuce bickering in the background, and Zane thought maybe he saw the emotion Ty was hiding behind the anger. Ty looked as if he wanted to say something to Zane as he sat there, but he looked away with a sigh and cleared his throat instead.

"We should start thinking about how we plan to get them out of here," he said loudly, talking over the other two.

Deuce looked over at him in surprise. "You don't mean to take them with us, do you?"

"We don't have a well to throw them down," Zane threw out crossly, feeling like something with Ty had been interrupted, something he might not be able to see again.

"We could dig one," Ty muttered as he flicked at the wire of the radio, his head still down and his knee bouncing rapidly.

"They need to go to law enforcement. They're already murderers," Zane said.

"You're one to talk, hero!" Redjacket yelled out.

Ty stood suddenly, the action throwing the flimsy chair he'd been sitting in backward, and he turned toward the two men tied to the tree with the obvious intention of heading over there to break things. Earl grabbed him and wrapped him up in his arms before he could get too far from the table. He lifted Ty off the ground and turned, setting him back down on his feet hard and holding him there as Deuce lunged up and put himself between them and the two prisoners, just in case Ty got loose.

Zane didn't move at first; instead, he stared across the clearing at Redjacket and then Earflaps, who had apparently chosen to exercise his right to remain silent. Once Earl had Ty still again, Zane pushed out of his chair and walked slowly over to the tree where the two men were bound.

"I wonder now about your chances," Zane said conversationally as he knelt in front of them to speak to them. "You know that I won't hesitate to shoot you. Now you've got the Marine ready to skin you. He was Recon, you know, discharged due to mental problems," he told them in a conspiratorial whisper. Zane looked back over his shoulder at Ty, who was barely staying in the seat with Earl right over him. "The Doc would rather leave you than risk having you around. That only leaves one in your favor, and he's not really a nice guy."

"We're four days' hike from anywhere! You leave us here we'll be dead in two!" Redjacket claimed in outrage.

"Gag them!" Earl called out. Zane had a better idea. He stalked over to the table Earl had stacked with supplies and grabbed a roll of duct tape, pulling off a good-size strip as he approached the tree. The two men struggled, trying to yank their heads away from Zane's hands, but they had been tied much too tightly to do them any good.

"Believe me," Zane muttered as he taped both their mouths shut, not merely using a single strip over their mouths, but rather wrapping the tape around and around their heads. "I could think of much more uncomfortable ways to shut you up." He turned his back on them and walked back over to the others, where he tossed the roll of tape on the table next to the first aid kit. "So. We should start thinking about how we plan to get them out of here?" he said, falsely cheerful.

Deuce cleared his throat. "The ATVs are the only way," he said after an uncomfortable minute. He didn't seem to want to comment on Ty's outburst or on Zane's nonchalant reaction to it. "We just tie them down and drive them out of here."

Ty sat with his eyes closed, Earl's hand on his shoulder. Earl's knuckles were turning white from the pressure he was exerting to keep Ty where he sat. Zane watched for a moment, partly moved because Ty's violent reaction had been to defend him, partly surprised by the vehemence of it. "Ty," Zane said, trying to get his partner's attention focused on something besides breaking necks. "Ty, we need to know what you want to do. If that's leaving them here or tossing them in the ravine, those can go into the vote."

Ty took in a deep breath and finally looked up, seemingly calm once more. Earl removed his hand slowly and gave Ty's shoulder a pat before he took a small step away. When Ty answered, his voice was pitched just loud enough for the two prisoners to hear him. "I say we take them with us," he decided grimly. "We may need them if we run out of food."

A muffled series of protests emitted from the tied prisoners. Zane had to turn his back on them as he covered his mouth to stop from laughing, careful of jarring his nose. Ty wasn't too far gone if that jackass sense of humor was still showing.

Deuce merely rolled his eyes and sank back into his chair. "Shall we talk about dinner, then?" he asked wryly.

~CHAPTER 12~

ZANE pushed through the brush, having escaped from the campsite to smoke after Earl and Deuce called it a night. He stopped maybe twenty-five, thirty yards back down the yellow-brick road and off the path a little ways, shook the cigarette out of the package, and lit up before leaning his head sideways against one of the trees he'd taken shelter under. He looked out into the dark, trying not to think, trying to shrug off the tension.

God, he was twitchy. After dealing with a long hike up into strange territory, the treasure hunters and their booby traps, Earl's repeated verbal jabs at Ty, the capture and showdown, and then the stressful walk to the camp, Zane's strongest instinctive response—besides wanting to curl up in a ball and protect his head—was to try to calm and comfort his partner. Ty would let himself be coddled when he was hurting when others couldn't see. But Zane doubted anything he could do at this point would help, if Ty would even let him try. It was frustrating.

Zane knew one thing: that sure as hell wouldn't happen with Earl around. Zane had never seen Ty react to anyone like he did to Earl. Zane had never even imagined Ty had it in him to behave the way he did around his father: sedate and quiet and eager merely to follow orders.

It was obvious that Earl Grady had been hard on his sons growing up, but it had been clear from the start that Ty and Deuce loved and respected him a great deal. They boys seemed to be more a product of tough love rather than abuse. And the Gradys hadn't struck Zane as a family that bickered and sniped to hurt each other until Earl had called Ty a coward.

The anger still flamed through Zane at the mere thought. The sheer audacity it took to even *think* that was stunning. And the fact that Ty had so obviously taken it to heart just because his father had been the one to say it made Zane want to hit something. He couldn't help but wonder if Earl was being cruel because he was reacting in some way to Zane's presence. Had he picked up on their relationship? Was he taking it out on Ty because he'd realized what they were doing and disapproved? Zane sighed and shook his head. He was pretty sure he was just being paranoid, and he knew he shouldn't brood over things he couldn't change. Leaning his head back, Zane blew a long column of smoke up into the air.

A twig broke somewhere in the darkness as someone moved behind him. Zane tensed and had one hand immediately on his gun as he whirled around.

"Don't shoot me," Ty requested quietly as he materialized out of the darkness. Zane relaxed and huffed at him, taking the cigarette from his lips. "Those things'll kill you," Ty said softly as he moved to sit on a fallen log near Zane. He stared out over the dimly moonlit valley below them.

Zane's lips quirked a little, and he relaxed back against the tree as he looked down at his partner. "I'm still expecting bullets anytime now."

Ty sighed with a hint of the downtrodden to him and nodded in agreement. He looked down at one of his boots and pulled a stick from the tread of it. They stayed quiet for a few minutes, with Zane gazing down at him. "How are you holding up?" Zane finally murmured.

Ty merely shrugged and looked off into the distance. There wasn't really much to stare at, as dark as it was. It was obvious from the line of his shoulders that he was not going to talk about his father or his feelings or much of anything else. He rarely did.

"I'm starting to think that we're better off at work than we are on vacation," Zane mentioned after a few more quiet minutes.

Ty was silent for a moment, but then he lowered his head and snorted. He chuckled ruefully, the sound loud in the still, cold night.

Zane smiled as he finished his cigarette and stubbed it out carefully on an exposed rock before he put it back in the slightly crumpled pack. "Next time we should tell Burns to send us on a case somewhere miserable. Fate would mean we'd be safe there."

Ty nodded in agreement as his laughter trailed off. He didn't seem to have much of anything to say, and Zane wondered why he'd sought him out. He stared off into the mountain blackness without moving again. It felt like a moment that deserved a beer or two, even though Zane knew he wouldn't have been drinking.

Finally, Ty looked over at Zane and sighed. "Got any more of those cigarettes?" he asked quietly.

Zane slowly raised an eyebrow. He got the pack out of his pocket and pulled out a cigarette, sliding it between his lips. After another moment, he had it lit, and after inhaling once, he offered it to Ty.

Ty shook his head as he reached out and took the cigarette. Instead of stubbing it out and flicking it away like he usually did when he took one of Zane's cigarettes, he took a long drag of it and handed it back to Zane wordlessly.

After a few heartbeats, he reached out and took it again, keeping it this time.

He was silent, unmoving as he sat with his elbows propped on his knees and his head cocked to the side, only occasionally putting the cigarette to his lips.

Zane didn't know what else there was to do. He'd learned that sometimes the best thing to do with Ty was to wait. Sometimes his partner needed time to work up to what he wanted to say, and sometimes he never said anything at all. So Zane kept quiet and sat down heavily next to him, facing the opposite way so their shoulders brushed as they sat, extending his legs, and lightly prodding the swollen cheekbone under his black eye with one long finger.

"How's it feel?" Ty asked him softly after several minutes of sitting in silence.

"Hurts like hell," Zane admitted. The aching throb in the whole side of his face was his pulse. He'd be really colorful for the next several days.

Ty looked over at him with a sympathetic frown. He was the only one who had remained uninjured through the whole ordeal; even after the can bomb, the grenades, the beating he'd taken, and the skirmish, he'd come out with just a bruise or two from the punches he'd taken. He didn't even have a scratch on him. Zane wondered if Ty was adding a bit of survivor's guilt to all his other current problems. He watched him worriedly. Ty didn't deserve this.

Ty lowered his head again and blew a stream of smoke down toward his feet. "You sure it's not broken?" he asked mildly.

Zane shut his eyes and made himself unclench his jaw, because that just made it hurt even more. "No," he muttered.

Ty turned his head to look at him, examining him in the darkness. It was hard to make out his features, so he probably wasn't seeing many of Zane's, either. After a moment, he nodded and looked away. "We'll get it checked out when we get back," he said softly.

Zane nodded. He knew better than to think that was the last he'd hear about it, but for now, he sighed. "It'll help when I can get some sleep," he said quietly. It was getting ridiculous how much he was saying and thinking that lately.

Ty glanced at him as he blew smoke to the side. "Still with the nightmares?"

"And then some."

"You stopped seeing the shrink?" Ty asked carefully.

Zane's nose wrinkled as he peered out into the darkness. "I had a disagreement with the Bureau therapist in Miami."

Ty was silent, mulling it over. "Like a... personal disagreement?" he finally asked.

"I suppose you could call it that," Zane said as he sank his cold hands into his jacket pockets. "I thought therapy was supposed to help you recover. It wasn't."

Ty looked down at his feet and back at Zane doubtfully. "Why didn't you talk to me about any of this?" he asked in confusion. "I was getting so pissed at you," he admitted as he looked away again.

Zane winced. "I don't know. I knew I'd be changing therapists anyway since I was moving to DC, and I guess I figured you'd tell me to suck it up. I was really hoping I'd just get over it, but…."

Ty glanced at Zane, seeming as if he wanted to say something. He hesitated, starting and stopping several times before he finally took a deep breath and said, "I'm sorry I haven't been a better partner to you, Garrett."

Zane blinked at him in surprise. "What makes you say that?" This was an odd mirror of the conversation he'd had with Deuce a few nights ago.

Ty exhaled another long stream of smoke and shook his head again. "I backed away when I knew you needed help," he answered in a low murmur. "I should have stuck with you, whether you wanted me to or not. You're not a quitter, good or bad," he said wryly as he handed Zane the half-smoked cigarette as evidence.

"Yeah, well," Zane drew out. He had no idea what to say to that, but he was relieved to finally get an answer to why Ty had been drifting away from him in DC. Ty simply nodded and looked down at his feet again. Zane huffed quietly, took a last drag off the cigarette, and ground it out on the rock underfoot. He studied Ty's profile. "You're a great partner," he added quietly.

Ty had been looking at his feet diligently, but then he glanced up, a flash of surprise in his expressive eyes. He studied Zane for a moment before nodding. "Likewise," he whispered.

Some of the tightness Zane had been feeling in his chest since he talked with Deuce relaxed. That wasn't something Ty would lie to him about just to make him feel better. That was one of the good things about having a partner who was so brutally honest and blunt. When he said something good, Zane knew he meant it.

"I'm working on it," Zane said just as quietly. When he closed his eyes, he saw that shotgun going off and a shot tearing into Ty's back as he crumpled forward into the dirt. He blinked his eyes open and reminded himself silently that he'd been in time to stop that from happening.

They sat in silence, feeling the chill settle in the air and listening to the soothing sounds of the mountain. Ty finally lifted his chin slightly and breathed in deeply. "I know how hard it is after you pull that trigger," he said quietly. "If you need to talk about it...."

Zane very carefully did not turn his chin toward Ty. The very words he'd spoken told Zane several things: Ty was surprised that Zane had shot the man—even though Ty's life had been at risk—that he thought it had to have been a difficult choice for Zane to make, and that he believed his partner was suffering somehow over taking a life. For a moment, Zane felt a pang of loss for the man he'd been years ago, a man who'd agonized after killing a murderer in the line of duty.

That man was long gone.

Zane sighed softly. Ty thought he was a better man than he really was. Zane wanted him to think that for at least a little while longer.

Ty glanced over at him, looking at him in a way Zane had never seen. He seemed to be contemplating Zane's reaction, trying to decide how to categorize it. Then he reached out slowly, taking hold of Zane's shirt and pulling him until their noses almost touched. He turned his head slightly, almost brushing their lips together. Zane could feel the prickle of Ty's grown-out whiskers against his lips.

"Next time you're struggling, you tell me," Ty said quietly. "Don't care what it's about. That way I don't have to guess what you need from me."

Zane's lips pressed together hard, and he swallowed with difficulty, not wanting to pull away from Ty even an inch. "I don't want you to think I can't back you up," he said, their lips brushing as he spoke.

"When I think that, you'll know it," Ty promised, and he leaned away from him just enough to be able to look him in the eye. "It's twice now you've saved my life," he reminded in a gruff voice. "Time you stopped thinking of yourself as the weaker half."

Zane spent a moment studying Ty's face, his eyes so close, their lips so close. "I'll try," he whispered.

Ty nodded, but he didn't let go of Zane's shirt, nor did he move away from him.

"You're pretty damn strong yourself, Ty Grady," Zane said softly, raising his hand to touch Ty's scruffy cheek gently. His beard had grown to nearly a full one. It suited him somehow. Zane thought maybe *anything* would suit Ty. Ty snorted in amusement and released Zane's shirt. "Strong enough to take care of yourself," Zane added pointedly.

Ty rolled his eyes. "You think I could have taken care of myself after being shot in the back with a twelve gauge?" he posed.

"That's why I killed him," Zane said bluntly.

Ty nodded, still looking into Zane's eyes unwaveringly. He smoothed down the material of Zane's shirt that had bunched under his hand and looked away almost regretfully. "That's why I said thank you," he pointed out.

"There aren't many things left that truly scare me, Ty," Zane said softly. "But that's one of them."

"What is?" Ty asked without looking back at him. There was a hint of dread in his voice as he stared devotedly at the ground.

Zane looked at him longingly, the words on the tip of his tongue: Not being in time. *Losing you.* But just the sound of Ty's voice carried a warning; they were too close to a line neither of them wanted to cross.

"Hell freezing over because you actually said thank you," he tried instead.

The tension in Ty's frame ebbed some as he looked at Zane, and he seemed almost relieved to accept the out, as weak as it may have been. "Well," he said after a moment. "Quit being a scaredy-cat," he advised in an almost gentle voice.

"I've had lots of practice," Zane tried to joke as Ty reached out and smoothed down Zane's shirt again. It was a tender gesture, one Zane wasn't sure Ty was even aware of performing. Zane felt the knot in his chest relax as Ty touched him. They so rarely shared tender moments like this. When they came along, they were at the same time welcome and disturbing. Zane was never sure whether he wanted more of them or wanted to run from them. Tonight, though, he decidedly wanted more of this one. When Ty was done fussing over the collar of his shirt, Zane lowered his head until their foreheads touched, and he brushed his nose against Ty's.

"Quit it," Ty muttered despite the smile Zane could feel on his lips. He pushed Zane away half-heartedly and stood.

Zane got to his feet, stepped over the log, and caught Ty's arm to pull him close again. "No more nuzzling," he agreed.

Ty gave a token struggle just like he always did as Zane wrapped him up into a hug. He enjoyed the game they played when it came to control and power and was often disappointed when he succeeded in eluding Zane's grasp. But it was obvious in the way he let Zane pull him closer now that he'd been missing the contact as much as Zane had while they'd been on the mountain. Zane closed his eyes, the feeling of relief almost palpable as he soaked in Ty's touch, his scent—even though neither of them had showered in days—and the warmth of his body. He smiled as he slid his arms around Ty's waist.

Ty sighed loudly and rested his chin on Zane's shoulder as he slid his hands under Zane's arms and around him. He gave his back a few manly pats. Zane knew Ty was humoring him. But at least he cared enough to be doing it.

To Zane's surprise, Ty's arms tightened around him, the humor of a moment ago turning into a true embrace. Ty turned his face into Zane's neck and hugged him close, his fingers pulling at the fabric of Zane's coat as he did so. Zane smiled in the dark as some little knot of tension inside him unfurled and began to flutter like butterflies instead. "I'll be glad when we get home," he murmured, his lips against Ty's cheek.

"Shut up," Ty muttered as he extricated himself and gave Zane's unhurt cheek a pat. A hard one.

Zane grinned but kept his mouth shut. He reached to grasp Ty's chin, turned his head, and claimed a short, solid kiss before letting him go.

Ty swatted at him as soon as he was free. "Just… don't get carried away," he reminded with a small smirk as he pointed in the direction of their camp.

Zane nodded as he tried to calculate just how many hours it would take them to get back to civilization and get naked somewhere nice and private. He'd even settle for semi-private at this point. Ty nodded as if he was thinking the same thing, but then he glanced off into the dark woods, squinting as if trying to find the campfire. They were far enough away that they couldn't see the glow of the flames, nor could they hear anything from the other men through the dense woods.

"Actually, fuck it," Ty decided as he reached out to Zane and pulled him close again to kiss him.

Zane's pulse picked up immediately, just like it always did when Ty kissed him passionately. He wrapped his arms around Ty and pulled him closer, equally comforted and aroused by having him so close.

Ty gave a low groan as they pressed against each other. "Been missing this," he said in a harsh whisper.

Zane squeezed his eyes shut and nodded before covering Ty's mouth again, his tongue pushing in to taste him, both hands dropping to grip Ty's ass and lift him until he stood on the tips of his toes, his arms wrapped around Zane's neck to meet his height and kiss him possessively. Zane was addicted to Ty's kisses. They were much like Ty himself: unbridled and spontaneous, warm and gentle at times, but with just enough bite to set them on fire.

One kiss from Ty never failed to make Zane want more.

Shifting his weight, Zane moved to press his groin against Ty. Despite being exhausted, dehydrated, and hurting, he was hard already. He wanted Ty to touch him so badly he was shaking. Ty's hands slid down his body, finding Zane's skin under all the layers. It seemed he wanted to take this further just as desperately as Zane.

"You sure you wanna start this way the hell out here?" Ty asked roughly, though. And he had a point. He was thinking about the logistics of it all: the hard ground was littered with sticks and dried leaves and God knew what else; the cold air would assault their bare skin as soon as clothing was removed; and it wasn't just Deuce or Earl who could interrupt them with their pants down. There were any number of other obstacles they were sure to find as soon as they went too far to turn back without parts turning blue.

Zane groaned as he ran through them in his mind. He didn't care about any of them. "Need it," he managed to say as he moved his lips along Ty's neck. "Need you."

"Did you come out here with a condom, Zane?" Ty asked in amusement as he continued to kiss Zane slowly, almost as if he was humoring him again.

"For fuck's sake, Ty, just touch me… please," Zane gasped out between the kisses. "That's all it's gonna take."

Ty took a small step back and searched Zane's face in the darkness. They could just make out each other's features in the moonlight. He rubbed his hands together vigorously, then cupped them and blew onto his palms. He smiled crookedly as he unbuttoned Zane's jeans and pushed them down. He reached through the opening of Zane's boxers and slid his fingers along the length of Zane's erection. His fingers were still cold, though, and even though it was such a relief to be touched intimately again, Zane was almost afraid it was too cold for the results they wanted. Then Ty kissed him one last time and dropped to his knees without warning.

Zane's breath hissed out in a rush, heat zipping through his body at the sudden sight of Ty on his knees in front of him. One of his hands delved into Ty's hair as he looked down at him with widened eyes. Ty had never even hinted at this before. It was something Zane had simply considered off-limits. But Ty didn't waste any time now; he took Zane into his mouth, pushing his head forward to drive Zane's cock deep into the warmth.

Zane choked on a cry, and he bit his lip to muffle the sounds threatening to tear from him. If they didn't fuck soon somewhere where he could yell as loud as he wanted, Zane thought he might have to resort to more violence. Both hands gripped Ty's short hair, and he couldn't help but move, thrusting into Ty's gloriously hot mouth. Rather than fighting against it, Ty hummed and pulled at his hip to encourage him to do it again.

Holy shit, he was going to lose it before he even had a chance to enjoy this!

Zane inhaled harshly through his nose as he tried to be careful with the movement of his hips. He wanted to give Ty control over the actions rather than merely fucking his mouth, using him to get off, and probably either drowning or choking him in the process. But Ty used his free hand to pull at Zane's hip again, urging him to thrust. He really wanted Zane to use him like that.

It was all far too much for Zane to process. The danger and stress they faced, the emotional tangles he and Ty fought, the need and desire, and now Ty going down on him for the first time in the middle of the goddamned woods was just driving every lucid thought out of his mind.

Zane lost track of everything but needing to move and remembering to breathe. His hips jutted forward, harder this time, and one of his hands scrabbled to grasp at Ty's shoulder. He felt Ty's cold hand on the back of his thigh, sliding up under his boxers, fingers digging into the skin as he did his best to take Zane's cock all the way in with every thrust. Zane couldn't see his cockhead disappearing between Ty's lips, and he cursed the canopy of trees that hid the moon from them. He could imagine what those sinfully full lips would look like as the head of his cock passed between them, though.

204 | Madeleine Urban & Abigail Roux

"Oh God," Zane groaned as he rocked his hips forward. "Ty—I'm gonna—"

Ty jerked his head back quickly and stood before Zane could finish the warning. He grabbed Zane hard around the back of his neck with one hand and kissed him roughly as he stroked him with the other.

It didn't even take two squeezes to finish him, and Zane shuddered as he pulled Ty against him, remembering the imagined sight of his cock between Ty's lips, thinking about how badly he wanted to come down Ty's throat. His shoulders bowed as he panted and came hard.

Ty gripped him tightly, holding him on his feet as Zane's knees went weak. He slowed his strokes to leisurely pulls, eventually stopping altogether as he continued to kiss Zane languidly. Floating along, Zane abandoned himself to Ty's hands for a long moment, soaking in the afterglow. "Ty," he breathed as they kissed.

Ty didn't respond, not willing to end the kisses by talking just yet. Zane started moving his hands gently over Ty's body. He felt Ty smile against his lips as he tugged at the button to Ty's jeans.

Ty's hand stilled his fingers. "I don't expect tit for tat, Zane," he assured Zane in a whisper. "Don't have to do anything but find your sleeping bag."

"And pull up my pants," Zane muttered as he shivered and did so, buttoning them back up. But then his hands were right back on Ty, and they didn't stop moving. One even delved into the back of Ty's jeans, cupping his ass possessively.

Ty snorted softly, shifting closer to Zane again and pressing their bodies close. He rested his forehead against Zane's and nuzzled their noses together before kissing him again.

Zane mumbled and shifted one hand around to cup the front of Ty's jeans, rubbing slowly. Ty sighed, his warm breath brushing against Zane's cold cheek. Zane kept it slow, listening to the soft sounds of pleasure from Ty's lips as he started to unbutton his jeans despite what Ty had said.

Ty reached down and caught his wrist; the fingers that grabbed him were cold and sticky. "Don't have to, Garrett," he whispered again.

Zane's lips covered his practically before the last word was out of his mouth, and he started pushing down the heavy denim. Zane had gotten a hell of a lot of blowjobs over the years, but he'd avoided ever giving one. Ty knew that much about him. What Ty didn't know was that Zane was willing to try it for him. But out in the cold, dark woods was not the time to experiment.

Ty moaned as he kissed Zane again, clearly willing to let him do anything he wanted. Zane just laughed again as he curled his fingers around Ty to pull his cock free of his boxer briefs.

Ty hissed slightly and laughed breathlessly. "Jesus, it's cold," he joked as he pushed his hips against Zane's hand. "Make it fast, and we'll go find that fire," he said in a lower voice before kissing Zane with renewed passion.

With a grunt of agreement, Zane began jacking him slowly as he lifted his other hand to Ty's mouth and pushed two fingers between those full lips. He could make out Ty's mouth now, see his fingers sliding inside, Ty's cheeks hollowing as he sucked them in. Zane's spent cock twitched at the mere sight of it. Christ, he'd have to talk Ty into doing that again somewhere with better lighting.

Ty smiled around his fingers and bit them gently before flicking his tongue across the tips and sucking on them slowly. He kept his eyes open, looking at Zane intently in the darkness. Zane moved his fingers over Ty's tongue, rubbing around it before pulling free. Stealing another kiss, Zane shifted so he could reach around and slide his hand over Ty's ass, fingers seeking sensitive skin.

Ty managed a muffled curse against his lips. He stood on his toes, giving him just that much more height, and he wrapped one arm around Zane's neck to keep his feet as he was fondled. Zane wanted to be all over and around him, inside him and feeling his pleasure pulse through him. But he settled for stroking and squeezing Ty's cock as he flexed his index finger against the clenching hole, sinking slightly in before pulling free and then repeating the motion.

Ty gave a wanton groan and let his head fall back, practically hanging on Zane.

"You feel so good, baby," Zane groaned as he kept his hand moving and pushed his finger in to tease Ty some more.

Ty didn't respond with anything more than a wordless moan and another languid, sensual kiss. He seemed to think if he moved one way or the other, some of the pleasurable stimulation would stop. His cock jumped in Zane's hand, and his entire body was tense and hard against Zane's. Zane growled in frustration. When Ty was tight like this, a hard bundle of energy and writhing pleasure, there was nothing better in the world than to shove deep inside him and watch him go off like a firecracker.

Zane's finger started to mimic his tongue, plunging in and out, deeper, as he tried to give Ty enough stimulation to push him over the edge. He twisted his hand over Ty's cock and slipped the pad of his thumb over the wet cockhead, moaning appreciatively. Ty gritted out Zane's name as he lowered his head and bumped his forehead against Zane's chin. His entire body trembled as he pushed his hips into Zane's hand, and his fingers tightened in Zane's hair almost painfully as he rutted against him. "Fuck!" he growled in frustration. He was obviously close to release, needing just a little more to find it.

Gripping Ty's cock hard as his hand shuttled over it, Zane shoved two fingers into him just as he dipped his mouth to Ty's chin for a quick kiss. Then he dug his teeth in at the crook of his neck and twisted his fingers around, pushing at the walls of muscle. Ty gave a short, sharp cry before managing to quiet himself, and he gasped and panted out several harsh breaths as he came into Zane's palm. His body arched and tensed until it had to be painful. Zane spread his fingers wide as the muscles pulsed around them, and Ty's knees went weak. He whimpered pleadingly, just as he almost always did when he came before Zane and Zane was still riding him hard to find his own release. It made Zane's cock throb pleasantly, and he cursed again for not being able to do anything more than this.

Zane shushed him as he gentled his grip and pulled his fingers free, petting the curve of Ty's ass before pulling his jeans mostly up and then curling his arm around Ty's waist to support him.

Ty cursed creatively, his lips moving against Zane's unbruised cheek and the corner of his mouth. Zane just laughed softly and kissed him as he finally let go of Ty's softening cock.

Ty gave a full-body shiver as he reached down to finish pulling up his jeans. Zane pulled out one of the individually packaged wet wipes he'd stuck in his back pocket for the next trip to the second tree to the left and worked on cleaning up his fingers and hands. He handed one to Ty as well got a wry smile from his partner.

"Fuck, it's cold," Ty breathed with a small laugh as he buttoned his jeans. They could see their breath now in the night.

"At least it'll explain why we're flushed," Zane said.

"Fuck it," Ty muttered as he made sure his shirt buttons were all straight. "Deuce already knows and to hell with Dad. He can't think much worse of me," he declared stubbornly as he reached out to fix Zane's collar.

Zane stopped still and watched Ty's eyes as he let Ty fuss. He wanted to say so many things: to call Earl a liar, to tell Ty he was the bravest man he'd ever met. He just didn't know what Ty would believe in the aftermath of Earl's words or what he himself had the courage to tell him. It was hard to open your heart to Ty; you never knew if you'd get a sincere response or a joke in return. There were some things Zane wanted to say that just couldn't be met with a joke, and so he kept them to himself.

"Don't think about it right now," he said softly instead.

Ty looked up from his collar and met his eyes for a few seconds. Zane didn't think he'd ever seen Ty's eyes more honest than they were in those short moments. They were sad and worried, angry and lost. Haunted. It made Zane wonder just how much of Ty's carefree attitude was put on all the time, how much baggage he truly carried with him and just never let on about. Zane told himself in that moment to remember this look the next time he wanted to strangle Ty for being an asshole.

Then the moment passed, and Ty's hazel eyes were clear again as he looked at him. He nodded his head. "Thanks, Zane," he whispered.

Zane nodded slowly. "Any time." After a long moment he reached out and let his fingertips trail down Ty's chest. "I think I'll go try to sleep while the endorphin rush is keeping the pain somewhat at bay."

"Good idea," Ty said softly as he lowered his head and looked away.

"You coming?" Zane asked carefully.

Ty looked back at him, his eyes flickering toward the camp in the distance and back to Zane. He nodded and smiled slightly. "We have a tent all to ourselves," he informed Zane.

"Was that Deuce's doing?" Zane asked drily.

"You complaining?" Ty asked with a raised eyebrow.

Zane shook his head. If it were anyone else under any other circumstances, Zane might have held out his hand. But even in his gentlest moods, that wasn't Ty's style. Zane slid his hands into his jacket pockets. "C'mon, Grady. I'll give you the warm spot."

Ty draped his arm over Zane's shoulders as they walked. "I've trained you well," he claimed, sounding very pleased with himself.

Zane chuckled. "You do realize the only warm spot in that tent will be under me?"

Ty turned his head to look at him innocently. "And?" he asked with a slight leer.

Zane bumped their hips together as they walked along. "Just saying," he murmured, trying to hold down the grin that threatened. He wanted to hold onto this warmth and comfort as long as he could. It was a feeling he'd experienced fleetingly after they'd been reunited in DC, one he'd mostly lost in the last few weeks as Ty had drifted away from him. He'd almost given up hope on recovering it until Ty had invited him up to these godforsaken mountains. Maybe the trip wouldn't be a complete loss if they lived through it.

Ty squeezed his shoulders tightly and then released him, letting his hand slide down Zane's back as they entered the silent camp.

A long glance showed Redjacket and Earflaps had finally wrangled around enough to rest their heads against the tree—although uncomfortably—and they both appeared to be dozing. Zane had the intense desire to chuck a rock at them and wake them up. He restrained himself, however, and after watching them for several seconds to satisfy himself they were secure, Zane looked to Ty and waved a finger in question toward the tents.

Ty glanced at him before looking back at their prisoners with a deep frown. He looked around the camp, his eyes reflecting the firelight. To Zane he looked haunted as he gazed around the darkness, perhaps seeing other camps and other prisoners from the past.

Zane let him be for a few moments, but then he took a half step in Ty's direction. "Hey," he said softly. "Still with me?"

Ty looked back at him and cleared his throat. He met Zane's eyes and nodded jerkily, and he brought his hand up to his mouth to rub at his bearded chin. "Let's get warm, huh?" he suggested, jerking his head toward the tent they were supposed to share for the night.

Zane nodded and walked over to the all-weather tent, where he crouched down and unzipped the front with a silent curse. It was difficult for him, seeing Ty like this. Zane didn't know what to say, didn't know how to relate to what Ty was going through. He glanced over his shoulder before crawling in over the thick sleeping bag that had been tossed on the taped-seam floor of the tent. *His* Ty seemed to be back, for now, and Zane wanted to hold onto him for as long as he could.

Ty remained standing outside the flap of the low tent for a few moments; then he ducked down and crawled in behind Zane. The tent was just high enough for them to be able to sit up. It was made for one person, possibly two who were very friendly, but it was warm inside, out of the wind, and appeared sturdy enough.

Ty zipped the flap up and secured the nylon covers on the mesh windows, making the interior a very small space with both of them in it. Zane wondered if Ty's issues with dark, enclosed spaces would rear their ugly heads, but Ty didn't seem fazed as he fussed with trying to get the sleeping bag unzipped while sitting on it.

Zane was sitting up, his head brushing the curved top of the tent, but it was easy enough to twist and get out of his jacket. He figured it would be warm enough with the two of them in there. He folded the jacket and dropped it about where his head would fall when he lay down.

Ty gave up on the zipper and merely sat next to him, his head lowered as he rested his hand on Zane's knee. He turned his head, looking at Zane out of the corner of his eye. He seemed to be holding his breath. Zane watched him, waiting.

Finally, Ty exhaled heavily and lifted his chin. "They started when Dad picked up that can," he told Zane in a low voice. "The flashbacks." Zane watched him closely but didn't comment. Ty lowered his head again and glanced back furtively at Zane in another nervous gesture. "I've only ever done this two or three times," he said. "Not sure how to handle them." His voice wavered as he spoke. He cleared his throat and looked away again.

Zane didn't know what a doctor would technically classify a flashback, but he'd call it pretty close to being awake during a nightmare, himself. Zane knew nightmares. He also knew there was nothing to be said. He didn't want to hear platitudes after a nightmare; he was sure Ty didn't need them now. So he waited.

Ty reached down and fiddled with the zipper of the sleeping bag again, fidgeting like he always did when he didn't know what else to do with himself. "Want to sleep on it or under it?" he finally asked roughly as he plucked at the edge of the thick sleeping bag.

"You're sleeping on it," Zane said, reaching out to tug at his arm. "Under me, remember?"

Ty moved with him, turning and reaching out to him to kiss him. Zane paused as their lips touched, pressed, and rasped against several days' worth of whiskers. It was easy to lift one hand and touch Ty's cheek gently as he let Ty control the kiss. As far as Zane was concerned, Ty could have whatever the hell he wanted right now.

Ty let his lips linger against Zane's as he pulled away, and then he pressed his forehead against Zane's and closed his eyes. "You mentioned a warm spot?" he whispered as he let his fingers curl through Zane's hair.

Zane hummed a positive note. He reached up to unzip Ty's jacket, and Ty shrugged out of it obediently. He tugged at Zane's shoulder, pulling him down on the padded sleeping bag. He pulled his jacket over them both, sliding his hand over Zane's waist and pulling him closer. The fabric of the jacket smelled overwhelmingly like Ty as the collar fell against Zane's cheek, and taking a long, slow, deep breath in was reassuring in ways Zane didn't want to examine too closely. Instead, he subtly shifted his body toward Ty.

"Tell me something," Zane murmured.

"Anything," Ty offered in a whisper as he brushed his nose against Zane's.

Zane's breath caught, revealing his surprise over Ty's reply. The sentiment behind the whispered word made his heart beat wildly for a few breaths before he could calm himself. He very certainly didn't want to ask his question about the flashbacks now. Not after that tender response. He had no idea what to say.

He pulled his arm out from between them to slide it under Ty's neck, urging Ty closer to his side. "I... I'm here. For you. You know that. Right?" And the shaky words whispered against Ty's cheek just stuttered to a stop.

Ty was still, the tip of his nose cold against Zane's cheek as they lay tangled together. "I know," he assured Zane, the words barely more than breaths against Zane's lips. "What were you really gonna ask?" he added as his fingertips slid under Zane's shirt, resting against the skin of his lower back.

Zane huffed and shivered as Ty's cold fingers hit his warm skin. Ty knew him too well. "What are they like? The flashbacks? Are they anything like when you're half-awake but still having a nightmare?"

Ty swallowed hard and pushed his head back a little, enough that Zane could just make out his eyes. Ty was looking at him in the darkness. "It's more like... a feeling," he tried to explain haltingly. "The feeling you get in the pit of your stomach when you're falling. Like I'm not sure which way is up."

Zane tightened his arms. "I won't let you fall." Then he winced apologetically. Very trite. He sighed. Trite but true.

He could feel Ty holding his breath. Then his partner snorted quietly and bit his lip, trying not to laugh. He tightened his hold on Zane and pressed his nose to Zane's again. "Thanks, Garrett," he managed to say, though his voice wavered with the threat of laughter.

"Go ahead and laugh. It was awful, I know," Zane admitted grudgingly.

"It's the thought that counts," Ty tried. He laughed suddenly and then kissed Zane impulsively, getting a smile out of him.

Zane was glad to hear the happy sound, short as it was. He relaxed again, enjoying the slight tremors passing from Ty's body to his own. "This wasn't exactly what I thought I'd be doing today," he murmured after a few moments of merely enjoying the embrace.

"No kidding," Ty responded wryly. He turned his head and began to burrow his face between Zane's uninjured cheek and the rolled up coat beneath them, using Zane like he usually used his pillow when they were at home. Zane smiled affectionately as he did it. It was like a puppy rooting through a blanket.

"What's so different about today?" Ty asked, his voice muffled.

Zane sighed and slowly slid his hand over Ty's back. "It's my birthday," he admitted.

Ty jerked his head back and looked at Zane in shock, pushing up onto his elbow and dislodging the coat that had been keeping them warm. Even in the darkness, his expression was plain to see. "What?" he asked in disbelief.

Zane would have laughed if he didn't feel so stupid about bringing it up. "My birthday. October fifteenth."

Ty stared at him for a second before he thumped him hard on the chest, and Zane gasped. "I knew I should have stolen your file!" Ty claimed angrily as he settled back down again, pulling the coat over them both with a yank. "Why didn't you say something?"

"What was I gonna say? Take me out for dinner, Grady, it's my birthday," Zane posed as he rubbed his chest.

"Better than not telling me at all," Ty said with sincere annoyance.

Zane snorted and shook his head. "See how you feel once you're past forty. It's not really something I try to celebrate."

"How's that working out?" Ty asked in a wry drawl.

"Well, they keep on coming, so I guess I must be doing something right." Zane slid his hand down to Ty's waist and pulled him closer again in order to give his ass a good squeeze.

Ty shook his head, but he didn't bat Zane's hand away like he usually did when he was annoyed and Zane tried to grope him. "You should have told me, Zane," he scolded as he shifted his shoulders, trying to get comfortable in Zane's arms. "Would have been the perfect excuse to tell Dick we were going to some nice little tropical island instead of coming up here!" he hissed.

"Yeah, all right. Mark your calendar then," Zane answered with a roll of his eyes. "And you can give me an IOU for this year."

Ty smiled slowly, a hint of mischief entering his tired eyes for the first time in days. "I could do that, yeah," he agreed slowly, his tone one that suggested he might have a better idea.

Zane tipped his head to the side as he looked at Ty speculatively. He was never sure whether to be worried or elated when he heard that tone of voice from Ty. "Or?" he prodded.

"The best presents are received in your birthday suit, Zane," Ty advised in answer. "But we'll wait 'til we get home to break those out," he decided as he pressed his nose to Zane's once more, obviously deciding to forgive him for not telling him about his birthday earlier.

"Sounds like good times," Zane murmured. He closed his eyes, unable to stop the smile as Ty began to burrow again. He sighed slowly, the warmth of having Ty right up against him actually working to lull him to sleep as his mind worked over the things Ty had told him. He couldn't imagine the kinds of things Ty had seen, the kinds of things he must have been reliving to evoke that look he'd had in his eyes earlier. He supposed when you got right down to it he didn't really know much about Ty at all. The few experiences they did have with each other that extended beyond the bedroom weren't what Zane would call personal. It seemed like there were more bad memories between them than good.

Zane thought maybe he should work on changing that.

~CHAPTER 13~

THEIR plan had been a good one, in theory.

Earl and Deuce had packed up several bags and lashed them to a couple of ATVs while Ty and Zane got the prisoners situated on the other two. Strapped down like cargo, they wouldn't be giving anyone any trouble, and Zane had yanked off the duct tape, figuring the engines would cover any badmouthing that might send Ty overboard. The group reviewed the maps Ty found in one of the satchels, and after Earl said he had a general idea of where they were, with the help of a beaten-up old compass, they'd set off a little after dawn with hopes of making it to something resembling civilization before dusk.

But at high noon, they hit a snag.

Zane stood several feet away from the raging floodwaters the storms had created, arms crossed, wondering why he was surprised. It wasn't like anything had really gone right yet on this nice little hike.

What had probably been a three-foot-deep babbling brook in the narrow ravine was now a rushing river full of debris, including broken tree branches as big around as his bicep. When it surged up toward him, it was probably rising about five to six feet out of the ravine. There was no way the ATVs would be able to ford it.

"I'm beginning to hate this vacation," Ty muttered to Zane as they stood and watched the water rage past.

Zane stifled a groan and rubbed his eyes. "How about after this we agree not to say the word 'vacation' again, okay? Actually, no, we agree to not even *think* the word 'vacation' again."

Ty glanced sideways at him. "We'll use code," he agreed. "Call it time off. Time off from hell."

"Hell would be more relaxing than this," Zane muttered as he glared at the water. "And I could get a tan."

"Well," Earl said with a heavy sigh as he came to stand beside them and look out at the water. "ATV ain't gonna cross that. Everybody in shape to hoof it?" he asked as he looked over at them. The sound of the rushing water forced him to shout.

"Yes, sir," Ty and Deuce both answered at the same time, their voices tired and defeated. Zane shrugged, feeling their pain. It wasn't like they had a choice.

"What do we do with them?" Deuce asked as he turned and gestured at the two prisoners.

"Toss them in, see how deep the water is," Ty suggested without looking away from the river.

"You really think we're going to be able to *wade* through that?" Earflaps asked, voice a little thin.

"I hope you can swim," Zane called back to them.

"We can't untie them and let them get across," Ty was saying distractedly. "We risk them escaping. I say we leave them."

"We can't let them get loose and go back to what they were doing," Zane agreed evenly.

"Neither of you is stable," Deuce muttered as he turned to watch the water rush by again. He and Ty stood shoulder to shoulder, squabbling quietly.

Zane turned slightly away from them. "We're going to have to take one each with us to cross," he said to Earl.

Earl nodded grimly. "We can't leave 'em," he said to Zane in a low voice. "But I'd be with Ty on this one otherwise," he confided. "Let 'em rot."

Shaking his head, Zane walked over to Ty and Deuce. "Guys," he said, "let's get going, huh? Bitching about it won't make it easier." Ty nodded and gave Deuce's cheek a pat before turning to head for the nearest ATV. Zane followed along after him.

"Kinda wish we'd kept some of that rope free," Ty said to him as soon as Zane came up to him. He looked back at the river, his eyes searching for the easiest place to cross. There wasn't one.

"Winch on the ATV?" Zane suggested.

Ty was already pulling out the blue synthetic rope from the Gorilla winch mounted on the front of the vehicle, wrapping it around his hand and elbow. "If we move it closer to the water, it might reach," he agreed. When it hit the end, he looked up and said, "'Bout fifty feet, thereabouts." He looked across the water. It wasn't actually a big river. It was just a creek overfull from the downpours and roiling along at too fast a clip to make it safe to cross. "It might make it," he wagered again as he looked down at the rope. He sounded nervous, though, as he weighed his chances of making it across.

"I could take it," Zane suggested, though he didn't really expect Ty to let go of that rope.

Ty looked at him and nodded. "I know you could," he said seriously.

The corner of Zane's mouth curled. That was a compliment. "You're probably a stronger swimmer than me," he allowed as he looked at the current. "You'll almost certainly be off your feet in that mess."

"Yeah," Ty agreed. He glanced up at Zane and looked back down at the rope as he slid it off his forearm and placed the coil on the ground. He untied his boots, stood back up, and began unbuttoning his jacket. "But someone's gotta anchor it on the other side," he said finally as he stripped off every piece of clothing he could afford to. "Maybe I can pull myself along the bottom rather than trying to swim it," he hedged.

"I know me saying I don't like this won't make a difference, but I'm saying it anyway," Zane said as he took each item as Ty handed it over.

Ty laughed softly. "Believe me, neither do I." The water wasn't the only danger. The logs and other debris it carried were moving at a fast clip, fast enough that a large piece could knock a man unconscious.

"Are we sure this is the only idea we have?" Earl asked finally.

"You want to get home?" Zane answered without even looking over at the older man, his voice a little sharp.

Earl didn't reply. There was no arguing that trying to find a different place to cross would be futile and time-consuming, nor was there any question that Ty was the best choice to make the attempt.

Ty got down to his briefs, folding his discarded clothing neatly before handing it to Zane so it could be packed and kept dry.

"Get the ATV going, Deuce," Zane ordered. "We'll need the nose right up at the edge of the water."

Deuce moved to mount the ATV, shaking his head and muttering about heroes. He nudged the four-wheeler closer to the water as carefully as possible, slipping and sliding in the deep mud.

As he positioned the ATV, Ty stood barefoot between Zane and Earl, already shivering in the chilly air. He held the end of the blue synthetic rope and clenched his jaw as he looked out at the water. After another long moment of nothing, Zane huffed, although the sound of it was lost under the rushing water. He turned to help Ty secure the blue rope to himself, tying it around his chest where it wouldn't hinder his swimming strokes. Then he stepped in front of Ty and reached out and cupped Ty's face with both hands. Ty looked up in surprise as his shoulders snapped back.

Leaning close to Ty's ear, Zane whispered, "Don't make me come after you. You get swept off, I'm eating your share of the pie."

Ty's eyes tracked sideways as he listened, and his lips quirked into a wry smile as he looked away. "Understood," he responded, loud enough that the river didn't cover it.

Zane nodded, squeezed Ty's shoulder, and took a couple steps back before looking out at the deluge. Well, at least it wasn't dark, he thought grimly.

Ty was checking the end loop of the rope when Earl took hold of his shoulder. Deuce looked up at them from where he sat on the ATV, holding his breath as he watched them just like Zane was.

"Be quick about it!" Zane heard Earl shout over the sound of the river. Ty nodded, said something Zane couldn't hear, and then turned to look over his shoulder, raising his chin at Deuce. Deuce nodded wordlessly at his brother in return.

Ty turned his head to look at Zane one last time before he glanced back out at the water, rolling his neck as he tried to convince himself that the cold water wasn't going to hurt like hell when he hit it. When he started wading in, broken branches and other debris almost immediately smacking into him, Zane flinched harder than Ty did and curled one hand into a fist. Ty visibly struggled as he waded in up to his knees, the water yanking at his feet and the larger pieces of debris trying to upend him. Zane and the others watched helplessly. Each one of them would have gladly done the task, but all they could do now was watch and wait as sticks and stones did their best to batter Ty to his knees in those cold waves.

Ty stood knee-deep in the water, wasting precious seconds before he went hypothermic, trying to decide the best way to continue. Zane knew what he was thinking: did he keep trying to walk it and risk getting broadsided by a log, or did he give up the footing and try to swim it, putting himself at even more risk for being swept away downstream?

As long as the rope stayed attached to his chest, though, the biggest danger was being dragged under and not being reeled in faster than he could drown.

Before Zane could ponder the dangers any further, Ty dove headfirst into the water, disappearing under the little whitecaps and the sticks and other debris that floated past.

"Goddamnit, Ty!" Zane yelled, even though he knew Ty wouldn't hear him. He turned and kicked the ATV's tire before running a hand over his head and beginning to pace. He looked back out over the water, every part of him tense. He hadn't thought it could be worse than watching his partner wade across the river. But not being able to see him at all? That was so much worse.

He knew they should be doing something—securing the ATV so it wouldn't slide, packing up their equipment into the ponchos to keep it dry as they crossed, manning the winch in case Ty got washed downstream—but he couldn't. He had to watch for Ty.

The blue coil of rope on the ground in front of the ATV unwound steadily, whether because Ty was actually making progress across the river or because the water was pulling it in was hard to tell. Zane found himself counting the seconds, wondering how long Ty could hold his breath. A few minutes at least, give or take.

After a full minute had passed, they caught sight of Ty's hand breaking the water much further downstream. It was the only glimpse of him, though. He didn't come up for air.

"He's going down instead of across!" Zane said over the river noise.

"Current's gonna take him that way," Earl yelled as he worked hard at packing everything he could fit into the packs to be carried across. "He'll correct it," he said with utmost confidence.

Zane spared a moment to wish Earl would say things like that when Ty could actually hear him. The confidence he had in his son bordered on blind faith sometimes. Zane wondered suddenly if Ty knew it and that was why he took everything his father said in stride. *Be quick about it*, his father had said. It implied complete confidence that Ty could make it across, didn't it? But it was also a fairly common psychological device, Zane knew, impressing onto others your belief of what should—and thus *would*—happen to achieve an end. He glanced at Earl, hoping that confidence was real and seeing their relationship in a slightly different light.

All their eyes snapped to the rope when the coil suddenly started rolling out far too quickly for Ty's progress. Deuce stood up on the seat of the ATV, trying to look downriver and find any telltale signs of his brother.

Something had to have snagged him for him to be moving that quickly. The rope was swiftly playing out. It would hit its end far too soon for them to do anything but hope Ty wasn't crushed by whatever had hit him and he could free himself without assistance.

But they were coming up on three minutes that Ty had been without air.

Zane wasn't watching anymore. Something was wrong. He jerked into motion around the ATV, skidded over the rocks and mud to get down to the water's edge, and went splashing in after the rope. He was up to his knees before Earl got him by the arm, hauling him back toward the bank with surprising strength. As Earl pulled him out of the freezing water, Zane glanced over to see Deuce gripping the winch controls until his knuckles turned white, trying to give Ty as much time as he could before pulling him back. They all knew the more attempts he had to make at crossing, the less likely he was to make it at all.

Just as Zane was about to get away from Earl and wade back into the river along the rope, Ty's head broke the surface of the water, much closer than Zane thought he would be. Deuce shouted as soon as he saw him and pointed.

Ty gasped for air and took a few strong strokes through the water, but he didn't go anywhere as the current beat him back. He ducked back under the water again, disappearing from view to use the rocks along the river's bottom to pull himself across.

Zane shook Earl off but didn't go any deeper; he watched where Ty had been, willing him to surface again, looking back and forth between there and the ATV, checking the rope, oblivious to the water splashing up his thighs and soaking his jeans.

After what seemed an eternity, Zane caught sight of Ty dragging himself out of the frigid water on the far side of the river, and the vise around his chest let loose so he could breathe again.

Earl stood there staring at his son for a long moment before turning to get himself out of the cold water. He began taking his soaked shoes and socks off, his eyes on the opposite riverbank the entire time.

Ty clambered out of the water, struggling over slippery rocks, probably frozen already and unable to feel the fingers he was using to scratch his way to dry land. Once he was clear of the steep riverbank, he turned and waved to them like they hadn't been watching him like hawks the entire time. The rope on his chest was visibly tugging him, obviously still caught on something large. After he was sure he'd gotten their attention, he yanked at the line a few good times until it came loose, almost sending him falling backward as the tension was released.

Deuce sat back down with a relieved thud and closed his eyes for a moment, rubbing at his forehead. Earl finally tore his eyes from the riverbank in order to finish rolling their supplies into dry packs.

"Lucky son of a bitch," one of the two prisoners muttered grudgingly.

Zane turned to slog back up onto the bank and looked over the four men with him. "Deuce, why don't you go next? Then there will be two of you over there when we send one of them." He jerked a thumb at Earflaps and Redjacket.

"Good plan," Deuce muttered as he began to strip his clothing just as Ty had done. They stuffed his and Ty's things into one of the waterproof packs with as many supplies as they could, and Deuce slung it over his shoulders as Earl worked the winch.

On the other side of the rushing water, Ty had found a tree to secure the heavy nylon line to. When the winch pulled it tight and it held, Zane could see Ty's shoulders slump in relief. He felt like slumping himself. But not yet. He watched as Ty picked up a handful of leaves from the ground and began rubbing his bare skin down, trying to dry himself before he got too cold. They needed to hurry.

"Ready to go?" he asked Deuce.

Deuce sighed as he looked at Zane, but his lips quirked into a wry smile as he nodded. "I just wish I could think of something clever to say," he admitted as he put his hand on the taut line and began to follow it into the water. "Holy shit, it's cold!" he called out as the water lapped at his bare ankles, but he kept moving anyway.

Zane rolled his eyes, put his hands on his hips, and turned on their prisoners. "Who's next?" he asked pleasantly. They both sat staring at him as if he was out of his mind. Studying them, Zane thought he might understand why Ty got that look of unholy glee in his eyes sometimes. "Right then. I nominate you." He pointed at Redjacket. "All in favor?" He raised his hand.

Beside him, Earl raised his hand as well without taking his eyes off Deuce. Earflaps quickly raised both hands, since they were lashed together.

Redjacket snarled at him. "Put your hands down, idiot."

"The ayes have it." Zane grabbed Redjacket by the arms and started propelling him toward the water.

Earl watched them distractedly, his attention torn between them and Deuce as he struggled out of the water on the other side. He breathed a sigh of relief as Ty grabbed Deuce by the forearm and yanked him up the slippery bank to safety. He turned to Zane and stepped close enough to speak to him in a low voice. "Don't you think we should cross with them?"

"Too risky for us," Zane reasoned as he watched Redjacket inch into the water. Earl looked at him in confusion for a moment and then turned to watch Redjacket's progress. The man had stopped and dug in just short of the water, and Zane shrugged. In one smooth motion, he pulled his gun and fired a shot that hit and skidded through the wet dirt at Redjacket's feet, sending him scurrying into the water with a yell.

"You asshole! You're gonna kill me!" he bawled. But he grabbed the rope, put it to his back to have support against the strength of the rushing water, and started moving deeper into the current.

Across the water, Ty and Deuce had stopped getting dressed and were both shouting unintelligibly at them. Zane glanced at Earl to see if he was making out what they were saying.

"I think they're asking you not to shoot at them again," Earl answered, his lips almost twitching into a smile.

Zane smiled and gestured significantly with the weapon when Redjacket looked back at them obstinately. The longer he tarried, the colder he would get. They hadn't allowed him to remove his clothing, and Zane didn't care if he caught ill. He raised his gun again threateningly. Across the water, Ty and Deuce both scrambled to take cover behind large trees in case Zane fired again. Earl actually chuckled as he moved to start collecting any leftover equipment he could gather.

Redjacket inched into the rushing water, holding tight to the rope with both hands and looking back at Zane with every other step as he waded through the water. He was about halfway across, being barraged by rushing water and all the small debris that came with it, when he stopped and looked back at Zane furtively. This look was different, and Zane tensed. Redjacket squared his shoulders and stood up straight—as straight as he could in the pounding waves— and he deliberately let go of the rope and ducked under it, letting the current take him. He was risking death at the hands of the river in order to attempt an escape.

"Damn fool," Earflaps grunted, loud enough that Zane heard.

Zane glanced downriver, seeing how the water crashed against the rocky sides of the ravine indiscriminately, smashing up branches and anything else in its path. "Ty!" he yelled, taking two fast steps down to the water and pointing.

On the other side, Ty and Deuce were both scrambling down the steep embankment, trying to get ahead of the man and snag him before he was swept away beyond rescue. Earl grabbed at Zane again as the current took Redjacket into the middle of the river and buffeted him against the whitecaps being made by the rocks underneath the surface. "Won't do to kill yourself over him," Earl said to Zane breathlessly as he held him back. They began running along the bank instead, trying in vain to find something that would stop his progress.

It soon became apparent that Redjacket was no longer swimming to get away. He screamed silently at them as he flailed in the rapids. He was caught in an eddy that swirled with broken sticks and debris, all swamping him as he struggled to free himself from the grasp of the whirlpool.

Ty and Deuce reached the bank where they were nearest him, but they were still too far to reach him and drag him out, and neither man appeared to be willing to swim into the maelstrom the water created just a little further downstream. The only reason Ty hadn't been swept away was because he'd kept himself close to the bottom, where the water was calmer and there were handholds to pull on. The treasure hunter hadn't stood a chance trying it like he had.

Zane closed his eyes, letting the roar of the water fill his ears after he saw a large tree limb crash into Redjacket's back and the man slipped into the roiling flood, carried limply away.

After a few moments of nothing but the overwhelming rush of water, the sound of Ty's voice finally drifted to them. They couldn't hear what he was saying even though he was shouting at them and waving, pointing toward the rope and the ATV.

"Let's go," Zane said shortly as he opened his eyes and walked back to the ATV where Earflaps was frozen in place, staring at the water.

"Best we send him next," Earl told Zane sedately with a nod of his head at their lone remaining prisoner. He still had to shout to be heard.

Zane walked over to the man, who eyed him warily. "Just hold onto the rope, and you'll be fine," Zane said in something resembling reassurance. And after a moment's deliberation of the man's mental state, Zane drew one of his knives and sliced through the rope and tape binding his wrists.

Earflaps blinked down at his hands and then at Zane. "Thanks. I think," he mumbled as he removed most of his outer clothing and then shuffled into the water.

They watched him make his way precariously across the burgeoning water, gripping the nylon line so tight his knuckles were white by the time he was a yard away from them. Zane slowly removed his own clothes, stuffing them into the bag Earl indicated.

Earl zipped up the last remaining pack and hoisted it. "That's all we're gonna be able to take with us," he told Zane worriedly. Their clothing and shoes had taken up much of the room in the packs, and only the necessary supplies remained.

Zane turned his attention to Earl. "How far off do you think we are?"

Earl sighed and squinted his eyes, shaking his head as if trying to remember a map. "If we're where I think we are, it's still a good two, three days' walk before we see a ranger," he finally decided. "And that's only if we're where I think we are," he repeated as he looked up at the sky. They hadn't been able to see the stars at night for some time due to the cloud cover.

"So another couple bags would be a good thing, just in case," Zane surmised, studying the older man.

Earl was already shaking his head. "Ain't worth the danger," he told Zane firmly. He pointed at the wheels of the ATV, which were already sliding dangerously toward the water. "Plus, you and Ty both already been wet for too long," he added as he pointed at Zane's soaked jeans. "This water's coming from the peaks. Go back across another time and you won't make it before you're frozen."

"Let's get moving then," Zane said, looking across the water and steeling himself to cross the frigid expanse. "We'll have to make do without the rest."

THE five of them sat hunched around a fire they'd all cussed over before getting started. After Zane and Earl had waded across the river with everything they could keep dry, they'd all been shaking so badly it had taken attempts from each of them before Ty had managed to get the matches to work.

Deuce was thankful they'd been able to keep the blankets and extra clothing. He was pretty sure they would all freeze if they were still wet, because it was getting colder as the sun set. After the trial of crossing the river—and losing the man they'd known only as Redjacket—no one mentioned trying to gear up and get any farther before nightfall. Dinner was slow cooking, mainly because they were all too listless and exhausted to mess with it. But as Deuce warmed a little, the psychiatrist in him began to have a fit.

So far two men were dead; Zane had shot one and they'd watched one pretty much commit suicide trying to escape justice. Deuce supposed Redjacket could be alive somewhere downstream. In his opinion it was unlikely. So unlikely that they'd elected not to waste time and energy trying to find him. He glanced to Earflaps, sprawled on the ground on the far side of the fire, trussed up and snoring noisily.

Deuce looked up across the fire at Earl, who sat staring into the flames with a frown set on his face. It didn't seem the time or the place to address any issues pertaining to his father and Ty, did it? Or was he just terrified of doing it and being in the middle? He shook his head and glanced to the side, where Ty and Zane sat next to one another. Ty was hunched over and rocking slightly, just like he always did when he let his self-control slip a little. And it was probably serving a secondary purpose of keeping him warm.

It was alternately fascinating and painful, watching Ty and Zane together. They fought and they argued, sometimes cruelly. But Ty had brought Zane up here, hoping Deuce would help him, and Zane had been willing to leap into that river with nothing but dumb luck as a lifeline just on the off chance that he might be able to help Ty. They were a study in extremes, and as much as they denied it, they seemed well matched. After watching Zane take Ty's face in his hands and lean forward to speak to him—when it had very much looked like he'd been about to kiss him—Deuce suspected they were better matched than they knew themselves. But that wasn't really a topic Deuce could bring up now, either, not in front of Earl.

Deuce squeezed his eyes closed and massaged the bridge of his nose, fighting a headache. "So, Ty," he finally decided on, tired of the tense silence. "That was some distraction ploy you used back in the camp," he complimented, looking at his brother closely in the flickering light. "How'd you know they wouldn't shoot you?"

Ty looked up at him blankly, appearing not to understand. "What?" he asked in confusion. Zane turned his chin, watching Ty with a small frown.

"Yelling at the assholes with guns," Deuce provided with a small smile. "Pretending you were losing it."

Ty pressed his lips together tightly and then looked back down at the tin plate he held. "Yeah," he answered flatly.

Deuce continued to look at him. So, mental breakdown and not a clever ploy, then. That was good to know, at any rate. Just as worrisome were the slight changes on Zane's face when Deuce glanced at him; the frown went flat, Zane's eyes narrowed, and then he squeezed them shut for a few seconds before reopening them and focusing on Ty again.

"You were pretending, right?" Deuce asked Ty.

Ty looked up and glared at him.

"He's a dumbass for doin' the yellin'," Earl stated, pulling his blanket tighter around his shoulders.

Deuce looked over at his father as his head began to pound harder. "Dad," he said in frustration. "Would you just shut the hell up for one fucking minute?"

Earl looked up slowly, looking at Deuce in shock. Ty stared at Deuce with much the same expression Earl was, his mouth slightly agape. Zane snorted and ducked his head as he rubbed at his eyes.

"Is there a reason you're on his case more than usual, or are you just getting meaner in your old age? 'Cause you sure as hell ain't gettin' smarter," Deuce snapped.

"Deacon," Ty said softly, his voice surprised and full of dread.

Deuce didn't look away from his father. He saw Earl's jaw tighten as he ground his teeth. Neither of his sons had ever spoken to him like that. In fact, Deuce was pretty sure *no one* had ever spoken to Earl Grady like that and walked away except perhaps for Mara. Earl looked as if he was about to say something, but then he began to nod slowly, and he sighed. He looked from Deuce to Ty slowly. Ty met his eyes, though he did so with clear trepidation, and he shifted nervously where he sat. Deuce thought he might have caught sight of Zane's hand gently settling on Ty's leg.

"He's right," Earl said to Ty in a rough voice. "I'm sorry, boy," he offered.

Ty stared at him in obvious surprise for long, tense moments before he nodded jerkily. "Yes, sir," he responded almost inaudibly.

Zane leaned closer to Ty and murmured something—he didn't look at all appeased. When Ty just shook his head, Zane leaned back and kept his mouth shut. But his dark eyes were filled with something menacing that confused Deuce. Not many emotions inspired that kind of darkness: fury, desperation... utter devotion.

One thing was certain. If Zane ever came to any family holidays with Ty, it would be interesting.

They ate in silence, all of them too tired and too hungry to argue any more or try to make idle conversation. As soon as Earl had finished, he stood with his bedroll. "Night, boys," was all he said as he turned and walked a few feet away to settle down for the night.

Deuce waited until his father had done so before he scooted closer to Ty and Zane and lowered his voice. "You didn't have a plan, did you?" he asked Ty. It came out as more of a statement than a question. Ty glanced at him sideways before looking back down at the tin plate in his hand. He shook his head in answer. Zane looked up as well, but this time there was no emotion to be read on his face.

Deuce watched them both in growing anger. "Do you two have any idea how completely dysfunctional you are?" he asked them.

"Dysfunctional?" Zane repeated, though his voice was low.

"You're both practically suicidal," Deuce pointed out, forcing himself to keep his voice low. The last thing they needed was for Earl or Earflaps to weigh in on this. "First Ty goes ballistic and starts begging people to shoot him; then you go off and try to dive into that river without even thinking about how you'd get back out."

Ty flinched and turned to look at Zane questioningly, but Zane was watching Deuce. Deuce rolled his eyes and looked away. "Dysfunctional" was an understatement.

"Look, can this wait until we're not all freezing our balls off?" Ty asked sedately as he continued to eat slowly. They'd taken all the MREs they could carry from the ATV, and that was all the food they had unless they wanted to forage. "Thought I was done with these damn things," Ty muttered as he poked at the food.

"Here," Zane murmured, handing over the little mini-package of M&Ms out of his meal.

Ty glanced at it and then up at Zane with a small, tired smile. "Keep your damn chocolate," he muttered gruffly.

Deuce put his chin in his hand and watched them silently. He couldn't read Zane, but he thought the man's projected emotions were fairly straightforward. When they were visible at all. Right now, Zane was focused on Ty, and that anger appeared to be totally gone, replaced by something milder. Warmer.

But Ty? Deuce snorted. Not in love, his ass. Ty could fool Zane, maybe. He could even fool himself for a while longer. But Ty couldn't fool Deuce, not anymore.

~CHAPTER 14~

"I GOTTA take a leak," Earflaps said petulantly.

Ty jerked and gasped, yanked from his doze by the man's voice. He shook his head and rubbed at his eyes, leaning forward to pile more sticks into the stuttering fire before looking over at the prisoner hatefully. "I should let you just piss yourself," he told the man irritably.

"Too bad you're a Fed," Earflaps observed.

Ty narrowed his eyes and sighed. Unfortunately, the asshole was right. No cruel and unusual punishment. He muttered to himself as he unfolded his stiff limbs and stood. He gave Zane's foot a gentle nudge. Zane's eyes opened immediately. Ty should have known he wasn't asleep. Maybe he should make Zane take the guy out in the woods.

"Playing escort," he told Zane softly instead as he fished out a flashlight from the nearest pack. It was one of only two left. "If we're not back in five, come shoot him," he joked.

"Sure," Zane said, a small smile curving his lips. "I've still got more than half a magazine."

"Good boy," Ty said with a patronizing pat of Zane's head. He moved to untie the ropes from Earflaps' ankles. He grabbed the man's coat and hefted him to his feet, bringing them nose to nose. "Any funny business, I'll leave you tied up out there, got it?" he threatened. Earflaps sneered at him, but then he thought better of his response and merely nodded. "Move," Ty ordered as he picked up the shotgun and pushed the man in front of him. He left the flashlight off, conserving the battery while the moon was actually peeking through the clouds to give them light.

He gave the man some leeway in his wandering, partly because he knew no one back at the fire wanted to hear this guy do his business any more than he did. But also because his mind was struggling to keep up; he was tired, cold, sore, and having more and more trouble giving a shit. The only thing he did care about at this point was getting home. These mountains could make unsuspecting victims out of even the most experienced of travelers, and Ty found that he couldn't stop worrying about Zane out here. It probably hadn't been the greatest idea, dragging him up here for his first hike. But Ty was sure he'd been enjoying himself before they were almost killed. Repeatedly.

He sighed heavily and slid his hands into his pockets, carrying the shotgun in the crook of his arm against his hip. He shivered slightly in the cold air. Hell. He was probably getting sick after that damn cold water. That would be his luck. Avoid the traps and the bullets and drowning and then die of pneumonia before they could get back.

The thought actually made him smile crookedly in the darkness.

He realized they'd been trekking into the forest for almost five minutes before he snapped out of it. "Hey," he said sharply. Earflaps took a few more slow steps before stopping. "This'll do fine," Ty told him.

Earflaps looked around. "Turn around," he told Ty.

"Go to hell," Ty replied easily.

"Well, can I go behind a tree?" the man asked irritably.

Ty glared at him. He glanced around the small clearing the man had found. If he did make a run for it, Ty could easily catch him. And if he somehow escaped, there was really nowhere for him to go that didn't involve freezing to death, being eaten by an animal, or getting lost and starving. He was about to tell the man to be quick about it when a noise that was out of place caught his attention and stopped him in his verbal tracks. He tensed, cursing himself for not paying more attention and allowing Earflaps to lead him so far from the fire.

"Come on, man!" Earflaps whined.

"Shut up," Ty hissed. He raised his shotgun slightly. "Do you hear that?" he whispered.

"You ain't gonna scare me, hillbilly," Earlfaps declared stubbornly.

Ty shook his head, hushing the man again and pressing the butt of the gun against his shoulder, at the ready. A twig broke somewhere to his left, then another.

"I heard that," Earflaps said, suddenly quiet and serious, looking off into the dark woods.

Ty tensed and remained motionless, a chill crawling up his spine. He instinctively felt they were being stalked, and by something with far more skill than the three treasure hunters they'd been dealing with.

"Come over here," Ty whispered, and Earflaps didn't argue as he began to move. "Slowly!" Ty hissed. Earflaps froze and glanced around nervously. Ty could relate. He resisted the urge to call out for help, knowing it might just trigger an attack. And whoever came to their aid would be in danger too. Ty couldn't have that. Even as he thought it, there was a rustling sound in the underbrush to his right. Jesus, it moved fast. That or there was more than one. A strange sound, almost like a purr, emitted from the darkness.

Ty's entire body went cold, and he began to shake almost uncontrollably as he gripped the shotgun. They were rare, but there was only one thing in these mountains that purred.

He tried to keep from breathing too heavily as he went over what little he knew about cougars. They were supposed to be endangered in these mountains, a population so sparse they were more of a myth than a fact. Ty supposed it was just his shitty luck to stumble over one. At least he now knew why there were no small animals in the area and what had been driving the snakes to lower climates.

A large cat emerged from the undergrowth, appearing suddenly and without further warning, its tan fur almost silver in the moonlight. It growled at them both, circling them warily.

"Oh Christ," Ty breathed as he watched it, not quite believing what he was seeing. The cat was almost two feet high at the shoulders and at least six feet long from nose to tail. When it moved its shoulders rolled and its tail swished sinuously behind it.

It was the most terrifying thing Ty had ever seen.

"Oh shit," Earflaps echoed.

"Don't move," Ty told him. He knew that to run or play dead would just trigger the chase and kill instincts in the cat, and he forced himself to stand there and stare at it. He hoped it couldn't smell fear, or they were both dead men.

Ty knew one thing: if it had wanted to kill them, they never would have seen it coming. They'd probably just stumbled too close to its babies and it was trying to warn them off. Cougars were ambush predators. He had studied the way they and other animals killed when he'd been on the Recon team, curious to see if he could learn anything from them. He had learned quite a lot. He knew that cougars were solitary hunters, so he didn't have to worry about a second one anywhere. But they could leap over twenty feet in one go and run up to thirty-five miles an hour; they had a vertical of nearly fifteen feet, and when they struck, they did so from the side or rear, severing the spinal cord and then either eating their prey alive or letting it bleed out to save for later.

The fact that he was staring at this one in the eyes was actually a good thing. It meant the cat wasn't sure if they were food. Yet. Not that the idea offered him a shred of comfort.

"You're, uh… you're supposed to stand tall," he told Earflaps breathlessly. "Stretch your arms out and make yourself appear as large as possible."

"Bullshit," Earflaps whispered back at him. "You first."

Ty shook his head minutely. He knew what you were supposed to do. But he just couldn't force himself to move as the cat stalked back into the underbrush and disappeared. Ty had never seen anything so big that was so adept at hiding itself, even if it was dark. A part of him, the part that may or may not have been suicidal and wasn't terrified into stupidity, took a moment to admire the ability.

"Oh God," Earflaps mumbled softly. Ty could see his breath misting in the cold air. He trembled with the urge to flee from the danger. Ty could understand the impulse.

"Don't move," Ty told him again. The man didn't respond, but Ty could see his body coiling in the moonlight. He knew he was fighting the same instinct to run that Ty was. He was losing the fight, though. "Don't move, man," Ty practically pleaded. He raised the shotgun, more for comfort than actually thinking it would do much good if the cat came at him from behind.

Earflaps jerked suddenly and broke into a run. Ty shouted at him, but the man either didn't hear him or didn't care. He hadn't gone four steps before there was a loud screech. The underbrush whispered with the movement, and the cougar yowled again as it pounced on Earflaps' back and knocked him to the ground. Earflaps gave a horrible scream as Ty brought the shotgun around and fired. The cougar flinched, giving another keening cry as it leapt away, disappearing silently into the darkness.

Ty stood breathing hard and staring, straining his eyes as he moved forward cautiously. He didn't think he'd hit the cougar, but the sound of the shot had at least scared it off. For now. After a brief moment, he rushed toward the fallen man and laid the gun to the side, yanking off his coat to press it to the gaping wound on the man's neck. Flashes of the past assaulted him, holding his camouflaged clothing to the wound of a dear friend as he died in Ty's arms, so far from home.

Ty gasped as the warm blood flowed through his fingers. The man grabbed at his wrists, looking up at him with terrified eyes, unnaturally white in the moonlight that filtered into the clearing.

"Hold on," Ty told him breathlessly. "It's not that bad," he told him, knowing the man wouldn't make it long enough to call him a liar. Even as he tried to stem the bleeding, the life drained from his prisoner's eyes, and Earflaps fell limp, the blood still gushing from the rips in his throat.

ZANE'S head jerked up and a shiver ran down his spine as the scream echoed through the trees. He was on his feet, gun in hand, without even thinking about it, turning toward where he thought the scream might have originated. Then his brain kicked into gear. That wasn't Ty screaming. It couldn't be. It was Earflaps. Shit. Had Ty actually lost it and shot him? Or did Earflaps rush Ty in the dark?

It all added up to him needing to be there, now, and see what was happening. See if Ty was okay. And if he wasn't, Zane would deal with it. They were both getting off this damn mountain alive.

"What happened?" Deuce demanded dazedly as he rolled to his hands and knees.

"Sounds like he shot him," Earl guessed roughly as he stumbled over the fire and grabbed for the second shotgun. "Garrett?" he barked as he stood and peered out into the pitch-black woods.

"I'm going, Earl," Zane answered flatly as he checked his gun. "Stay with Deuce."

"Garrett," Earl said again sharply. When Zane looked up at him, Earl was staring at him determinedly. "You bring him back," Earl told him quietly.

Zane stared at him for just a moment, surprised at the lack of argument, but then he nodded curtly and turned to lope into the darkness in what he hoped was the right direction. If Ty had killed the man, he might not be in the most stable state of mind. Zane hoped Ty seeing his partner would be enough to snap him out of it.

Ty CLOSED his eyes as he moved his bloody hands away from the dead man, but then his eyes were on the underbrush once more as his hand groped blindly for the shotgun. If he was going to be eaten, he wanted to see it coming. And he would damn sure to put up a fight. He knew the others would have heard the shot and probably the screaming. But that didn't mean they would find him in the dark woods. Not in time, anyway. He even thought maybe he could hear them calling out, but he didn't dare call back.

His hand landed on a decent-sized rock. Ty palmed it, still feeling around with the other hand for the gun. What the hell had he done with it? He tore his eyes away from the trees to search the ground. The barrel shone dully in the moonlight, roughly six feet away. As he crawled slowly toward it, he found a thick tree branch that was still fairly green and hefted it. The more weapons he had on him until he made it to the gun, the less he felt like kibble.

Ty felt the movement at his side rather than saw it, and he turned and tried to rise to face it, striking out with the stick as the cougar came at him with horrifying speed. He didn't make it to his feet, though. The impact knocked him to the ground, the big cat landing on him and knocking the breath from his lungs. He saw stars as his head banged against the hard ground. The cat caught the stick between its sharp teeth, and it snapped in half like a desiccated twig, showering Ty's face with bits of wood. The cougar's claws scraped across his shoulder and tore into the skin.

Ty screamed in agony even as he held what remained of the stick in front of his throat, trying to protect himself. He cried out again as teeth sank into his hand. He dropped the stick as he lost feeling in the hand but rounded with the stone in his other hand, smacking the cat in the side of the head with it. It made a dull thud when it hit, and the cat leaped away and hissed at him angrily, lashing out with one giant paw. Ty rolled out of its reach, narrowly missing being lacerated by the impressive claws. He found himself on top of his shotgun, and he grabbed it gratefully, rolling again and coming to sit with it clutched to his chest.

The cat shook its head, pawing at its ear where Ty had landed the blow, tail twitching as it sized him up again. Ty pushed up onto his knees and threw the rock at it, sending it scampering backward a few feet with a low growl. He gripped the gun and struggled to his feet unsteadily, surprised when he weaved a little, wielding the shotgun almost like a baseball bat with both hands until he could grip it correctly and aim it.

The cougar continued to watch him warily, obviously deciding that he might not be an easy kill after all. Ty could feel blood dripping down his fingers as he gripped the gun, and he didn't know if it was his blood or the other man's. The cougar made a grumbling, growling sound in its throat as it slinked toward the body lying in the brush. Ty realized belatedly that the big cat must have thought he was after its meal.

"Take him," Ty told the cat breathlessly. "Eat him. He won't care now," he said as he began backing away.

The cat hissed one more time, bared its impressive teeth, and then took Earflaps by his ruined neck and began dragging him into the forest. It locked eyes with Ty, neither looking away until the cat dematerialized into the woods.

Ty listened intently, holding his breath as he waited for the telltale breaking of twigs that signified the cougar making a hasty retreat. He heard none, though. It was still out there. Watching him. He lowered the shotgun as his entire body began to tremble. He'd just been attacked by a fucking mountain lion.

And he was not handling it well.

"Ty!" It was Zane's voice, somewhere close, coming out of the darkness. Ty could hear rustling approaching from behind him.

Ty held his breath a moment, weighing the benefit of calling out versus being eaten. "Garrett!" he called back after a few seconds. His voice was filled with panic and near-terror. He backed away another step. The shotgun shook in his trembling hands.

There was an immediate shift of direction in the movement behind him, and he could hear Zane running toward him, amazingly sure-footed in the darkness, he thought distantly. Time dragged as

Ty tried to watch all around him, listening hard, but it couldn't have been more than thirty seconds before Zane skidded to a stop not too far away and called his name again.

"Slowly, Garrett," Ty managed to call back, though his voice was still shaking with fear and adrenaline.

Zane went still for a long moment before he started moving, one step at a time. Then he appeared out of the darkness at Ty's side, his gun held ready. "What the hell?" Zane said under his breath, surprise and something darker in his voice. "I heard gunfire and screaming."

"It ate him," Ty answered without moving. Somewhere in his mind, he knew it sounded astoundingly stupid. But it was the best he could articulate.

Zane, for some reason, didn't act like it was odd at all. Maybe it was the stunned look on Ty's face, or the fact that his entire body trembled, or that he was covered in blood.

"Can you get back to camp?" Zane asked, turning so his back was to Ty's as he looked at the darkness around them.

Ty nodded jerkily, backing up until his back was pressed against Zane's. "Count of three," he said shakily. "We run." He remembered the last time they'd counted to three, cornered by kids with paintball guns. Ty had used Zane as a distraction, as a human shield. Ty gritted his teeth as the shaking in his hands subsided suddenly. He'd take on that mountain lion with his bare hands before it touched Zane; he knew that much for certain.

"I'm facing twelve," Zane said to him quietly. "We're going to three o'clock." Ty nodded in acknowledgment. "Count," Zane said.

The brush shivered in the moonlight as Ty watched it. He swallowed hard and said a shaky, "One."

Zane shifted his weight in preparation to move. "Two."

Ty spared the dark woods one more careful look before he reached behind him and pushed at Zane's hip. "Three!" he shouted, and they turned and ran as fast as they could through the darkness.

Zane led him back to the camp, where Ty knew the fire and the scent of more people would provide safety. Adrenaline still rushed through him, and he didn't know how badly wounded he might be. Nothing hurt yet, at least. He just knew they needed to get to safety before the cat came back for more.

When Ty and Zane broke through trees and into the circle of light and warmth from the fire, Earl was waiting with a flashlight and a large hunting knife. As Ty stumbled, he grabbed the shotgun out of his hands; Deuce stood with his shotgun drawn, looking out into the woods, ready to fire at anything that came after them. Ty slid to the ground and grabbed at the end of one of the sticks in the fire, turning with the flaming branch in his hand and breathing hard as he waited. For whatever reason, he felt better with the branch than he had with the shotgun. Probably because he'd missed with the fucking shotgun the first time.

But the forest was quiet. Nothing came out of the woods after him. A bird chirped somewhere in the distance, and another happily answered the call. The fire crackled merrily, and the only sounds were Zane's and Ty's harsh breaths as they tried to pull air in.

Finally, Ty lowered the stick in his hand and looked down at it abashedly before tossing it back in the fire. The others lowered their weapons and turned to look at him doubtfully, like he might have finally had that mental breakdown they were all expecting.

"I'm okay," Ty mumbled to them. "I think."

"Where's—"

"He's gone," Ty said flatly, cutting Deuce's question off.

"Gone? What happened?" Deuce demanded.

The flashlight played over Ty, and Earl stopped it at his hands. "Jesus Christ, boy," Earl grunted as he came closer. Zane appeared at Ty's side, shoving his gun into his waistband, putting a steadying hand against Ty's back.

Ty looked down to see that blood was dripping down his fingers, running freely and obscuring the sources so they couldn't see how many punctures there were or how badly his hand was torn up. His entire front was covered in blood, in fact. Some his, spreading from the scratches on his shoulders, but most of it belonged to the dead man.

He held his hand up and peered closely at it in the wavering firelight. "Fuck, man, I just got that out of a cast," he said in annoyance. "Bring that light," he requested as Earl stopped in front of him and shined the light down on his hand. He could discern at least four separate punctures, one of which was so deep that Ty thought it might actually have hit the bone. His fingers were stiffening up quickly, and his hand was beginning to throb. The knuckle of his ring finger was swollen and turning blue. "Hell," he cursed in defeat. He supposed he was lucky that he still had the hand at all, considering he could have yanked out the cat's tonsils at one point.

"What happened?" Deuce demanded.

Ty shook his head as Earl yanked the buff off Ty's head and used it to make a rough tourniquet around his forearm. The buff wouldn't go tight enough to do much good, though, and Zane went to dig in his backpack.

"What'd you do?" Earl asked as Ty tried to calm his breathing.

"Cat jumped us," Ty answered in a surprised voice. "Ate him."

"A cougar?" Earl asked in shock.

"Yeah," Ty answered, still in disbelief. He held his hand up as it began throbbing angrily, trying to slow the blood flow to the wounds.

"I thought cougars in these parts was just hearsay," Earl said in surprise.

"Well, we'll be sure to report the sighting to fucking Fish and Game when we get home," Ty snapped as he sat down heavily beside the fire. His entire body was shaking. The firelight flickered off the blood streaming down his hand and forearm.

"Hey," Zane said quietly as he knelt beside Ty with a shirt he'd yanked out of his backpack. Ty recognized it, actually. Zane had worn it the day they drove up here. It was one of Zane's favorites. "Look at me, all right?" Zane used the shirt in one hand to start mopping up the blood on Ty's shoulder and down his arm, and the other hand settled on Ty's knee to squeeze gently.

Ty looked up at him obediently. His hand trembled in Zane's. He'd been trained to face danger of all kinds, but he supposed nothing overrode the very distinct knowledge that you were about to be dinner.

"You're okay," Zane said quietly but clearly. "Just focus on me for a few minutes. What's the first thing that comes to mind?" While talking, he was gently wiping away the blood.

Ty blinked at him, opening his mouth as he thought the very first thing that came to mind when Zane prompted him. *I love you.* He snapped his mouth closed and stared at Zane, unable and unwilling to answer.

Zane frowned a little. "Ty?" His head tipped to one side as he looked Ty over, probably for more injuries. "Are you hurt somewhere else?"

Ty swallowed hard, his mouth suddenly dry as he tried to answer. He cleared his throat and shook his head. "I don't think so," he finally managed to utter. The truth was, he had no idea. His entire body was numb, not to mention his mind was reeling as he watched Zane.

"Deuce, would you get a canteen, please?" Zane requested, his eyes not wavering from Ty's face.

Ty cleared his throat uncomfortably and tore his eyes away from Zane's, afraid of what he might say if he continued to look at him. He glanced around uncertainly. Earl was rummaging through the first-aid kit, not paying them any mind as he searched for ointment and bandages, but Deuce was standing over them with his hands on his hips, watching them closely, and he nodded at Zane's request as Ty looked up at him.

"Sure," Deuce said, and he limped over toward his backpack.

Zane's hand on Ty's cheek brought his attention back to his partner. "Hey. You with me?" Zane asked, the concern clear on his face and in his eyes. "You have any more of the... falling?"

Ty swallowed hard again. "I've never seen anything like that, Zane," he admitted roughly.

Zane didn't try to make light. He nodded and continued to wipe at the blood on Ty's shaky hand. "I've got your back," he promised.

Ty nodded jerkily. He cleared his throat again, finally feeling the embarrassment. He looked down at his hand for lack of anything better to do. "It's bleeding a lot," he said in a surprised voice as he looked at his fingers in the light of the fire.

Zane must have noticed his discomfort, because he released Ty's hand as Deuce lowered himself carefully to a knee, offering the canteen to Ty.

"A cat?" Deuce asked dubiously.

"It was a big cat," Ty insisted as he held his hand up. He watched as several drops of blood dripped off his wrist. It looked like he'd stuck it in a blender.

Earl muttered as he knelt beside Deuce and took Ty's hand. He raised it up to look at it. "Won't be able to get this fixed up real good until daylight," he said grimly. "Should cauterize it."

"Oh, hell no," Ty protested as he tried to jerk his hand away. Earl's grip tightened, and he looked at Ty pointedly. "We'll just clean it real good and double-time it in the morning, okay?" Ty bargained.

Earl raised an eyebrow but nodded in agreement. "Wash it up real good," he warned.

"Yes, sir," Ty muttered. His father handed Deuce the ointment and bandages and then went to get water. Ty glanced over at Zane, who was watching him silently. "Shut up," he muttered.

~CHAPTER 15~

As Zane and Earl packed their bags at sunup, Deuce hunkered down, took Ty's hand, and frowned at the wounds. "Does it hurt?" he asked as he poked at Ty's palm. Ty nearly choked on the water he'd been gulping down and wrenched his hand away with a hoarse curse.

"I'll take that as a 'yes'," Zane said wryly as he stopped next to them.

"We need to wrap it," Earl advised. He turned around, his hands on his hips and a scowl set on his face. "You need to protect it while you're walking. You need to keep it as still as possible, keep it up. We'll have to immobilize it somehow."

Ty resisted the urge to growl. It was a nuisance, but he knew his father was right. Bites were nasty business at any time, but out here where they were miles away from anything resembling sanitary conditions, it could turn deadly very fast. Of all the wounds the others had suffered during their escapades, this was probably the most dangerous, as embarrassing as it was. "Yes, sir," Ty muttered with a nod.

"I'll get a clean T-shirt," Deuce mumbled as he climbed to his feet.

Zane's lips twitched as he stayed there next to Ty. He crouched down next to his partner. "So. Just a nice stretch of the legs on the mountain. No problem," he said conversationally.

"It's not entirely going to plan," Ty muttered as he looked away from Zane, flushing a bit.

Zane snorted. "With us, when does it ever?"

Ty glanced over at him, met his eyes for a moment, and smirked crookedly. "I can think of a few times."

Their eyes met briefly, and Ty felt more words on the tip of his tongue, but the jarring sound of material ripping interrupted any further conversation. Deuce was methodically cutting a brown T-shirt into thin strips. "Hey!" Ty called out. "Not that one!" he protested as he pointed at the shirt. The Schitt Creek Paddle Co. shirt was one of his very favorites. "That's a lucky shirt!"

"Deal with it, Meow Mix," Deuce advised as he carefully draped the strips over his shoulder to keep them clean.

"The Phillies will never win again if you tear up that shirt," Ty told Deuce threateningly.

"We don't need your lucky shirts," Deuce claimed with a smirk. "Save those for your damn Redskins."

"You can get a new shirt," Zane pointed out. "New hand, not so much."

"New hand, nothing," Earl broke in as he knelt and began rummaging through his pack. "It gets infected and you won't make it off the mountain."

"Being a little dramatic about it, aren't you?" Ty asked him with a small, hopeful smile.

His father turned his head and met his eyes. "No."

Standing up, Zane took Ty's good hand and pulled him to his feet. When Ty stood, though, his head swam, and he wavered. Zane placed a supportive hand on his lower back. "You okay?" he asked, his voice exposing new concern.

Ty nodded and brushed him off. "I'm good," he muttered as he looked down at his hand. "Okay," he sighed as he started trying to think of a way to immobilize the wounded fingers. Earl was right—the less he moved them the better. If an infection did get into the joints, it would spread faster if he were using the fingers. Besides, they hurt like a bitch.

Ty looked around the clearing, frustrated by how muddled his thoughts seemed to be. The pain when he kept his hand at his side was distracting, and he raised it up and cradled it to his chest unconsciously.

Finally, he turned and looked back at Zane appraisingly. "How much of your gear do you really need?" he asked.

"Just the canteen. Everything else important is on me," Zane answered. Ty knew he meant his weapons. "The duffel we can leave behind."

"No, no," Ty corrected as he made a "hand it over" gesture with his good fingers. "The duffel's what I need."

Frowning again, Zane shrugged and took the several steps to snag it and bring it back, holding it out for Ty to take.

Ty nodded his thanks and took the bag, unzipping it with difficulty as he knelt. He dumped the contents onto the ground and then slid the hunting knife from its sheath at his thigh and began slicing into the thick padding of the shoulder straps.

Zane watched as Ty started cutting up the bag. "Are you making a sling?" he asked after a few moments.

"No, but that would have been brilliant of me," Ty answered as he glanced up at Zane and smiled slightly. "I'm making a splint," he added as the smile fell. "Pretty sure something broke in there. A little wrapping with that damn duct tape and this padding should be hard enough to do it."

Nodding, Zane knelt down next to him and grabbed the roll of silver duct tape they'd been using to tape the prisoners up. "Let's get you wrapped up then," Zane said to him.

Ty knew that he couldn't manage the feat with just one hand, and he relented with a grunt of displeasure. "Try to mold it as you wrap it," he advised as he held out his injured hand in the shape that would work best. "Just curve the end of it."

"Leave the man alone, boy, he's got sense enough to know basic first aid," Earl chastised as he clunked down a small plastic box.

Zane raised an eyebrow as he followed Ty's instructions, making the mold fit the natural curve of his hand. Ty watched him as he wrapped it rather than watching his progress. Every time he thought too hard on it, an uncomfortable tightness formed in his throat and butterflies assaulted him. At least he now he knew the truth about himself and Zane. Looking raptly into Zane's dark eyes, Ty wondered why he hadn't realized he loved the man earlier.

"How bad is it? Really," Zane asked, looking up to meet Ty's eyes.

Ty swallowed hard. "Hurts worse than I thought it would," he answered in a barely audible voice. Whether he was talking about his hand or something more, he really couldn't have said.

He shook off any more thoughts along those lines and cleared his throat. He would let himself ponder that once they were off this mountain and in the clear.

He looked down at his hand and examined it, holding it out toward Zane. His shoulders ached where the cougar's claws had sunk in, but his hand was the true problem. The side of it where the shallowest punctures had been was bruised and swollen, and the entire hand was red and painful. The two knuckles of his pinkie and ring fingers were twice the size they were supposed to be, and all his fingers were swollen and bruised as well. There was a puncture on his palm that made it impossible to grip anything hard. And since he'd wrenched his hand away from the pain when the cat had bitten down, the punctures weren't just deep, they were rips that had torn up the skin, making it harder for the wounds to close. In fact, he'd had gunshots that were less painful than his hand was right now.

"Hurts," he repeated. "It ain't infected, though," he surmised with a shake of his head.

"Keep an eye on it, tough guy," Zane murmured as he kept wrapping the modified brace with the tape to bulk it up and make it stiff. "I don't want to have to carry you out of here."

"Wouldn't be the first time," Ty assured him as Earl stepped closer and handed him a small tin of Rawleigh's antibiotic ointment. "Thanks," Ty said as he looked up at his father and took the tin.

Earl swished a bottle of water at him. "Time to clean it again," he said grimly. Cleaning it the night before had been painful enough. Ty thought he might have whimpered through the whole process.

"Great," Ty muttered as his father chuckled and took the mangled backpack and Ty's knife just as Deuce held up the cloth, indicating for Zane to take the canteen.

"Ready?" Zane asked.

Ty glared at him. "Just do it quick," he requested.

Glancing to Deuce, Zane waited until he nodded to start pouring the water in a thin, slow stream. Deuce held the cloth under it briefly, took Ty's hand, and began scrubbing at it, hard and fast. Ty just closed his eyes and turned his head slightly, breathing in the cool air of the mountain as the little torn bits of skin were ripped up and away. It wasn't as bad as he'd been expecting. He supposed most of the pain was coming from the bruising rather than the open wounds. He was almost positive the nerves around those were all dead, now, anyway.

When he looked back down at it, most of the dried blood that had caked his fingers and palm was gone, and Deuce was slathering it with ointment and wrapping it carefully with the strips of his T-shirt.

Ty sighed and looked up at his father, who was standing aside and watching with a frown. He met his dad's eyes and gave a weak smile. They both knew how bad this could turn.

Zane picked up the mold he'd made and held it out. "All right, into the splint," he said.

Ty placed his hand into it, wincing as his palm settled. Deuce waited until Ty gave him a nod; then he began anchoring the splint to Ty's arm with an Ace bandage from the first aid kit.

"I gotcha a sling, here," Earl announced as he held up what had once been Deuce's spare pack. "Might be better off without it," he advised.

Ty shook his head. He needed to keep it up more than he needed that hand to walk. "Let me have the damn thing," he muttered as he pulled his hand away from Zane and stood slowly. He'd found if he rose too quickly, his head would swim and his vision would blur. He pulled the straps of the mangled backpack close to his body, essentially tying his arm to his chest. It would fuck with his balance and probably end up making him fall on his face, but it was better than the alternative. When he'd adjusted it, he flopped his good hand to his side and looked around at the others. "Let's divvy up the shit and get going," he suggested.

As Earl and Deuce picked through the rest of the supplies spilled on the ground, Zane stood slowly, only a couple feet from Ty, keeping his eyes on him the whole time. He took a step closer and reached out to untwist one of the straps and tie it more securely. "There you go," he murmured.

Ty found it difficult to meet his eyes as he thought about a similar action Zane had taken in a New York hotel room almost a year ago. Now, just as then, his heart beat a little faster because of it. But he nodded in thanks and smiled as he tried to fight back the hint of warmth it caused. *I love you.* The thought had haunted him all night, almost as much as the sound of the cougar's scream.

Zane's fingers lingered where Ty's T-shirt met his neck, pressing against the warm skin for just a few moments longer than necessary. "Come on. There's beer and apple pie waiting," he said.

"Can't wait," Ty muttered. He reached out and socked Zane in the stomach as soon as the other two men had turned away and started off down the trail.

"Ow!" Zane huffed, rubbing the spot as he hefted the remaining backpack. "Asshole."

Ty grinned crookedly and began laughing softly. "You're carrying my shit over mountain trails. You're officially a jackass."

Zane skipped a step to catch up as they started walking. "I vaguely remember you carrying *me* around. What does that make you?"

"A hero," Ty countered with a smirk.

Zane snorted as they sped their steps, hiking after the other two men. "So now you're going to admit it, huh? None of that 'I was just helping my partner' shit you gave in the reports?"

"Shut up," Ty grunted, suddenly uncomfortable with the discussion.

"Humility doesn't suit you, Grady. Now step it up," Zane said as he stepped over a log fallen across the narrow trail.

Ty muttered to himself as he walked ahead of Zane. His hand throbbed angrily with every beat of his heart, and the punctures burned under the makeshift bandages. He didn't say anything to the others, though; he just tried to keep pace with them. The closer they got to civilization, the better off they were. And they had a long way to go.

"MRS. Grady, I understand that you're worried," the ranger was saying patiently as Mara and Chester stood together in front of him. Mara's jaw was set firm, and her green eyes flashed as Chester stood beside her, leaning on his shovel. "But they're not even a day late," the ranger continued, looking askance at the shovel. "Earl's missed his schedule by a lot more than this before."

"This time's different, Dale," Mara insisted stubbornly. She had awakened that morning with an odd feeling in the pit of her stomach, and she couldn't seem to shake it. She tried to tell herself it was just the change to her routine that was causing it, or the fact that Chester had been awake and dressed, ready to ride with her to the ranger station. But deep down, she knew she'd never convince herself. Something was wrong on the mountain today.

"They're not technically missing yet," Dale tried to reason with her, putting his hands out almost defensively.

"Twenty-four hours could kill a man in those mountains, and you know it!" Mara told him angrily.

"Been awful cold up there," Chester informed him calmly.

"Your boys are more than capable of handling themselves on the mountain," Dale reminded with a hint of admiration. Dale had gone to school with Ty and Deuce; he knew them and what they were capable of. "There's nothing I can do until we get some kind of word that there's trouble," Dale told them in a voice that was almost pleading with her to understand. "We're short-handed as it is in the offseason."

Mara lifted her chin and glared at him silently, looking around at the other two rangers who stood in the office, trying desperately not to get in the line of fire. "You're not gonna go search for my boys 'til morning?" Mara questioned in a calm voice.

"Mrs. Grady, please—"

"Well then, we're gonna need to borrow two guns, some britches, and a daypack," she interrupted as she looked back at Dale.

He stared at her with his mouth hanging slightly open. "What?" he asked dumbly.

"You heard the woman, sonny!" Chester shouted as he brought the shovel up and slammed it onto the desk beside Dale, narrowly missing his fingers. Dale jumped and flinched away from the sharp tip.

"Yes, sir, but—"

"Well, I certainly can't go up there in nothing but my dress," Mara reasoned with him, "and I don't have time to go driving all the way back home to get Earl's rifle."

He continued to stare at them, shaking his head helplessly.

Chester hefted the shovel and rested it on his shoulder, narrowing his clear blue eyes. Mara crossed her arms stubbornly. "And some extra ammunition," she requested of Dale.

Dale sighed and slumped his shoulders, sitting back against his desk and rubbing at a spot of tension on his forehead. He looked back up at her as she stood there waiting, his eyes flickering to Chester and his shovel warily as he cleared his throat.

"Jerry, call down and have them start up the search-and-rescue team," Dale requested of one of the other rangers in the office. The man hopped up gratefully and went to go get the local volunteer search and rescue squad on the horn.

Mara nodded at the young ranger. "Thank you, Dale. You're a good boy," she told him.

"Thank you, ma'am," he said in defeat as she and Chester turned and made their way out of the office.

ZANE paused next to Ty for a couple deep breaths at the top of another hill on the grassy path. When he stopped, Ty glanced at him, and Zane got a good look at his partner. His face was flushed, but other than that, he looked like he was taking a walk in the park. It made Zane worry that the flush was from fever and not exertion.

"Okay?" Ty asked him.

Zane nodded even though he was slightly winded. "You?"

"Hurts," Ty responded as he lowered his head again.

That worried him. It was the second time Ty had admitted to the pain, and Ty wouldn't admit to pain unless it was bad or he wanted to be coddled. And Zane knew he didn't want to be coddled in front of his father and brother. He studied Ty's face. "Throbbing? Burning?"

"Little of both," Ty answered curtly as he looked out over the trail ahead. "Hey, Dad," he called as he unscrewed the top of his canteen with his thumb. "I think we need to check this."

"Hurts?" Earl asked worriedly as he brushed past Zane on his way back to Ty.

"Hurts," Ty echoed as Earl's back obscured Zane's view of what they were doing. He could tell Earl was unwrapping the makeshift cast and examining the wounds, though.

"What's the verdict, Dad?" Deuce asked after a quiet minute.

Earl was silent for a moment, still holding Ty's hand and looking at it closely. Finally, he shook his head. "Hand's hot," he answered grimly.

"Infected?" Deuce asked.

"Red's just setting in," Earl responded. "If I had to guess, I'd say that cat lost a bit of tooth in that knuckle," he added as he turned Ty's hand over and began rewrapping it with extreme care. Zane's stomach plummeted with the news.

"We just need to get within range of a cell tower or ranger station," Deuce offered calmly. "And hell, Ma and Grandpa probably got the cavalry all riled up by now."

Zane glanced up at the canopy. There was no fucking way they'd be able to see a cell tower through all the trees. He looked back at Deuce and Earl. Neither man seemed at all bothered by the news. Ty's hand was probably infected, he was already showing signs of fever, and they still had two days of hard hiking before they could reach help. Ty would probably be septic before then.

"We go," Zane said firmly. "And we go as quickly as we can."

BY THE time Earl stopped them for the night, it was long past dark. Normally, as soon as the sun began to set, he would have called a halt. Hiking in these mountains was dangerous enough in the daylight. But he could feel the heavy hand of time pressing at his back now, and so he'd pushed them until he could no longer discern the path in the moonlight.

They had made decent time, but Earl knew they weren't going to get far enough fast enough, even with the pace he was setting. By morning, Ty would be even weaker, possibly even unable to continue on. Earl knew he couldn't carry his son with broken ribs. If Ty became too weak to go on, it would be up to Zane to pull him through. And Earl was beginning to think that perhaps Zane could manage the feat. He'd certainly gotten Ty out of those woods with no regard for his own safety going in and had been willing to do the same in the river. He'd killed a man to save Ty's life without blinking an eye. Earl wasn't worried anymore about Ty having a partner worthy of him, not after this week.

As Deuce got a small fire going, Earl sat on a fallen log and watched Ty closely. He was shivering, tired and listless as he sat next to his partner. Earl glanced from Zane to Deuce and back. They'd both spoken up for Ty, and Earl knew anyone who would stand up to Earl had some steel in them.

His eyes settled on Ty again. His oldest son had never done anything to deserve all the weight that had been put on his shoulders. Earl knew he'd never been easy on either Ty or Deuce. He expected certain things from them, expected them to be strong and capable, self-sufficient and dependable, loyal and fair. He expected them to think and do for themselves, to be good to and protect their mama, and to respect those who deserved it.

Earl's eyes closed slowly. Ty was a good son. He was a good man. He'd been a good Marine and he was a good federal agent. He was a lot of things. But he was no coward, and Earl had never even dreamed of thinking he was. Earl had said it in the heat of the moment, knowing it would put Ty into action, and he'd been angry at himself ever since for doing it, continuing to take the unfamiliar emotion out on the boys because he didn't know what else to do with it. He would have to make it right with more than a simple apology. Soon.

Ty was getting along with everyone's help on the trail. He was pale, though, and every few minutes, he would simply shiver violently as his body fought the infection spreading through it. It was painful to know he was hurting and not be able to do anything about it. His boy might die up here, and there wasn't a damn thing he could do but sleep until daybreak.

His boy might die up here, all because Earl had called him a coward.

Earl lowered his head, telling himself not to think too hard on it any longer. Not until the danger had passed. Tears wouldn't cure Ty's wounds.

"How's it feeling?" Deuce asked Ty as he poked at the flames and fed two more small sticks into the fire.

"Hurts," Ty grunted. "Feels like my fingers are on fire. Feels like my whole body's on fire," he corrected as he leaned slightly to one side against Zane's conveniently close shoulder.

"We could try cleaning it again," Deuce suggested doubtfully. His tone of voice said he knew it wouldn't do any good, and he knew Ty would turn down the offer.

"Hell, no," Ty muttered.

"We should keep going," Deuce said as he turned to meet Earl's eyes, asking for permission to do so. "Me and Ty, we should keep going and—"

"You can't watch the trail and me at the same time," Ty broke in.

"We still have the one flashlight, we could make ten miles by morning," Deuce argued.

"We're safer together," Zane ground out.

"He's dying, Zane. We should be going as fast as possible," Deuce insisted.

"I can't make that pace," Ty pointed out derisively. "I can barely walk a straight line."

Deuce opened his mouth to respond, but Earl held up his hand and closed his eyes. Both of his sons snapped their mouths shut and lowered their heads, the argument ending before it could get in full swing.

"We stay together," Earl ordered in a gruff voice. "We head out at first light. Not before. Ty's right," he said pointedly as he looked at Deuce. "He's too weak to be trusted on a dangerous trail," he said as he turned his eyes to Ty. Ty visibly flinched at his words, lowering his head. Zane watched his partner and then looked up to stare at Earl through the firelight.

"Get some sleep," Earl continued, not commenting on the reactions. He could feel the unspoken accusations in Zane's eyes. But despite what Zane Garrett might think, Earl knew his own son and how to handle him. Ty would walk through Hell and back to prove he could do something he wasn't supposed to be able to do. Earl was determined to keep him walking no matter how much it hurt both of them. "Four hours to daylight," he said roughly. He didn't look at Zane or his sons again, instead stretching out on the bedroll with his back to the fire.

He didn't want them to see the tears that threatened in his eyes.

WHEN Deuce awoke to the sound of chirping birds, his first thought was to chuck a rock at them. When he talked himself out of that, his mind turned to his brother, and he rolled over with a groan to check on Ty. He and Zane had placed Ty between them the night before, hoping to keep him warm during the chilly night.

Ty had thrashed and grumbled almost the entire night, fighting the fever and the periodic shivers that ran through him. But he was resting peacefully now, curled against Zane's left side as if he were cold. Zane's arm was wrapped around him, holding him close and keeping him warm. It would almost have been sweet under other circumstances, but Ty was too still. A bolt of cold fear shot through Deuce as he reached out to touch him.

He calmed when Ty mumbled at him and tried to bury his head under Zane. He was hot to the touch and far too pale, but he was still breathing, and that was all Deuce could ask for this morning.

"Ty, wake up," Deuce said as he sat up and shook Ty's arm. Ty groaned and rolled, burrowing further against Zane, who opened his eyes to look at Deuce blearily. "Come on, G-Man," Deuce grunted as he shook his brother harder.

Ty awoke with a jerk and a gasp. He tried to sit up and reach for a knife Deuce knew he used to keep under his pillow, but the pillow wasn't there, and neither was the knife. He looked around wildly for a brief moment, obviously trying to figure out where he was, why his hand was tied to his body, and probably wondering why he was awake. That was, if his fevered mind even allowed him to think instead of instinctively reacting.

For all Deuce knew, Ty might think he was back in the Gulf with his Recon team.

Zane sat up and slid a hand gently up and down Ty's back, trying to calm him with soft murmurs Deuce couldn't make out. It seemed to help, and Deuce carefully watched reality seep back into Ty's eyes before he said or did anything. Even hurt and unarmed, Deuce knew his brother could be a dangerous man, especially if he was disoriented. Deuce would never have risked touching him in that state. Apparently that danger didn't apply to Zane Garrett. Something else to add to the list of things that didn't quite add up.

"You okay?" Deuce asked evenly.

Ty nodded and swallowed hard as he looked down at his hand.

"Dizzy?" Zane asked quietly. "Hot?"

"Yeah," Ty answered immediately. He didn't even try to make up a lie or deny that he was sick.

Zane lifted one hand to touch the backs of his fingers to Ty's forehead and then his cheek. Ty closed his eyes with the contact. Shaking his head slightly, Zane glanced to Deuce. There was worry shining clearly in his dark brown eyes.

"We need to get going," Deuce said needlessly.

"Let's get you up," Zane said to Ty, climbing to his knees and sliding his arm around Ty's back so he could help him stand. Ty wrapped his arm over Zane's shoulders and didn't even bother trying to hide that he couldn't have gotten up on his own.

"Fuck," Deuce muttered under his breath as he watched. He saw Zane's face slide into an immobile mask with flat, emotionless eyes as he took Ty's weight onto himself. Deuce wondered for a moment about an ability like that, to so completely suppress and hide emotion. It wasn't at all healthy. A groan from Ty drew his attention again. "You going to be able to go?" Deuce asked him in a low voice. Earl was already up and gathering their equipment.

Ty merely nodded jerkily and looked up, letting his arm slide away from Zane's shoulders. His fingers dragged slowly across the back of Zane's neck, as if he didn't want to forget what the contact felt like. Deuce felt a pang of anger and sadness as he watched them. As sick as Ty was, the two of them were still careful of showing too much intimacy for fear of how Earl would react to it. Deuce swallowed against a knot in his throat and gritted his teeth.

Zane reluctantly let Ty go, but he only took one step back as he watched Ty waver slightly. Ty closed his eyes and swallowed hard, steadying himself before he nodded to them both. Deuce knew his brother was in bad shape just by the fact that he didn't seem to be ashamed of needing help to stand.

"You ready?" Earl asked gruffly as he stood on the other side of the fire pit watching them.

"Yes, sir," Deuce and Ty muttered in unison. Zane just gave him a nod as he hefted the backpack awkwardly.

Once they crested the ridge they'd decided not to attempt the night before, the trail was too precarious to go anything but single-file. Deuce limped heavily as he kept pace with Ty, who trudged in front of him. Their father was taking point, but he kept having to stop and turn to wait for them as they lagged behind his pace.

Deuce wasn't really surprised when Ty finally came to a slow, almost rambling stop a couple hours later and merely fell to his knees without further warning. Still, it scared the hell out of him when he saw it. The fear and adrenaline overwhelmed any other emotion as Deuce clambered to get to him. Zane, bringing up the rear, almost barreled over him trying to do the same.

Ty was on his knees, eyes closed and breaths coming in harsh, pained gasps. He supported himself with just the one hand. He was sweating profusely even though he was shivering violently, his cheeks flushed with fever, and his eyes were glazed and distant, almost gray in color as he stared at the ground. Deuce reached for him, preparing to help him up.

"No," Earl barked suddenly as he went down on one knee in front of Ty. He didn't touch him; he merely ducked his head and met his son's eyes, forcing Ty to look up at him. "Get up, Marine," he ordered, his voice stern and angry.

Deuce saw Zane bristle visibly, but Deuce put a hand out to calm the man as Ty's shoulders snapped backward and he raised his head. Deuce couldn't see an ounce of recognition in his brother's eyes as he looked at Earl.

"Dad," Deuce said uncertainly, reaching out again.

"Get on your feet, Marine!" Earl growled angrily, batting Deuce's hand away before he could touch Ty and getting right in Ty's face.

Ty's chest was heaving as if he might be about to hyperventilate, but as Zane stepped forward to intercede, Ty lowered his head determinedly and pushed himself unsteadily to his feet again. Zane backed away and watched apprehensively, and Deuce stared at his father and brother in awe. The appeal to something ingrained deeper in his brother appeared to be what Ty needed. From one Marine to another. It was probably the only thing that would have kept Ty going, and Deuce wondered how Earl had known.

"You keep your feet, Staff Sergeant," Earl told Ty, pointing to the ground.

"Yes, Gunny," Ty managed to say in response, his voice a rough and tortured whisper.

Earl nodded curtly before turning and heading back down the narrow path. Deuce glanced from Ty to Zane, who looked just as unhappy as before, but that anger he'd held in his rigid shoulders was gone. He must have figured out what Earl was doing too and realized it was working better than anything they could have done. Deuce placed a calming hand on Zane's arm. Earl's words had gotten Ty to his feet. That was what mattered for now.

TY'S entire body was on fire. It felt like a sunburn that emanated from his fingers and burned out of control wherever clothing touched him. He burned, but he was so cold he had to clutch his heavy coat around him to keep his teeth from chattering, and even then he was shaking and shivering uncontrollably. The rational portion of his mind, the one that was trying to figure out how to survive, told him that the shivering was a waste of his energy. But then, so was walking. And breathing.

He distantly recognized that it wasn't the cool wind that made him shiver. He was going into septic shock. It had happened much faster than he'd realized it would, but a part of his addled mind told him that the exertion of trying to get off the mountain was sending the poisoned blood racing through his body faster than it would have if he'd been lying in a bed being given sponge baths by a pretty little nurse in white Crocs.

He concentrated on the footfalls of the man in front of him. He thought it might be his father, but if he was wrong he risked calling the Gunny "Dad," so he just kept his mouth shut and tried not to fall.

Keep your feet. Keep his feet, they'd told him. It was shameful, not being able to keep his feet in front of the others because he'd been bitten by a kitty cat.

Keep your feet, Meow Mix.

If he fell, no one could carry him. Sanchez and O'Flaherty would drag him out, but... no. No, they weren't here. Elias Sanchez was dead, shot over a year ago in New York City by a serial killer Zane Garrett had later killed. And Nick O'Flaherty was a cop in Boston, discharged just like Ty had been, thrown into the real world to make his own way. This wasn't a Recon mission. He had to keep his wits about him. He had to grasp at a thread of reality and hold onto it.

Zane Garrett. Zane was reality. Zane was here, and he was clear enough for Ty to hold onto. Zane appeared at his side from time to time as they walked, taking his arm as they went over particularly rough terrain, but then he would move away again. Still, Ty could grasp at that thread and hold it.

Ty's steps finally slowed, faltered. He stopped walking and closed his eyes, his head pounding. He wavered as a rush of noise assaulted his ears, and heat swept through him in sickening pulses. When he opened his eyes again, the edges of his vision were dark and sparkling.

His father turned around and looked at him, the man's steel gray eyes hard and disapproving when he realized Ty had stopped moving. "You keep walking, Marine," Earl said to him.

Ty's entire body trembled, and the waves of heat kept coming, but he swallowed hard and nodded obediently. He took another agonizing step, and his knee gave out. He sank to the ground against his will, his knees and his one good hand hitting the rocky ground hard as he tried to catch himself.

He tried to push himself up and failed.

"Ty!" Earl cried in alarm as he darted toward him. He no longer looked stern or angry, just as worried and scared as any father about to lose his son.

"Yes, sir," Ty managed as he tried to push himself back to his feet yet again. He lost his balance on the slight rise of the embankment, toppling over as his father caught him. He rolled to his back, knowing with a certainty that came with encroaching death that he would not be getting back up under his own power.

"They're coming for us," Earl assured him as he pulled Ty into his arms and sank slowly to the ground along with him. "I can hear 'em now, boy, just stay with us."

In the floating distance, he could hear shouts, but Ty found that he couldn't move. He fought to stay conscious. Shame washed through him, just as painful as the fever that ravished him. He had failed spectacularly in front of the only person he'd ever wanted to make proud of him. But even that shame wasn't powerful enough now to get him to his feet.

"Stay with us, son," Earl murmured into his ear pleadingly. "Hold on."

"Grady, don't you fucking dare give up after I dug you out of that basement," Zane growled from somewhere close. "You didn't give up then, and you won't give up now."

Ty's eyes fluttered open, searching for Zane's eyes. Above him, the sky was a startling blue. The scrub pine was a bright, almost neon green, and the few trees in view boasted brilliant leaves of orange and yellow and red. Ty had never seen such colors in his life. It was beautiful. The faces looking down on him looked like airbrushed photos, taken and perfected and stylized until the colors were stark contrasts of highlights and lowlights, making them look ethereal.

He met Zane's dark eyes, the eyes he'd been searching for. "Zane," he managed to gasp. He tried to think of something to say, an apology for dragging the man up here and thanks for all he'd done. *I love you.* But nothing came to his lips. He just closed his eyes, seeing Zane's face imprinted in the darkness. He held to the material of Earl's coat, trying to keep himself from spinning and swaying on the ground. "Mountain's moving," he told them all in alarm, the words slurred horribly.

"Ty," Zane barked, his voice a mixture of anger and desperation. "Open your eyes," he ordered. "Get up!"

Ty did open his eyes, but when he tried to sit up, his limbs wouldn't cooperate. He put every ounce of his energy and will into getting off the ground, but he realized with a sinking sensation that he hadn't even managed to lift his head.

"Get up, Beaumont, it ain't your time yet!" Earl called to him, sounding far away and gauzy.

He was dying. After all the things he'd been through that could and probably should have killed him, he had to go and get attacked by a goddamn mountain lion. Someone somewhere was going to find that funny.

Ty's eyes focused on the impossibly blue sky overhead as he felt himself slipping away, and the pain faded too. He idly thought that angel wings sounded a whole lot like the rotors of a chopper, and he'd really have liked the chance to tell Zane that.

~CHAPTER 16~

ZANE reflected on the past painful twelve hours as he walked tiredly down the long, door-lined hall. Mara Grady, with an assist from Chester, had lit a fire under the local search-and-rescue people as soon as they hadn't shown up on the day they'd planned—she'd actually mentioned a bad feeling; Zane was pitifully glad that she hadn't ignored it—and several rangers with dogs had found them on the mountain just as Ty collapsed. A rescue helicopter had been in their wake, and Ty had been airlifted off the mountain to this hospital in Charleston.

He'd barely made it.

The doctors assured Earl and Mara that Ty was now out of danger. He'd woken once so far to be told what had happened, only to immediately fall back into unconsciousness.

Zane turned the corner at the end of the hall and slowed as he saw Earl outside the door to Ty's hospital room. To Zane's eyes and satisfaction, Earl Grady seemed to be agonizing over the state of his son. The elder Grady stood with his arms crossed and his head down as he rubbed at his newly shaved chin and frowned, looking into the room where his son slept. He hadn't gone too far from the room, but he hadn't gone inside much, either. It was like he couldn't make up his mind. As far as Zane was concerned, he could stay outside. He wasn't feeling too charitable toward Earl Grady. If the man hadn't gone overboard insulting Ty—and fuck, Earl couldn't have thought of a worse thing to call Ty than a coward—then his son, Zane's partner, wouldn't be lying practically dead in this goddamn hospital.

Even though it had been Earl's unusual methods that kept Ty walking much longer than he should have been able, Ty's father had still been seriously out of line. Zane would never wish him real harm, but he seriously hoped the man understood and regretted what he'd done.

"Everything okay?" Zane asked as he stopped next to the older man, meaning it in general terms.

Earl turned his head slightly and gave him a weak smile and a nod. He turned back to look into the room, covering his mouth with his hand and sighing. Ty was asleep in the bed, hooked up to several IVs and his color looking better than he had even an hour before. Deuce sprawled in a chair beside the bed, snoring softly. Zane had just walked Mara downstairs to the truck; she was heading home with Chester to pack them all some clean clothes and would return in a couple hours.

"Do you know why Ty joined the FBI?" Earl asked Zane abruptly.

Zane shrugged as he leaned against the doorframe. He had lots of little pieces to Ty's puzzle: the "official" story of why he'd left the Marines, which was complete bullshit according to Ty; that his last partner had been killed in the line of duty, even though Ty had tried to take the bullet for him; that he'd known Dick Burns since he was in diapers.

"Not exactly," Zane answered.

Earl glanced at him and smiled sadly. "He joined the FBI 'cause his daddy's best friend asked him to," he told Zane softly, looking back into the room to make certain Ty and Deuce were both still asleep.

Burns. Zane didn't comment; if Earl needed to spill his guts, he could do it. But Zane was the wrong person to be looking to for any sort of absolution. He didn't forgive and forget easily, not when he could still see the pain in Ty's eyes.

Earl nodded in response to his silence, his eyes still on his sons. "Richard was paying me a visit one weekend a while back, and he was talking about work," he told Zane. "He didn't like what he was doing. Said he didn't trust any of the agents he was working with to get the job done. I remember sitting there and him looking at me with defeat on his face. He was talking about early retirement. He said to me, 'Earl, if I had just one good man I could count on, I could get a lot of good done'."

Earl swallowed heavily, cocked his head, and then turned and met Zane's eyes. "I told him where to find Ty."

"You say that like you think it was a mistake," Zane observed, shaking his head.

"It didn't give Ty much choice, me sending Richard to him," Earl answered flatly.

"No. It didn't."

Earl nodded again, as if knowing he deserved the harsh words. "Richard and I never gave a thought to what he wanted or to how dangerous it was," he said, the words quiet and solemn. "We just... we just thought Ty could handle it and carried on from there. And Ty... he'd do anything to meet what he felt like were our expectations," he told Zane as he lowered his head in apparent shame and turned away from the door, beginning to walk slowly down the hall. "Even when he was a young'un, he never made an excuse not to follow me into those mines. He was scared to death of 'em," he told Zane with a tremble in his voice. Zane realized the older man was on the verge of tearing up. "I almost lost him today," he said, almost to himself. He gave a soft snort and shook his head. "A damn wildcat," he murmured.

"I guess he figured he'd done everything spectacular already," Zane said, looking over his shoulder to glance inside the room. He didn't have to study Earl to know the man was worried. He was worried, himself. Zane frowned. As angry as he was, he couldn't bring himself to be cold and cruel to a father so obviously torn up over mistakes he'd made with his son.

How many harsh words had Zane himself said to Ty to light a fire under the man? Anyone who knew him knew that the best way to make Ty dangerous was to make him angry. It made him a useful weapon.

"He's going to be okay," Zane finally settled on. He didn't want to think about the alternative. He wondered if this was how Ty had felt when it had been him three-quarters dead in a hospital bed. Right now he felt helpless. He was hurting. He was scared that he might have lost something he wasn't even sure he'd had, and there hadn't been a damn thing he could've done about it. "He's strong," he said to Earl confidently.

Earl stopped with his back to Zane, and he looked up at the ceiling of the hallway. "I know he is," he responded with a hint of pride in his voice. "But he thinks that's enough," he said as he turned and met Zane's eyes again. "I'm relieved to see he has a good man with him," he told Zane solemnly. "Someone to watch his back."

Zane flinched in surprise. That wasn't something he'd have expected to hear from Earl Grady.

Earl nodded as he observed Zane's reaction. "I don't just say pretty words to hear myself talk, son," he informed him. "I mean it. Thank you for...." He was forced to look away and swallow hard as his voice faltered. He pressed his lips together tightly as he fought to regain control.

It was clear, seeing Earl's emotions bubble to the surface, that Earl was being truthful. It gave Zane an odd, bittersweet feeling of vindication. He'd proved himself to Earl Grady—but Ty had been seriously wounded in the process. "Yes, sir," he said quietly, watching the older man, wondering if Earl planned to apologize to Ty as well. "You might keep that in mind the next time you talk with Ty."

Earl looked back at him and lifted his chin, obviously still fighting back his emotions. "Keep what in mind, son?" he asked, managing to make his voice even once more.

"You owe him a hell of a lot more than just pretty words." Zane paused, his banked anger melting into a quiet, pained sadness. "I don't know what you thought you were doing, but you couldn't have said anything that would have hurt him more."

Earl was silent as he took a few steps toward the doorway and stared into Ty's room. The guilt and worry were clear on his face, written in the lines around his eyes and mouth. "I know," he whispered. "I'll never be able to apologize enough. I'll never be able to make that up to him. But never for one second have I thought my son was anything but what he is."

Zane was silent. There was a big difference between thought and deed, and what Earl had said up on that mountain was unforgivable. Earl sighed heavily and nodded in agreement as if he'd heard Zane's last thought loud and clear.

Deuce came shuffling out of the room, rubbing his eyes and yawning, and Zane wondered if he'd heard any of his conversation with Earl.

"How is he?" Earl asked in a whisper.

"Talking in his sleep," Deuce answered in a low voice.

"What's he saying?" Earl asked with a frown.

"I don't know," Deuce answered with a shrug as he looked at Zane and gave him a small smile. "I don't think it's even English."

"Might be Farsi," Zane murmured.

"Could be," Deuce responded with a closer look at Zane, as if he hadn't expected Zane to know Ty spoke Farsi. "But I think it's just slurred cursing."

Zane snorted. "You going to sit with him?" he asked Earl as he stepped back to give Deuce room to get through the door.

Earl's expression became more guarded, and he looked back into the room where his son lay muttering to himself. He shook his head in answer. "Not just yet. I'm gonna go hunt down some coffee," he said gruffly, and then he turned away and headed down the hallway, walking with his shoulders squared and tense.

Zane turned his eyes to Deuce. "He needs someone to talk to," he said with a sigh before rubbing his eyes.

"Dude," Deuce responded wryly. "I'm a fucking psychiatrist, and he won't talk to me," he pointed out.

A short laugh got out before Zane could stop it. "Deuce, you know we love you. But we *hate* you."

"Yeah, yeah," Deuce muttered as he turned around and looked back into Ty's room. "The whole family likes to screw with other people's heads. I'm just the only one who took it pro. But," he added with a slightly darker undertone as he looked at his brother, "Dad can sit and stew over this one for all I care." He turned his head and peered at Zane. "What'd he say to you?" he asked.

Zane took the opportunity to move into Ty's sterile-looking, sparsely decorated room as he considered how to answer. He didn't want to get into a mini-showdown with Deuce, even though it sounded as if Deuce was just as angry at Earl as Zane was. The only person who didn't seem to be seething over what had been said was Ty. Still, Zane didn't want to insult their father and make Deuce feel the need to defend him.

"He's worried about Ty," he answered as neutrally as possible. "About this and maybe his mental state in general. He was talking about why Ty joined the Bureau."

Deuce looked at him closely, then sighed and shook his head. "Yeah, I've heard that one before," he muttered dejectedly. "Dick's little side jobs," he said bitterly. "Ty's told me he's afraid one day we'll get word he was killed in a car wreck or something equally innocuous because he was on some secret mission they can't make public."

Zane glanced at Deuce, frowning hard. He had no idea what the man was talking about. He'd never heard about any secret missions or side jobs, although he supposed that might have been what Ty was doing when they were separated after the Tri-State case and Zane had been unable to track him down. He himself had been thrown back undercover, after all. With Ty being so close to the Assistant Director, there was no telling what sort of work he was trusted to undertake.

"The thing that always made Ty so good at everything he did was that he had no fear. Makes Ma and Dad sick with worry," Deuce continued with a sigh.

"He's afraid of things just like we are," Zane said as he turned his eyes on his restless partner. "He just hides it well."

"Yeah?" Deuce asked in what sounded like honest surprise. Whether it was surprise that Zane knew that or surprise that his brother was afraid of things, Zane didn't know. "Like what?" Deuce asked.

Zane didn't look away from Ty as he resisted the urge to touch him, just his arm, his shoulder, something to reassure himself that Ty really was there and breathing. "The mines, for one," he answered. "Seems reasonable to me. Small, dark spaces to get trapped in."

Deuce watched Zane as he sat down beside the bed again. "He tell you that?" he asked.

"Yeah," Zane glanced up as he slid his hands in his pockets. It was easier to keep them to himself that way. "I made the mistake of waking him up once, when he was doing this." He nodded down to Ty's active sleeping. "Figured it was a bad dream."

"Made the mistake," Deuce echoed. "What happened?"

Zane finally looked over at Deuce. "Oh, he didn't hit me or anything before he woke up," he said as the corner of his mouth turned up. "But he sure was cranky once I got his attention." His eyes slid back to Ty. It had to be the IV keeping him under now, he thought clinically. Ty usually woke up in a snap if he sensed someone close. That, or he wasn't getting better, and that didn't bear thinking about at all.

"You're lucky you just got cranky instead of hit," Deuce told him fondly.

"Yeah," Zane agreed. "After he woke up, we had a talk about things we were afraid of. How we might die. Heights. Small places with bugs," he listed off.

Deuce smiled and nodded. He looked back down at Ty, but the smile fell as he watched his brother toss and turn. "Ty has a lot of bad dreams," he said to Zane, his voice sad.

Zane wondered what Deuce expected him to say about that. Of course, the man had no idea that Zane was living with the same problem. "That's why he keeps quiet, you know."

Deuce looked up at him, still frowning. "Why?" he asked.

"So you don't have bad dreams. So your mom and dad don't have bad dreams."

Deuce looked at him for a long time before the corner of his mouth twitched into a smile. He nodded and returned his attention to Ty. "You know him better than you think you do," he said thoughtfully. "You want something to drink?" he asked as he pushed himself out of his chair.

"Yeah, sure," Zane answered as he rolled his shoulders back and realized he still had his jacket on from his last cigarette break. He shrugged out of it and tossed it over the small rolling tray table that had been pushed to the side.

"Back in a minute," Deuce said to him as he left, patting Ty's bare foot as he passed the end of the bed.

Ty groaned as the door to the room clicked when Deuce opened it, and his foot twitched where he'd been touched. Zane shook his head. The last time they'd been together in a hospital room, it had been him in the bed. He remembered it hazily because he'd been so drugged. But he could still see the upset expression on Ty's face when he'd announced that he had to leave while Zane had to stay. He remembered a short, gentle kiss. And he remembered the guilt on Ty's face when he'd told Ty to go while he was too drugged to stop him.

Sighing, Zane paced around the bed and sat in the chair crammed between the bed and the window. As he sat down, the chair jarred the bed a little. Ty flailed under the thin hospital sheet, both arms and both feet coming off the bed like a baby who'd been startled. His IV rattled, and the plastic side rails of the bed banged noisily as Ty gasped and tried to sit up.

Zane leaned forward. "Be careful," he cautioned. He reached to try to catch Ty's flailing arm and save the IV. "It's okay; you're okay."

Ty hissed as the IV tugged, and he put his hand over the line and looked up at Zane accusingly. Rolling his eyes, Zane sat back. "Welcome back to the land of the living."

Ty responded with a grunt as he looked down at the cast on his hand and the IV in his arm. He looked around at the room and then over at Zane with narrowed eyes. "Hungry," he muttered, his voice rough and hoarse. "You ate my lunch, huh?" he asked.

"And it was yummy too," Zane drawled. He was relieved to find that Ty must have remembered the last time he woke when they'd told him what had happened. Ty had not taken it well when he'd been told the cast would have to stay on his hand for a minimum of three weeks, and Zane had been dreading the possibility of having to tell him again. There was a chipped bone in there somewhere, and the doctors wanted the entire hand immobilized just to keep any infections from spreading further as the antibiotics did their job.

Ty glared briefly before allowing a slow smile. His eyes drifted closed, and his shoulders slowly began to relax. "How long have I been asleep?" he asked as he forced his eyes open again.

"Twelve hours, give or take," Zane said as he leaned back in the chair. "How much better than roadkill do you feel?"

"Depends," Ty muttered. "Never felt roadkill."

Zane's lips quirked as he leaned forward and propped his elbows on his knees. "Deuce is real torn up," he said seriously. He wasn't even going to mention Earl.

Ty's chin jerked to the side, and he looked at Zane with wide eyes. "Why, what happened?" he asked worriedly.

"Over you, jackass." Zane bit back the rest of what he was about to say before shaking his head. "It was close. We almost didn't get you here in time."

A hurt look flashed through Ty's eyes before he looked away, concentrating on the hand that was resting in his lap instead. "Oh," he responded, abashed.

"Yeah, oh." Zane rubbed at his eyes again. He would have to sleep soon. He hadn't managed more than a few minutes stolen here and there since reaching the hospital, and he'd never slept more than a couple hours at a time on the mountain. He was still too jumpy, even being so exhausted. All he wanted was Ty in a bed next to him and a week to do nothing. "He wasn't the only one worried," he muttered, although he figured Ty wouldn't appreciate it.

Ty glanced at him and winced. "Wasn't exactly the relaxing vacation it was supposed to be," he agreed slowly as he began to poke at the plaster of his cast and pluck at the tufts of gauze sticking out of it.

Zane just had to chuckle. "No, it hasn't been. Christ." He shut his eyes and leaned back against the chair.

"Well, it would've been," Ty insisted under his breath. He sniffed and looked around before asking, "They go home?" He sounded forlorn.

"No. Deuce is getting us drinks. Mara's back home with Chester, but she's coming back soon. And Earl's taking a walk."

Ty sighed and closed his eyes, resting back into the bed. "Taking a walk, huh?" he asked, resigned.

"Would you please look at me?" Zane asked. Ty needed to understand how Earl was reacting to this mess. If he chose to keep lying to him after, that was his business. Ty forced his eyes open and turned his head to look over at Zane blearily. "He's not angry," Zane said. "He's upset about what happened up on that mountain and about what he said to you. All this hospital shit just put some lovely little icing swirls on that apple pie of your mom's. Understand?"

Ty stared at him blankly for several beats before frowning. "Someone brought pie?" he finally asked in confusion.

Zane stared at him passively for a long moment before standing up and walking around the bed. "All right, lay back down," he murmured, pulling the pillows back into a pile for Ty to lean against. "I should've remembered you're still drugged to the gills. And I forgot what you've said about meds making you funny sometimes."

Ty made a noise of agreement and carefully turned onto his side, taking advantage of Zane's help to find a more comfortable position. "They don't make me funny," Ty argued. "I'm always funny," he told Zane as he fingered the IV line. Then he turned his face up to look at Zane. "Do I get any of the pie?" he asked earnestly as he reached up to pull out the oxygen line that rested under his nose.

The rest of the irritation drained out of Zane as he calmly retrieved the line and replaced it. "Yeah, sure," he answered, straightening out the sheet so it wasn't bunched up around Ty's legs. When he was done, he reached out to rest the backs of his fingers against Ty's forehead.

Ty's eyes fluttered closed at the contact, and he gave a heavy sigh. He didn't even try to pull out the oxygen line again. "Tell Dad I'm sorry," he requested sleepily.

"Don't worry about that right now," Zane chided gently as he rubbed along the beard Ty had grown. In his opinion, it was Earl that owed the apology. Only a real fool would call Ty a coward in *any* situation. Ty nodded, but it was obvious that he was already drifting off again. "It's all right," Zane murmured, still petting. "It'll keep."

Behind him, someone cleared his throat softly to announce his presence, and when Zane turned, Deuce smiled slightly at him. "Got you a Coke," he said as he held out a bottle. "Was he awake?"

Zane shuffled a little as he straightened, surprised that he'd been caught off guard. But Ty had a way of holding all his attention. He accepted the bottle with a nod. "Thanks," he said, wondering what, if anything, Deuce might have seen.

Deuce twisted off the cap to his own bottle as he walked around the end of the bed, his head down and a small, worried smile on his face. "It's more than convenience, isn't it?" he asked Zane as he sat down.

"What's more than convenience?" Zane was deliberately obtuse as he opened his own bottle.

"You and my brother," Deuce answered bluntly.

"As partners, it's generally advisable that you at least tolerate each other most of the time," Zane spun out. "Sometimes it takes more effort than others."

"You're not as good at evading a question as he is," Deuce advised with a nod at Ty. "He knows there's no pie," he told Zane with a small smile.

"You sure about that?" Zane asked, raising an eyebrow.

Deuce shrugged and leaned forward to put a hand gently on Ty's shoulder. Ty twitched with the contact and muttered something unintelligible. Deuce pursed his lips and looked back up at Zane. "He knew the drugs would get him soon. He was just stalling until he fell back asleep. He'll never talk about dad to anyone. Never has, never will." He leaned back and threw his feet up onto the edge of the bed. "I'm not trying to put you in a tight spot," he assured Zane quietly, reverting back to their other discussion. "I've just never met anyone he was serious about," he explained.

Zane forced himself not to react, to just take a drink. *Serious.* Then he let himself look at Deuce. "And you think you have now?"

Deuce shrugged nonchalantly. "When I say never, Zane, I mean it. I've known him all my life. He never had a junior high crush. He never had a high school sweetheart. Even when he was in service and going through college, there was no one he was even remotely hung up on. There was always something more important to him than being in a relationship. The Corps. His Bronco. Football. His favorite Crayola sleeping bag," he said with a hint of a smile. "I like you, man. I think you must be good for him. But just remember what I'm telling you before you start thinking too hard. I don't think he'd even know what to do with himself if he loved someone."

Zane's heart tried to pound harder, and he took a slow, steady breath, reminding himself that Deuce's comment about love didn't apply to him. He still had to swallow hard. "I know what's important to him," he finally settled on. "And his partner's not at the top of the list." He actually gave Deuce an honest, though wry, smile.

Deuce returned it with a sad one of his own and looked down at his brother once more. He waited for a moment before glancing back up at Zane. "I would argue differently," he stated finally. "Just don't let Dad find out," he advised in a near whisper.

"You know, I have no idea what you're talking about," Zane muttered, turning his gaze back to Ty, who was tossing fitfully again. Zane thought his own stomach was tossing just as badly now as he looked at his partner. At his *lover*.

"Yeah, I get that a lot," Deuce replied with a long-suffering sigh before taking a drink from his bottle of Mountain Dew.

"Because there's no way I'd willingly talk to a shrink about my partner," Zane added, still not looking at Deuce as his hand crunched the plastic Coke bottle a little.

"Certainly not," Deuce agreed amiably. "Not that you have anything you need to get off your chest, anyway, am I right?" he said.

"Not a thing. All is right in the world," Zane continued, making himself ignore the tightness in his chest and focus on what he and Ty did best. "And Ty and I might just get through two days without a fight. Now, I said 'might', mind you." He looked at his watch. "Two hours to go. It'll be a new record."

"You fight a lot, then?" Deuce asked in a casual tone.

"That's an understatement," Zane groused before taking another swallow of his drink.

"Is this on-the-job fighting or after hours?" Deuce inquired curiously.

"I have yet to determine that there is any difference." Zane paused. "Any *appreciable* difference," he corrected himself, thinking about how they got along at the office as opposed to in the bed in his hotel suite.

"I gather it's not unresolved sexual tension," Deuce observed. "Could it be, deep down, maybe you enjoy the fighting?" he suggested in an offhand manner.

Zane snorted. "It's not deep down. We really do enjoy... fighting." He made himself take another drink to stop the smile, his eyes still focused on Ty. God, he wished Ty would wake up and argue with him right now. It would go a long way toward reassuring him that Ty was going to be okay. He could really go for a good fight, one where they yelled about something stupid and pushed each other around and ended up fucking each other silly and then holding each other all night after. He remembered their quiet talk in front of the fire in the trail cabin, where he'd deliberately told Ty something about himself that he knew full well Ty would take advantage of. More ammunition.

"So your observation that you may go forty-eight hours without a fight is actually one of disappointment," Deuce surmised clinically. "The way you express your appreciation of each other is through insults and barbs. Once you start being nice to each other, it signifies an ebb in interest," he pointed out with a smirk.

"We're never nice to each oth—" Zane cut himself off and twitched. He couldn't tear his eyes away from Ty, even knowing Deuce was watching, and Zane knew right then and there that he wouldn't be giving Ty up without a fight. Ever. He squeezed his eyes shut for a moment before turning a glare on Deuce.

Deuce merely raised one eyebrow and smiled in return. "And how does that make you *feel*, Special Agent Garrett?" he asked in a slow drawl.

Zane rolled his eyes, reached out, and popped Deuce on the back of the head, just like his mom did. "Asshole," he muttered as he tried to suppress the panic threatening at the edge of his awareness.

Deuce laughed softly and twisted the cap back onto his bottle. "You're welcome," he said smugly.

"You better hope he's really asleep," Zane threatened.

"Because you don't want him knowing how you feel about him?" Deuce asked.

Zane's shoulders tightened. "He knows enough. Why else would we fight all the time?"

Deuce examined him for a long while before turning his eyes back to his sleeping brother. "I don't know about that. Has he already started being nice to you?" he asked gently.

"We have our moments," Zane allowed reluctantly, knowing he was contradicting himself.

"And you don't know if that's just him being a decent human being or if it's that he's lost interest in trying to goad you on," Deuce supplied softly.

Tipping his head sideways, Zane met Deuce's eyes. "We're partners. We don't have to be at each other's throats all the time," he said with a slight shrug.

Deuce sat with his feet still propped on the bed and his arm resting on the side of the chair. He ran his finger back and forth across his lower lip as he watched Zane. "Ty has a protective streak a mile wide," he finally said. "He always has. He takes a lot on himself. He doesn't like to be leaned on because he's terrified of letting people down. So being charged with protecting something, especially if it's a job he's not sure he can do, it's something that weighs heavy on him. So when he has a choice, he only protects the things he holds close to his heart," Deuce continued, giving his chest a pat.

"And?"

"That's for you to figure out, Zane," Deuce answered with a shrug.

Zane didn't have anything else to say. He was pretty sure Ty cared about him, just as he cared about Ty. They were partners. They watched out for one another. They depended on each other. Only Zane was finding himself more and more attached to Ty—and that was something that scared him.

Deuce sat silently as Zane mulled it over, the hiss of his bottle cap as he twisted it off the only sound he made. "I'll send Ty the bill," he finally said with a small smile.

~CHAPTER 17~

"SHOULD he be traveling as sick as he is?" Mara Grady asked worriedly as she fussed back and forth between Ty and the pies she was preparing in the kitchen. "Maybe he should stay here until he's feeling better."

"I'm feeling better, Ma," Ty called out from where he sat on the couch, covered in blankets and holding a mug of hot chocolate his mother had shoved into his hands.

"You are not," she insisted from the kitchen as she banged a pie plate onto the counter and began rattling utensils and plates.

"God hates me," Ty muttered from under one of the heavy quilts she had draped over him.

Zane snorted from where he was sprawled in a rocking chair across from the couch, under an afghan of his own. Mara had taken to mothering him too. "If God hated you that cat would have bitten you somewhere more sensitive," he said, teasing.

"Yeah, wait 'til the drugs wear off and I can tell which one of you is real," Ty grumbled at him. He sniffed at the air as the smell of apple pie began to waft to them.

"When do you have to go?" Mara called.

"Leave the boy alone," Earl told her from his seat in the kitchen, and their voices dropped as they continued talking quietly to each other. Ty sat and scowled at Zane.

"I'd say it'll freeze that way, but you might like it to," Zane murmured as he rocked, the chair squeaking a little.

"When are we leaving?" Ty asked.

Zane was quiet for a long moment as he watched Ty. "I'm leaving tomorrow."

Ty inclined his head and frowned harder. "You're not leaving me here," he whispered harshly.

"Don't you think you need to rest and heal up instead of driving all the way back to Baltimore?" Zane asked. "It'll be a hell of a lot easier for you to fly home. It's only a short drive to the airport in Charleston."

"Don't you think you should be baking pies or something?" Ty responded gruffly.

"I bet you already know how," Zane said. *"Deliverance."*

"What the hell does that have to do with pie?" Ty asked in annoyance.

"Just a comment about your wide and varied skills." Zane paused. "Of which healing seems to need some practice."

"I heal just fine," Ty argued. "And you're one to talk," he added, pointing at the colorful bruise that stretched from his very black eye along the full line of Zane's cheekbone, which was apparently so painful that Zane hadn't shaved his beard off yet. Zane wrinkled his nose and winced.

"You boys want more hot chocolate?" Mara called out as Deuce came thumping into the living room and threw himself onto the couch beside Ty.

"No, ma'am," Ty and Deuce both called out.

"I'm good, thanks," Zane answered as he gave Ty a disbelieving look.

"What?" Ty asked him defensively.

"All I'm saying is, you have a chance to kick back and relax, have someone take care of you. Maybe you should take advantage of it."

Ty blinked at Zane slowly and pushed the quilt off his head as he leaned forward. "Do I look relaxed to you?" he asked in a low voice.

Beside him, Deuce began to chuckle softly. Zane raised an eyebrow, still rocking gently. Ty began to struggle with the heavy quilt, trying to get out from under it. Deuce moved beside him, pulling the edge of the quilt out from under himself in an attempt to help, and Ty growled as the throbbing in his hand got worse and worse.

"What do you need?" Mara asked as she came into the living room with a tray of more hot chocolate and set it on the coffee table. "Stop your fussing," she ordered as she swatted Deuce away and re-covered Ty with the quilt he'd just managed to get off.

"You're killing me, Ma," Ty protested as he began struggling with the quilt again, fighting against the cumbersome cast on his hand. "Killing me," he muttered with emphasis as she tutted and headed back to the kitchen.

Zane watched the circus with a slight smile, looking back and forth between Ty and Deuce.

"Stop it," Ty told him in a growl.

Deuce began to laugh softly. "She just misses you," he offered. "Let her baby you some. She'll let up," he advised.

"I'd be more tempted to listen to you if you weren't snickering gleefully while you said it," Ty told him. "Garrett, when are we leaving?" he asked Zane stubbornly as he gave up the fight against the quilt and started trying to go the other way instead, lifting it up over his head.

"Your family wants to spend some time with you," Zane reminded him gently. "Without someone around to remind you about work, I'd guess."

"I can see them any time," Ty countered.

Deuce cleared his throat pointedly, and Ty growled at him as he finally extricated himself from the quilt and tossed it on the floor triumphantly. Zane was shaking his head slightly, the look on his face pretty much classing that answer as bullshit. Deuce was looking at him in much the same manner.

Ty rolled his eyes at both of them and sighed. He sat silently for a moment, trying to ignore them and the intense throbbing in his hand. Finally, he looked around the room and pursed his lips. "It's kinda cold in here, huh?" he muttered as he leaned forward and retrieved the quilt to wrap up in it again.

"Zane'll take care of your Bronco. If you don't want to fly, I'll drive you home at the end of the week," Deuce offered.

"And I promise I'll take care of your Bronco," Zane repeated.

Ty sighed and glanced sideways at his brother. He couldn't honestly say he wanted to go anywhere but to bed. "Don't look at me," Deuce told him as he leaned forward and picked up a mug of hot chocolate. "I'm not a couples counselor," he reminded.

Ty jerked in surprise, but he recovered quickly and jabbed at his brother in retaliation, causing him to spill the hot liquid in his mug all over his lap.

Zane chuckled at their antics. Without warning, he shifted and stood. "I'm going to see if I can sleep until dinner," he murmured. "I can't drive home like this." And he started toward the stairs.

Deuce was standing and patting gingerly at the fronts of his thighs, and Ty watched Zane go as he hid himself behind the quilt. When Zane's feet disappeared up the steps, Deuce turned and swatted at Ty, gesturing that he should follow.

"What?" Ty asked defensively.

"Go talk to him," Deuce ordered in a whisper.

"You go talk to him," Ty hissed.

"Go talk to him, and I'll keep Ma and Dad off your back while you're here," Deuce bargained.

Ty glowered at him, but after a moment he sighed and stood, tossing the quilt aside. "What do I talk to him about?" he asked uncomfortably.

"Figure it out," Deuce answered as he shoved his mug into Ty's hands and headed for the kitchen to get a towel.

Ty looked down at the marshmallows that swirled in the mug and then up at the stairs with a deep sigh. He set the mug on the table and headed for the stairs unsteadily, trudging up to his old room in search of his partner.

He knocked softly on the door before pushing it open slightly. Not only had Zane left the door unlocked, but he was lying on the bed, on his side, with his back to the door. Ty stood in the doorway for a long moment, frowning. It was unusual behavior from his very paranoid partner. Maybe that meant he felt safe here. That thought actually made Ty smile. "You want to tell me why I owe my brother five hundred dollars?" he asked finally as he began moving into the room. Zane didn't even twitch, his cheek pushed against the pillow as he lay totally still. Ty sat on the edge of the bed next to him. "Did it help?" he asked softly.

"Did what help?"

"Talking with him," Ty answered as he leaned to one side, trying to see Zane's face.

Another long pause, and Zane's shoulder moved slightly. "More than I'd rather admit," he muttered.

"You think it might help to talk to him again?" Ty asked carefully.

"Can your wallet handle such abuse?"

"If it would help."

Zane finally moved, rolling toward Ty to look up at him. "I think Deuce has the wrong idea about us."

Ty resisted the urge to ask for further details. If it had to do with whatever he'd talked about with Deuce, then it needed to stay with Zane for now unless he wanted it out. Zane had to know that if he did decide to seek out help with Ty's brother, what they said was safe even from Ty.

He was also scared to ask what the *right* idea about them might be.

"He knows we're screwing around," Ty finally responded with a negligent shrug. It was the only thing he could think to say.

"You told him?" Zane asked.

"He's smarter than I am," Ty argued.

"Clearly," Zane murmured. "You should listen to him sometimes."

"What makes you think I don't?" Ty asked.

Zane studied him for a moment before shifting to lie on his back so he could look up at him, and he rubbed his eyes again. "I'm too tired to play word games right now."

"I'm not playing games," Ty assured him. "Look, Garrett," he sighed as he turned and leaned over him. "Wouldn't you rather talk with Deuce than some random Bureau shrink?" he asked, wincing inwardly as he waited for Zane's reaction.

Zane sighed, reached up to curl his hand over Ty's nape, and tugged down gently. Ty allowed it warily, not certain what to expect. When Ty was close enough, Zane kissed him gently for mere seconds and then released him.

"Thanks," Zane whispered.

Ty pressed his forehead to Zane's with a hint of relief. This was one step in the right direction, anyway. The sooner he got Zane back on track, the sooner they'd be in the field again. He cocked his head, looking into Zane's exhausted eyes. He wanted to say more. He wanted to ask Zane what he'd meant earlier when he'd mentioned "them" as if they were a unit. But he supposed his father was right; he was too much of a coward to ask.

"I can see your thoughts running in circles in your eyes," Zane said softly, his fingers ruffling in the hair at the base of Ty's neck.

Ty pulled back, his eyes darting back and forth as he looked into Zane's. He was too worn out to think of anything to say in return other than to ask, "What?"

"You're thinking hard about something," Zane said. "Something you're not happy about. It shows. To me at least." He smiled, but it immediately faded. "Probably because I've seen it so much lately."

Ty sighed and shook his head. "Usually I hide the thinking thing better," he tried in a wry voice.

"You don't have to hide from me," Zane told him quietly. "Lord knows I've probably seen you near your worst."

Ty gave that a small smile. "You're right," he acknowledged. "But I'm not hiding from you."

"So what are you thinking about? Will you tell me?"

Ty held his breath as he considered the request. It wasn't out of line. And Zane was right; he'd seen Ty at his very worst. Any opinions he might form about Ty's weaknesses, either physical or mental, had long ago been formed.

"I was thinking about being afraid of things," he admitted.

Zane didn't say anything right away. He tipped his head slightly to one side as he studied Ty, and then he moved, scooting over on the bed and drawing Ty down to lay next to him. "Things like dark rooms," he said softly. "Small spaces," he clarified. "You seemed to handle being out on the mountain in the dark okay."

Ty was already shaking his head in answer. "Do you... do you think turning back up there would have been cowardice?" he asked slowly.

"No," Zane answered immediately. "You heard me disagree with Earl from the start. We were four men of various capabilities, very lightly armed, in unknown territory with no resources and no idea who or what we were facing. We should have gotten to safety and sent back people who were equipped to handle it." His fingers clenched where they draped over Ty's hip. "We were lucky. Real damn lucky."

Ty didn't respond as he met Zane's eyes. Those were the same things he'd been telling himself up until he'd run into bigger things to worry about. But the hint of doubt lingered. He was too tired to try and conceal the emotion.

Zane lifted his hand and cupped Ty's cheek, turning Ty's chin so he couldn't look away. "You listen to me, Beaumont Tyler Grady. You are a wise-cracking, stubborn, annoying pain in the ass who lives to cause trouble. You're also a brave, courageous, and valiant Marine who puts his life on the line for what he believes and for those he loves. There is no way you have ever been or ever will be a coward. It simply isn't in you."

Ty stared at him in shock. It was the nicest thing Zane had ever said to him. Possibly the nicest thing *anyone* had ever said to him. He had no idea how to respond, and he realized his mouth was hanging open slightly as he tried to think of something to say. The corner of Zane's mouth curled up into a half-smile, and he moved one hand to slide his fingers lightly over Ty's lips. Ty blinked rapidly at him. "Thanks, Zane," he finally managed to say. It felt silly to say it. But it was the only thing coming to mind. At least he was no longer afraid of making a fool of himself in front of Zane. He wouldn't be able to function at this point if he worried about *that*.

Zane hummed slightly, and his eyes remained trained on Ty. When he spoke, it came out a little deeper. "Well, don't get used to it. I expect a lot more fighting in our future. That's how we get along best, remember?"

Ty gave him a weak smile and nodded.

Zane shook his head and poked Ty in the ribs. "Quit thinking so hard," he said as he tried to muffle a yawn. He curled his arm around Ty's waist and dragged him close enough that their bodies bumped gently from chest to knee. "Sleep," he murmured, his lips close to Ty's temple.

Ty swallowed hard and closed his eyes, turning his face into Zane's and inhaling his scent deeply. Just as it always did, it sent a thrill through him and caused a dull ache to start in his chest.

What he was afraid of, he'd come to realize, was not dark spaces or falling from great heights or being buried alive. His greatest fears, in the end, were letting down those he loved and saying the words "I love you" without any hope of hearing them in return.

He knew, deep down somewhere, that if he fell for Zane Garrett, he'd be falling alone.

RICHARD BURNS sat back in his chair with a long sigh. He waited a few moments to ponder what Earl Grady had related to him on the phone. It had been a week since Earl and the boys had made it off the mountain, but he was just now getting the full story. At first blush, it was hard to tell whether the debacle would fall under FBI jurisdiction. It might be handled by the Parks Department or the local law enforcement. Hell, treasure hunters and a booby-trapped mountain could even fall to the National Guard. Burns really hoped the Bureau wouldn't need to deal with it.

A team of rangers had located two of the dead men, although they'd had to comb several miles down a ravine for one of them. The shooting was being half-heartedly investigated, but Burns had no doubt Zane would be cleared. He had three good men vouching that he'd saved Ty's life and that deadly force had been required. There was no trace of the third hunter. And so far four bodies of missing hikers had been found in the area of the main camp.

The only thing that concerned Burns was how Earl and the boys were handling themselves since they'd come off the mountain. Burns knew there was going to be some fallout over the events Earl Grady had described. Earl had sounded close to tears as he'd told Burns about what he'd said to his son. Burns had been dumbfounded as he listened, unable to do anything but call his old friend an idiot and tell him to fix it.

Whether Ty or Earl would ever get around to fixing it was the real question. And knowing Ty like he did, it might just roll off him like water off a duck. It was hard to predict what would hit that boy hard and what would glance off. Ty had been through a lot of things like they were a walk in the park, things that would have mentally destroyed a lot of people. But when his cat had died of old age a few years ago, Ty had been inconsolable for a week.

Burns told himself not to worry. Things would be resolved, or they wouldn't. It was one family affair he would stay out of if at all possible.

They were all home safe now, anyway, which was sort of a miracle considering Ty had stayed in West Virginia for a third week of vacation along with Deuce. Burns kept expecting to hear about a mushroom cloud appearing over the West Virginia mountains.

Zane Garrett had returned to DC earlier than his partner, but as Burns had ordered, he hadn't turned up at the office at all and hadn't made a single noise about the extra week of vacation tacked on to his original three. Burns did know, through regular channels, that Garrett had shown up at the Bureau clinic and requested an appointment; he'd been attending the therapy sessions like clockwork, and the results were already very promising. Apparently, whatever had happened up on that mountain had convinced Zane that he needed to get himself together.

Burns sat staring at the packet of transfer papers on his desk, tapping it with his finger. Zane had passed all his evals earlier that day—blowing the academic end out of the water, as per usual; showing an excellent score on the physical; and squeaking by on the psych exam, to Burns' relief. Ty was almost fully recovered from his ordeal with the cat, although he'd be in the cast for a couple more weeks, probably. They were about ready to be reinserted into light fieldwork. Burns needed to sign these last papers, and the transfers to Baltimore would be final.

He just needed to know one thing before he could in good conscience put Grady and Garrett on another assignment together. He picked up his personal cell phone and hit the speed dial.

"Talk to me, son," Burns requested after the man answered. He pushed the button to turn on the speaker and set the phone on his desk. "I need you to tell me about them."

"First of all, sir, I feel the need to reiterate my extreme discomfort with this situation," the voice emitting from the speaker said seriously.

"Believe me, son, I know it feels a little dirty. But it's for his own good," Burns responded wearily. He was so tired of worrying, and he knew that while it felt slightly wrong to be doing this, it would also ease his mind both professionally and personally. "You know how hard-headed he is, he'd never let us do this with his knowledge. Now tell me what you know."

"Sir—"

"Deacon," Burns bit off sharply. "I would not ask this of you if it weren't important. Please. I don't want to hear about Garrett, there's doctor/patient privilege involved now," he said before Deuce Grady could remind him of the fact. For all the rules the Grady brothers had stretched, bent, crossed, and broken over the years, Deuce was admirably inflexible when it came to his work.

"Ty also speaks to me with the expectation of confidence," Deuce murmured. "It feels wrong to talk about him to you, Dick."

Burns knew how Deuce felt. Dirty and dishonest. Burns had felt that way when he'd all but ordered Ty to go home. He'd felt that way when he'd called Deuce to request he observe them closely. But he knew that if the Gradys weren't as close as family to him, he wouldn't be dealing with these issues at all. He'd just send Ty to a therapist and get a nice clinical evaluation of his mental state and then send Ty and Zane together to determine how they worked as a team.

But Ty had too much psychological training to go to a psychiatrist and not say just what needed to be said. He had to be tricked into it. And until just recently, Zane had to be pushed with a cattle prod to even get him into the doctor's office.

"I don't want to know what Ty talks to you about," Burns assured him softly. "Just tell me," he continued sympathetically, "is he still—"

"Sane?" Deuce provided flatly.

290 | Madeleine Urban & Abigail Roux

Burns sighed loudly. "Is he?"

"I've never seen him like he was up there on the mountain, Dick," Deuce confided. "But then, I've never seen him at work, so that could just be how he handles the stress of nearly being killed all the time. Hard to say. In my professional opinion, he's nuttier than squirrel shit," he claimed. Burns laughed before he could stop himself. That was what all the Bureau shrinks thought too. "But as his brother, I'd say he's as sane as he's ever been," Deuce continued confidently. "I'm not certain how many more of your little special cases he can go on and remain that way, though," he added disapprovingly.

Burs pursed his lips and scowled. "I don't want to know how you know about those cases," he grumbled. "When he's done he'll tell me," he stated in a voice that said that line of conversation was done. "Do they function as a team?" Burns asked slowly. "That's all I want to know, Deacon. Can I, in good conscience, keep them together and expect them both to live through it?"

Deuce was silent. Burns could hear him tapping a pen on a pad of paper as he mulled over the question. "I think," Deuce drew out hesitantly, "'function' is perhaps too strong a word."

Burns closed his eyes and placed a hand over his forehead, feeling his heart sink.

"My brother would take a bullet for his partner," Deuce added assuredly. "I mean, we know that from experience. The thing is, it wouldn't matter who his partner was. He just thinks that's part of his job. And his goal in life is to do his job well."

Burns nodded silently. Anyone who knew Ty even a little bit knew that much. He had always been driven toward something no one else could see, and he still was. It seemed like the man felt his purpose in life had always been to die for a cause. He had been trying to get himself killed ever since he could walk.

Burns could count on one hand the number of times Ty Grady had told him "no" in the past six or seven years. He was always ready, always willing, and always more than capable of doing whatever Burns needed. It was one reason he was so valuable. And one reason he scared the ever-loving bejeezus out of Burns.

"The real interesting thing, though, is that Zane Garrett would do the same for Ty," Deuce concluded.

Burns raised his head and stared at the phone. "Really?" he asked in unconcealed surprise.

Deuce laughed softly. "I believe so, yes. As a unit, they are largely uncooperative, unorganized, antagonistic toward each other, stubborn when problems arise, and they conceal their weaknesses from each other and sometimes from themselves. But somehow, it works for them. They trust each other. They're fiercely loyal to each other, as well. When there's an outside force working against them, they pull it together in one way or another and defend one another. Viciously, if need be. Zane Garrett stood up to my father, Dick. More than once." He paused to allow that information to sink in and then continued. "In my professional opinion, they aren't fit to be partnered with anyone *but* each other," he said wryly. "They'd drive anyone else crazy."

Burns sagged his shoulders in relief, sitting back in his leather chair with a sigh. He hadn't even wanted to consider the nightmare of trying to find Grady and Garrett new partners. They would've had to have both gone solo, and that meant undercover for Ty and a desk for Zane. Neither of which would end well.

"The only issue I can see arising in the future is... personal," Deuce said in a careful voice.

"How do you mean?" Burns asked with a frown.

"I still can't tell if they like each other or not," Deuce answered with a small laugh.

Burns smiled slightly. "Well. We'll just have to see, I suppose. Thank you, Deacon," he murmured. "I owe you one."

"Yes, sir, you do," Deuce assured him. He ended the call before Burns could respond.

After a long moment's consideration, Burns reached to press the intercom button on his desk. "Get me Ty Grady on the phone, please," he requested of his secretary.

"Um, sir?" she responded uncertainly. "He's here."

"What?" Burns asked in surprise.

"Special Agent Grady is sitting out here, waiting to see you," she said with a hint of suspicion in her voice.

"He's *waiting*?" Burns asked in disbelief. Ty had never sat out there patiently and waited to be seen. "Send him in," he requested, alarmed. He stood as Ty was shown into the office.

"You look better than I thought you would," he told the younger man as soon as the door was closed.

Ty gave him a game smile and moved to take a seat across from Burns. Burns slowly sat down again.

"When I started with the Bureau," Ty said without further small talk, "you told me there were three situations where I could quit your... personal missions," he said haltingly.

Burns nodded slowly, a hint of worry forming. "If you ever got married, had a child, or felt you were physically or mentally incapable of performing," he listed off in slight trepidation.

Ty nodded. He looked determined, and Burns wondered how much time Ty had taken to work up the nerve to have this conversation. "Sir, I'm not getting married," he said. "And I'm not a father. And I can honestly say that I do believe I'm still capable, physically and mentally," he said firmly. "But I would like to request a temporary break to the assignments, nonetheless," he said in a voice that was confident, if a little sad.

Burns could see clearly that Ty had anguished over this decision. His heart went out to the kid, and he wondered what had happened to precipitate this sort of decision. Was it what had happened on the mountain or had this been a long time in coming? Either way, Ty had lasted longer than Burns had ever expected.

He found himself nodding. "Care to share the reason?" he asked. Ty blinked at him, the only change to his expression as he sat stiffly in the seat across from Burns. Burns cocked his head sympathetically. "Would you tell me as a friend, rather than your boss?" he asked softly.

Ty lowered his head, linking his fingers together. "It's nothing… bad," he assured Burns finally. "There're just some things I need to take care of—personal things—before I give any more of my time," he explained, looking up to meet Burns' eyes from under lowered brows.

Burns found himself nodding again, realizing that he'd grant any request Ty made right now. He looked determined, if nothing else, and Burns wondered what could have finally found a place in Ty's life that he put ahead of his job. Burns would never have thought it possible. He hoped Ty wasn't lying to him and that it really was something good, rather than something that had happened on that mountain.

"Thank you, sir," Ty murmured as he stood again.

Burns stood with him, coming around the desk to walk him to the door. "Ty," Burns said worriedly as he reached out and took Ty's shoulder to stop him. "I heard about what happened," he said with a deep frown.

Ty nodded, meeting Burns' eyes apprehensively. "Dad told you?" he asked.

"He did. You did well, son," Burns told him sincerely. "You made us both proud." Ty merely nodded again, swallowing hard and turning away. "He told me what he said to you up there," Burns told him unflinchingly.

Ty froze, his fingers gripping the handle of the door until his knuckles turned white. He turned slightly, his head still bowed. He looked as if he might want to say something, but Burns realized with an ache deep in his chest that Ty wasn't capable of speaking as he tried to regain control of his emotions. Ty and Deuce were the sons he'd never had, and it pained him to see one of them struggling like this.

"You're no coward, Beaumont, and your daddy knows that better than anyone," Burns told him softly. Ty bowed his head and closed his eyes. Burns fought the impulse to pull him into a hug.

"Sticks and stones, sir," Ty finally managed to respond. He raised his head again, nodding at Burns. While he looked resigned, he actually smiled before turning and leaving the office. "But words will never hurt me," he recited in a singsong voice as he walked away.

Burns stood in the office door, watching him go with a small smile. Ty was truly a resilient man. He enjoyed life too much to let anything get him down for long.

Burns remembered suddenly that he hadn't told Ty about the reassignment he had for them. Ty would be ecstatic to hear that Zane Garrett was already settling into a new Baltimore apartment and that the Gummi worms he'd hidden in his old desk in the Baltimore field office had been located and cleared out in anticipation of his return.

"Grady," Burns called, gesturing for Ty to come back. He smiled widely, causing Ty to raise an eyebrow warily as he stopped in the doorway that led out of the front office. "I almost forgot. I have some good news," he said, gesturing him to return and slapping him on the back as he directed him to sit back down.

STACKING another empty box off to the side of the couch, Zane looked around at his progress. Not that he had all that much to unpack—he'd gotten rid of more stuff over the past few years than he'd acquired. So it was mostly books, not knickknacks or pictures. It wasn't cozy or decorated, but it was home now.

His new apartment in Baltimore was a ground level walk-up with a back door, which he liked. He always liked back doors. There was enough room out on the back porch for a small grill too, and he thought he might enjoy doing something that mundane for a change.

Zane hummed slightly and slid the last of the books onto the shelf, and his fingers lingered on the volume of Edgar Allen Poe stories before he headed to the kitchen for a drink.

A knock at the front door stopped him. Frowning, Zane turned to look at the door before glancing at his gun where it lay on the table with his wallet. A look at the clock confirmed it was the middle of the afternoon. He'd hate to pull a gun on somebody welcoming him to the neighborhood, so he went to the door without the weapon and pulled it open.

Ty stood on the top step, his head cocked slightly and a small smile on his lips. "Nice neighborhood," he offered.

"Hey," Zane said in surprise. He hadn't seen Ty in almost two weeks, though they'd talked on the phone a few times. He'd missed seeing Ty, more than he thought he should.

Ty merely gave him a smug smile. "Can I come in?" he asked.

"Of course," Zane said, stepping back and leading the way into the apartment. It wasn't a big one. A decent-sized front room with a couch, coffee table, and TV was separated from the kitchen by a bar, and a doorway to the right opened to a small hallway that was just big enough for four more doors: two bedrooms, a bathroom, and a closet. A washer and dryer were in a closet by the back door. It was more than he needed.

Ty looked around the living room as he walked into the apartment. He slid his hand into his jeans and shrugged uncomfortably as he turned and faced Zane again, giving him an uncharacteristically nervous smile.

"How are you feeling?" Zane asked, looking him up and down. Despite the slight show of nerves, Ty looked pretty good, actually: clean-shaven, color back, not so worn out, mostly relaxed, though not totally. The only time Zane had seen Ty totally relaxed was after he fucked him into the mattress. It had been a while.

"Better," Ty answered with a nod. "No longer dying," he added with a small smirk. The quirk to his lips fell, though, and he raised his chin slightly as he looked at Zane. "I need to talk to you," he stated, his voice calm, but his posture screaming he was dreading the coming conversation, whatever it was about. Zane wondered if Ty realized how much he showed his partner through his expressions and body language. He suspected not.

The apprehension was catching, apparently, because Zane felt it tighten around his chest. "Well. Sounds like a reason for a smoke break," he said, gesturing to the door at the far side of the kitchen. Ty nodded, not even offering a disapproving word about the cigarettes. He followed Zane out, glancing around at the bits and pieces Zane had unpacked as they went.

Zane stopped outside the screen door and picked up the pack he'd left sitting out on the railing. He shook it, sliding the lighter out, and lit up as Ty joined him. He looked over his partner's face, trying to see some sort of clue about what he had to say.

Ty was looking out over the backyard, his lips pressed into a thin line, his eyes worried. He looked around and then sat down on the top step with a heavy sigh. "I had some time to do some thinking," he said after a moment of silence.

"Deuce kept Mara distracted, hmm?" Zane tapped ash off into an ashtray he'd left on the wooden porch railing.

"The shovel did, actually," Ty answered as he looked up at Zane and smiled fondly. Zane grinned and chuckled as he watched the smile light up Ty's eyes. It got him in the gut, and he took another drag off the cigarette to combat the feeling. Now wasn't the time. Ty continued to look up at him, watching him hesitantly as if trying to gauge his mood. Finally, he dropped his eyes. "I know what I'm about to say probably isn't what you want to hear, and I'm sorry. But I need to say it, regardless," he said apologetically.

Sighing softly, Zane sat heavily beside his partner. It didn't sound good, what Ty was hinting at. They sat side-by-side silently for a moment, Zane still with his cigarette, both hesitant to continue the conversation.

Finally, Ty cleared his throat. "I don't know how else to say it, Zane, so I'll just come out with it," he said quickly as he raised his head and looked at Zane with a stubborn set to his jaw. "Despite the desk work and the near-death experiences and the bullshit in the mountains...." He took a deep breath and blew it out heavily. "The last couple months have been some good ones, and it's solely because of you," he told Zane slowly.

Zane raised one brow, surprised. But before he could think of anything to say, Ty shook his head.

"I like being able to wake up to you. I like knowing you'll be there if I need you," he continued, obviously uncomfortable with what he was saying but refusing to be deterred now that he'd begun. "I like *being* with you, Zane. And I'd like to keep that up now that you're here," he admitted shakily. He met Zane's eyes determinedly. "I want you."

Stunned, Zane found that all he could do was sit there. Despite how they'd gotten closer, some things were just unspoken; he wouldn't have imagined hearing this sort of thing from Ty again. The last time had been when they were reunited in DC—more than two months ago—and that had been during a seriously emotional outburst on both their parts. That certainly wasn't common. And the slow but steady drift apart afterward had made that memory, that warmth and knowledge, fade. But here Ty was, saying it again.

As for himself, he'd said as much to Deuce up on that mountain. He'd wanted Ty since the first time Ty had met his eyes evenly and given him a soft smile. When Zane allowed himself to think about it, he had to admit that he was a hell of a sucker for the man. The realization had hit him right between the eyes before he left West Virginia. But he tried *not* to think about it—tried not to think about *more*—because it was far too close to feelings that terrified him, deeper feelings he knew could cause so much pain when things went bad. Deuce had been right. Feeling too much was what Zane was afraid of. But wanting....

Ty nodded at Zane's silence, light color spreading across his cheekbones as he looked down again. "I just wanted you to know," he said quietly.

He stood up and reached out to affectionately pet Zane on the head as he walked by, heading back into the apartment. Zane reached out to grab his wrist and he stood. His gut clenched with delight. Hell, there had never been any question that he wanted Ty. Surely Ty knew that without Zane having to say it.

"I'm on board with that," he declared.

Ty blinked at him, his fingers curling around Zane's hand as Zane held his wrist tightly. "Really?" he asked in honest surprise.

Zane smiled warmly. "Really. I want you here, with me," he assured him. "I'm glad you're home," he added softly.

Ty actually managed to blush further, and he swatted at Zane's head as he backed away. Zane grinned as he reached out and caught Ty again around the waist.

"Rumor has it we're being put back into fieldwork next week," Ty told him as he let himself be dragged back close to Zane.

"We've got to be safer there," Zane responded wryly as he pressed his forehead to Ty's and brushed his nose against Ty's cheek.

Ty laughed, the sound rich and honest and carefree. True to form, all the problems and hangups and issues that had been thrown at them had already slid right off his back, and the Ty Grady Zane knew so well was here with him again, alive and well, and they were together. Now Zane had every reason he needed to get himself straightened out.

No way was he going to fuck it up.

Check out this exclusive sneak peek at the sequel to *Sticks & Stones*

FISH & CHIPS

By Madeleine Urban & Abigail Roux

THEY sat at McCoy's conference table, behaving themselves and attempting to appear abashed.

Ty figured Dan McCoy knew him better that that, though. He was probably still getting a read on Zane, though, just like everyone else in the Baltimore office. They'd only been actively assigned to Baltimore for a few weeks now. Ty was at home. Zane was still an unknown to most everyone, despite the stories that had filtered through about their past escapades.

McCoy knew enough to know they were up to no good, anyway.

"I hope you got it out of your systems," McCoy finally said to them in annoyance.

"We were just putting on a demonstration," Ty explained easily. "Zane calls it, 'How To Get Your Ass Kicked.' It goes over real well with the rookies," he drawled, overly pleased with himself.

Zane just sat there looking cool and comfortable in his well-fitted suit. He had a small smile on his face as he shook his head slightly at his partner.

"Shut up, Grady," McCoy requested flatly.

"Right," Ty muttered. He shifted in his seat and leaned forward. "You said you had an assignment for us?" he asked eagerly. He would take anything over the "getting up to speed" deskwork they'd been doing the last three weeks. Despite one blip up in the mountains of West Virginia, the last eight weeks of Ty's life had been godawful boring. Even Zane couldn't keep Ty's wavering attention for very long unless he had something shiny to wave around. Ty needed to be *doing* something or he began to go stir crazy.

McCoy's lips curved into a slow, slightly malicious smile. "I do," he answered. "Corbin and Del Porter," he said as he retrieved a file.

"Who?" Ty asked, unimpressed.

McCoy smiled and reached to the middle of the table for a little white remote. He turned slightly and pushed a button, causing a small flat screen to flick on. A picture of a large cruise ship appeared on the screen bolted to the wall.

"Oh shit," Ty found himself blurting before he could stop himself.

"This," McCoy said with a gesture to the screen as if he hadn't heard Ty, "is the *Queen of the Mediterranean*," he told them with a wave of his fingers at the ship. "It is currently docked in Baltimore, preparing for a fifteen-day cruise to the Caribbean."

"You're not making us take a vacation, are you?" Ty asked in something close to panic.

Zane's chin snapped up in alarm. "Jesus, Grady, we agreed not to even *think* that word, much less say it."

"Corbin and Del Porter," McCoy said loudly to curtail any more conversation, "were supposed to be on that ship tomorrow. But we finally got enough on these two to detain them," he said as he slid a file toward Ty and leaned back in his seat with a grin. "There's a laundry list of no-nos we can pin on them with a little more evidence, and we'll get it soon enough. What we want from you is something concrete on a few of their contacts."

Ty scratched his head absently as he looked over the file. The two men were implicated in numerous thefts: art, antiquities, rare gems. All stuff that was hard to steal and harder to fence. It was difficult to tell whether they were collectors or middlemen, but either way, if the FBI leaned on them, it could produce a lot of information on a lot of different high-end thieves and dealers.

But Ty and Zane weren't leaners. They didn't interrogate suspects who weren't part of their own investigations. They didn't know anything about this case and would be lost if they were asked to do the interrogation. Information wasn't why they were here. He glanced to his side, where Zane shrugged one shoulder, having obviously come to the same conclusion.

"I'm not sure I understand why we're here," Ty said in confusion as he gestured between himself and Zane, still looking down at the file.

"You are here because you both roughly match the physical description of the two men we now have in custody," McCoy answered with a wide grin.

Ty looked up at him suspiciously. McCoy seemed to be enjoying himself too much for this to be good news for Ty or Zane. Zane leaned forward in his seat, though he didn't speak up.

"We look like them," Ty reiterated flatly.

"Vaguely," McCoy agreed. "Same build, mostly. Zane's coloring."

Ty glared at the man. "I'm not following," he said slowly. "You want us to assume their identities? How's that gonna work?" he asked.

"Corbin and Del Porter were booked to leave on that cruise tomorrow," McCoy said again. "We have it on good authority they plan to meet several of their buyers and sellers while on this cruise, taking advantage of somewhat lax security and customs and what have you. And since this will be the first instance of the two of them ever showing themselves physically in their business dealings, their contacts only have virtual interactions to go on. They won't know you're imposters. We can get a lot of information out of this if you two take their places and play your cards right."

"I'm not sure I like the sound of this," Zane said. "We've not got word one on the case until today, and now we're supposed to impersonate these guys?"

"You'll be given a crash course. And you're both professional bullshit artists, you're perfect for it," McCoy replied carelessly. Zane frowned at him.

Ty scratched slowly at his cheek. "Okay," he said carefully. He still didn't understand why McCoy seemed to be enjoying the prospect so much. There was a catch coming.

"You leave at nine in the morning. The rest of your team has already been put in place," McCoy told them as he pushed another stack of files toward the center of the table.

"Our team?" Zane repeated. Ty sighed heavily and closed his eyes. There was the catch.

"You know the drill, Garrett, a team. Team leader, two more field agents, and tech support. Read the files so you don't end up shooting one of them when you meet them. And Grady, we'll be needing you to make just a few... alterations... to your appearance before you go," he said as he studied Ty critically.

"What the hell are you talking about, McCoy? It's not like he can gain fifty pounds overnight," Zane said crossly.

"Nothing like that. Some hot wax and a little bleach, and he'll be set," McCoy continued, barely keeping himself from laughing now.

"Hot wax?" Ty asked in alarm. He heard Zane stifle a snort.

"Del Porter is what you would call... arm candy," McCoy drawled with a smirk.

"Oh hell," Zane muttered, leaning back, rubbing his hand over his face, and shifting in his chair uncomfortably. Ty glanced at him, not following.

"I see that Garrett has figured it out," McCoy said, his voice nearly bubbly. Ty shook his head in confusion.

"I didn't mention that?" McCoy asked in feigned innocence as he flipped through his notes as if he needed to check his information. "Corbin and Del Porter aren't brothers, gentlemen. They're lovers. Legally married, in fact." He reached out and placed two silver rings on the desk in front of them. "Go ahead and put those on," he instructed.

Zane went totally still, his eyes locked on the jewelry. Then his chin raised slowly as his gaze shifted to McCoy. "Are you sure this is necessary?" he asked flatly.

Ty very carefully didn't say anything in response as he stared at the shiny rings. He'd worn a wedding ring before as part of a cover. But this was different.

"The Porters are a very out gay couple," McCoy continued, ignoring their reactions to the news. "The fact is well-known to all their contacts. It would be an alarm bell if you weren't wearing the rings," he said to Zane. "Corbin is what you'd call the brains of the operation. Del is… pretty."

Ty still sat motionless, staring at McCoy with a churning in his gut as he realized what they were being thrown into. A very out gay couple amongst people who would expect them to act as such— including a team of their own people. He slowly reached out and picked up one of the rings, turning it over in his hand. It was a simple silver band, flat and wide. He glanced at Zane apprehensively. Zane still wore his own gold wedding ring on his finger. Ty didn't know how his partner would react to replacing it, even temporarily. But Zane didn't move a muscle, didn't even twitch as he stared at the single ring still there in front of McCoy.

"Now understand, this may put you both in a few uncomfortable situations," McCoy went on sincerely. "But I'm sure you'd both rather have to kiss each other than be shot at," he joked. Ty cleared his throat and tried to restrain a smile. McCoy had no idea how right he was. "Those rings are all we're going to provide you for this one," McCoy said. "We've appropriated the bags they'd already packed for their cruise, so you're set on being clothed and otherwise outfitted. Lucky for us you two are even roughly the same sizes," McCoy rambled as he stood. "Everything they needed for the deals they were making is in that luggage. You'll have to smuggle weapons on board; we'll come up with some sort of concealment for them in the luggage. The captain and head of security on board have been informed of your involvement, but you are not to break cover even with them unless absolutely necessary. Ty, if you find yourself in the brig, you stay there until they make port. You'll have the rest of your team there if you get in trouble, but when you make land, you're shit out of luck."

McCoy stood at the end of his little speech, looking down at them with a raised eyebrow and a smile. Ty and Zane sat staring at him, their mouths hanging open as they listened.

Dan McCoy had been a good field agent, and he was a good Special Agent in Charge. Ty had even worked on a few cases with him before McCoy had been promoted, and they'd gotten on well. Which was probably why McCoy was enjoying this so much and letting it show. Ty sort of wanted to hit him.

"Come with me," he invited with relish as he swept out the door.

A few moments after McCoy disappeared, Zane stood abruptly with a sniff and straightened his jacket. Ty saw that he was grinding his teeth. He lowered his head and looked at the ring in his hand, not sure what to do or say about them. He supposed he would just put his on and let Zane work it out himself. He slipped it on his finger discreetly as he stood up. It was a little tight; he had to force it over the knuckle that was still a little swollen from the surgery he'd had to remove a piece of cougar tooth, but once it got on, it fit well. Ty very carefully didn't give it any extra attention after that.

Zane reached out and plucked up the other ring, closing it into the fist of his right hand before turning on his heel to leave the room. Ty followed them out silently, dreading the hissy fit that would come soon enough.

They followed McCoy down a few floors to an interrogation room and filed into the observation half of one of the suites where an agent, Harry Lassiter, already stood at the glass. Ty and Zane nodded to the man as McCoy pointed through the two-way mirror. "Gentlemen, meet Del Porter."

The man sitting at the table was handsome, probably about Ty's height and build, just a little slimmer. He had short, spiky hair bleached an unnatural platinum blond that contrasted oddly with his dark tan. He wore a sleeveless vest that tied with a simple cord of leather at his ripped chest, and his entire upper body was well muscled and toned. He was also clean-shaven and completely devoid of body hair.

He looked to Ty like he should be standing under a waterfall in a gay porno.

Zane paused in place, eyes a little wide, looking from Del to Ty to Del and back.

Ty blinked rapidly at the guy. "I'm supposed to be… *him?*" he finally asked in a stricken voice.

"Good thing you're a hell of an actor," Zane murmured as he continued comparing them.

Ty glared at him briefly and looked back at the man behind the glass. "I'll never pull this off," he said to the other men in the room.

Zane tipped his head to one side, openly appraising Ty's body. "I don't know," he said distractedly. Ty looked back at him hatefully, feeling himself blushing under the scrutiny.

"He's not what I'd call stupid. But he sure as hell isn't the brightest bulb in the pack," McCoy informed them. "He knows just enough to keep his mouth shut. But that and the fact that he's pretty and got himself a rich husband are about all he's got going for him."

"Holy fuck, man," Ty finally muttered. "I'm gonna be this dude for how long?"

"Relax, Grady. You have the easy end of this," McCoy assured him. "Garrett's guy is the real brains here, and no one who's familiar with them will expect you to do anything but lay in the sun and work on your tan. Garrett? In the field, you're the lead on this one. You're calling the shots. Grady is just there as scenery and backup."

Zane snorted as Ty turned to look at McCoy in outrage. Backup? They were partners; there was no lead and backup!

"Ty, we've booked you an appointment at some spa with a name I can't pronounce," McCoy went on as he handed Ty a slip of paper.

Ty reached out woodenly and took the certificate. "I'll get on board with the hair color," he bargained pleadingly. "You're seriously gonna make me wax my chest?"

"You see that guy in there?" McCoy countered with a point of his finger at the man in the interrogation room.

Ty swallowed hard. He had done a lot of things he wasn't proud of in order to assume identities that weren't his. He'd changed his appearance, changed his behavior, treated decent people horribly to make an impression on a scumbag, prepared crack cocaine for others to smoke, taken lives, and any number of other things he didn't care to remember. He knew how important a part the smallest thing could play when trying to convince a stranger that you were someone they already thought they knew. He looked down at the silver ring on his finger and back up at the man behind the glass with a heavy sigh.

"There's a good man," McCoy said with a pat to Ty's shoulder.

Ty glanced at Zane as he felt himself blushing slowly. Though Zane's face was composed, Ty could see the laughter in his eyes.

"I don't know how they'll get rid of the tattoo, but they've assured me they can," McCoy added with another pat to Ty's shoulder.

"What?" Ty cried as he looked at McCoy in outrage.

McCoy just smiled at him. "This guy was obviously never a Marine," he reasoned. "Now, Grady, you get going," he ordered before Ty could have a meltdown. "You're getting the works, so you'll probably be there all fucking day. Garrett, come with me," McCoy said as he gestured for Zane to follow him. "I'll introduce you to yourself," he said wryly as they headed out the door.

Ty felt the sudden urge to beg Zane not to leave him there. He could feel the raised writing on the slip of thick, cream-colored paper in his hand. He looked down at it, thinking of all the procedures the makeover would entail. Salon Láurie… waxing, tanning, bleaching, manicures, lotions, scented mud….

Del Porter said something suddenly, complaining about being left in the room for so long. Ty turned to look at him in shock. He pointed his finger in outrage and turned to the other agent in the room. "He's British?" Ty cried.

Lassiter, who'd been standing there silently the whole time, covered his mouth with his hand and merely nodded in answer, unable to keep from laughing any longer.

MADELEINE URBAN is a down-home Kentucky girl who's been writing since she could hold a crayon. Although she has written and published on her own, she truly excels when writing with co-authors. She lives with her husband, who is very supportive of her work, and two canine kids who only allow her to hug them when she has food. She wants to live at Disney World, the home of fairy dust, because she believes that with hard work, a little luck, and beloved family and friends, dreams really can come true.

Visit Madeleine's blog at http://www.madeleineurban.com/. You can contact her at mrs.madeleine.urban@gmail.com.

ABIGAIL ROUX was born and raised in North Carolina. A past volleyball star who specializes in pratfalls and sarcasm, she currently spends her time coaching middle school volleyball and softball and dreading the day when her little girl hits that age. Abigail has a loving husband, a baby girl they call Boomer, four cats, three dogs, a crazyass extended family, and a cast of thousands in her head.

Visit Abigail's blog at http://abigail-roux.livejournal.com/.

Visit

http://www.urbanandroux.com

Read about how the Grady-Garrett partnership started in

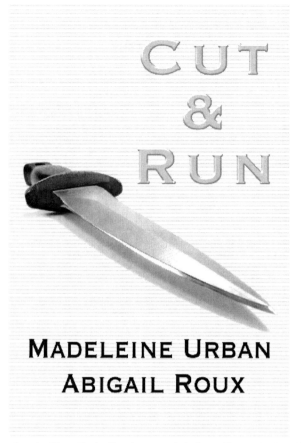

MADELEINE URBAN
ABIGAIL ROUX

A series of murders in New York City has stymied the police and FBI alike, and they suspect the culprit is a single killer sending an indecipherable message. But when the two federal agents assigned to the investigation are taken out, the FBI takes a more personal interest in the case.

Special Agent Ty Grady is pulled out of undercover work after his case blows up in his face. He's cocky, abrasive, and indisputably the best at what he does. But when he's paired with Special Agent Zane Garrett, it's hate at first sight. Garrett is the perfect image of an agent: serious, sober, and focused, which makes their partnership a classic cliché: total opposites, good cop-bad cop, the odd couple. They both know immediately that their partnership will pose more of an obstacle than the lack of evidence left by the murderer.

Practically before their special assignment starts, the murderer strikes again—this time at them. Now on the run, trying to track down a man who has focused on killing his pursuers, Grady and Garrett will have to figure out how to work together before they become two more notches in the murderer's knife.

http://www.dreamspinnerpress.com

Other Bestsellers by
MADELEINE URBAN and ABIGAIL ROUX

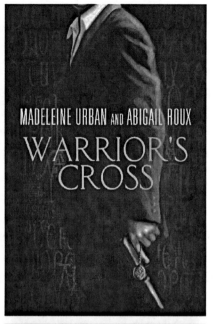

http://www.dreamspinnerpress.com

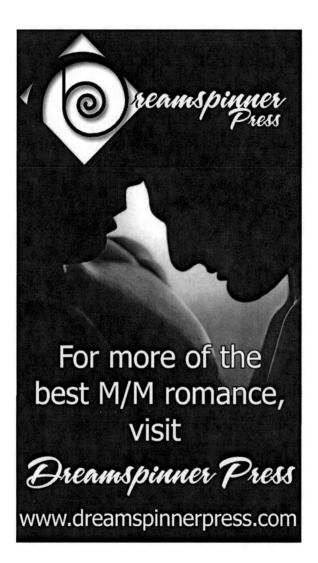

CPSIA information can be obtained at www.ICGtesting.com
Printed in the USA
LVOW05s0458030414

380140LV00004B/621/P